FIRES OF NUALA

KATHARINE ELISKA KIMBRIEL

POPULAR LIBRARY

An Imprint of Warner Books, Inc.

A Warner Communications Company

POPULAR LIBRARY EDITION

Copyright © 1988 by Katharine Eliska Kimbriel
All rights reserved.

Popular Library®, the fanciful P design, and Questar® are registered trademarks of Warner Books, Inc.

Cover illustration by Don Dixon

Popular Library books are published by
Warner Books, Inc.
666 Fifth Avenue
New York, N.Y. 10103

A Warner Communications Company

Printed in the United States of America

First Printing: December, 1988

10 9 8 7 6 5 4 3 2 1

For John,
Who is always dragging me out of the Dark Ages

Nualan Time

The planet Nuala has a twenty-five-hour day, retaining the ancient sixty-minute hour and sixty-second minute, although Nualan timekeeping appears hazy to off-worlders. It can be extremely difficult for planet visitors to keep track of time, since moonrise and moonset can vary enormously. In Amura (Nuamura), the hours are canonical. Elsewhere, however, the moon cycles are closely watched, and it is possible for second bell to precede first bell—or follow third bell, depending on moonset. The same situation applies to moonrise.

Matins	— First bell and the deepest point of night
Lauds	— Second bell, moonset (firstmoon)
Canonical	— Between matins and starrise
Prime	— Third bell, starrise (Kee)
Tierce	— Fourth bell, midmorning
Sext	— Fifth bell, high noon
None	— Sixth bell, midafternoon
Vespers	— Seventh bell, starset (Kee)
Compline	— Eighth bell, moonrise (firstmoon)
Canonical	— Between starset and matins

The Nualans' sequence also changes fractionally with the seasons. Compline and Lauds are rung at their median points during the dark of the moons.

Nualan Calendar

The Nualan year is an ecliptic orbit of 432 Nualan days, based on a twenty-five-hour day. Ancient Terran hours are used as the base measurement. Nualans divide the calendar into four seasons of 108 days each. These divisions are based on the rainy seasons; it rains almost 36 days straight at the beginning of spring and autumn. A Nualan month is 36 days. Nualans do not use any smaller fraction of the calendar between "month" and day. They refer to the passage of time according to festivals and religious feast days.

New Year	Firstday (first day of fall)
Festival of Masks	Thirtyfiveday
Feast of Souls	Thirtysixday
Yule	Onehundred Twentysevenday (midwinter)
Feast of Atonement and Anointing	Onehundred Eightyoneday (first day of spring)
Ascension Day	Twohundred Fortysixday
Midsummer's	Threehundred Fortythreeday
Feast of Adel	Fourhundred Twentyfiveday
High Festival	Fourhundred Twentysixday through Thirtytwoday

Chapter One

"Wake up, Darame. Wake up, now."

Wake up? I'm not asleep . . . am I? Not asleep . . . not awake. Concentrating on the familiar voice, Darame willed her body to move. It ignored her command.

A low hissing sound reached her ears, and something was placed over her nose and mouth. "Breathe, girl—breathe deep. Gotta remind your lungs how to breathe."

Ah, Sweet Saints, it was oxygen—a rich mix. And something to help clear her out—was it gas or fluid they used to fill the lungs? She had never really cared about the procedure, as long as she trusted the person running the barracks. *Mona . . . Why is Mona waking me? Is something wrong? She's the pilot, I can't do a damn thing shipboard—*

"Up, girl, up. Only six hours until we're boarded. See the hot planet on the comp screen, feel the heat. Need me topside soon—" Another hissing sound erupted through the cabin.

Final restimulant. A red gel light over the cot, praise Mona, she was so kind sometimes, at odds with her gruff appearance. Eyes attempting to open, to focus, blinking rapidly, then slowing . . . Darame stared through the dim light at the solid blur with Mona's voice. Grayer than she remembered . . . When had Mona come out of Sleep?

"Hal-sey . . ." The name came out funny, almost stretched.

"Waiting for you, girl. Received a transmission from Brant a few hours ago. Need your final briefing." The older woman folded her arms over her flat chest and gave Darame a hard stare. "Never seen anyone take to Sleep like you do. . . . Make a good ice cube."

Managing a thin chuckle, Darame flexed her fingers, enjoying

1

the sensation of warmth from the cot—med table?—she occupied. Always so cold; it was almost unnatural the way she was always so cold.... "I'm ... ready to ... sit."

Mona obliged by nudging her up from behind. Still trembling from the restimulant, Darame settled her hands firmly behind her and drew in deep breaths of oxygen. In a few moments the old pilot removed the face mask. "Someday your luck will leave you, girl, and it will take you a full day to recover, like normal folks. Halsey shouldn't trust it so much. Fine mess we'd have if we had to carry you to the lander!"

"I'm tougher than I look, Mona, remember?" Darame managed to croak. Better—her voice was coming back. Always low, it'd be hoarse for a few hours, but that was a small price for the stretch of Sleep. How many years lost on this trip without it? Ten? She never paid attention. All people in her line of work used Sleep—her friends would still be around when *Gypsy Rover* returned to Caesarea Station.

Her brain finally started working; she turned slightly, facing Mona's sharp, almost bony features. "Why are you doing barracks duty?" Halsey had hired some medtech since it was a long trip and a large crew. Where was he?

"Just you," the woman said stiffly. "Didn't like the way that fella was looking at you. Didn't want any funny business with your revival."

An inward smile, but Darame did not let it reach her face. "I took a contraceptive gel before we left, Mona—it should be good at least a hundred days Terra."

The familiar sniff ... "Principle. Don't like him. Not so much to him that women like you cross his path regularly."

Smiling, Darame reached up to lightly touch the pilot's arm. "You are mother and father to me," she teased, listening as the lilt sluggishly returned to her voice.

Keen hazel eyes raked her features. "Better to you than that old scoundrel Halsey. Make it to the water by yourself?"

Even after all these years, Mona's clipped, Emerson speech could still confuse her.... Questions or commands? Smiling, Darame said: "Yes. I can reach the box without help."

Another sniff. Mona didn't approve of those secret smiles. "Topside, then. Keep hold the rails, there's a problem with the artificial gee." Nodding once, the pilot moved off into the darkness of the room, and Darame heard the hatch wheel spin.

Problem ... Gee was probably intermittent again. Where did Halsey buy (buy?) this heap, anyway? It had more problems than she cared for, but Mona had been satisfied, which meant that it was secure where it counted.

Flexing fingers, flexing toes... Always a few moments longer to come out of it. Was she reaching her limit already? Despite what science said, she believed the old stories: only so many Freezes to a customer. Human tissue could only be pushed so far.

And Halsey? *He* took it well, that was certain. Darame shuddered to think how old the man might be.... Sweet Saints, he had known her great-grandmother! But kind to her, doting on her—taking her in when her father tried one trick too many, and overplayed his last game.

"Should've stuck to mining," she muttered as she always did when thoughts of her father crossed her mind. Time to try out the feet.

They worked just fine, Saint Jude be praised. Standing brought on no dizziness.... Good. How about walking? A few wavering steps made her reconsider. And consider again. Changing direction, Darame headed for the boxes.

Bathing always helped, hot water getting things moving again. Amazing, the drugs they used, that the body could go through such extremes in only a few hours.... Shivering against the cold of the room, Darame stripped off the thin shift covering her body and stepped into the shower box.

At least the seals worked—she closed the door firmly and started the flow. *Relief.* She could taste the pleasure. Going through Freeze always killed off her surface skin, like sunburn—scrubbing it away with soft soap made her feel more like herself. Such delicate skin, surprising it was so tough....

"Wake up," she ordered idly, knowing the mind wandered after Sleep and as always annoyed by it. The job at hand, what was the job at hand? She worked the soap into her long, fine hair, almost scratching at her scalp. It was Brant's scheme, this one, not Halsey's, for all her old friend had protested. *Brant—dear God.*

"He's never betrayed me," Halsey had said cheerfully at their last briefing before entering Freeze. Which was true; Brant had always been careful with Halsey, for many reasons.

He has betrayed others. Abandoned allies at Emerson, running for space and the safety of Caesarea Station. Claimed there was no choice, but Darame was not so sure. She had friends in Emerson system, friends who had seen what had happened.... And their version of the event did not match Brant's later tale. Of course his partner was dead, and dead men rarely tell their side of the story....

Nuala is different. There is trine gold. The thought made her hands momentarily still. Wealth beyond any imagination. That long-elusive kin to platinum, so far found only in a few systems, already mined out everywhere else. Rumor had it that on Nuala trinium was as common as iron ore. *That* she doubted. . . . But the veins must be massive to have led to such a rumor.

And the Nualans didn't care! They used it for *jewelry,* by the Seven Virgins! And to plate components in their satellites. As an alloy, sometimes, or— Dear God. Maybe outside interest had made them more careful with it.

No corrosion, no tarnish . . . It was even immune to radiation, God alone knew how, she was no chemist. A gram worth . . . What had Halsey said? A canister of cut diamonds? A cargo hold full? Something incredible.

Slowly she rinsed the soap from her hair, wishing for something gentler than ship's issue. Well, maybe on Nuala. They exported a lot of luxuries. A smile rose to her lips. Maybe syluan would be cheaper there. An entire wardrobe of syluan, as elegant and durable as silk, but with that sheen that practically glowed in the dark . . . and such colors!

Punching the vacuum, Darame leaned against the wall, waiting as the recycling system sucked the box dry. A Nualan ship would meet them, take them to the surface, because of the radiation belt circling the planet. Only Nualan ships could breast the dangers, and they didn't share the secret. *How much gold can we carry out in our pockets? Brant, have you found a Nualan ship with averted eyes and a price you could meet?*

Carefully stepping out of the box, Darame pulled a wipe from the wall dispenser and wrapped it around her hair. Still quiet; Mona must be keeping that medtech busy. Good . . . she needed some private time.

Slowly finding her balance, she moved to her locker. A quick inspection told her that someone had tried to force the lock. Foolish. Did they think a thief of her caliber would leave her own unguarded? The pulse must have given the would-be burglar quite a jolt—maybe even marked him. She'd have to keep an eye out for recent burns. Spinning through the code, she popped the door.

A pale visage greeted her, the brightly polished metal a poor mirror. Darame reached to press a moist finger against the back of the cabinet. Her pallid twin mimicked her action, reaching outward. Tiny, elfin, bearing a beauty at odds with her long-dead, tall, fair cousins. *To be my mother's daughter, a valkyrie among women*. Still, the dark good looks of her father had served her well, just as her current odd condition brought fruitful results.

Loosening the wipe, she let the mass of silver hair fall around her face and shoulders. Something unexpected from Norwood—everything about that system had been unexpected. In the food, it had turned out; both her partners that trip also ended up with silver hair, although both currently dyed it. Darame had found her combination of silver hair and basalt black eyes especially effective when seducing men. And, after all, her part of these jobs usually included a bit of such activity.

A slight shrug; she was good at it, it was part of the game. Graduating from simple deceptions to the big money had cost her a few bargaining tools, but she did not regret the price. PPR—Public Promotion and Relations. That was her department, its title a shield from the probes and sensors used by a dozen law enforcement groups. Halsey and Brant worked the Victorian Technique: no matter what the game, their team knew only what related to their own responsibilities—no more. And what she did was not illegal, it was simply a part of current business techniques.

Of course Halsey's part could get them life imprisonment or "adjustment" on almost any civilized world. Worse, on some parts of Emerson. But that was not her business. Great gain . . . great risks.

She studied her wardrobe for appropriate clothing. Activating the screen, she searched for the clothing requirements portion of Brant's communiqué. Ah— No pictures, only a terse narrative. Quaint. Fortunately she could read Caesarean. . . . Could the person who sent the message for Brant? Probably—Caesarean was used throughout the Seven Systems as the language of trade and diplomacy.

No real requirements. Nuala was mainly a hot place, but the season was over halfway through autumn, well past the pre-winter equinox. No proscriptions about clothing, although something clothing the loins was considered good taste. . . . Then pants were perfectly acceptable. And someone stepping off a deep-space transport was never thought out of style—indeed, often set new trends.

Pulling on a white, sleeveless stretch-top to hold her full breasts firm, Darame dug for her white pants. Fortunate she was delicate enough to wear white—it made Halsey look like a freight hauler. The silk pants were tailored but not skintight; never advertise without reason, especially on planet landers. A collarless turquoise overshirt with long sleeves completed the outfit. Knotting the tails in front, her fingers lingered on the smooth Cathay silk, blousing the garment to hide "one of her best attributes," as Halsey teased.

From him, she would take it. It was kindly meant, the affection of a doting grandfather image who was as proud of her exquisite body as he was of her intelligence and natural cunning. From Brant . . . Brant had learned never to make personal comments.

Drained of water, her hair billowed up in the dryness of the air, refusing to hold any shape. Smoothing the tips against the small of her back, she finally ignored it and turned over a hand, comparing natural pallor to acquired tan.

Sufficient. Enough color to look healthy, at least. She wanted to look casual, yet effective enough to attract attention, should one of her chosen marks see her while en route to her lodging. Curiosity never hurt her work. . . . A touch of rose cake to her lips and high cheekbones, and then off to check in with Halsey.

Strange how she was never conscious of ship movement. Somehow it was slowing, now. . . . Topside Mona would be arranging their last trajectory, calculating the mass ratios, taking care of the millions of details Darame had never understood and never cared to understand. Now followed the part she hated, the long, cold night in the belly of the ship, before an in-system lander docked with their vessel. This time that image seemed ominous. . . .

The corridor was deserted, which suited Darame's current frame of mind. No use for that medtech, or any of the others on this trip. Why so many new people? That still bothered her: so many new to the fold, or part of Brant's team. Only Halsey and Mona were long-standing partners. . . . Darame tried to calm her growing unease. Surely Halsey knew better than to trust Brant! To even work with him again, except that the stakes were so high—

Holy Virgin, this was *Nuala*, not a mere hop to Emerson. Furthest of the Seven Sisters, a law unto itself, only remotely tied to the alliance which bound mankind together. Maybe not even human . . .

She shoved the thought back into her subconscious. Too late to worry about it, they were hours away. Surely people from off-planet weren't allowed near the dangerous places. Surely people tainted with radiation were isolated. . . . The thought of being touched by a genetic nightmare brought vivid pictures to mind.

Reaching Halsey's room, she pounded on the door to drive away the image.

"Enter, enter," came a brisk, cheerful voice, the annoyance edging it disappearing when he recognized her. "Such a racket, Davi! Ready for action, are you?" His round face beamed as he extended a meaty arm to offer a brief hug. Not a contact person, Halsey—she was the only one he touched when others were present, and even alone the embrace was frugal. He was tanned, which he certainly had not been back on Caesarea, but otherwise he looked the same. Always the same . . .

"Ready for anything Brant can dish out, old man," she murmured, testing the range of her voice. The low notes were returning already—good, all would be normal by planetfall. "Changes already?" She settled into the seat next to his, accepting the warm broth he was pouring into a mug. Halsey was the last alive who remembered "Davi," the ten-years-Terran child dumped into his lap by grudging relatives. That nickname no longer seemed a part of her, except when Halsey pulled it out of storage. Where her mother had found the name "Darame" was not known, but its multisyllabic roll of letters had served her well, and this time it would serve her better.

"Some changes, but nothing we can't handle. Before we start final memory, what name will you use this trip?"

"Darame." This caused Halsey's thin eyebrows to lift. "Didn't you tell me Nualans are the best in the Seven Systems at sniffing out truth?"

"It is said their people do not lie." His expression was serious.

Darame grimaced. "Wonderful. I can smell worm-rotten fruit already. But I imagine they have the best interrogation equipment, as well. If a false name trips a stress, they'll dig deep; even *my* shell might crack. Better to give them no doubt about the foundation of my story." She grinned suddenly. "After all—I've nothing to hide."

Her mischievous grin was infectious; Halsey's smile blazed like a torch at nightfall. "Boast, boast." But he straightened his shoulders, his pride in her a glint in his eye. No world had a record of her, no agency a shred of evidence. Darame had been cautious during her lengthy career, and thus had no secrets. How could she feel any guilt for her line of work? Those she fleeced were greedy fools, exploiting their own people and planet for gain. Halsey chose his prey carefully, choosing only those who previously had been predator. It was a very old human tradition, the mirror game; cheating a mark with his own greed. . . . The

Caesarea Force turned a blind eye to Halsey's scams, a fact which simultaneously amused Darame even as it confirmed her suspicions about most authorities. The greatest philanthropist of the planet could be forgiven the source of his money, since he only struck at those the Force could not reach, the wealthiest and most devious of the underground economy.

"Very well—*Darame*," Halsey continued, stressing her name. "Let us get to the vitals. The only 'change' from what we decided back on Caesarea is in the long-term portion of the plan. We may be able to turn this into a trade agreement." His pleasant tenor voice rolled smoothly through familiar code words. Darame nodded her understanding. The truth of this con would only be known when they hit dirt—Brant could not trust any sort of message. But the original plan had involved a simple "in-and-out" scheme, attempting to use an insider's greed as a weapon. If someone could be bribed into awarding them a middleman contract, they would simply disappear with the shipment, leaving the official with the first installment of the bribe and a great deal of explaining to do. But if those involved could be induced to "join" their team . . . this could become a lifetime position, a bent elbow in the trade laws, the perfect niche to skim cream from milk.

That farm image, a remnant of her distant past, brought a smile to Darame's face. And a tiny shrug. Either way made no difference to her. Brant and Halsey could retire on the original agreement. If things became long-term, perhaps the rest of the crew could live like kings as well. Halsey would tell her no more—he never did. *The same routine as always. . . . Why am I nervous?*

"Brant is disappointed at the timing. . . . It would have been better if we had arrived earlier. We will be met momentarily by a trinium transport, which will take us to a drop point outside Atare."

"A mining transport?" That was not simply unusual, it was abnormal.

"The only passenger station is far to the south, a small, neutral city called Amura. Brant's 'sponsor' did not want to wait the days necessary for a ship to bring us north, and so arranged for a special lander to meet *Rover*." Smiling at the added questions in her eyes, Halsey paused to sip his kona. Darame waited silently and wrinkled her nose at the mere thought of drinking the bitter brew. Halsey had few annoying habits, and fewer vices. She'd allow him a bit of mystery in his schemes, and his stimulants.

"Disappointment?" she prompted finally, when she realized he wanted a leading question.

"The Festival of Masks, a rather . . . boisterous . . . celebration, will be over by a planet day by the time we enter the city. It would have been a good time for us to arrive, a chance for you to strike up conversations with no suspicion. The night following begins the Feast of Souls, a somber religious holiday."

"Religious holiday?" Darame repeated casually, submerging her tension. Memories of Gavriel flitted through her mind—of portions of Emerson and Kiel. Just what they needed, a religious complication.

"It's all right," Halsey said hastily, as if reading her mind. "The Nualans are very religious, but tolerant—even of their own schisms. As luck would have it, it is an heir's birthday, and Brant has arranged for us to be invited to the private celebration."

"An ambassador's aide arranging invitations to royal parties . . . He moves quickly, as always," she murmured, pouring another cup of the nutritious broth. Easy on the stomach for a few hours . . .

"The communiqué was signed off by Second Ambassador Brant," Halsey offered, a definite twinkle in his eye.

"*Second Ambassador?* Good heavens, Halsey, did he marry someone?" Her surprise was genuine. The Caesareans were lax about some things, but usually strict about seniority and promotions. Brant had not been with their foreign branch of government that long. Of course, with Nuala so isolated, the rules could be different for this outpost.

"Or perhaps a death . . ." Halsey did not continue on that path; he always avoided reminding Darame that Brant's methods were occasionally very direct. "At any rate, he has hold of several important ears. The code breaks down into the names Iver and Caleb—they'll be your marks. But the emphasis is light on the last code, so I think you can simply get your bearings the first night." He smiled as he spoke, leaning back in the flexseat with an audible creak. Darame half-closed an eye, waiting for the snap, but the mold held. "Good. You need some time to play. Your last job ran past the deadline."

"Past?" she said innocently, and he laughed, his huge frame shaking. Darame had boarded scarce moments before takeoff, the authorities in close pursuit. It seemed like yesterday. . . . It might as well have *been* yesterday—she was bundled into Cold Sleep right after briefing. *Time off after this job. When was my last vacation? A year ago . . . More than that . . .*

She let him enjoy the joke, while she pondered a few more questions. Usually she preferred to find out things from the natives of an area, but basics had to be observed. "Halsey..." she began.

"Yes, Davi?" The big man patted moisture from his red face.

"The succession in Atare—on the entire planet. Your notes say it is a matriarchy?" If power was in the hands of women, why play up to the men?

"Yes and no. Descent is matrilineal. You remember that eighty percent of the population is sterile?" he asked in turn.

"The inherent genetic mutation problem."

"Exactly. It's one of the reasons we've brought gene packets as part of our trade package; they always need new strains. But they prefer the natural process, and so fertile people have power—it's as simple as that. Certain families have historically had great fertility, and this helped them move into positions of great power. The Atare family not only controls the trine mines, it is also one of the strongest and most numerous clans. Power is shared between the eldest male and female of a single generation who are children of the last eldest female. The man carries the name of the clan as his title—in this case, Atare—and the female, whatever the clan, is called The Ragaree, the mother of the heir. Does that make sense?"

"Then... the man's children do not figure into the next ruling generation?" she continued.

"No. I think they become the head of the judicial branch or something, but they have nothing to do with the rule. The ruler's sister's children will rule, and must be trained for their role. They are living repositories of what the Nualans value most: healthy, fertile genetic material." Halsey had his superior look on his face.

"I heard somewhere that they dote on their children," she murmured aloud. "I doubt that they look at their offspring as living tissue cultures."

"Their children are everything to them," Halsey stressed, serious once more. "Each royal family has their own system to protect their heirs. Among the Atare, it is an organization called the *guaard*. It's modeled somewhat on the janissary system; they are *totally* loyal to the ruling Atare and Ragaree. *Guaard* have existed over a thousand years, and there is not one recorded incidence of betrayal. Brant claims they are incorruptible by any normal means. Fortunately the royal family and its hangers-on are not so virtuous."

Smiling slightly, Darame straightened in her chair. "Halsey ...I... need to prepare myself on something. Are the Nualans

. . . Do they look human?" she said quickly. "Not that it's a big problem, but—"

"My dear child!" Halsey said, seizing her hand. "Do you think I'd throw you to dogs like a bone? Of course they look human! I'd call the Atares quite human. After all, they've been bringing back spouses ever since they succeeded in passing the radiation belt. By now their heredity is mostly off-worlder." Then he winked. "Not bad-looking, either."

"If you had your choice of materials for a baby—"

"No, no! Not the Atare clan. At least not the ruling line. Their looks are solely from generations of having their pick of mates. After all, even if some of the ragarees weren't much to look at, the idea of all that wealth, prestige, and security must have tempted a lot of people. They have become an unusually hand-some line. This assignment won't be a chore."

"At least it will be a feast for the eyes?" she suggested, lifting her mug as if to toast him.

Halsey raised his steaming kona, gently bumping it against her molded cup. "Probably better than that—they are known as scholars and lovers, my dear Davi. Bored you shouldn't be, in *any* fashion!" His merry laugh rang out again as he sipped his kona.

We'll see. They value fertility among some sects on Emerson, too . . . so they only have sex during certain times of their year, and it's poor sport, my alpha male friend. But men rarely think about how a woman sees such things. Something bothers me about this job, old man.

As if by command, memory finally returned. . . . She had not worked with Brant since she heard about that Emerson fiasco. Darame answered Halsey's smile, not wanting him to worry, even as she calculated how much credit she could withdraw from her account without causing comment. This place was too much of an unknown to make any better plan. Trust and adore Halsey she might, but she wanted enough money on her person for a ticket to Caesarea, if something went wrong. . . .

ATARE, NUALA   THIRTYSIXDAY   VESPERS
GUAARD HOUSE   NUALAN YEAR 2007

"*Mailan!* Where are you? The vespers bell just rang!"
The shriek penetrated her formless dream, and Mailan was

suddenly on her feet beside her cot. "The *vespers* bell? Nev's bones, I am dead late!"

Jude's solid form grew out of shadows. "No one has called in; I think you have a pad. What happened to your wake-up call?"

A pad? The extra time existed only until White called for his replacement. How could she be so careless? Muscles bunched and sprang and she charged through the door and down the corridor, even as she heard Jude's cry of "Your clothes!"

Moments of black disorientation followed. In and out of the shower in scarce minutes; it was necessary, she had been too exhausted at starrise to think of bathing. And the sanitation, she *had* to empty her bladder, duty would be until after lauds— Jude appeared so abruptly Mailan threw out an arm in defensive posture.

"Whoa! Friend!" Jude said quickly, blocking the movement with one of her own. A towel was extended from her other hand, and Mailan gratefully accepted it. There was concern in the square, dusky face. "I have the night off. Do you need a second?"

"Enjoy your freedom; I will be fine. It is just . . . Last night was bad," Mailan said finally. No point in elaborating; Jude was not part of her assignment, and any other discussion would be gossip. One did not gossip about Atare business, even the simple daily occurrences. They reached the cedar wardrobes even as she spoke. Mailan tore through her things, finally locating a clean camisole and drawers.

"Dress uniform," came Jude's reminder.

"Dress? By The Path, why tonight? And he is certain to be exhausted. I wish—"

"Pipe dream—try some smoke next time you are free, your luck will be better." Jude's advice was oblique, but Mailan took her meaning. The Serae Leah was touchy about points of courtesy, and that meant every single throne-line Atare had to attend the heir's birthday party. There was no suitable excuse. Even Sheel was excused from his hospice duty, and rumor had it Caleb was returning from his mountain retreat for the affair. No one risked offending the eldest daughter of the Ragaree.

The tailored black uniform of syluan slid over her lean form like a wisp of cloud, cool and delicate. Glancing in a mirror, Mailan rumpled her dark curls and groaned. "It will suffice. How can I get a roster without—"

Jude held up a flimsy information ring.

"Best of friends!"

"It is not your fault!" Jude said suddenly, fiercely, as she pressed the roster ring into her hand.

Turning to slide the ring into a wall screen, Mailan hid her expression. It would not do to criticize the Captain—Mailan knew better. Surely Captain Dirk was still not angry over her appointment. Old Fion, her trainer, had been so proud and pleased that they would be working together. And one did not deny the request of an Atare. . . .It was not done. True, it was unexpected, so few Atares this generation cared who their regular *guaard* might be. . . .

"Still at home, good. Better to explain only to the seri," she muttered.

"And White." Jude was not rubbing a sore point, only warning. White was firmly attached to the Captain, and would delight in telling Dirk about this latest chip in the veneer of their elite troop.

"To the Last Path with White, that mangy *katt* of a man!" Mailan retorted, popping the ring from the wall and sliding it into a pocket. "I owe you, Jude. Have a good break, if that man of yours can still breathe after last night!"

"I told him to save a bit o'self for me," Jude said elegantly, trying to control a giggle. "Off! Hurry! Cut through the temple grounds! Oh—I forgot! That Claire woman finally delivered, a manchild, and Seri Sheel is definitely the father!"

It was already dusk beneath the towering neudeya trees which covered the slopes behind the Mendularion. Mailan rushed along the path, heedless of the crunch of dry needles and seed cones. Somewhere off the path a waterfall beckoned, probably one of the tiny ones created by the temple guardians, but she ignored it. A thirteenday without a break, and fiveday yet to come—Fion would be angry, but even his presence would not have dented the will of the captain. Somehow Dirk felt slighted, and he had no one to vent his anger upon except his underlings.

Her thoughts were jumbled as she left the temple grounds and approached the restricted sector. Why was Dirk so angry about her appointment? Surely *Dirk* did not think of guarding an Atare as a reward for . . . for what? Of course their pride and joy was to guard the royal family, and Mailan would not trade her post for any price, but it was hard work, to be especially Chosen. Rotation was supposed to be a constant fivesome, each covering two bells of time. But Sheel had chosen only two so far, and since he had not requested a standard shift, Dirk perversely let Mailan and

Fion share the assignment alone, four bells apiece, an inhuman load.

Could anyone except Dirk change it? Probably not, she reflected, starting up the steep hill to Sheel's home. The Atare or Ragaree, of course, but The Ragaree was secluded, dedicated to Mendulay's altar now that her children were grown, and Cort Atare had enough to keep him busy without handling a feud among his *guaard*.

Mailan stopped abruptly at the path gate, taking a deep breath and ordering her thoughts. She privately suspected Dirk was furious that Sheel had not asked for the Captain's advice in choosing official *guaard*, and intended to run them into the ground over it. When he had broken their health, he would probably relent, and set up a regular rotation. Fortunately Fion had been due for furlough. He was a tough old bird, but four shifts at constant alertness was a tremendous strain. The roster showed White had stood only two bells... that son of a nameless mother. She was tempted to substitute "knife" for mother, but that was an insult great enough that the law ignored a duel of honor over it. Better not to get in the habit of such thought.

Settling her mind into the proper framework, Mailan pressed her thumb against the lock, waiting for it to acknowledge her presence. She kept her walk down the path silent, in case Sheel still slept.

The mirrors in the front hall did not startle her; was that one of the reasons Sheel chose her? Because his house did not—distress, annoy, amuse?—her. Or because he had forgotten the protocol of dealing with the captain of the *guaard*, or never learned it before he took the Cold Sleep to Emerson, over thirty-four years Terran round-trip.

He left before I was born, Mailan thought as she slipped through the elegant, sparsely decorated friendship parlor and toward the sleeping quarters.

White was a bronze statue at the door, his broad face immobile. No reaction, no greeting as she entered; he always took the strictest interpretation of regulation when changing shifts.

As he wished. She, too, could take the absolute interpretation —which in the case of a sleeping subject was no speech at all. Nodding once in the manner which indicated accepting duty, she gave the slight bow of respect to a trainer and took the other side of the door. Without taking her eyes from White's face, she knew Sheel still slept: the breathing was relaxed, even, slower than his waking pattern.

Something flickered in White's eyes, but they did not meet hers. "You are late," he said concisely in an undertone.

Her expression warned him. Sheel was a very light sleeper, and the exhaustion of last night's work was no guarantee the *guaard* level of whisper would go undetected. Mailan knew he saw the warning; he chose to ignore it.

"You realize I must report this incident," White went on, still looking through her.

She considered waving him into the corridor, but thought better of it. If Sheel would wake, he was already awake. "White . . ." she began softly, evenly.

"Trainer White." He managed the emphasis without raising his voice.

Mailan did not respond. There were only two ranks in the *guaard*, trainer and captain. The captain was usually, but not always, chosen from the group of trainers, and was the only *guaard* spoken of by rank. But only students addressed a trainer by title—and Mailan was no longer a student. Seniority meant nothing except courtesy. She refused to take the bait.

"Trainer White." The soft, slightly weary voice came from the rumpled bed. Not tired, really . . . It was more the weariness of the world that she always heard, as if Sheel had seen too much in his short life, and had become cynical. And fine-tuned, controlled, like a bow drawn across the strings of a cello . . . "I suspect Mailan was as exhausted as I was, after last evening. Surely there is no need to speak to the captain. Four bell shifts is a strenuous assignment, or so I would imagine. Perhaps I should speak to my uncle about current *guaard* rotation."

It took all Mailan's self-control to remain expressionless, although exultation sang through her blood. White did not fare so well, his face momentarily startled. The Captain would not be amused . . . not at all.

"As you wish, Seri," White said, the tone lacking emotion. A brief nod to Mailan, a bow in the direction of the bed, and White disappeared. Only the tap of leather against the tile porch betrayed his passing.

Several long moments passed, but Sheel did not speak. Wondering if he intended to sleep until the banquet, which he was known to do, Mailan repositioned herself against the doorsill White had vacated. She now had a view of the entire corridor and bedroom, as well as part of the friendship parlor. Paranoid, she scolded herself. But she watched alone, and she was tired. Better to be overcautious. Sixth in line to the throne he might be, but

Sheel was still an heir. The Atare–Dielaan clan war had ended scarcely three years ago. . . .

A slight rustle from the sheets . . . "Mailan, it is possible I will be able to drag myself out of this bed, but it will be easier if you adjust the blind so there is more light."

A quick glance down the hall, and Mailan moved to comply. Technically she was required to do nothing but guard her charge —anything else was the prerogative of the individual *guaard*. But she knew Sheel's strange eyes were sensitive to abrupt light changes, and after the nightmare of last night's emergency center, she was ready to indulge him a bit. Slightly cracking the blinds, she returned to her post.

"That is the first," she said gravely, stifling a desire to laugh. They constantly "owed" each other favors, when they presumed upon each other's rights and responsibilities. It amused Sheel, in a positive sense—and so little actually made him laugh she was quite willing to humor him . . . when other *guaard* were absent.

"No, we are even. I seriously doubt White will mention this incident. Or if he does, he will include my offer of adjusting *guaard* rotation." Shifting onto his side, Sheel rolled upright, crossing his legs in a flurry of cotton bedding. The curled lumps of fur scattered across the bed reacted in varying degrees, one unfolding and stretching hugely, one stalking off in a huff, a third giving him an injured look before curling up once again, and the fourth jumping into his lap and purring. Absently stroking the tiny cat's beryl-tinged fur, Sheel suddenly lifted his head and gave her a direct look. "Let me rephrase that. . . . I am in your debt many times over, I suspect. Why did you not tell me that Dirk was making problems for you?"

This was definitely not in the regulations. Dear Mendulay, why did he have to treat her like a person instead of like part of the wall? The formality of the *guaard* made some things easier. She did not meet his eyes. It was difficult to meet Sheel's eyes even on good days.

An instant's relaxation, Sheel's equivalent of a shrug. "It did not occur to me that *guaard* selection had changed so drastically in my absence. Yet if I retracted the choice, I suspect it would be worse for you. If it is a problem, I offer my apology." Tickling the cat to make it move, Sheel unwound his long legs and jumped out of bed.

Always controlled, his movements. When the Temple taught the basics of Elkita, the ritual dance which was also warfare, it rarely found such responsive material. Sheel was incredibly graceful, every move accounted for as he flowed through his daily routine. Mailan did not have to watch him vanish into the sanitation to know the beauty of his movements.

Not good to follow that train of thought—she definitely needed a furlough. She had never thought him attractive, those first few months after his return from Emerson. First to admit she was as easily influenced by trends as any person of her generation, Mailan found his older brother Iver's beauty overwhelming. Classic from every angle, with the broad shoulders and narrow hips that made him look like a Terran statue, Iver was also blessed with what many thought the most pleasing type of Atare eyes: one iris blue, and one green. Curly blond hair completed Iver's physical charms, and he was not lacking in other graces.

Talking to him was like talking to a stone pillar, if one desired to talk to stone, Mailan reminded herself, trying to push the topic from her mind. But who would waste time talking to Iver? Gorgeous, an Atare, and a proven 20—women fell at his feet. His pregnant bride, a maiden from a conservative country on Emerson, turned a blind eye to his wanderings, understanding that Atare husbands were either disconcertingly faithful (as far as other women were concerned) or incurably straying, like Iver. But there it was; of the younger men, Iver was by far the one women dreamed about.

Yet Sheel was the one they set traps for, made excuses to meet, had even fought over. Part of it was his rampant fertility. All Atares were fertile; Iver had had three acknowledged children before he went seeking his wife. Sheel, incredibly, had twelve, between Atare city and lovely Maroc, and Mailan had heard there were several more in the mountains, where women did not rush to a physician to prove their child's proud ancestry.

What did that remind her of?... Oh, yes—another child. Claire reb Guin had been especially persistent. Remembering how persistent, Mailan felt irritation rising and stifled it. Sometimes it was an unpleasant sensation, the feeling that Sheel often slept with a woman to get rid of her. *I protect him as much as he will allow. . . .* But he would want to know about the new child before tonight; would not want to find out from the "wrong" people. Like his sister Leah, her jealousy a drawn dagger against his throat . . .

Mailan could not resist a sudden smile as she saw steam drift out of the sanitation and heard snatches of an old ballad. *They are fools, the ones who look no farther than the child they hope for. . . .* Any woman who had ever met him, talked to him—

surely they saw more than genetic advantage. Something about Sheel drew the eye, the spirit. The calm, even detached air he projected, maybe? Restless intelligence and flippant wit had endeared him to both his mother and her brother, Cort Atare. Mailan had finally decided he was very attractive, but not in the current fashion. Tall, taller than his *guaard*, who was considered tall among men and women. And thin—terribly thin, almost unhealthy at first glance, until one saw the tight muscle lining every curve and angle of his body. *I can count every rib, and the striations of muscle tissue*, she thought idly, moving to draw the vertical blinds and open the doors to the balcony. *That slender face, so remote ... and of course the eyes*.

Legend had it that Captain Habbukk of the starship Atare, founder of their tribe, had had such eyes. Very light, they changed color: now pale green flecked with amber, at other times hinting blue. But only half the left one matched its mate. The lower half, almost a horizontal split, was a warm topaz brown. The effect was tricky: in dim light one eye was light, the other unexpectedly solid dark as the reflecting properties of the iris blended. Face to face in full day, it was unnerving.

He sauntered back into the room, already half-dressed, reaching to stroke a cat's arched back as he walked toward the balcony. As predictable as starrise, Mailan followed, aware they were defenseless against snipers. *Our trainers intend us to become paranoid. Yet few Atares have died violently since our tenure began*.

The setting star turned Sheel's sandy hair to gold and drew fire from Mailan's chestnut curls. He settled upon a stone bench lining the railing and gave her a long look. "You ... need a furlough," he said calmly, and turned to look out over the drop.

Transparent. Always, in his presence. *At the least, I need a good man*, she admitted. Mailan had no delusions about her position. She was a borderline 20, as yet and perhaps always infertile, and a native. *And the first guaard he has selected since his return home*, she reminded herself. Let others compete for his attention and children. No blame there—if she were fertile, and not a rural mountain girl, the temptation would be great. Instead, she would settle for the honor of guarding his body and providing comic relief.

"Have I missed anything exciting, being unconscious an entire day?" he asked mildly, draping an arm over the railing as he moved into a stretching exercise.

Hot healers should not work emergency center. They are too precious.

He looked up when she did not immediately answer, and again, seemed to read something in her gray eyes. "Those three in shock would have died if I had not been there, Mailan. Be charitable."

"It is fortunate you are off duty tonight," she responded carefully. To approve of Serae Leah's party was more than Mailan would admit, but to criticize Sheel's decision to serve as a regular physician would also be poor form. Her responsibility was his health and safety. Hysterical accident victims did not make her job easy.

"I intend to stay inaccessible. Rob asked to borrow the house tonight—I shall stay at the palace long enough to avoid offense and then find some place quiet to sleep." He covered his eyes a moment, and Mailan was appalled. He rarely revealed such exhaustion, even to her.

"As you wish, Seri. In answer to your question, I truly slept through the vespers bell. The only news I caught was that Claire reb Guin delivered a manchild. Number thirteen." She placed the slightest of pauses before her last statement, wondering if he would catch it.

The barest hint of a dimple, heralding the possibility of a real smile. "Definitely mine?"

"I believe the ancient saying is . . . a baker's dozen?"

A chuckle escaped him as he once again surveyed the view. "Unkind, Mailan, unkind. Still another birth gift; I may need a loan at this rate."

"It is Mendulay's gift," Mailan said steadily, not sure she liked what overwork was doing to his attitude.

"Mendulay's will, at least." His attention was suddenly caught. "The Caesarean transport apparently arrived. I heard Leah sent a mining lander after it."

Mailan moved to the railing. Below, they could see the steps of one of the most exclusive hostels. The brilliant green of Caesarean diplomacy was highly visible, and she recognized the tall redhead Brant. Ah, that one, playing up to both daughters of the House. A dangerous line he trod. . . .

Flashing silver and turquoise focused her gaze, and Mailan's expression narrowed. An uncommonly attractive female. Glancing out the corner of her eye, she watched Sheel for a reaction.

Sheel lifted an elegant eyebrow. "An ice princess. Brant certainly attracts beautiful women. Do you think he will remain after his tour is completed?"

An idle question; Sheel probably did not expect an answer. Mailan chose to give him one. "I am uncomfortable in his presence."

Sheel's gaze was level. It was widely assumed that Brant was Serae Leah's current lover, and his attentions to Avis, the youngest daughter, had been noted. His dilemma was understandable; Leah was married, while Avis, like Sheel, had failed to find a spouse on Emerson. An Atare bride was quite a prize. . . .

"Avis favors Stephen," he said tranquilly.

Stephen . . . Second Ambassador Stephen Se'Morval, from Garrison System. Certainly in attendance . . . An order to shadow? Uncertain, Mailan locked the information away within.

Another stretch, and Sheel jumped up, moving back into the bedroom. "I doubt I can find service this late in the day, and clean sheets *would* be a courtesy. Do you think, Mailan, I can impose upon you to assist me?" He moved into the hall and opened the linen hatch.

Mailan gave him a long, haughty stare worthy of White. Then she reached for a stack of sheets and said gently: "That is the second."

Chapter Two

ATARE PALACE, ATARE   THIRTYSIXDAY   COMPLINE

FEAST OF SOULS

Sheel stepped backwards until he came up against the stone wall, doing his best to hide within the swirl of color that was the crowd. Only eight bells, much too early to depart. Several women were especially persistent tonight, Crystle reb Lesli the foremost, and he was determined to leave alone. If only Leah would send her son to bed; when the guest of honor said good night, Sheel would feel free to slip away. Dear Mendulay, what a mob. Anyone who was *anyone* in this city was present. A compliment to young Tobias, or fear of offending Leah? *You have gained a great deal of power in the last few years, sweet sister. I wonder what you intend to do with it. . . .*

"How can you stand this noise without a drink to fortify you?" came a familiar voice. Sheel tilted his head in his brother's direction.

"You are fortified enough for both of us," Sheel replied in the same language, Caesarean, giving Iver a wry look.

The man was puzzled at first, and then laughed broadly. Iver was normally a bit slow to understand Sheel's often deadpan humor; alcohol was guaranteed to drag out his comprehension still further. But Sheel liked his big, brassy older brother. Iver was not overly intelligent, to be sure, but he was honest, and had a kind heart. A decided weakness for attractive women and the party circuit were minor faults.

Finally regaining control of his mirth Iver said: "You look tired. What have you been doing with yourself lately?"

"Emergency Center. A festival is always a bad time in a hospice," Sheel answered, keeping his tone casual. He was not in a mood to discuss it.

"You know you should not do that," Ivar said seriously. "Cort does not like it."

"If our uncle had any real objections he would voice them."

Iver shook his head expansively. "Cort never objects to anything you do—not *anything*. Sometimes I think he wishes you were his son—or first heir."

Sheel lifted an eyebrow and gave Iver a withering look, which he missed completely.

"But that is not possible, so he lets you have what you want, instead," Iver continued, taking a swig of his grocha. "I envy you, Sheel. At least you have something they cannot deny you. A healer must heal. I have to wait until someone important enough dies before I can serve as a judge." Gesturing with his drink, Iver turned to face Sheel squarely as his brother took a cautious step to the left. Grocha was a powerful concoction, and could draw the dye right out of material. "I volunteered to take that position up in the mountains a few months ago, but Baldwin said it 'lacked prestige.'" Irritated, Iver took another drink. "He just wants me somewhere important so when he is Atare, he can control the post. I know I will be terrible with big decisions. . . . Arbitrating disputes over goats and pastureland is something I could do!"

There was little Sheel could say in response. Iver had neither false modesty nor ambition. He probably would have done a fine job in that post, Sheel reflected. It did not lack prestige, it was a regional post . . . but it was an area where Baldwin was not interested in maintaining direct control. And Cort Atare was a very old man, he could die before the winter was out. . . .

Reaching to give Iver's shoulder a sympathetic squeeze, Sheel said: "You would have done a fine job there, Iver. Baldwin could have re-appointed you later." That was as neutral as he could make it and still give his brother support.

Iver's face brightened. "He could have! Why did he not think of it? I wish he could see as far as you—it is all that reading you do."

"I confine my reading to theology and legend," Sheel said, laughing. "I only turn my mind to these things when you point them out to me. Baldwin, however, is always thinking—it is what he is best at. Trust him, he will not place you over your head." The last was soft, to spare prying ears. No sense admitting that Iver had no talent for the law. "Now, on a happier note; did you see the ice princess who arrived around vespers? She is apparently attached to the Caesarean consulate."

A broad grin crossed Iver's face. "As delicate as a snowflake! And Sheel, she has eyes as black as coal, as bottomless as a well. . . . You could fall into them and never climb back out."

"If you do not climb back out, I believe your wife will become annoyed," Sheel suggested.

"Well, true, but I do not mean anything serious! She is so tiny and perfect—look for yourself!" Grabbing his brother's arm, Iver pulled him to one side and pointed through an opening in the crowd.

"Pray do not be obvious, Iver. It will spoil your hunt," Sheel said. He looked, however. Silver hair was not common—it was currently not popular, at least on Nuala. Nor on Emerson . . . And she appeared young, too young to have tried any of the treatments to put off aging. She was too far off for a glimpse of the amazing black eyes, but she was wearing an interesting dress that was holding the attention of men around her. Shimmering like turquoise silk, it was what some cultures called a wrap, the long skirt slit up the back to the matching short pants. A second piece of material tied behind the neck, wrapped across a promising front, and crossed in back over the ribs, tying in front at the waist. Open-toed black shoes with a tall heel finished off the effect.

"Are you sure she is your type, Iver?" Sheel said curiously. "You have never—"

"What is life without variety?" Iver interrupted. "And she smiled at me earlier, Sheel! A nice smile." His expression grew sad. "I am already too drunk to introduce myself, but I think I will ask Brant to make sure I meet her sometime soon."

"Excellent idea, Iver," Sheel said, resting his hand on his brother's shoulder a moment. "Take care—I should pay my respects to Cort." Iver nodded a casual farewell as Sheel moved off into the glittering crowd.

Cort Atare, forty-eighth ruler of his line, eldest survivor of his generation and far older than he liked to admit, was bored. He was doing his best to disguise that fact, but Sheel knew that as Cort had aged he had had less patience with "idle chatter," as he termed socializing. Summoning his official smile, Sheel walked up slowly to the small group around his uncle, waiting for a courteous opening. As he approached, he heard the beginning of a "Cort explosion": "I want no further discussion of it—the Atare–Dielaan war is over, and the extremists are—"

Motion caught the man's attention. Cort immediately turned to Sheel, a smile lighting his fierce hawk face, a glint of humor in his green eye. Surveying first Sheel's clothing and then the impassive reserve of the *guaard* shadowing him, The Atare said: "Chose her because she glowers at people, eh? Fion says she will be the best someday."

"I thought so," Sheel said casually, not embarrassing Mailan by looking at her. A quick glance around the circle revealed Cort's companions to be the archpriest Ward, second in authority to High Priest Jonas and his likely heir, and Cort's own heir Baldwin, eldest of Ragaree Riva's eight surviving children. *You are an old man, Baldwin. You look to be Cort's brother, not his nephew. Go climb a mountain, brother, or take your grandchildren to the southern beaches. You need to feel young again.*

As if sensing Sheel's thoughts, Baldwin shifted, touching the collar of his formal shirt as if to ease its constriction. Few people made Baldwin doubt himself, but Sheel knew just the look that could make him uneasy. Actually, he liked his eldest brother: Baldwin was a steady personality, and would make a competent Atare. Little imagination, of course, and a tendency to be overbearing when he exerted his place as head of the immediate family, but a good man. And Baldwin returned his regard, if despairing of his lack of interest in the politics of Atare City.

"Archpriest Ward keeps trying to explain the importance of

ritual in our religion," Cort said easily, apparently unaware that Sheel had heard his last words. "As usual, most of it went beyond me."

"Do you truly pay attention, uncle?" Baldwin asked, no hint of humor in his face.

"Of course he does not," Sheel said quickly, a genuine smile pulling at the corner of his mouth. "Theology has always bored Cort. He would much rather watch the seri and me argue about the necessity of ritual in our religion." He glanced toward the priest as he spoke, and was rewarded with one of Ward's rare smiles.

Baldwin raised both eyebrows, but chose not to fence words. *Sixty-five Sans Sleep is not old, Baldwin. Stop aging yourself.*

Chuckling, Cort said: "Well, I need to say good night to Tobias and to Leah. I may be as tough as old leather, but even leather needs rest from friction. A good evening to all of you." He reached to gently touch Sheel's smooth, sharp-boned face, clapped Baldwin on the shoulder, and smiled in passing to the archpriest. All gave their nod of fealty at his leaving, his two *guaard* tight on his heels.

When Cort was out of earshot, Baldwin favored Sheel with one of his frowns. "Your attire is a bit casual for the occasion."

"A boy's birthday party?" Sheel arched one eyebrow because he knew Baldwin could not. "On the contrary, I think I am the only one appropriately dressed." Glancing down at his pale green syluan tunic and pants, simply and elegantly styled, he took in Baldwin's suit of tussah silk.

The new style of jacket, lacking lapels or pockets, did not suit Baldwin. The brown was a good color for him, matching his gray-flecked hair, but he was neither tall enough nor lean enough for the cut. The archpriest was dressed in robes of white silk, his second best ensemble—but then Ward always looked impressive.

Baldwin could be generous. "If I could look presentable in anything other than a state suit—" he started.

Sheel held up his hand in warning. "His name is Ryce. Over on Second Street. And not many have discovered him yet, so keep it to yourself!"

The heir pursed his lips thoughtfully, but did not speak. A smile pulled at the corner of his mouth, a smile almost never seen, and he nodded his thanks as he started off toward where Leah was holding court, his *guaard* matching his pace.

Ward actually looked amused as he watched Baldwin wander away. "You always know how to handle him. He is quite fond of you, you are aware of that?" the priest murmured, sipping his warmed wine.

"I am fond of Baldwin. He will make a good Atare," Sheel responded, thinking warmed wine sounded relaxing. "You are in good spirits tonight. Is Jonas feeling better?" The High Priest's health had been fragile for many days. Sheel suspected that Jonas was older than even Cort, but had courteously refrained from checking the records.

"Yes, he was much stronger today. A few visitors would cheer him, and he is ready for them. Come by when you have a moment."

"I have been on night duty, but now that I am back on days I will be able to see him," Sheel said obliquely, hoping Ward had no plans to lecture.

Not about the emergency center, at least. "Jonas still hopes to bring you back into the fold before he dies," Ward announced, glancing casually at Sheel out of one dark brown orb.

Controlling the smile which fought to spring forth, the same smile Baldwin always fought, Sheel said: "And you?"

Ward actually shrugged. "I would rather have you as you are, an unbeliever asking questions, than have you disinterested, like your brother Seri Fabe, or politely going through the motions like Seri Iver. I do not worry about your soul, Seri; only your peace of mind."

"Your concern is kind, but unnecessary," Sheel said, keeping his tone neutral. Ward had been within the palace walls during a few family arguments, and was well aware of Baldwin's fury over the unmarried state of his youngest siblings. "Perhaps I can stop in before work tomorrow. I will be trespassing tonight, I was generous again."

Ward was the only one who knew that Sheel occasionally bedded down in the temple guest rooms. "Maybe you should just send them to me?" Ward suggested, his face impassive.

Suspecting Ward was making a joke, Sheel said: "I do not think his pride could stand it. The 'borrower' would probably fear questions about when the child was due."

"If it is who I think it is, such questions would do him good," Ward announced, using his official tone. Shaking his dark head, the priest started toward Caleb, still another throneline brother. "You are about to be accosted. A good evening to you, Sheel of Atare."

Staring after the man, Sheel automatically tensed, expecting Crystle reb Lesli's delicate hand on his shoulder.

"Found you! I was not sure you would come, I heard last night was long!"

Relaxing, Sheel turned to face his little sister. He never called her that; he knew better. Avis was fully twenty-one Terran, and after nine moons of Baldwin and Leah's condescension had endured enough abuse as the youngest of eight children. The shortest of the family, almost a head smaller than Leah, and slender, Avis good-naturedly bore up under enough advice to send Sheel fleeing for the hills.

Laughing eyes gazed up into his, tinted in delicate pastels, one blue, one green. Her full head of curly blond hair drew men without effort, but Avis was unconscious of her beauty. Leaning into him, she whispered conspiratorially: "I need you to check something." Without ceremony she seized his hand and placed it on her stomach.

"Is this really the time or place?" Sheel asked innocently as Mailan and Avis's *guaard* moved to shield from prying eyes. It was common knowledge that Sheel's healing gift went beyond the usual limits—indeed, into the womb, where no probe could see without inducing a miscarriage. He was in great demand for predicting the sex of children. That he also knew whether they would be Sini—radioactive—or not was a secret he kept to himself. Along with other secrets. . . .

"Well?" Her impatience was charming. Wondering if she would actually stamp her foot in frustration, Sheel concentrated on the search. No, no conception, but . . .

"Where is Stephen?" Sheel asked, removing his hand and glancing over her shoulder past her *guaard*.

"Sheel!"

Laughing, he hugged her. "Not yet," he whispered into her ear. "But I suggest you find Stephen and spend a large part of the next three days working on it!"

Her wide, delicate eyes lighting up, Avis impulsively kissed him on the cheek and dashed off again. Unable to control the smile which crossed his face, Sheel turned toward the bar and looked for someone pouring refreshment. Wine? No, not yet . . .
"Soda with a lemon wedge," he said easily to the young man pouring drinks.

"You cannot be merry on soda, Seri," the youth replied, his tone almost scolding. "Can I interest you in a grocha?"

"I think my brother is covering that area nicely," Sheel replied, his expression bland. Laughing, the bartender opened a new container of soda and poured him a tall glass.

The touch on his spine was light and cool. "A moment for good nights, Sheel?"

"I took care of congratulations early on, in case Iver's socializing overcame me," Sheel said as he turned to face his older sister. Stooping without ceremony, Sheel extended his hand to Tobias. "Turning in, guy?"

Tobias made a face. "Mother says it is very late, but it does not *feel* late!" He carefully shook hands with Sheel, watching his mother with his one brown eye.

Her eyes a mirror of her son's, Leah's strong, square jaw tightened and then relaxed as she smiled. "Go ahead, it is your birthday—I will not scold!"

Grinning, Tobias tossed his arms around Sheel and hugged him. "It is undignified," he explained with a serious face.

"Yes," Sheel agreed, his own expression just as sober, "but birthdays are rare occasions. Sleep well, Tobias!" Standing and nodding politely to the boy's nana, they watched Tobias troop off toward the family wing, his *guaard* and attendant in tow. Turning to give Leah his attention, Sheel said: "A great success, Leah!"

"Tobias or the party?" she returned with a smile, the gold in her green eye glinting.

"Both, of course. You can be proud of him. May I compliment you on how well you look? Childers' potions did not kill you after all!"

"Sheel!" Looking over her shoulder and finding only her *guaard*, she gave her brother one of her stern expressions. "I know you do not like the man, but he is a certified doctor, and has been a great comfort to me since I lost the child." Her voice was slightly colorless at this last statement, and Sheel took her free hand in sympathy.

"I simply think there are some things a healer can do best, and since you have one at your disposal, it is a shame to keep him patching together careless revelers instead of tending to his family's health." Leaning over to lightly touch her cheek, aware of her tensing beneath his touch, he said: "I meant it. You look stunning in dark green."

This brought forth one of her genuine smiles, almost a shy smile, and a toss of long, flowing, dark tresses. "Knowing how rarely you make any comment on appearance, I am quite flattered." Her eyes wandered over the crowd, restless as always. "I am not yet beyond notice! The dark and the light, Avis and I—"

"And the most attractive women in the room," Sheel assured

her, sensing she was worried about something. *Leah, if you would only trust me enough to see if I can help....*

"Avis is cheerful tonight," Leah said softly, locating their sister near the windows. "Did you have good news for her?"

For those with eyes to see and ears to hear, it was there.... "No, but you know her exuberance. After that disaster on Emerson . . . Stephen and Brant, among others, have renewed her self-confidence. It will make our trip to Caesarea less humbling," Sheel said carelessly, sipping his drink. *If you do not yet realize that Stephen has won the game, you will have to plumb the depths of other sources.* But to stay? No one had asked Stephen, as far as Sheel knew. Even if it was but a passing thing, Sheel hoped that Avis conceived. Waiting on the birth would postpone the Caesarean trip. Leah would not be pleased about that child . . . not at all.

"You will find someone acceptable to you, Sheel. I am confident." Leah's voice intruded into his thoughts, years of experience weighing her voice. Choosing not to respond to her comment, Sheel casually met her eyes. Her expression rueful, his elder sister took leave of him with a cool touch to his face.

No change. The thought drifted to the surface of his mind, and he was glad no telepaths were in the room. No one knew how sensitive his talents really were . . . no one except Cort Atare. Shortly after his return from Emerson, his uncle had set him a task: determine if Leah could bear more children. Not would . . . could.

The fear, the *danger* such a question brought on was stifling. Yet Cort's suspicions had proved correct. Leah reb Riva Atare was sterile, and Sheel had no idea why it had come about, or if it could be reversed.

That *off-world* idiot Childers certainly could not do anything for her—she brought him back from Caesarea because she could control him, through his desire for position and wealth. Whether hot healing could help her was an unknown, and Sheel could not maintain physical contact with her long enough to test his theories. It had been hard enough to make the initial determination. Finally arranging to sit behind her at an informal family gathering, he had rubbed her shoulders while seeking answers within her bloodstream.

Reduction in hormones . . . premature menopause. No wonder she was so edgy; she was terrified. Leah defined herself by her house status. As a sterile member of a very fertile house—no wonder she was desperate to keep it secret. And she knew little about the three youngest of her siblings—why should she trust any of them with the information? But pretending to have had a miscarriage! Knowing exactly what he was seeking, the answer to that question had been instantaneous: Leah had not been pregnant recently.

What could he do to help her? . . .

He was oblivious to the crowd, and therefore not expecting to have someone practically thrust into his arms. A gasp penetrated his thoughts even as something cold splashed across his back and arm, drenching the woman clinging to him.

"It is grocha!" came the bartender's cry as he thrust a bottle of soda into Sheel's hand. Not pausing for explanations Sheel promptly dumped the entire contents down the front of the woman's dress, even as someone soaked his own back.

"By The Path what a mess!" came Iver's voice. "I most humbly beg your pardon, I forgot about the step up!"

Turning slightly, Sheel saw Iver wore an agonized expression. Glancing down, he realized the woman using his arm as a support was the exquisite ice princess. Her expression was one of complete bewilderment as she stared first at the bottle in his hand and then at her wet garment. Iver's apology was lost on her.

Her gaze finally reached Sheel's face, and he found it odd that she did not change expression; most off-worlders were startled by his eyes. Sweet Mendulay, Iver was correct, she *did* have eyes that pulled the viewer in. . . .

"It was grocha," Sheel heard himself say. Realizing that would not help much, he added: "Grocha can remove dye from cloth. Soda neutralizes this effect." He glanced over his own shoulder as he spoke.

"We caught it, Seri, but the fiber has probably been weakened." The bartender looked quite stricken.

"It happens," Sheel said gently, his tone dismissing the problem. Turning to Iver he said: "Perhaps you should escort our rather damp guest to a place where she can change clothing? That dress should be in soda immediately."

Just then two familiar faces came into focus: Leah, and Iver's wife Bette. Seeing the mess, Leah shook her head graciously. "Iver, you must pick women built more like Avis or myself if you expect us to be able to loan them clothing."

Not good—people were starting to gather, and Iver's spouse was very unhappy. At least the ice princess was not becoming hysterical or abusive. "If you will come with me, an attempt will be made to save that lovely garment," Sheel said quickly, lightly taking her elbow and allowing Mailan to force a path through the crowd.

In moments Sheel felt the ancient, rough-hewn stone of the first floor corridor beneath his fingertips. Silence rang in his ears after the din of the party room, but he did not slow his pace. No footsteps followed, but he would take no chances. Not knowing this woman's rank or authority, he could not risk any public embarrassment. Brother Baldwin would fry Iver's ears if this woman had any complaints. Always careful of the proper procedure, was Baldwin. . . .

"Here, Seri," came Mailan's voice out of the dimness ahead. The *guaard* was holding open a door to a guest room, her slender body straddling the doorsill. Staying his swift pace, Sheel gestured for the woman to precede him.

She was very small, scarcely 150 in height, he guessed. Finding suitable clothing would be a problem. Perhaps sending a *guaard* to her room . . . Proceeding straight into the sanitation, Sheel turned on the lights, revealing a large room tiled in pastel blues. A touch at the control eye and the closet door slid open.

"There is a robe here, and the wipes are on the ledge next to the shower cabinet," Sheel began, bending to find the delicate soaking cleanser. Stocked as always—he sealed the basin near the door, started the water, and dumped the packet in. Setting the dial for barely warm, he turned back to the woman.

She was studying him, a slightly bemused expression on her face. It was a searching gaze, missing little. Iver would have quite a chase with this one. . . .

"Completely submerge the dress in this—" Sheel gestured to the basin. "It will stabilize the dye and strengthen the fibers. I will see if there is anything appropriate to be found to replace it, or if we must send to your hostel."

"Do not put yourself to great effort, Sir," she said softly, her voice very low and vibrant. Natural or chemicals? That the question should distract him momentarily amused Sheel, and then he said:

"I am Sheel of Atare. Do you need . . . help?" He was suddenly at a loss, realizing he might have offended a personage used to attendants.

"No . . . Seri. I will manage quite well, thank you." She was already moving toward the sanitation, pulling free the wrapped skirt as she walked.

"As you wish," Sheel said quickly, feeling his own surprise

pulling into a smile and controlling it. Moving toward the corridor, he slipped past Mailan and said: "Put someone on the door."

How Mailan was able to put a *guaard* on the guest room and still catch him within a dozen strides was one of the innumerable mysteries of *guaard* training. Fortunately the storage closets were only in the next corridor.

. Nothing of Leah's would do—his elder sister was nearly Mailan's height. And Avis was much rounder. But he remembered an old silk tunic of his own.... Yes. Pulling it out, he studied it a moment. Flaming red, of jacquard weave, it had long, full sleeves and was slit up the sides. Not the current style at all, but at least she could retire to her own apartments and wardrobe in it.

It was not until he was once again at the guest room door that he realized he had not caught her name. Had she offered it? Had there been time? Curse The Path, Baldwin would be furious.... Mailan was already knocking, the second *guaard* ignoring them both. Sweet Mendulay, his back was damp.

"Come in."

Mailan led, stationing herself against the supporting wall between sanitation and entry way. Sheel found the woman had already bathed and was wrapped in one of the thick, absorbent robes provided for all Nualan guests. She turned away from the tall windows at his return, a faint smile crossing her face. "I did not realize anyone still used wipes exclusively. It is a novelty rarely appreciated."

Sheel had time to notice how rigid Mailan appeared—*she thinks it was an insult*—before answering: "In a climate as hot and dry as ours, vacuums can cause the skin to flake. Wipes take less energy to maintain." He laid the tunic on the center bed. "This is not the latest style, but it will allow you to return to your hostel in comfort."

"You need it back immediately?" she asked, moving to examine the material. "I would not want to offend the hostess by leaving early."

"A damaged dress is a perfect excuse to leave," Sheel assured her.

The woman struggled to control the wry expression which crossed her face. "Returning to the party might be awkward... and I have spent the last ten years in Freeze. I need something tonight besides rest! I hoped to discover more about the city and your customs before paying my evening respects." Loosening the woven black belt knotted around the tunic, she walked into the sanitation. "Accurate information about your world is scarce, in the Seven Systems, and my employers expect me to be well-versed in Nualan courtesies before the night has ended."

As he moved toward the window to gauge the night, a whisper of silk reached Sheel's ears. He turned his head to see her reappear in the tunic, methodically rolling up the sleeves, the belt tossed over one shoulder.

He was momentarily appalled. Never had he thought of himself as anything but thin—he was so narrow through the shoulders Avis could not wear his shirts—yet this tunic engulfed the woman. She seemed unconcerned. Giving the sleeves a final tug, settling them at her elbows, she tied the long belt around her waist and began weaving the ends across the front in a braid. Fascinated, it took Sheel several seconds to realize he was staring. Pulled in by the belt, the tunic did become a dress, but gave evidence of being designed purposely oversized, in a style popular in Dielaan. He had not expected it to look so elegant . . . but this woman had made a robe of toweling elegant.

"You have only to ask. What would you like to know?" he asked gently, wishing the Caesarean tongue used a greater range of civilities.

"Very gracious," she said smiling. "Are you with PPR?"

He considered the acronym, and then a smile of state crossed his face. "Public Promotion and Relations?"

"Yes—that is what I do for Rover Consortium. I doubt I could have smoothed over a scene any better than you handled this one."

"You . . . are a guest of the house. But it would not be proper for my sister to leave the assembly," Sheel said carefully, not sure how much she really wanted to hear about Nualan custom. "If you would prefer someone from Service . . ."

"Not at all. You're easily the most interesting person I've met this evening; I have no complaints," she said, coming to stand next to the window. As she passed him, the scent of cloves rose to his nostrils.

Suddenly at a loss as days of poor sleep descended upon his head, Sheel thought desperately for the proper question. As he mentally tore through various introductions, he caught her eye. She was extremely amused, he was certain—and he was not sure she had intended him to notice that fact.

"I'm not bored," she added quickly, even as he considered the same words.

Sheel felt a familiar smile tugging at his lips, but he suppressed it.

"I can tell you're dying to slip away—that soda must be sticky. Give my regards to whoever it is, and have someone show me the route back to the hall. I can send this back to you here?"

"I am not bored," he found himself saying gently, aware the humor was trying to leak through. "Though I am tired, and may not be very good company this evening."

"You sound weary," she agreed. "I won't keep you."

"My sister Avis claims I always sound weary," Sheel admitted, "but I am as good a guide as any you will find tonight. Probably better . . . I am still sober."

"We could do something about that—unless . . ." Her low voice trailed off. "All those bottles behind the bartender that glowed like jewels—they're native liqueurs?"

"Yes. The water is treated, if you wish to try them," he said neutrally.

"Well . . ." She managed a faint smile. "I'm not much of a drinker, but I love to try exotic-tasting things. I saw one with the name . . . sunjewel?"

"A type of flower . . . and a *very* exotic liqueur. We can rim the bottom of a glass or two, and you can compare it to wild suckle-berry, which oddly enough is similar. Except for the aftertaste," he added, still uncertain. Very different, this woman, keeping him off-balance. At first there was a hint of seduction in her manner, but now . . . friendly yet without promise. Why? . . .

"Only if you explain to me what a 'seri' is," she said. "There seemed to be a lot of them running around that party, but I received differing impressions about rank and status."

She sounded almost cross, as if someone had made up a game and refused to tell her the rules. Sheel could not hold it in any longer, and his laugh rang out. Startled, the ice princess grinned. Not her practiced smile; a real grin.

"Only if you tell me the proper means of addressing you."

She actually looked disconcerted. "I've never told you, have I? My name is Darame Daviddottir."

"No longer the ice princess." He started for the doorway.

"I . . . beg pardon?" he heard her say in the Caesarean manner.

"You glitter from a distance. It was as good a title as any," Sheel answered, waiting at the entrance for a reaction.

A pause, as if considering . . . "I feared you were referring to my personality," she told him, a hint of asperity in her voice.

"Indeed. *Are* you an ice princess?" he asked brightly.

Not likely . . . Her laughter was very warm.

MATINS

"I thought the previous bell rang eight times," Darame said abruptly, startled out of her concentration. The bird calls were fascinating, like nothing she had ever heard, and she found the interruption annoying.

"It did," Sheel replied placidly, kicking a stone down the paved path.

"How many kinds of birds sing at night?" Darame continued, peering up through the tall foliage dancing above their heads.

Sheel chuckled, drawing her attention. "That makes four."

"Four what?" she asked, wondering what tangent they would pursue next.

"Four conversations we are carrying on at once. You keep bouncing among the university and its grounds, the prospect of rain, the fauna, and now the bells. Do you continue these conversations in your head? Sometimes the next question in the category does not fit the sequence."

She stopped walking, folding her arms and giving him a firm look. *Blessed Nualan is very clever,* she couldn't help thinking. *I never relax this much with strangers.*

Sheel also paused, seemingly oblivious to her expression, and she saw the outline of his head tilt upwards. "Here comes your rain."

The drops reached them before he finished the comment. "Where do we go?" she said aloud, wondering uneasily if the rain could hurt her somehow. Radioactive rain . . .

"This way." Seizing her arm, he guided her swiftly along the trail.

Darame had no idea where they were. Tiring of the party, which had increased in gaiety as the night progressed, she had convinced Sheel she really wanted a tour of the city. To her surprise, he agreed. An even greater surprise was the discovery that they were going to walk. Accustomed to long hours in awkward shoes, Darame found this no hardship. The shadow in black which matched Sheel's pace had been harder to accept.

Atare City had been a marvel; buildings were tall and crowded close together, although the stone streets were quite wide. Intricate detailing made each structure a work of art, yet the overall blend was harmonious. Sheel had been strangely at home as they walked the nearly deserted streets, explaining with simple eloquence the design of the community. There had been no empty buildings; a store Sheel claimed was eight hundred years Terran had contained a bustling chocolate bar which made Darame long to try Nualan delicacies. Something in her manner had said "off-world," however, for the shopkeeper sadly informed her he currently had no imports she could sample.

A kinship between the university and the palace was not merely architectural skill; at one time the palace had been a part of the learning center. There Sheel had seemed most relaxed, the shadows and stark edges of the campus of a kind with the sharp angles of his face. It was there that she had discovered, almost in passing, that he was a doctor, and sometimes taught classes in medicine.

Only one other building had been open this late—the museum —and it had been closing as they arrived. Sheel had paused to speak with the curator, and had arranged for them to visit one exhibit before the lights dimmed. It had been an unusual display, the guts of a control room laid out before their eyes. Bits of plastic, ceramic, rubber, and silicon had glittered against pieces of clear acrylic, the plastic command chairs of faded red mounted on . . . acrylic? Then she had noticed the sign. Not merely a display; the fragments had been the remnants of the control room of *The Atare,* one of the three ancient ships which had landed upon Nuala and then been unable to leave . . . unable to escape. The metal of the hulls had been swiftly destroyed by whatever was present that rotted normal alloys. Radiation was involved, the same radiation which had mutated their children and almost destroyed them all. . . .

A shiver which had nothing to do with the rain and rising breeze traced Darame's spine. Sheel had not spoken to her at the museum, except to explain that the acrylic represented the metal which had been devoured by the mutated microbes. Lost in thought, choosing not to ask him what microbes he spoke of, Darame had followed him back to the streets as the museum had faded into gloom. To have been trapped here with no hope of rescue, forced to make a new civilization or die in the attempt—

What a mysterious place, Darame could not help but think as the *guaard* sprinted past them both, dragging her thoughts into the present. Allowed landfall with a prick of her finger and a walk down a flashing metallic corridor, yet those attached to the royal line were followed constantly by bodyguards. And no one asked questions here . . . not of anyone. People volunteered their names upon first meeting—and if they didn't, no one in the circle asked. Even Sheel had asked only for her preferred mode of address. His few questions had been immediate, and often teasing. No one had asked why she was here, or for particulars about her work. . . . And then there was that one man at the party. . . . *Why don't they ask questions? Is the secret in that somber relic of* The Atare?

A box of light appeared before them, and Sheel pulled her through a doorway into some sort of lounge. The *guaard*—what did he call her, Mailan?—was arranging colored sticks in a fire-pit, even as Sheel crossed to a small bar. Turning slightly to the *guaard,* Sheel softly spoke to her in Nualan. She answered briefly, and the man laughed in response. Pulling a wine carafe from a cabinet, he said in Caesarean: "Would you like wine? Chilled or warmed is possible."

"You talk to her," Darame heard herself say, and wondered where her common sense had flown. Sheel twisted slightly, giving her a puzzled look. "The guard. Everyone else pretends they aren't there, but you talk to her." *So maybe she's your mistress; Sweet Saints, where is my mouth?*

"Guaard," Sheel said easily, drawing out the vowel. He poured some wine into a mug and hesitated over the second mug, raising an eyebrow at her.

"Warm, please," Darame said quickly, grateful he was overlooking her breach of the invisible Nualan boundaries of courtesy.

"They are not exactly guards. They are shadows, in a sense. They do nothing but exist to protect us, yet they may choose to do as much or little else as they wish, as long as it does not distract them from their charge. Mailan and I . . . owe . . . each other favors, and keep track of them. Every time she does something a *guaard* is not required to do, yet saves me effort, she puts me in debt. When I do something my family normally does not do, I put her in debt." Sheel placed the mugs in a hot box and set the timer. "Fire-tending is outside her duties. I suggested it was her third of the night, and she reminded me that tracking odd garments through the halls was not *guaard* duty."

"Four, then?" Darame said, relaxing slightly.

"Perhaps. I think *you* owe her one, actually, but we will settle that some other time." Removing the mugs from the hot box and carefully offering her a handle, he added: "It is my father's fault. He was an extremely gracious man, and felt it rude to act as if *guaard* were not present. All those running conversations! His *guaard* was as patient as Mailan—although I try not to speak to her in public, or when other *guaard* are present. It implies she is too casual at her duties."

"Which she is not," Darame finished for him, sipping carefully at the spicy pink wine. "Thank you, Mailan, I am always cold," she added as the multicolored flames sprang from the stone basin. Bending over, she examined the "logs" closely. Pressed . . . what? Fire crystals, someone had said at the party? The fire burning there had been huge. She turned back to Sheel, and found he had changed expression. It was detached, almost professional.

"If you are often chilled, wet clothing will only make it worse. There is undoubtedly a robe in the closet, and the shower is that way—" He gestured through an arch as he sat down on one of the low, cushioned benches circling the firepit. Recognizing her protest before she could voice it, he said: "Please, it would be very embarrassing for me if you caught a cold in my presence!"

She could see the sense of it; tossing him a smile, she moved off toward the sanitation.

Everything was as promised; twisting her hair into a knot upon her head, Darame stood under the spray until warmth returned to her body. Damn Brant, and damn Halsey for letting the fool upset him. . . . She had not thought the evening would turn out so pleasantly. The first night was traditionally hers—Halsey encouraged her attitude on that point. *Make sure Iver and Caleb see you*, Halsey had said. *But play hard to get—Atare clan finds that attractive. The rest of the night is your own.*

Until Brant had decided she wasn't obvious enough. Curse of the Star of Morning on that man! Since when did he know more about finding a man's weak point than she? And that business with the drink—it had not gone as Brant wanted, and she'd hear about it. Indirectly, of course. "They" had decided that Halsey and Brant were friends, but she and Brant only casual acquaintances. *Damn right*. Now instead of being charmingly embarrassed over bumping a pretty woman's drink, Iver would be either upset or trying to forget he'd made a fool of himself and destroyed a woman's dress—either way, likely to ignore her next time they met. It would take a lot of work to undo Brant's heavy-handedness. If he was going to push a member of the royal house, at least find out what he was drinking!

And Sheel was not part of Brant's plan. Baldwin, Caleb, and Iver were the only sons of the house Brant had mentioned by name, yet Sheel was obviously close to the royal family, if not an heir himself. The ruler plainly thought a great deal of him, and the marks all conversed with him during the evening. The Ragaree's little son obviously adored the man. Then to have that drink fly all over him as well. . . . She had already decided on

Sheel; fortunate it had turned out as it had, or Brant would rue his interference.

Turning off the water, she concentrated on that first moment she had noticed Sheel, trying to decide what had drawn her to him. There was grace in his movements; nothing wasted, in speech or gesture. And his beauty was something rarely seen, remote, chiseled, by turns androgynous and then arrogantly masculine. But she had seen both traits in those who followed medicine as a field: the detached, assumed confidence, and the gentler, healing qualities.

He certainly wasn't dull, she decided, reaching for a wipe. She had honestly enjoyed the tour, and the rest of the evening as well. So much to learn about the Nualans, and she'd barely disturbed the surface of the water. Of course she suspected he hadn't wanted her around . . . not at first. Still politely neutral, touching her only to speed her out of the rain. There had been that gorgeous brunette throwing herself at him earlier—he had seemed oblivious to it. Could he prefer men? No—surely that incredibly beautiful woman would not have made such a fool of herself if there was no hope. Scholars and lovers, eh . . . *I'll settle for what I've had, but it's worth a try.* He had very nice hands. . . .

"And sunjewel *was* an exotic taste," she murmured aloud. Wrapping the robe around her slender figure, she released her hair with a flick of her fingers and walked back into the lounging room.

Mailan was not immediately visible. A quick glance around showed her to be in a recessed area of the corridor, a wide view at her disposal. The flames had settled; fire crystals apparently were both quiet and smokeless. Sheel was still by the firepit, although he had dragged the cushions off the benches and arranged them on the floor. He had also removed his shirt, spreading it to dry over the back of a chair.

"I put your mug back in the hot box," Sheel said without turning, sipping his own drink. Outside the tempo of the rain increased, spattering against the glass terrace doors off in the adjoining room. Nodding absently, Darame moved toward the one tall window of the room, leaning against it.

"Doesn't look like it will stop soon. Can you stand sharing any more instruction in the Nualan culture?" she said softly. "I rinsed that tunic in cold water and hung it up, by the way—I don't think it will spot. Do you want to soak that shirt?"

"In a bit," Sheel replied. "It is syluan, the watered variety. It will not spot, although I should rinse out the soda. If you want

more culture, you may have to ask questions. I have given you
the usual tourist information."

Wandering over to the hot box, Darame pulled out her wine
and sipped it. "I was told Nualans were known as scholars and
lovers. You have lived up to half that image. Is there anything
about this city you don't know?" She seated herself on the edge
of a bench, off to one side of him. "You'd better find another
robe, or a blanket. You'll catch cold, and that would be more
embarrassing than me catching cold!"

He managed a smile. "I am never cold."

"Never?"

Something in the way she said it sharpened his attention. "Not
physically, at least." He held out his hand; touching it, Darame
felt her eyes widen.

"You are like that fire! Why are men always warmer?"

"Not always. Better circulation, sometimes." He seemed evasive for the first time that night, and she chose not to pursue it.

"Why don't people ask questions here?" It seemed safer than
any other line of conversation. He turned his head toward her,
and she watched as the left eye moved into shadow, the split iris
blending into a solid darkness. The man's expression was a question. "No one has directly asked me my name, or what I'm doing
here. . . ."

Sheel's face cleared. "You mean *personal* questions. No, no
one asks personal questions, usually. . . . You know that we are a
sanctuary planet?"

"Yes." She waited while he sipped at his wine.

"Do you know what it means?"

"Political and religious asylum," she started tentatively.

"Here it is more. It is a clean slate. Your past dissolves when
you walk through the pillars. Once you have told the authorities
why you seek sanctuary, and they accept you, you can become
another person. There is no record of what name you choose to
use once you take up residency."

"Then that's why—" She stopped. Sheel's expression invited
confidence, but he did not speak. "There was this man at the
party. Not of the royal line, I guess; he had no *guaard*, but he
appeared wealthy. He never asked any questions, but he was . . .
hinting at something. I couldn't figure out what he was suggesting." She realized it would make no sense to him, and
elaborated. "He said—casually—that he was a 20, and part of
the Bellen mining family, which I gather is wealthy—"

"Very. Silver mines."

"The sort of thing people make up to impress people," she went on, aware it sounded inane. "It . . . felt awkward. . . ."

"If you had immigrated to Nuala in hope of marrying well, someone would have explained such code words to you," Sheel said simply. "He was not making it up. Atare—indeed, Nuala—is too small a place for exaggeration. There was a young Bellen at the party. He found you attractive and was trying to save himself the burden of a trip to Caesarea. Was his name Kobb?"

"Yes! He told me his name right off."

Sheel started to chuckle. "Poor Kobb. Wealth or wife, what a dilemma!" Seeing her expression, he continued: "Kobb is a 20. That means he is fertile. And from a wealthy line. He is highly placed in his house, a branch of Atare, and important in the mining industry. But if he goes to Caesarea, he will lose his position in the business, since he will be absent twenty years Terran. Yet his house is prestigious enough that he wants an off-world wife, not a Nualan. His few children are healthy enough, but his line has produced no healers. Therefore they prefer non-Nualan genes. If he is going to marry, why not the best?"

"And if he can find an 'off-world' bride visiting Nuala, so much the easier?" Darame said, grinning. "But what if I'm sterile?"

"You are not. Among all those tests run from your blood and energy field, we also test for disease and sterility. The guest board in the palace lobby lists all diplomatic visitors in black or blue print—in Nualan, of course. The occasional black means sterile or unacceptable. Become involved at your own risk."

"A bit presumptuous, don't you think?" Darame said with icy civility.

"You asked," he reminded her gently. "Eighty percent of our population is sterile. Women fight over fertile men, and men have been known to duel over fertile women. Since being the product of a married couple is only important in inheritance cases, many people come to the embassy hoping to . . ."

"Get lucky, as they say on Caesarea Station," Darame finished. "Well, I can't criticize. I've been working straight—sans sleep—for a long time. He could have figured into my recreation, if . . ." She decided to leave it dangling. *Forget it, he's not helping at all, he's not interested.* "I steered him toward that brunette in silver netting, but she wasn't interested. Poor Kobb isn't bad looking, but he's not my type, either."

"Brunette?" Sheel said, his mug pausing halfway to his lips.

"The one who stared at you all night," she said deliberately, wondering if that was too familiar.

"Crystle reb Lesli. Poor Crystle . . . If only she was not so obvious, I might oblige her. Tonight I simply could not stomach it."

Darame stared at him. "She's gorgeous. Kobb's crazy, he should shower her with silver."

"Kobb wants an off-world wife. And Crystle wants a child to solidify her line. . . . Kobb's house is not as clean as mine."

"You *are* an Atare?" *I need* some *political specifics tonight*.

"Yes. For over a thousand years Terran, my family has been required to take off-world spouses for their legal line. I am mostly off-world, now, and my Atare genes were tough in the beginning, withstanding the planet's heat." He seemed to be considering something. "I do not think it would be violating a confidence to tell you this. . . . Everyone knows it. Crystle's family is one that has trouble breeding. Every other generation they must turn to the knife."

"The knife?"

"The labs, to stabilize the genetic tissue and produce viable offspring. It has no real stigma, but it is painful for the families, to still be so variable. Crystle is second generation. . . . That means she will probably need help from the labs to bear viable offspring."

"Unless she finds someone who is extremely fertile and extremely healthy," Darame said finally. "You fit both categories. Why not another Atare? Iver has women falling all over him, and he doesn't resist."

Sheel actually looked embarrassed. "Iver . . . has only three children. A few on the way, since returning, and of course his wife's unborn child."

"And you?" She could not resist the giggle in her voice.

"I knew I would regret the direction of this conversation." Sighing, the man continued: "Thirteen documented. A few more yet to be born, and a few whose mothers see no reason to have it on record. Those unrecorded are grown and married, with strong lines of their own."

"How . . . oh. You went to Emerson. . . ." She moved down closer to the fire, stirring it with the poker lying near the rim of the pit. *So you are the best, and she wants the best. Can't blame her for trying.* Something about the discussion nagged at the back of her mind, but she lost the thread of thought. Then something else occurred to her, and she looked over at him. *Sweet Saint Jude, you've smiled on me.* "So you're sick of playing stud, eh?"

He jerked slightly, but did not turn toward her. "I suppose you think it is a little thing to give her."

"How many Crystles are waiting in line, hoping to catch your attention? I'd think you'd be exhausted, not to mention . . . bored. The great Turabian lost track of his lovers, but he finally became a celibate, didn't he?"

A hint of a smile . . . There was that dimple again, fighting to remain stern. "I am not that familiar with the great lover. But at least he was in demand because . . ." Tensing suddenly, he set down his mug and folded his long fingers, resting his chin upon them.

Dear lord, they've bled the playfulness out of you. How do the others stand it? Are you more sensitive—introspective—or is there something more? "It's nothing of you, is it? They want your genes, not you. It wouldn't matter what kind of person you are, or what you've accomplished in your life. Just the genes. Are they taking their temperature while they get your attention?"

That made him laugh. "No, not yet. They probably take care of it beforehand. I have never shown any interest in a permanent relationship with a Nualan, you see, so they waste little time in preliminaries." There was a sharp edge to his voice, hard enough to cut to bone. "On Emerson it was just the opposite: all games, no one interested in a family."

"But you have extremely advanced genetic techniques." The puzzlement in her voice made him turn his head. "I mean . . . can't you just . . . give them some material to work with and send these women to the lab?" She had never thought herself squeamish concerning fertility, but then such frank—no, brutal—discussion was not common on other worlds.

"I do. But the lab splices everything, to better mix the gene pool. We trade cultures with other city-states as well. Some do not want the advantages of the pool, they want pure throne line Atare. But too many Atare descendants would upset the balance, cause inbreeding . . . so the lab does not fill those requests. A woman must pursue a royal Atare herself."

"Well . . . I am not in any hurry to start a family, if that's any consolation. I was planning on meeting you without any idea of the . . . long-term advantages of such an introduction?" She considered her words. "I don't think that came out right." Sighing, she decided to try bluntness: "You seemed amusing and interesting and attractive. And I've been sleeping alone and very cold the last ten years Terran."

Laughter bubbled out of Sheel, and he tried vainly to smother his amusement. Finally he looked over at her, but words clearly eluded him.

She went on ruthlessly, peeling at his mask: "I like your mouth . . . especially those dimples you're always fighting, when you really want to smile at something. And you have great hands—" Abruptly she reached for one, unfolding it from its mate. Long, slender—more than competent. An unusual odor trickled past her nose . . . sandalwood, with a touch of dry musk. . . . "Anything else is dessert."

That puzzled him. "Dessert?" There was humor in his voice.

She felt a foolish grin slip out. "Not on the regular menu . . . not expected, or included in the price of the meal."

"I have never thought of myself as a delicacy. . . ." he started dryly, and Darame collapsed in laughter. "You, however, are unusual. I . . ."

"Go ahead, say it. If it's too personal, I won't answer," she said wickedly, and saw a trace of embarrassment touch his features.

"I have never seen a young woman with silver hair before. . . ."

"You've never been to Norwood. The food does it—permanently. I could dye it black again, but I like the novelty."

"How long have you traveled in Sleep?" he said quietly, his expression unreadable.

That required thought. "You know, I don't know?" she said finally. "I lost count a long time ago. Over a hundred years Terran easily. I must be hovering around thirty Terra." She studied his thoughtful face, and as if divining his thought said: "It's a lot of places to be. I've never found anything to hold me. . . . I always wanted to see the next planet."

"Beyond the Seven Systems?"

"No, not yet," she protested. "I'm not that old! Maybe next . . ." She considered the idea. "That would be a great leap in the dark. What if I couldn't get work there? What if they limit how often you can Sleep, and I couldn't return here?"

"Neglect to tell them your Terran birthdate," Sheel suggested.

"Lie? I can't believe a Nualan suggested that!" She gave him her best wide-eyed look.

"I merely suggest you fail to volunteer information. It is the Nualan thing to do," he corrected gently.

She was still holding onto his wrist, but as he did not seem to mind, she dismissed the worry. It was a strong wrist, all bone and tendon. "Of course . . ." Then she remembered that sect on Emerson which considered it a sin to waste seed. *Now how can I propose that with a witness?* Releasing him, she sat up and tied the robe securely. "I find myself remembering Mailan's presence."

"She sees and hears only threats to my person," Sheel said, looking away.

"So is one old lady a threat?"

A long pause. Finally he spoke: "How old a lady?"

Darame thought she detected that trace of humor once again. "I was born in 2216 A.R.," she said evenly.

"One hundred seventy-three years should command some respect," Sheel said dryly. "If Mailan was worried about you, she would not stand so far away."

Far away? The *guaard* was within leaping distance. "How do you make a pass at someone with a *guaard* present?" she asked, injecting some of her old lilt into the phrase.

The man gave her a long, thoughtful look. Then he reached up and delicately touched her cheek. "Very slowly. . . ."

Chapter Three

MENDULARION S ATARE   THIRTYSEVENDAY   LAUDS

It was not the first nightmare since his return from Emerson, but it was the most vivid. Sheel threw himself off the bed in one fluid movement and was on the terrace before he realized he had left the bedroom. Brisk night air caressed his skin, drawing a shiver from him. The last image of the dream hung before his eyes like a dye canvas, bleeding into the night, slipping away like dew at starrise.

Motion caught his eye; he glanced over to see Mailan hovering at the doorframe.

"A dream, Mailan," he said easily, knowing she would understand. No one knew that the nightmares usually had a thread into reality—at least he thought no one knew. Mailan had listened to him recount a few. . . . Had she ever put them together with current events and seen the parallels?

Bleeding into the night . . . shaking, Sheel moved back toward the bedroom. Why so much blood? He had seen Cort Atare's death. . . . But why so much blood? An old man, Cort Atare, and likely to slip away at any time. Would dissension follow Cort's reign? And there had been *guaard* present, he had seen *guaard*. *Guaard* covered with blood, even as Cort had been. . . . *Guaard* still alive?

He had never thought of himself as having prescience—not really. It was intermittent, and always violent. Yet every nightmare of his childhood had a parallel in its immediate future. Could it be coincidence? Had he forgotten the incidents which were false dreams?

Suddenly Sheel remembered the woman. Damn The Path! She could not have slept through his hasty departure. . . . Where had he—oh, yes. Now that he considered it, he had been using her stomach as a pillow. *A very comfortable pillow.* . . . Hoping she was a heavy sleeper, he glided back into the wing of the temple, pulling the terrace doors closed behind him.

It was a fruitless hope. A rustle of cotton sheets, and a rose glow erupted from a tiny nightlight next to the bed. Sheel folded himself onto the mattress, a tangle of long, hard limbs, and studied Darame.

Her hands shielded the gleam, allowing their eyes to adjust. Not bothering to pull the blankets up beyond her ribs, she settled comfortably on her side, a statue of pale bronze, her hair tumbling down to pool brilliant against the dark blue sheets. Deep, shadowed eyes studied him dispassionately, their question unvoiced.

It took a moment for Sheel to remember she did not speak Nualan. "A dream," he said softly in Caesarean.

"A nightmare," she corrected, her gaze still dissecting.

"I suppose . . ."

"A common occurrence?" she asked, her expression guarded, aware that the question might be too personal.

"Not really. . . . I have not had one in many moons." Suddenly he was tired, very tired, and let his head drop down to his arm. Correctly interpreting the gesture, Darame twisted her supple form and reached to extinguish the nightlight. Sheel noticed a shiver as the room plunged into darkness. "If you are cold, there should be an extra blanket on the shelf in the closet."

"I . . . I was afraid it would make you hot," came the simple reply.

He considered it. "Possibly," he admitted. "Come over here, instead; surely I have enough heat for two people."

"Blankets are not restless sleepers," she replied, sliding next to him and bringing with her the scent of allspice and cloves.

"When I am not having bad dreams, I am a quiet sleeper," he promised, slipping an arm around her back.

At first unwilling to relax, her form stiff, cautious, Darame finally shifted to meld herself against his side, snuggling into his shoulder. "You're better than a hot water bottle," she muttered.

"A what?"

"Something used in the Gavriel system—a soft plas container filled with hot water and wrapped in a cloth. It's used to warm up sheets, or sometimes for a sick person," she explained, letting her fingers glide across the smooth skin of his chest. "You're not very fuzzy, you know."

Sheel fought back laughter. "No, few Atare men are . . . fuzzy."

"That's all right. There are some disadvantages to all that hair. A woman can end up covered by morning. You're so warm you don't need it." She sounded half-asleep, murmuring a confidence that probably would never see the light of day. Then she stiffened again. "Where's Mailan?"

The laughter bubbled out, and Darame reached to touch his face. "You're laughing at me," she said crossly, her delicate fingers finding the betraying dimples.

He was; she was quite funny, the way odd things popped out of her mouth. But he chose to say: "Nualan women also find the *guaard* disconcerting."

"Common sense," she said, burrowing against him. "I think I'll attach myself here for the rest of the night."

It had been a long time since anyone had spent the entire night. The thought was pleasant, and Sheel folded his arms around her in response. Beneath the woman's calm, elegant exterior was a personality which liked to be cuddled. A personality that meant what it said, and kept its promises, unlike the women of Emerson. . . .

Unfair. He could not know that; he had been wrong about Constance. Disastrously wrong about Muriel. . . .

At least this woman had pushed for no more than he wanted to give, had been quite content with play that had no purpose save mutual joy. Right now, that was enough. Someone to hold was enough.

Later, it was not quite enough . . . but she politely refrained from commenting on his change of heart.

PRIME

At first Mailan thought the bell-ringer was confused. Third bell had rung only moments before—the light of the rising star was barely filtering through the trees. Then the tolling continued, and it was plain something was wrong. A three-minute ring at the death of someone important. . . . Why did the peal persist?

Finally she moved to the omni, punching up the silent mode in case Sheel was sleeping through the noise. Some listings were not yet broadcasting, and others were finishing their darkside programming. Only two had news, and the brief message the coastal channel passed on was not totally unexpected: Cort Atare had taken The Path. It was the local station's report that slowly numbed Mailan's senses.

Cort Atare had not died naturally, the obvious assumption. It was murder.

The announcer's lips moved slowly, maintaining professional calm. Forcing her mind to read the words flowing across the bottom of the picture, Mailan let the crisis register: *Others of the royal family were also attacked.* No other specifics were forthcoming.

First order of business is the Seri, she reminded herself, even as she moved to the wall box to contact the center command. Sweet Mendulay, she had forgotten to report in last night. It was not required when an Atare left home, but she had to tell center where her successor—

To her surprise, it was the barracks, not the center, her fingers had tapped into the membrane.

"Jude," she heard herself request, even as a terrible thought formed in her mind. To kill the Atare, they—surely more than one—would have had to kill his *guaard*. What was powerful enough, skillful enough, to overcome *guaard*?

"This is Jude." Only Mailan would have noticed the rawness in her voice.

"Mailan here. What has happened, Jude? Who was—"

"Mailan?" It was soft, a squeak, drawn raggedly from the depths of her solid frame. *"Mailan?"*

"I sound like Fion or Crow, maybe? What—Jude? What is wrong?" Suddenly the woman's reaction was not merely unexpected, it was disturbing.

"But . . . but Dirk said . . ." There was a long pause. "Hold the line." Jude abruptly disappeared.

Remaining on the wall box, Mailan wished for a vid. These inexpensive lines in the temple rooms were totally inadequate when dealing with *guaard*. One had to see the person to know what they were feeling.

Another click on the line, and Jude's rough voice once again seized her attention. "Mailan? Damn The Path! *They said you were dead!*"

That took a moment to assimilate. Standing in a daze, Mailan finally heard Jude say: "Mailan? Are you still there? Mailan?"

"Why?" It seemed the obvious question. "*Who* said?" That would do for a follow-up. . . .

"May, The Atare is dead!"

"I saw, on the omni. But—"

"So is Seri Baldwin. And Seris Caleb, Dimitri, and Fabe. Seri Iver was injured, but he lives. May, they said Sheel and the woman with him were dead, and you were missing and presumed dead! They are dragging the pond by his house!"

"Sweet Mendulay." It was barely a whisper. Mailan leaned back against the wall. After a time she realized Jude was speaking once again. "Jude, I am with Sheel. He did not go home last night, he—he loaned the house to a friend. Dear Lord of Life . . . You are certain about the heirs?"

"Not only the heirs, but their *guaard*. I saw Martin's body when I was sent to Baldwin's home. Also Baldwin's wife, and Dimitri's wife. The others either were not in town or not sleeping with their husbands that night—no one heard anything, Mailan!"

Her mind was churning, light exploding from within. Shaking her head to clear it, she asked: "Are you on duty?"

"Not yet. I am an alternate today."

"I need you. Come to the obelisk in the temple gardens. I will meet you there in, oh, twenty minutes. Do not ask anyone about anything, just enter a request from Sheel taken through the current *guaard*. Do not list a destination. Just come."

"Mailan, I—"

"I am dead on my feet, Jude, and it will take me some time to remember what is wrong. I need someone with Sheel I can trust." She took a deep breath. "Please. I will explain when I know what to tell you. Sheel will cover for you."

"You know you have only to ask. . . . Are you *sure* you are all right?" Jude asked carefully, as if expecting her to suddenly give a death rattle.

"Twenty minutes." The wall box disconnected with a jangling, discordant sound. Mailan leaned against the smooth controls, reaching with one hand to blacken the omni. Far above them, in one of the twin towers, the bell was still ringing. . . . Three minutes for each member of the royal house, for each *guaard* who died in the line of duty. . . . Dear sweet Mendulay, how many had died?

"Well?" Sheel's soft, weary voice penetrated the tolling of the bell. Glancing over at the entrance of the sleeping room, Mailan studied her sworn lord and master. He had found one of the thick, warm robes always provided in the temple guest rooms—his slender frame was lost in the folds.

How does one say this? She straightened slowly and turned with exquisite grace, her face frozen in its stillness. "This is one," she started.

"One? How have you managed to indebt yourself to me before Kee has fully risen? Or am I indebted to you?" The smile was slight; careful. He had heard some of the conversation, then.

"I promised another *guaard* that you would countenance my request for a back-up," Mailan continued.

"And we need a back-up because . . ."

"Because The Atare was murdered last night, as well as several other members of the line. Jude believed both you and me dead until my call." She studied his expression, looking for reaction, but at this distance even his pale blond stubble was invisible. "Something I have learned this morning, either from the omni or from Jude, has stirred an incongruity. I need time to think; I cannot do it unless I know you are safe." There was really nothing more to be said, except . . . "Seri, I am sorry."

"Murdered?" Sheel's inflection was not exactly a question. Moving slowly to the window, he leaned against the sill and surveyed the pale morning.

"It was the word chosen by the local listing, Seri." There was a long silence. *Dear Ones, he is going into shock.*

"Why kill him in a manner that is obvious? He was not a strong man; they could have smothered him with a blanket." The question was odd, coming from Sheel at this moment, even as it crystallized one of Mailan's thoughts.

"Seri . . . are the *guaard* so feeble on the scale of the Seven Systems that strangers could have devastated our ranks in one night?" Perhaps it was arrogant; very well, she would admit to inordinate pride. But she was *guaard*, damn it all, and she had yet to learn of a technique that could stop her. A mag gun, maybe. . . . But only a distance weapon. What else could kill a *guaard*?

There was a sigh from the window, and Sheel sat down in a chair facing the glass. "No, Mailan. I have yet to hear or see anyone or anything that could overpower a *guaard*." Another long pause, and then he said: "If they thought us dead . . . there must not be much left of Rob. . . ."

That startled her; she had completely forgotten the implications of Jude's phrasing. If they had assumed the bodies were Sheel and a night visitor, then . . . Mailan felt momentarily ill. The young nobleman had been Sheel's closest friend; he had even accompanied the Seri to Emerson.

"I suppose it is too late to play dead." Mailan felt her eyes widen as Sheel looked her way. "No, do not blame yourself, I would not have thought of it, either. But if someone went to this kind of trouble to kill off the family . . . I doubt it will end here. Unless they were careless and left evidence of their deed."

"Do you wish to remain here, Seri? I have arranged for my alternate to meet me a few moments from this place. No one knows of our whereabouts."

"Except possibly Archpriest Ward," Sheel murmured. For a moment he looked very old. "Who else is dead?"

Tempted to vacillate, Mailan hesitated. But then Sheel would know if she withheld information. . . . "The Seri Baldwin, his wife, the Seri Caleb, the Seri Dimitri, his wife—"

"Enough." Anger threaded the word, and Mailan hoped he would let more of it out. A wintry smile crossed his face, and he turned back to the window. "I should have asked who lives."

"The Seri Iver apparently lives, as well as your sisters."

Sheel's eyes closed in response, as if exhaustion swept through him. "Poor Iver," he murmured. "The last thing in this life he would want, and now it is his. . . ." Folding his hands across his knee, he asked: "Suggestions?"

As though she were the Captain himself. . . . "Caution costs nothing, my Seri. Something is wrong, although I have yet to solve the mystery. Remain here, with another *guaard*, while I make inquiries. Fion worked very hard on my intuitive capabilities. It would be foolish to ignore this . . . itch . . . in the back of my consciousness." Thinking it sounded lame, she added: "I am sorry I am so vague, Seri, but *something* struck me as wrong, and until I figure out what it is, I will be worried."

"My life is always in your hands," Sheel said gently, not lifting his eyes from his knee. "What of Darame?"

Ah . . . the woman. Mailan had consciously forgotten her, even as her ears had listened for the rustle of sheets. "I doubt she could be a part of this, else you would not have lived to see the dawn. But undoubtedly she will be questioned. I will stop at her hostel and bring her a few things. Is there anything you would like me to bring you?"

"A change of clothes, if it is not too much trouble. My medical bag, when you stop to check on Iver. Tell Avis and Leah I am well, if chance allows it. And Mailan . . . If you are in the vicinity . . . see if they killed the cats." Finally glancing up, he added: "If so, it tells us something about the individuals behind the violence."

Nodding, Mailan automatically examined the window and doors of the room, making sure they were secure. Leaving an Atare unattended, who would have thought it? Why was she so nervous? What had Jude—the omni?—said to distress her subconscious? As her gaze passed Sheel, she noted the odd expression on his face. "Seri?"

"Mailan . . . Do you trust the *guaard* who is coming?"

Mailan stared at him. What kind of question? . . . "Seri?"

Vaguely waving her on, Sheel looked back toward the window. "It is nothing . . . only a dream I had last night. The angle was wrong. . . ."

She waited, but no more was forthcoming. What had he meant? Nodding again, she moved toward the bedroom.

Awake, yet waiting silently. Mailan paused in the doorway, meeting the off-worlder's eyes. Somehow the woman had reached for the other robe without making an audible sound. Now she was wrapped in it, slowly moving into a sitting position. Did she speak Nualan? Unlikely. . . . Few were the ambassadors who learned the language. This planet was not sought as a permanent post. That point would have to be explored, and soon.

"There has been an altercation in the city," Mailan said clearly in Caesarean. "You will have to remain closeted for a time. I will try to secure your possessions before returning to this place. Please do not attempt to leave or to use the wall box. For now, come with me." Nodding formally to the woman, Mailan slipped back into the lounge.

Drawing one of her cat knives from its upper arm sheath, she extended it hilt-first to Sheel.

Sheel merely lifted an eyebrow as he accepted the knife.

Turning to the off-worlder, who stood uncertainly in the bedroom doorway, Mailan reached for a handful of robe and firmly guided the woman through the outer door.

Still deserted and filled with early-morning fog, the temple grounds were unnaturally silent. Only the bell intruded, driving away fauna and visitors alike. Approaching the obelisk from a side path, Mailan slowed as the off-worlder stepped on something sharp. No cry of pain—she, too, felt something oppressive about the scene. Eyes wide and face white with strain, the woman pulled the robe tightly around her tiny form and limped on.

Jude waited in the shadow of the pillar. Continuously turning, alert to any movement, she saw them long before she heard them. Gesturing with her free hand, Mailan moved further into the shadow of the trees. "Have you heard anything more?" she asked in Nualan.

Her friend shook her head and reached into a pocket. "They increased the guard on the survivors—here is the revised schedule." Pressing the filmy ring into Mailan's palm, Jude said: "Should we call others?"

"Not yet. I am sorry I am being so mysterious, but—" Suddenly she was at a loss for words; if Fion had been there, he would have understood. . . .

"It is nothing," Jude said, interrupting. "If Fion, if an Atare, can trust these moods which take you, why not a fellow guaard?" Glancing around, she continued: "Where is he?"

"Temple guest rooms, third from the left." Indicating the off-worlder with a jerk of her chin, Mailan added: "I told her not to leave or to contact anyone. No trouble so far." The exhaustion was catching up to her; she was having trouble thinking straight. "I am no longer on official duty since third bell, and they will be annoyed that I did not call in during the night—"

"Whatever is bothering you, see to it," Jude told her. "Then come back." Pausing a moment to grip the other's arm, Jude set a firm hand on the off-worlder's shoulder and gestured back toward the temple. Moving silently down the side path, the two faded from view.

Mailan stood very still, her inaudible cursing a litany that finally roused her feet. Why was she so fearful? What was making her so irritable? No matter what she did, there would be trouble. On one hand, there was Dirk, looking for a chance to show fault; on the other, Sheel, who would protect her . . . but at what cost? If her subconscious fears fizzled into nothing, would Sheel ever trust her again?

Why did they assume the body in the bed was Sheel? Dirk knew of his habits as well as any *guaard*. A check of the files would show the temple as one of Sheel's retreats. Had they contacted the temple even as she and Jude conversed?

Did the people doing the killing know so little of Atare that they saw no difference? Or was it something else?

Something she had heard, something was not right— The words beat a drum tattoo to accompany her pace as she headed for the hostel. Easy things first; time enough to think out her path.

There was no problem gaining access to the off-world woman's room. Not a lot of possessions, thankfully. Worth searching? No. Quickly packing a small roll with a few days' necessities, Mailan stopped by the mail drop for messages.

Only one—it was a frage. Controlling the frown that hovered behind her calm, Mailan carefully accepted it and signed the receipt. They were being extremely cooperative for hostel employees—had other *guaard* been here before? But to ask was to reveal that her own visit was irregular. Let them think an off-worlder had finally caught Sheel's eye. Nodding a polite farewell, grateful the uniform kept them from including her in their whispered speculations, Mailan moved out the door.

Silence. The bell had ceased. She could see Sheel's home from where she stood. And a few *guaard*, patrolling the perimeter. No such luck—the barracks would be easier. No conversations with any *guaard* until she found Captain Dirk. Spinning on her heel, Mailan took off toward the barracks.

As she had hoped, it was deserted. Tossing some uniforms into the off-worlder's roll, she pulled out the packet containing a change for Sheel and slipped it in as well. Fortunate she had thought to store some things here, the last time Sheel had left town for the mountains. Then she paused to check the roster Jude had given her. . . . Dirk was listed as at Baldwin's home. A tiny sigh—now or later, it made no difference. Plucking the ring from the wall screen, Mailan stuffed it back into her shirt. Still in dress black, very conspicuous for daytime use, but no time to change, she feared to change—

Voices in the corridor. Seizing the bag, her hand dropping to the sill, Mailan was out the window and among the foliage before they ever approached the room. *At least my reflexes are still good.* Turning south, she started toward the palace and the heir's —former heir's—home.

There was something...ah. The frage. She touched the pocket where it rested. An unusual sort of message, a frage. The tiny cylinder actually unrolled, a delicate filament carrying a transmittal wrapped around the center peg. But to know its contents was to destroy it; a frage could only be read once. Somehow Mailan doubted it was incriminating....A frage attracted too much attention as it was...

Damn you to The Path, Dirk! The thought was sudden—savage. Tired, too tired, and it was because of his pride, his stubbornness, that her seri was in danger, in the hands of *guaard* both exhausted and inexperienced— Mailan pushed the thought away, concentrating on the path beneath her feet, oblivious to the crisp autumn morning.

Behind the palace, a winding stone path led to the sprawling, gracious home which had belonged to Baldwin reb Riva Atare. *Guaard* swarmed over the area, engrossed in their search for clues, for evidence pointing toward a motive, a suspect. To her surprise they ignored her; all were meticulously studying the ground, the entranceway, the windows.

"Mailan?" The voice was incredulous. She turned, seeking a source, and realized that one of the searchers was Crow.

How could I have missed— "Crow?" Why she made the word a question she was not certain. The young man's dark form sprung up from the step he was examining. Dark, like tarnished copper, this one, and smooth-skinned, his dark eyes looking out from a face as broad as Jude's. But sharper— Crow's cheekbones stood out prominently, contrasting with his strong jaw.

"Do I look like the Captain?" Impatient, always impatient, was Crow. Always in a hurry, reaching for the last word, the final gesture, the ultimate experience—even in a woman's arms, he reached ahead of himself....

Except when I slow you down...Aware that exhaustion was gaining the upper hand, Mailan stiffened her spine.

"Where have you been? What happened? Where is Seri Sheel—"

"Safe," she said flatly in a voice which did not encourage speech. "I need the Captain. Have you seen him?"

"Gone. To the hospice, I think, to check on Seri Iver. Mailan, what is going on?"

"Do you think I know?" The explosion was soft, terse, but her expression caused him to take a step backward. "Do not push, Crow, I can barely see straight, much less think—"

"Who is with Sheel—"

"Jude. He is fine." Stubborn, to keep insisting, but Jude could take care of him. "I must report to Dirk. When did he leave?"

For once Crow's words did not flow over her own. This surprised Mailan enough that she paused, facing down his stare.

"You are in trouble again," he stated, and she could hear the clean breaks between each word. "How can I help? Extra *guaard* are needed on every Atare."

"You cannot—" She broke off, considering. "Yes, you can. Will you take a message to Serae Avis and Serae Leah? Tell them Sheel is alive and well. That will be a great help."

A tilt of the dark head, reflecting the blue-black of a faxmur's wing. "And?"

"It will be enough," she murmured, momentarily seeing him as a double image. "It has to be. Crow . . . How long have you been here?"

"Since they carried Martin out feet-first," was the prompt answer. "Mailan, you do not—"

"Do you know if they killed Sheel's cats?"

This final interruption brought Crow up short. "What?"

There was a reason Sheel had asked that question, but Mailan could no longer remember it. "Never mind. Thank you for finding the serae." Turning quickly, Mailan started back along the winding trail, grateful she did not have to breach the palace. No chance of leaving the palace without being caught, questioned . . .

"Mailan, wait!" Fortunately Crow did not raise his voice, but Mailan refused to turn. Too easy, to dump it on another unsuspecting victim. Who knew what Dirk would do to Jude when he got the chance? . . .

Crow did not follow. Tapping down the part of her that wished he had, Mailan hurried toward the hospice. She tried to use the side roads, avoiding major throughways; it made no difference. Few people were out and abroad, and those who chose to travel averted their gaze. *Do we reek of blood and death this day?* she wondered. Grateful at their silence, she swerved onto another path, heading for the rear doors of the building.

The hospice was packed with *guaard*. A few trainees actually registered surprise at her presence. Her stony gaze quickly brought them back into proper expression. First order: Sheel's medical bag. Then she would deal with Dirk.

Familiarity with the layout of the floors was a help—she avoided meeting any other *guaard*. Sheel's office of muted greens was as they had left it, basically neat, a few papers scattered across the desk. He was rarely there, preferring to spend hospice time with patients. Throwing open a storage bin, Mailan found his medical bag. A quick examination revealed it stocked with basic supplies. On impulse she slipped in a few packets of rav pills. The off-worlder woman might find adaptation to Nualan food convenient. . . .

Mailan's hands stilled as she closed the bag—all the *guaard*. Of course, Iver was in the building. It occurred to her that Sheel wanted a firsthand report of his brother's condition. So, was access restricted?

Iver was indeed on the restricted level, but her thumbprint admitted her without machine comment. Her destination was not far; she could see *guaard* uniforms before the doors slid shut. Gar and Ayers had glints in their eyes. . . . They were dying to ask questions. Too bad; they stood guard before a private room, and Mailan was grateful for it. No chatter in such an intense situation. Wondering if they would stop even her, she nodded and pushed open the door.

Four *guaard* within, and a delicate whiff of perfume . . . ah. Bette, Iver's wife. She sat motionless next to the bed, her usually cheerful face swollen from weeping, her strong hands twisting in the edge of the sheet. Fortunate for Bette that she was sleeping restlessly, the unborn child keeping her awake nights. . . . That she chose to sleep alone until the birth. *Hope this does not trigger a premature delivery,* came an idle thought.

Mailan nodded her respect to the woman and to White, who was one of the four attending *guaard*. Two she did not recognize —perhaps young reserves brought up for the emergency—and the last was White's eldest son, Teague. Bearable, that one, if overconfident of his charms. Not like the younger son, who imitated his father shamelessly and had never had an original thought.

Before White could even open his mouth, Bette said: "You are Sheel's *guaard*, are you not?"

"Yes, Serae. I came to see to the Seri's condition. Sheel is concerned about him," Mailan said simply.

"If only he had Chosen someone," she whispered, "this might not have happened. . . ."

"I am certain that those who died for his life were no less devoted, Serae. Do not distress yourself with imaginings," Mai-

Ian told her gently. Glancing at the chart hanging above the bed, Mailan saw a familiar scrawl. The healer who had trained Sheel. No problem there— Iver suddenly stirred.

Idiot, you woke him. Waiting for permission to speak, Mailan studied the fluttering eyelashes, the monitor next to the bed. Injuries were not severe. . . . A punctured lung, it seemed, some lacerations and bruises. *I think it is lucky you are a light sleeper.*

Iver's first reaction startled her, although she kept it from her face. There was no doubt . . . it was fear that ravaged his expression, pulling his mouth tight. Recognition dawned, and Iver began to speak.

"You . . . are . . . Sheel's . . ."

"Yes, Seri. I thought I should check on you. Seri Sheel is worried about you."

"Tell him . . . tell him—" Iver stopped, and a look of terrible confusion crossed his face. His eyes seemed clouded, as if by painkillers. Why painkillers with healers on the staff? Sheel could stimulate the body's natural painkillers.

"You are tired, Seri. I will return—"

"No! Tell him . . ." Bette reached sympathetically and touched his arm, drawing his gaze to her face. Behind them, Mailan heard White move forward.

"You must rest, Seri. You are not well," White said evenly.

If anything, Iver looked more frightened. He reached for Mailan's hand, tugging at her, his eyes darting back and forth between their faces. Suddenly discovery leapt in his eyes, and Iver actually smiled. "Praise Mendulay." His tone was a prayer of thanksgiving. Mailan bent over, for his voice was soft. "Tell Sheel that Irulen should have believed. . . . Tell him exactly that. He will . . . know. . . ."

Mailan was alarmed. Iver's expression had passed abruptly from sheer wonder and pleasure into concern. Something had upset him dreadfully, and— Then she noticed where he was staring. At White and the other *guaard*. Was he delirious? She glanced at the monitor—his heart rate had increased tremendously. Her eyes flicked back as she leaned closer still, for Iver was mouthing words.

He reads. That was all; Iver closed his eyes against the effort.

"Rest, Seri. Do not concern yourself with anything. Serae Leah will take care of things until you are stronger—Sheel and Avis will assist. Concentrate on health." Mailan spoke in a firm tone, as one might speak to a delirious child.

"What did he say?" Bette asked, the strain clawing at her

voice. Turning her head, studying Bette's fear and White's annoyance, Mailan realized that she had blocked their view—the others had heard and seen nothing.

"I think he is delirious," Mailan said slowly, letting the puzzlement slip into her voice. "He muttered something about Sheel reading."

"Do you think he wants me to read to him?" Bette sounded almost hopeful, and Mailan was shaken out of her own daze by the woman's need to help.

"Not quite yet, I would think, Serae," Mailan said quickly. "Your company is surely enough. Later, I am sure it would give him pleasure."

Rearranging her burdens across her shoulders and hefting the medical bag in her left hand, Mailan nodded to the serae and went back out the door. Stopping to face one of the *guaard*, she asked: "Where is the Captain?"

"He was here within the hour," Ayers responded. "He did not inform us of his destination. I suggest you check the daily roster."

Nodding, Mailan noted in passing that Ayers's eyes were redrimmed. The son of Martin, was he not? And fond of his taciturn father. . . .

Thoughts clicked together in her head even as she took her leave of the two blond, burly *guaard*. The key is Martin. *The key is Martin*. Swiftly she left the hospice, searching for a ROM.

A Read-Only Module was located not far from the exit gate of the hospice. Inserting the schedule Jude had handed her last vespers, Mailan quickly scanned the assignments. There—the discrepancy. Surely she had heard correctly; both Jude and Crow had mentioned Martin's body as having been at the house of the heir.

But Martin was guarding The Atare last night. Not the heir. The screen blurred momentarily, and Mailan seized the metal overhang support to steady herself. Popping the ring, she inserted the update Jude had provided scarcely an hour before.

No. Minutely she examined the image. Not just Martin, then —several people were now listed in different places. *Now why?* . . . The authorization block stopped her musings. Last-noted changes were at mid-afternoon the previous day . . . long before Jude had handed her the first schedule. Time of changes, person who made changes, authorized by . . . No one made that many changes without logging. . . .

Popping the ring, Mailan carefully tucked them both into various pouches of her uniform, securely fastening the lips. Realizing her hands were shaking, she applied mental pressure to calm them. *Too tired, just too tired.*

Whatever it meant would have to wait. No longer seeing straight, Mailan knew that soon her physical and mental sharpness would fade, if it hadn't already. *Would I detect the decline?*

A Random Access Module; she needed a RAM. How to word the message? Was it even important enough to send a message? Of course it was—at the least, The Atare and his immediate heirs had been murdered. They needed Fion. *I need Fion....*

Further in toward the center of town was a functioning RAM. Fion was probably at his parents' farm, he considered it home since his wife died.... A relay was necessary, through Maroc to his village.... Pulling her coin strip from her leg pocket, she carefully counted coins. Enough for a call? The meaning of her actions gave her pause. *Why not use credit? Credit means identifying yourself to the machine....* Perversely refusing to explore the impulse, she checked the pay list hanging by the module. Just enough for a brief message.

It would be brief. Stop and think—what was Fion's callback? Ah—Dragonwatch. She thought a long time, and finally her fingers moved toward the message membrane. *Dragonwatch, we need you. Foxes in the henroost.* No room for a signature, even if she'd intended to leave one. Fion certainly would recognize the phrase from one of their favorite drinking songs. *And they said I could never be his student, that only one who could match him drink for drink would be acceptable!*— Would he remember the most recent meaning for the phrase? That Mailan had taken to referring to her oppressors among the *guaard* as foxes?

A giggle bubbled out of her as she started shoving coins into the module slot. All those years of her mother despairing of her tomboy daughter.... Learning to hold her liquor at her father's knee.... Who would have thought— Realizing her gasping chuckles were becoming hysterical, Mailan gave herself a shake and waited for the transmission lights to clear. Then back, back to Sheel, to give him Iver's contorted message.

TIERCE

Mailan had reached the terrace when she heard the crash. Instinct took over; dropping her assorted bundles, she drew a cat knife and threw herself through the open doorway.

A jumbled scene littered the floor. Seeking Sheel first, Mailan found him on his knees, her cat knife gripped tightly in one hand. He had the tip of the blade pressed into the throat of a *guaard*. A *guaard?* Glancing around quickly, she saw Jude crouched, both knives held in throwing position, her eyes on—

"Crow?" Mailan's surprise sounded shrill. Vision widened, taking in the entire room. Pressed against the inner door, the off-world woman waited, the color of her face rivaling alabaster. Crow was almost as pale—and confused. He clearly had no idea—

"Seri?" Mailan ventured, wondering if she should speak, and if so, what were the proper words. Sweet Mendulay...

"Did you send him here?" Almost conversational, Sheel's tone.

"No. I sent him to the palace to speak to your sisters."

"Did you tell him where we were?"

"No."

"Then what"—Jude, rising now, her exasperation evident—"were you doing creeping around in the bushes?" Her voice easily rose an octave from start to finish, even as she gestured for Mailan to close the terrace doors.

Afraid Jude would lunge at the young man, Mailan quickly said: "Crow . . . how did you ever guess? . . ."

"Common sense. I checked a few other places on my way. Where you spent the night was not important—the current location was the major thing. And unless you went to the Ragaree's retreat—" The knife pressed closer, and Crow stopped his careful recitation. "I doubt anyone else would guess. . . . I have met you after duty before, Mailan. I knew where to look."

"Why were you creeping around the windows?" Again, that gentle speech pattern, which always meant Sheel was fighting anger.

Crow actually rolled his eyes. "Because I did not want anyone to see me sneaking around the temple grounds, of course. I did not intend for the entire *guaard* and local enforcers to find the place. Mailan wanted it kept quiet."

"Then why did you come?" There was no way for Mailan to warn Crow that his life depended on the answer to her question. Why Sheel was acting this way was unimportant. . . . To those who knew him, he was on the edge of violence.

"Because . . . whatever you were doing, you needed help. You were—are—a mess, and one alert *guaard* on an heir is not enough." The youth was completely relaxed as he directed the last to Mailan; he had even dropped his knife, drawn instinctively when he was jumped, if his story was true. *If?* Could she doubt him? Why had she not confided in him? ... In more lucid moments she would have known he would read her worry.

"Seri ... what do you need?" Mailan started, still afraid to move.

"The oath will do."

All three *guaard* stared at him a moment. Mailan was lost. ... What oath? Did he ...

Glancing over at Jude's defensive posture, Sheel drew his steel away from Crow's throat and reversed the blade, holding it point down between them. Crow did not risk looking away; his eyes still meeting Sheel's, the young *guaard* reached to wrap his right hand around the offered hand and hilt.

"On this I swear," Crow began, the whisper slowly gathering volume, "by life and honor, by blood and trust, that with this oath I will serve the son and daughter of Atare, obeying all words and following all leads, shielding their line and prizing their secrets as Mendulay guards mine own, for so long as they hold to their charge."

Mailan's knees felt weak. *That* oath—the sharing of oaths, the duty accepted by each at the feet of their Atare, the moment they were chosen to become *guaard*.

Sheel responded by folding his left hand over Crow's. "On this I swear, by life and honor, that I will take you as a *guaard* to serve Atare within the bounds of your oath, holding your trust as I hold to my charge—head, hand, and heart of the heirs, now and forever."

The group remained frozen in their tableau for several moments. Finally Mailan moved, reversing her grip on her cat knife. Noticing her action, Sheel sat back on his heels and shook his head.

"No, Mailan. ... I only ask for that oath once. And you ... 'spoke' ... for Jude." Grinning suddenly at Crow, he released his grip and added: "You did not have time to speak for him." Standing and turning his back to Crow, Sheel stretched, loosening massively constricted muscle. Glancing at the off-worlder, he said in Caesarean: "It is all right. No one is going to die."

Crow seemed to wake out of a dream. Taking up his discarded cat knife, he muttered: "Die ... the sack!" Jumping up, he sprang to the travel pack which had landed on the cushioned bench. "Seri, I found them! At least the ones still alive."

This caught Sheel's attention. Immediately at Crow's side, he asked: "Them?"

"I used those skin patch things in your medicine cabinet to knock them out." Crow opened the stretch fastenings and carefully lifted out a brown and white ball of fur. Taking the cat, Sheel held it a long moment; checking its internal state, Mailan was certain.

Moving toward the off-worlder, Mailan held out the small roll containing her possessions. Her other hand fumbled for the frage. "Do you know how to use one of these?" Mailan asked slowly, studying the woman's face. The stranger's response was negative. "Slip your fingernail under the exposed edge and unroll the cylinder. Use good light—it can only be read once, it is very fragile. It was waiting for you at the hostel. . . . The doorkeeper said a heavyset off-worlder left it for you." Remembering her other impulse, Mailan popped open Sheel's medical bag and handed the woman a packet of pills. "Rav pills. You may find acquired immunity to our planet desirable." Leaving the woman studying the pill packet, reading the Caesarean instructions—she could read Caesarean, interesting—Mailan turned to gain Sheel's attention.

Faust, the forest coon cat, was now curled on the bench, the delicate short-haired calico next to him. Sheel was holding the tiny, pale-green oriental, and Mailan noted with alarm that there was blood on the animal's coat. She glanced in the pouch—empty. No sign of Fathima, the elegant, haughty Somali. What had Crow said—"ones left alive"? Damn. . . . Sheel was fond of the creatures.

Her seri was wasting no time. Slipping into that state of consciousness which surrounded healing, Sheel bent to his task. Could he heal an animal? Why not? It was just a different collection of fluid and tissue. . . . It was rare that Mailan was able to witness a healing, and the event had yet to lose its lure.

Checking the gash for infection, a solution to cleanse the edges of the ragged wound, and then . . . Mailan watched intently, forcing herself to focus, grateful Jude was on duty. The injury drew together, carefully closing, free of hair and debris—

A sharp intake of breath startled her. Turning, Mailan found the frozen visage of the off-worlder. Her back once again pressed against the inner door, the woman's gaze was glued to the scene before them. As Sheel finished, relaxing, checking the tiny creature's heartbeat, the off-worlder wrenched her eyes away from the tableau, focusing on Mailan. The *guaard* was astonished at the terror reflected from those black eyes.

Now the woman's attention turned to the packet of rav pills still clutched in her hand. Staring at them blankly a moment, she released her grip. Clattering, the packet's fall threw echoes into the high, arched ceiling.

Chapter Four

| GUAARD HALL | THIRTYSEVENDAY | SEXT |

"And you have worked for Rover Consortium for how long?" the voice continued, maintaining a pleasant neutrality.

"About twelve years Terran, Sans Sleep," Darame replied easily, her eyes focused on her bracelet of tiny freshwater pearls.

"Have you always worked in the promotion and relations branch?"

"*Public* Promotion and Relations," Darame stressed, knowing that word was important in some legal dictionaries.

"What branches of Rover Consortium have you worked with?" the voice asked specifically.

"Various branches. All trainees serve in multiple positions, until their skills can be matched with the proper department," Darame went on, her eyes tracing an intricate whorl of pearl. "I served in every branch in existence at the time I was hired, and was placed in PPR about eight years ago Terran."

A bundle of nerves this time out. How could things fall apart so quickly? Where was Halsey? Brant certainly knew she was here; she had asked for a representative of the Caesarean Embassy to be present while she was questioned, and the senior ambassadors assigned all "monitors." If Brant did not know, he would know soon.

They are asking the wrong questions, a tiny voice whispered within. Darame knew a myriad number of techniques, had been

investigated more times than she cared to remember. This inter-
viewer had glossed over her actions last night. Because a *guaard*
was present then, and was expected to keep a close eye on her?
Because a man with the power of a prince claimed she was with
him, and it sufficed?

Her fingers remembered the roughness of the frage, in Caesarean but not for casual eyes; written in a very ancient code, meant
for those with no eyes to see. *Always have options.* Halsey had
drummed it into her head at an early age, but he never stated it
save when he was very concerned. *He doesn't know what's going
on, either.* Not comforting—Halsey was the brains of the outfit,
the one person who should know every aspect of the job. If one
of their own operatives was not involved, then who? . . .

"I think that covers everything for the time being," the *guaard*
said quietly, his voice void of emotion. Reaching, he gently disconnected the probes running to her arm and temple. "Leave
word where you will be staying, and please do not attempt to
leave the city until further notice."

Staying? She controlled a wince. Good question. Probably the
hostel. Saints be damned, how could she have lost control so
completely? And in front of the one person she could not risk
offending. Glancing up as the door slid open, Darame stood and
moved out into the hallway, the silent Caesarean aide following.

They call it healing. . . . Even the fertile people are mutants.
Darame could not stop the shiver that ran through her. Dropping
those pills—that she could explain away, ignore, even. But running into the bedroom . . .

Sheel knew. He *had* to know. How often did it happen? Were
there even Nualans who questioned his talent? Could it change
him in some strange way, make him one of the irradiated sinis?

Could it change the people around him?

"Woman?" The aide's purely Caesarean mode of address
pulled her back from her thoughts. Had she caught his name?
Careless, very careless today.

"Yes?"

"Second Ambassador Brant would like to speak with you."

"Of course." Darame hesitated, wondering if she should send
some sort of word to Sheel, at least to let him know his word was
still worth something. *As if she had doubted it* . . . Then she
flinched as she heard movement behind her. There he was— Had
the youth been in the room the entire time? *Guaard* certainly
moved silently.

She did not even know his name. First Sheel was going to stick a knife into him; then he was sent to—guard? shadow?—the off-world woman. *Me*. Why? No way of knowing right now, but she was starting to recognize Nualan syntax, and some major nouns and verbs. Had to get her hands on a language probe immediately. . . .

Glancing at the dark, smooth face, Darame spoke to him in Caesarean: "I need to go speak with one of the ambassadors. You don't need to come if you have somewhere else to be."

"Seri Sheel requested I remain with you until you returned to the temple," the youth replied in a low, musical tone.

"As you wish," Darame said, nodding to the aide to lead the way. Requested? Instructed. . . .

Embassy Row was close to wherever she had been taken for questioning. The building owned by Caesarea Station had been designed, if not constructed, by Caesareans: it was lasered stone, the ledges sharp and clean, glass windows covering the west wall and skylights facing east. No doubt the furnishings would also be Caesarean in style—minimal.

"Just how cold does it get here in winter?" Darame asked the aide, trying to remember the median temperatures for this part of Nuala.

His eyes settled on the building, and he gave a rueful smile. "Not very practical for the North," he agreed. "The windows are heavily insulated, and there's a fireloft in every room. We have the best of both worlds." An odd expression, one of unease, crossed his face, and he began walking faster. "The ambassador doesn't like to be kept waiting."

How little he's changed. Darame did not speak her observation aloud. Dozens of people could have been on this job, and Brant had to be Halsey's choice. Granted, no one was better at winning confidences and squirming into places of trust, but right now she wished that they'd taken the slower route, with Halsey endearing himself to their contacts. *If any of the marks still live*, she amended with a shiver. Iver, and who else? Her eyes flicked down the curving stone street of Embassy Row. Not a single Nualan clan represented. . . . Interesting.

Green uniform blurred before her eyes, and Darame slowed, waiting for the aide to open the door. The locks responded to his thumb imprint, and he ushered both Darame and her silent shadow into Caesarean domain.

A few wood and metal benches, many green plants, high ceilings of stone—very Caesarean. It was the most convenient passport for a traveler to have, but Darame found native Caesareans rather sterile in both imagination and outlook. That was what made Brant such a successful manipulator: his Caesarean features were at odds with his powerful vision. Not imagination, precisely; more a feel for multiple possibilities, and the initiative to carry out his plans. But no imagination. Which was why Darame had no use for him. Brant had tried to wiggle into her confidence when they first met—had also tried to presume on their physical proximity. Making it plain she wasn't interested had not particularly helped; Brant had some obscure list of traits he used to judge people, and once he'd placed someone into a slot, they rarely moved from it.

Just as well. Safer for him to underestimate me. . . . He certainly doesn't overestimate my abilities. Darame hid her irritation under a soft half-smile. Thinking of Brant always did this to her . . . and now she came basically as a supplicant. By Catherine's Wheel, what a nasty position she was in! How to land on her feet? . . .

Brant was waiting for her. Not obviously, but Darame saw him jerk as the aide paused at the door and announced her name. A tilt of the head, the familiar arrogant stance . . .

"Send her in. The *guaard* can wait in the lobby." Brant dismissed the aide with a barely perceptible nod of his auburn head.

Redheads always seemed to be very attractive or homely—seldom was there middle ground. Brant was attractive by almost any human measurement; tall, fair, thick-haird, with penetrating green eyes that had the trick of looking remotely at whatever he was currently contemplating. *Do you have any idea why I took an immediate disliking to you?* she caught herself wondering as she gracefully entered the room. Probably not; strangely enough, unless Brant was trying to con someone, he was insensitive to the minute clues of reaction that everyone had. Of course he was usually trying to con someone.

He had examined and dismissed her as unimportant, those many years ago when they'd first met. One of the crowd, that's all she'd appeared to be; Darame doubted that Halsey had told him, before or since that meeting, what Darame truly meant in the scheme of Rover Consortium. *I'm salaried, and I get a cut of the take before the split.* That meant top flight, in the company she kept.

As Brant turned to greet her—formally, in case anyone was listening—an odd thought crossed Darame's mind. Was there a specific reason Halsey let Brant believe what he wanted about her? *Not a test for me . . . a test for Brant?*

"Darame Daviddottir, what a pleasure to see you again. It's

been a long time," Brant said in his rolling, mellow tenor, indicating that she should step to the back of the parlor. "I trust the *guaard* were as polite as possible in their choice of questions?"

"Both efficient and gracious," Darame responded, trying to let her half-smile reach her eyes. Now was not the time to pick a fight with Brant. She took a quick inventory: tanned; weight about the same; a new haircut feathered back from his face in short layers, much like Sheel's. . . .

He looked worried, very worried; there were new lines pulling his mouth into a downward curve. That meant he didn't know what was going on, or at least not completely. And was hoping she knew something. Ah—a bargaining chip. Spend it well.

Moving to an offered chair, Darame pretended not to notice when Brant reached to activate a small button. The faint blue light in the room told her all she needed to know.

So Halsey gave you one to bring on ahead. Does it block Nualan probes as well as Caesarean? Just as well—she had no idea how this conversation would fall out. Glancing at her roman strapped to her wrist, she made a vague comment about how long they had questioned her while privately noting a pale gray sheen appearing on the luminous dial of the timepiece. Brant was recording their talk. Interesting . . .

"Where were you last night?" he said, his undertone irritated.

Darame raised her eyebrows slightly. "Vacationing. The first night is mine, unless otherwise specified. Good thing. . . . If I had spent it with any of your marks, I'd probably be dead."

"Ia's Rings, child, don't remind me," he muttered, taking a long draught of the fluid rolling around in his mug. Moving to a narrow table pushed against the wall, he offered her a drink by gesturing at the ice dispenser.

It might offend to decline. . . . Darame nodded, indicating an unopened bottle of wine in his cooler located beneath the table. It was a fairly common vintage, but not one of her favorites, and it was unlikely it contained any chemicals to make her more "agreeable" to his way of thinking.

Converation ceased until Brant handed her a chilled glass. Smiling faintly to indicate her approval of the wine, Darame waited for him to start. He was busy with his ale, however; a thread of relaxation seemed to enter his manner. *I relax you, and you make me nervous.* It took control not to snicker at the irony.

"Well," Darame finally said, considering and discarding a half-dozen phrases in the brief moment the word passed her lips. "Now what?" *More neutral than you deserve. You must have*

*known something about last night, you're aware of everything
that happens in a marked city. What is the alternate plan?*

"Good question," Brant replied, standing and moving toward
the wall of windows. "Things will be a mess for some time, what
with Iver injured. His sister will keep the government running—
until Cort's rule, Atare basically had a shared throne. You know,"
he continued, turning back to face her, "we may actually do better this way. Iver was one of my major objectives, anyway; he's
insecure, and I think I can get a trade agreement out of him with
little or no trouble. But things will be confused until they find the
assassins."

"Originally we were going to work through . . . Caleb?" she
asked, watching him in the mirrors over the drink table.

"Caleb would have been his brother Baldwin's prime minister. It's not always a sibling, but usually. He could have gotten
us the contract—Caleb had expensive habits, and his allowance
from the family went through his hands like water." Brant
shrugged. "Now we concentrate on Iver. Leah will share the
rule, and I have considerable influence with Leah. Eventually
you'll work on Iver, but he needs to recover fully first. With
luck, you'll have him in your pocket before his wife is back
out of childbed."

"Is the minister still important for our purposes?" Darame said
idly, agitating the goblet gently to release the bouquet of the
wine.

"The importance of the prime minister varies, depending on
the strength of The Atare and the strength of The Ragaree," Brant
answered, frowning at something in his mug.

"Does Iver's sister have more influence with him than his
younger brother?" Taking another sip of the wine, Darame waited
almost a minute before looking up. She recognized the remote
look on Brant's face as he seemed to look over her right shoulder.

"So you were with Sheel. You were quite lucky, my dear—I
hear Rob reb Dorian of Drake was unrecognizable, as was the
woman with him."

"Yes. . . . Apparently they thought it was Sheel until his *guaard*
called in," Darame agreed. "But where does he fit in this game?
If Iver is so nervous about ruling, won't he want Sheel as his
minister? They seemed congenial enough at the party."

Brant waved his mug vaguely and turned back to the windows.
"Sheel is a hot healer—little is allowed to interfere with that
talent, it's too valuable."

"Yes. . . ."

That word was not as controlled as she'd have liked; Brant actually chuckled, although Darame was not certain whether amusement prompted his reaction. "Does the idea bother you, my sweet Gavrielian? All that religion before Halsey picked you up, Iver suspect. Surely you've seen stranger things in the Seven Systems." He moved back toward the chairs, his expression sardonic. "But not masquerading as human, eh?"

"Considering their laws about Atare marriages, the royal family must be mostly off-world," Darame said gently, slowly lifting her glass to her lips.

"True. But the Nualan traits are strong—look at their eyes, for example, and the healing gene keeps popping up in their clan. Of course Nualans pray for the healing strain. . . . Apparently it means the heat is gone from the line. No more sinis for a healer's descendants."

"Unless the other parent is Sini?" she asked, intrigued despite her unease.

"You'd have to ask a geneticist, I have no idea. Just be very careful: on Nuala, terminating a pregnancy is considered premeditated murder. Don't get careless."

"Unlikely," Darame said, her smile thin. "What shall I do until Iver is out of the medical facility?"

Leaning back against his desk, Brant tapped his fingernails against the polished wood. A remote expression was once again on his face. Even as he opened his mouth to speak, a tiny bell chimed.

"Ambassador, she's coming in," said a disembodied voice. Darame recognized the particular note of strain: the aide who had guided her to the embassy. An unannounced guest?

"Brant, where's Halsey?" Darame asked suddenly, suspecting their conversation was about to be cut short.

"Probably back at the hostel by now, they questioned him first—"

A whisper of sound, and the door to the front office slid open. Darame barely had time to react as the woman swept in, a *guaard* in tow. Leaning onto the balls of her feet, Darame rose gracefully and waited for Brant to speak.

Sheel's older sister. There had not been much time to study her last night; although gracious to the women visiting Atare, Leah preferred to converse with the men. Tall; her head rose above Brant's shoulder. Her features were strong for Darame's tastes, but many would find her quite attractive: pale, dark-haired, the right eye a warm, deep brown, the other emerald green. Not as full-figured as her younger sister, but ample; Leah had a great deal of style and flash.

She walks as if she owns the ground she touches. . . . Darame controlled a smile. If the stories about the Atare mines were true, Leah's wealth was such that she might as well have owned the very soil beneath their feet.

No youth was watching the mother of the heir—the man following Leah looked at least thirty Terran. Where had he been last night? . . . Surely she couldn't have missed him. His dark, forbidding good looks would have caught her eye immediately. The *guaard*'s impersonal gaze flickered over her and settled on the windows, but Darame thought he recognized her. *Why would you know me? Where have you seen me, that I missed you?*

Turning slightly, Darame let Brant come into her line of vision, waiting for his cue. The momentary anger in his face startled her; what? . . . Then she realized Leah was speaking.

"Brant, you must speak with Iver, he is raving on about last night and demanding an inquiry—" Noticing Darame, Leah stopped abruptly.

Does she know we work together? That was one of those things they had not yet discussed. The expression on Leah's face was not exactly hostile—more displeased.

"Have you already met?" Brant said smoothly, his anger vanishing at his words.

"I am Darame Daviddottir, Serae, from Caesarea Station," Darame continued for him, nodding deeply. "I was among the multitude at the party for your son. My condolences for the great loss your family has suffered."

Leah's face was vague at first, studying her without recognition. Then: "My brother spilled a drink on your dress."

"Yes, Serae."

"I hope the cleaners will be able to save it," Leah said cordially. "Grocha is a potent brew."

"The Seri Sheel found a neutralizer; please do not concern yourself," Darame said quickly, waiting for Brant to take control of the conversation.

"You should have sent for me, Serae," Brant said, extending his hands to take Leah's fingertips. "There was no need for you to come to the embassy. Please, you are distressed, sit down." He turned his head toward Darame. "Could you wait outside a moment?"

Nodding her acquiescence, Darame set her glass down on the end table and moved gracefully toward the exit. Invisible hands slid the panel aside; as Darame stepped through the doorway, Brant and Leah both began to speak.

"Just what is she to you?"

"Where in Seven Hells have you been?"

Darame paused as the room sealed behind her. Two different conversations, addressed to . . . whom? Leah's comment was surely to Brant; she could not have seen the *guaard*'s recognition of Darame, she had her back to him and was facing no mirrors. To whom was Brant speaking?

Moving to a bench, she sat down, considering not just the words but the tone of speech. If Brant was plying his seduction skills on Leah, he would not speak to her in that manner. . . . Besides, the daughters of the line were holed up in the palace, that had been announced on the omni news. It made perfect sense; surely the palace was the most secure place in the city. So . . . Brant was most likely speaking to the *guaard*. What had been different about him? Something. . . . She glanced up and studied the young man who had waited for her in the lobby. Same matte black uniform, a shadow itself, nothing to reflect. . . .

Nothing? There had been something on the other's collar. . . . An officer of some type, then. Made sense, since she was mother of the heir. How important a person? *I wonder if they will dismiss all the officers after this attack.*

"What is your name?" Darame asked abruptly.

The young *guaard* knew she was speaking to him. "I am called Crow, lady," he said politely in Caesarean.

"Is there a line I can use to call the hostel?"

"I am instructed—" Crow began.

"I wish to speak to a friend."

"This way, lady." He started over to a niche in the wall. Both vid and wall box—the embassy did not stint its guests. Crow quickly punched in a number. "The hostel where you are registered, lady." He moved to one side.

A picture flashed across the screen. Darame recognized the woman who had been on duty when she had checked in, seemingly years ago. A few quick questions left Darame with no more information than before the call. Halsey did not answer at his room—he had left no other messages for her. He had left early in the morning with several *guaard*. Darame told the woman for Halsey to seek her at the temple, and then switched off the vid.

Perhaps a shred of information . . . *If a guaard is watching me, and they know where I was last night, then certainly guaard are watching Halsey*. The thought that he was still being questioned —or questioned again—was not comforting, but there was no help for it right now.

"Crow, was that *guaard* tailing the serae an officer?" Darame asked casually, wondering how long Brant would be closeted with his guest.

"The only officer, lady. Dirk is captain of our troop," Crow said steadily.

Before Darame could continue her questioning, the panel to Brant's private room slid open and Brant's face appeared. "Maintain status quo, will you, please? Don't worry about anything, no accusations have been hurtled toward you or your party. I will be contacting all Caesarean citizens and nationals as soon as I have any information. Thank you for coming."

So. Translated, that meant: *Keep doing what you were doing, I'll get back to you as soon as I can*. Huh. Keeping a smooth face, Darame rose to her feet. *What about Halsey, you fool!*

Always have options. No sense in relying on Brant; it could take days for him to get back to her. She might have better luck finding out about Halsey through Sheel. How to smooth things over with Sheel? . . .

She was silent so long, frozen in thought, that Crow's uncertain voice finally intruded: "Lady? Are you ready to return to the temple?"

Swiveling her head, Darame fastened a bright black gaze on Crow's face. "What kind of animal was killed last night at the seri's home?"

Crow simply stared at her. Exasperated, Darame started to repeat her question. "A .cat," the youth said quickly. "A sorrel Somali, a female."

"How did she die?" Darame asked the question gently, stepping closer to the *guaard*, to keep their voices lowered.

The youth paused before answering. "Her throat was cut. Why, we will never know. Perhaps she was startled by the intruder and called out. She was a gentle animal, she would not have attacked . . ." Puzzlement shaded his voice; realizing he was falling out of duty character, Crow once more became impassive.

"I want you to take me someplace where I can buy a Somali kitten," she announced, starting to walk toward the exit.

"Lady?" This time Crow actually sounded bewildered.

"He's obviously fond of the creatures, and he'll have enough on his mind without brooding about that cat. The best thing to do is bring home a successor immediately." Glancing over her shoulder, she added: "You *can* find me a breeder, can't you?"

MENDULARION'S ATARE   THIRTYSEVENDAY   NONE

"That was all he said?" Annoyed, Sheel rearranged himself on the couch and reached for his mug of saffra.

"All he verbally said, seri," Mailan replied, her voice falling into neutral duty mode as Jude moved into the other room to relax. "I truly believe he was mouthing words, there at the end. Perhaps even whispering, but I was the only one close enough to hear, I am sure of it."

"And he seemed afraid . . ." This was more to himself than to Mailan, but the woman heard it and said: "Yes, seri—he was quite frightened until he recognized me. It may have had nothing to do with me, however; he was half-asleep when he noticed me."

"Irulen should have believed . . . and I will understand. . . ." Sheel took another long sip of the warm red fluid. Irulen. . . . Sweet Mendulay, from where did he know that name? "There had to be more!"

"No, seri." Mailan paused, and then added: "He stared at the other *guaard* present for a long moment before he added the 'He reads' portion. When his wife asked what he had said, I mentioned that he sounded delirious, and that he had muttered something about reading. Neither Serae Bette nor the *guaard* heard his words."

"Did you ever find Dirk?" Sheel asked abruptly, pushing Iver's words into the back of his mind. Maybe he was delirious . . . or drugged. Why use drugs when Capashan was on duty? What could Iver have been thinking about?

"No, seri. I was . . . distracted." Something in her voice made Sheel look up. "I finally realized what had disturbed me this morning. Both Jude and Crow confirmed that the body of *guaard* Martin was found at the home of the heir. But I saw Martin last night at the party, and he was assigned to your uncle." The woman pulled a film ring out of her pocket. "This was given to me yesterday afternoon, to check your location before going on duty. Martin was one of those assigned to Cort for the evening."

"Could he have gone to Baldwin's home after it was obvious Cort was dead, to be sure of Baldwin's safety and to warn the *guaard* on duty?"

"Why not use a call box, seri?" Mailan replied. "But he was not the only one in an odd place last night." Loading the ring into the ROM set in the wall, she removed the flimsy coder and then loaded still another ring. Adjusting the files, she split the screen and brought up both charts on the huge wall screen. "The second ring I acquired this morning, when I was looking for the Captain. Notice how many changes have been made . . . and that there is no listing of time of changes, authorization, who actually made the changes. . . . "

"Is not access to this screen limited?" Sheel said mildly.

"Usually. Only the Captain or a trainer can make changes, except for location of charge—we can call that into the computer ourselves. Dirk makes up assignments several days in advance."

Sheel studied the screen for several minutes. Finally he realized it was fading from him, blurring before him. Shaking his head to clear it, he spoke the first thought which came into his head.

"It is more than a blow in the night. So the code has been broken," he murmured. "Why? What game is being played? How far was it taken? . . . Mailan, do you know all the active *guaard?*"

"Most, seri, at least by sight. But new ones are always coming up, and people going on leave and such," Mailan said quickly.

"But if you were relieved by a *guaard* you did not know, would you not think it odd?" Sheel continued, uncertain of what he was seeking.

"I am *your guaard*, seri. I would immediately find a RAM and request to see the roster, to find out who it was . . . since normally I would know anyone who would be allowed to personally watch an Atare," Mailan said firmly, straightening once again and moving back to the doorframe.

"Who could order such a change? Promote a *guaard* to personal watch so suddenly?"

"Only the Captain could authorize it; any trainer acting under his orders could enter it." Sheel gave her a hard look—she was sounding more neutral by the moment.

"So . . . it is possible, if slightly improbable, that if a *guaard* came up to Martin and told him that Dirk had shuffled the roster

... and sent him to Baldwin's home, he would believe it, and go?" Sheel continued, his voice almost contemplative.

Mailan did not answer for a long time, her face expressionless. Sheel knew it for her thinking silence, and did not prompt her. Finally, a bit hesitantly, she spoke: "I might think it irregular ... but we have been at peace for several years, and there have been no threats from any disgruntles lately. If I had been guarding The Atare, I would have called up a screen and checked the roster."

"And seen this second chart?"

"I ... have no idea when it was changed, seri. Between vespers yesterday, and when I called up that roster this morning. Possibly," Mailan offered, her voice even more uncertain.

"If you had been Martin, and seen your name moved to Baldwin's home ... and seen at least one familiar name left for Cort ... would you have bothered to check"—Sheel leaned forward, examining the categories—"the time of changes?"

"Probably not...." Her voice actually trailed off. Sheel glanced her way once again.

"In other words, probably yes, but you cannot speak for Martin's frame of mind," Sheel corrected gently. "You cannot incriminate him in his death, Mailan—and I am aware that only the best normally would *guaard* the Atare. Which means Martin would know anyone with enough experience to be switched out—"

"Unless he thought it was an emergency," came a voice from the bedroom. Jude stepped into view. "Forgive me, seri, it is difficult not to listen to such a puzzle. But if someone told him something was wrong, that they were short *guaard* or something —especially if it was at the change, when he normally would be ready to leave anyway!—he might accept a second shift in a row."

"I forgot a normal shift is only two bells," Sheel said, lifting an eyebrow at Mailan. Another of Dirk's little tricks.... One finger began to tap as Sheel considered the problem. Someone getting into the computer, and someone masquerading as *guaard*. "Do you not have numbers?"

"Yes, seri." Jude walked to the screen and indicated herself, as the morning shift for Sheel. "Name and number."

"Would the computer accept the wrong name with a number?"

Jude's broad, square face creased as a frown crossed her features. "When a number or a name is entered, the other automatically appears. I ... doubt the computer would—could—accept a false name."

"Unless someone tampered with the code for the program."
Worse and worse, but still possible. One skilled technician, a
handful of assassins posing as *guaard*, and a story good enough
to get one assassin into each position. And then simply jump
Caleb's, Dimitri's, and Fabé's *guaard?* He offered up this theory
to the pair.

The *guaard* exchanged glances. "You do not care for the
theory? Where is the hole?"

"It sounds unnervingly possible, seri—except . . ." Jude began
slowly.

"Martin would have been on the call box immediately, asking
why a green recruit was on Cort," Mailan finished for her.

Sheel jumped to his feet and strolled across the room, running
his fingers across the many boxes of rings left out for visitor
viewing. Martin was a *guaard* of many years experience, old
enough to have two children in service. A cautious man, to be
entrusted with Cort's care. "A disguise?" Sheel muttered aloud.
"It would have been dark. . . . " His eyes scanned the case set in
the wall, titles sweeping past his fingers. Between these and the
on-line entertainment channels, an entire library was at a guest's
fingertips.

His eye paused on one title: *Tales of Horror.* The off-world
edition, not the Nualan, which had several stories horrifying only
to natives—

Suddenly Sheel felt very cold. A claustrophobic sensation
closed in from all sides, and he could hear ringing in his ears.
Reaching out, his hand closed on the protruding edge of the
omni. *Irulen . . . Of course, Irulen!*

"Seri?" Jude had moved in his direction, alarm in her question.

Irrational terror seized him, that she might touch his arm, and
he waved her off with a brisk, concise gesture. *Do I look that
bad?* He stumbled toward the sanitation.

Light blazed at his touch, ignited in passing on his way to the
sink. He put too much weight on the foot control—the water
came out in a rush, full force. Heedless of backsplash Sheel
cupped his hands beneath the faucet, burying his face in the icy
offering. Only when his skin was numb and his senses calmed
did Sheel lift his gaze to the mirror behind the sink.

Jude was right: he looked awful, as pale as cow's milk. Dropping his gaze back to his hands, he saw they were shaking. *Sweet
Mendulay, now what?* Could he confide in anyone? What could
he do? Had Iver told Leah and Avis, directly or in the same

manner? And if he used the story to tell them, had they understood? *Can I trust even Mailan?*

Straightening slowly, Sheel took his foot off the controls and watched the water diminish to a trickle. Lifting a towel from the side rack, he returned to the lounge, gently patting he moisture away. Forcing himself to sit, he reached for his mug only to find it missing. Steam intruded from the side of his vision—Jude had refilled the cup. *Do not be a fool, if she meant to kill you, she would have done it this morning.* Taking the offering, he sipped carefully, and found she had spiked it with wine.

Did Cort have time to realize he was betrayed? Sheel roughly pushed the thought aside; no time for grief, not yet. If Iver saw what he claimed to have seen, then the entire family was in incredible danger.

"Mailan," he started softly. "Have you ever heard the tale of Irulen Atare?"

Both *guaard* looked puzzled. "I do not remember there ever being such a ruler, seri," Mailan admitted calmly.

"There has not been. . . . It is in a story, an old story, at least a thousand years old. It was Iver's favorite when he wanted to be scared to death, although it always made me sick to my stomach —I was younger, and more impressionable. . . . It has never been a favorite of the *guaard*, and there was quite an outcry of criticism when it was published." Jude studied him intently, while Mailan's expression indicated she had one ear trained in his direction.

"Perhaps this will nudge your memory." Sheel forced his body to relax, his pulse to slow. "Irulen Atare had the same *guaard* for twenty years, a rather unusual man; taciturn, zealous in his duty. . . . He was an albino, and always on the outside, so to speak, in social—"

Jude's gasp interrupted him. Mailan made no outward sign, but in the late afternoon light she looked a bit pale.

"Ah . . . I have always suspected the trainers hold that one over your heads," Sheel said mildly.

"'Irulen should have believed. . . . ','" Jude whispered aloud.

"You understand what he meant?"

Silence. It was Mailan who finally answered the question. "When Alger finally lost his mind, and attacked Irulen Atare, the ruler could not believe the man had turned upon him. He hesitated too long before drawing his own weapon, and so he died for his disbelief," she said steadily.

"Yes. And that was what Iver must have tried to tell me . . . tell me in the presence of *guaard*. That the person who attacked him looked like a *guaard*." Something occurred to him; he looked over at Mailan. "A compliment for you, Mailan, that he trusted you enough to give you the message."

"Whoever attacked him must have appeared male," Jude said thoughtfully.

"Or was someone he recognized," Mailan offered steadily. "Perhaps someone he felt I did not know, or disliked. . . . Someone I would not have been in alliance with . . ."

Sheel stood at this, tension knotting his body. "You can accept a traitor among your own more easily than an impostor?" His voice was too harsh, but he could not withdraw the question.

At this, Mailan actually relaxed her vigil momentarily, turning her head to give him her full attention. Sheel was shocked to see tears running down her face, although her voice was still level. "Your brother is not a brilliant man, seri, but he is not a coward. He would have announced that someone dressed as a *guaard* attacked him, and left others to ferret out the truth. Seri Iver must have recognized the person who stabbed him, and had visions of a conspiracy. . . . Why else hesitate to speak to four competent *guaard* carefully watching over him?"

A knock at the corridor entrance spared Sheel from answering her. Jude moved to stand in the vestibule.

"Identify," Mailan demanded as the *guaard* on duty.

"Crow, with the lady Darame," came the response. Jude used the security device on the panel and, satisfied with what she saw, opened the door.

The two entered quickly, a box with holes in it under Crow's arm. He promptly handed it to the off-worlder and composed his face, which was anxious but laced with a touch of mischief.

Calming himself, Sheel sat down and gestured for Darame to do the same. He had expected her to appear more wary, after her behavior that morning—typical behavior for an off-worlder witnessing a healing; they should have removed her, careless—but of course this woman was trained in protocol. Whatever she was privately thinking, she now had control of her expression. How— A tiny squeak, almost a squall, reached his ears, and Faust, who had been sleeping in a chair by the window, lifted his head.

Turning toward the sleepy animal, Darame said firmly: "Don't even think about it, cat. This is neutral territory, you've only been here a day yourself." Glancing at Sheel, she asked: "Where are the others?"

"The cats? Probably hiding under the bed. Cats do not travel well," he replied, wondering what she had in the box.

"They don't?" She immediately folded back the longer of the two flaps on the box top, and peered inside. A smile touched her face, and she carefully inserted her hand into the opening. "Don't scratch," she instructed an unknown creature.

It was not what Sheel expected, this off-worlder arriving with an armful of packages. A native bird? No—Darame lifted a tiny, dark bundle of fur from the container. Stroking it, she chirped softly at it, enough to make it stir, and then, suddenly at a loss, extended it toward Sheel.

He stared at it, and then at her. "It's for you." When he did not move, she said: "I figured things were enough of a mess. No sense in decreasing the cat population as well. They didn't have any, eh... 'orrels' females, but I...I didn't think you would want one that looked exactly the same."

Her last words relaxed his face. Even if she had never cared for animals, a common enough reaction among spacefarers, she understood that humans could become attached to them. *That I was attached to her* ... Not trusting his face, Sheel kept his eyes on the kitten. A ruddy Somali, very young, by its size. He found himself reaching for the ball of fur.

Older than he thought, simply small for her age. He offered the kitten a finger, which she licked several times and then proceeded to chew thoroughly. "Your teeth are quite good," Sheel remarked to the animal, loosening its grip. Still studying the kitten, he fumbled mentally for something to say. He was not sure he was ready for a successor, but it was here, and...was probably a peace offering.

"Thank you," he finally said. "It was a kind thought." Lifting his head, he met the off-worlder's eyes and said: "You will need to comfort her for a time, she will be frightened. I will put Faust in the bedroom, so she can prowl around in here and become accustomed to the odor of the other cats." Gently handing Darame the kitten, he scooped up Faust before the big Coon cat could either greet or attack the newcomer and dumped the animal into the other room. As Sheel shut the door, he said: "I must go to the hospice and check on my brother, and then to the palace. You are welcome to stay—or if you would prefer Crow to escort you back to the hostel?" He turned as he asked the question.

Her eyes seemed to light up at his words, but she only said: "Whatever you prefer, seri."

"Mailan. If you are reassured as to what distressed you this morning, it is time for us to leave this place."

Nodding to the off-worlder, Sheel started to indicate that Jude should stay when Mailan pointed to Crow. "You come with us." Moving to the door, Mailan checked the hallway and opened the door. Glancing down the corridor in both directions, she turned, her face now dry and composed, and said: "Seri?"

Taking a slow, deep breath, Sheel started out the doorway.

HOSPICE   THIRTYSEVENDAY   VESPERS

The obelisk was in sight before the tolling began. Mailan, leading the way, tensed visibly; Sheel could not see Crow's reaction. Four, five, six . . . seven. Vespers bell. Relief made Sheel momentarily weak. He hoped Mendulay had no prominent deaths planned for this day—the bell-ringers' nerves were undoubtedly already frayed.

Gray skies continued to haunt the city, casting an early shadow beneath the conifers covering the temple grounds. Sheel let his eyes drift up toward the tops of the neudeya, trying not to feel vulnerable. *We should have taken a meth' car.* . . . He actually paused, wondering how long it would take to call up a vehicle, and then discarded the idea. How was he going to throw out the *guaard* in Iver's room without creating a scene? Should they stop and ask Leah to join them? . . .

Suddenly Sheel realized the grounds were deserted. In the temple? All the priests and priestesses? And half the town, he decided, as they turned onto a sparsely populated street. *To me, Cort was family, but to them, he was the rock this city was built upon.* . . . Not good for the land, not good for the people. Iver had to get things moving again as quickly as possible—Cort would have been incensed that the city had stumbled into silence.

Feeling drawn, Sheel was grateful when they finally approached the footpath to the hospice. Halfway up the flagged stone walk, he heard the temple bell begin to toll. Frantically casting through his mind for a name, any name at all—anyone recently ill who was prominent enough to rate a passing bell— Sheel drew a blank. *Sweet Mendulay, what has happened now?*

Mailan opened the main doors, and the confusion hit them in a wave. People were rushing about shouting questions, and Sheel could hear the distant sound of someone in hysterics. A strange, sinking sensation touched him, riding to the pit of his stomach. Stepping to his side, Crow cautioned one of the approaching men with the flick of a hand. *Guaard* had one advantage over any hired bodyguard: if a *guaard* chose to flip someone into a wall for pressing too closely, there was none but The Atare to reprimand him.

The pair of *guaard* bored a passage through the crowd to the lifts. Sheel had the code of the restricted level punched in before the doors closed. Ringing finally intruded on his thoughts. Could they hear it, or was it his own ears playing tricks? Blood pumping too fast. *The shock is finally settling in*. Control, he had to maintain control. . . .

Doors slid open to reveal a corridor packed with *guaard*. Strong odors assailed him—of medicine, and disinfectant. The shrieks had disintegrated into muted sobbing—Bette, Iver's wife, her face flushed and swollen. So . . . it was not over, not yet. *Worse and worse* . . . Sheel recognized Leah by her side, as pale as the other woman was florid. His sister looked up at the sound of the lift, her eyes meeting his squarely. The expression was not comforting; Leah looked as if she had been struck. *No strength there . . . But you never expected to find it there, did you?* The inner voice was mocking. Sheel shoved it aside once again; now was not the time to evaluate his own perceptions of Leah.

He did not pause to ask questions. Pushing past the stunned attendant partially blocking the doorway, Sheel entered the private room.

The monitors were silent. Iver no longer looked quite right. . . . Death was settling upon him early. Automatically Sheel reached for him, checking the minute processes of the body even as a familiar voice said: "He simply stopped breathing."

There was little to see while he made his search. Sheel flicked a glance to one side and saw his old mentor Capashan seated near the bed, head in his hands. "Suddenly the monitors . . . went dead. We rushed in. The *guaard* were already trying to revive him. I tried every possible stimulant. . . . Nothing." The man smoothed his thick white hair, his hands still trembling slightly, and asked: "What do you think, Seri? It does not appear to be a heart attack."

"No. . . ." Sheel was losing himself in the pathways of the body. It was difficult to do, seeking anomalies in a dead man.

Things were already too far along. . . .Sheel straightened. "When did the machine cut off?"

Capashan's brow furled momentarily. "Less than five minutes ago."

"Impossible. The body has almost completely shut down," Sheel snapped, returning to his investigation. "He has been dead almost an hour." Nothing specific, no injury to put a finger on. . . . Sheel's fingers stumbled over the probe attached to his arm. Carefully removing it, he examined it. The frequency switch . . . ah.

For a moment Sheel was frightened, afraid of his neutral response. Someone had murdered his brother, and almost succeeded in making it look natural. Why did he feel so cold?

"I will find the persons who did this," he said conversationally. Capashan rose and stepped to his side. "And when I find them, they will regret the finding. . . ." The softness of his own tone made him shudder. For this, and for Cort, there would be a reckoning.

Capashan had been distraught over the sudden loss of an important patient; he had never been intimidated by the simple presence of royalty. Reaching, he took the probe from Sheel's hand. A brief examination caused his breathing to catch. *"Switched off?"* He stared at Sheel. "It was this way when you removed it?" Even as he spoke, he was reaching for Iver's arm.

"Very clever," Sheel had to admit as he smoothed the sheets over his brother's still form. "With everyone so distressed, it was possible no one would notice . . . or would think it had been bumped off when it was removed. But I was very careful, Capashan. It is as it was when I removed it. I do not know who you have been monitoring for the past hour, but it was not Iver."

"Then . . ." Capashan touched the body again.

"His heart stopped from lack of oxygen. Smothered, or an injection—there are too many violations of the flesh to find it that way, we would have to go over the surface. Perhaps a chemical like Avion."

"Avion is highly regulated, Seri," Capashan said, his face closing with anger.

"Yes. But for the right price, it can be found. Probably stolen from a storage depot still unaware it is missing. Have someone check the known sources." In microscopic doses, Avion was used to regulate heartbeat. Too much would stop all major organs in mid-function. It would fade quickly, which meant—

"Autopsy?" Capashan asked, as if reading his mind.

"It may be too late. But, yes. If we can determine how it happened, it would be better. The *guaard* were outside the room?" Sheel turned around as he spoke.

It was Dirk, captain of the *guaard*, who materialized before him. "Two were outside each of the two doors entering the room, Seri," he said quietly. "There were *guaard* inside whenever he was visited."

"Get me the technician in charge of the monitoring station," Sheel told the young *guaard* standing in Dirk's shadow. The maiden disappeared swiftly. "I want a detailed list of all visitors since Iver was brought into the hospice, which *guaard* have been on duty, length of stay—"

The pale maiden was back, a trembling tech in tow. Sheel turned his attention to the man.

White as a fish's belly. *Dear Mendulay, do I look that angry?* Closing his eyes, Sheel forced himself to become calm, to push aside the fury building within. "Can you change the frequency of any given probe from the station, or must you set each probe by hand?"

"I can change it at the opposite end of the hospice, Seri," he whispered, nodding deeply. "Each frequency is unique, and a list of ones in use is also in the computer."

"Can it be overridden?"

Puzzled, the man stuttered a moment. Finally getting a semblance of control, the tech said: "The closest signal is picked up, Seri. It simply erases any interference."

Do you understand what this means? He glanced at Capashan, who was giving orders about Iver's body. *Measured Avion, given hours ago . . . and then simply override the frequency until they want the body discovered.* "His readings were good until the machine stopped functioning?"

"Excellent, Seri. He was recovering from his injuries handily."

Dismissing the man—the group—with a gesture, Sheel stood silent, staring at nothing, wondering if Bette could bear the shock of the word "murder," or if he should keep silent for now. He realized he was trembling within, and wondered if it showed. Mailan's face rose out of the shadows, and her words were soft.

"Atare . . . I took the liberty of recalling Fion, earlier today." There was a trace of unease in her voice as she added: "That is at least two."

"No, Mailan," he said, his voice scarcely audible. "We are even."

Chapter Five

". . . and rumors of both off-world and outclan intrusion continue to circulate in the wake of Iver reb Riva Atare's death," came the voice of a Caesarean translator as Mailan unlocked the door into the temple suite. There was a pause, as the translator waited on the announcer. Blinking quickly in the dim light, Mailan oriented herself; the off-worlder was still up, and Sheel apparently not back.

"Unconfirmed sources have suggested that a possible conspiracy was played out with disastrous effect. That Iver reb Riva may have been at the center of an attempt to seize the throne through—"

Fury seized the *guaard*. Only two steps to the omni and her fist was in the controls, slamming against the power switch with such force that the button wedged in its socket. Burping, the machine blinked out abruptly, and the degree of light in the room decreased by a third.

"Lies!" she snarled at the machine. "All lies!" The anger drained as swiftly as it rose; appalled at what she had done, Mailan backed slowly away from the dark screen and turned toward the off-worlder.

Curled in one corner of the sofa circling the firepit, the woman had not moved. Only her eyes suddenly glittered, wary, as she stared back at the *guaard*. Mailan doubted she could move; there was a bottle of fine whiskey at her elbow, and the contents had dipped noticeably since Mailan had left the room hours before.

Mailan considered apologizing, and then decided against it. If the machine had been on all evening, the woman had seen the same report several times over. Not really viewing—listening, perhaps, more for company than anything else. She was facing the one tall window of the room, the Somali kitten curled in her lap. Overcast outside, but no rain, fortunately. *Tomorrow will be depressing enough as it is....*

Too many funeral pyres. Normally taken care of before starset on the day of death, the autopsies would postpone things a day. And of course Riva Ragaree would come down from her retreat for the ceremonies. Sheel was probably off helping with arrangements, or barricading his sisters into their homes. Who was with him? Jude and Ayers—a fast choice, but the safest one Mailan could make on such notice. Somehow she felt she knew Ayers well enough to say he would not have any part of a plot which included murdering his father....

Where was Crow? Moving to the window, she glanced out; the man's profile was just visible, beyond the light of the room. So, he'd locked the inner door and was watching her from the outside. Why? Did he fear distractions? Was she a talker—simply too attractive? Mailan glanced back at the woman.... What was it, Dara-me?...

Not just silver hair. Delicate silver eyebrows, arching elegantly, naturally, and long, thick silver lashes. Even her arms bore a sheen of silver. Truly her own, then. Body dyes were coarse at best; surely a woman of her experience would have chosen a depilatory before body dye.

I should try to sleep. Two *guaard* when he was outside this room, one with the doors locked, otherwise. The Captain had added two others as an honor guard, but Sheel had informed him that he was "keeping" Jude, Crow, and Ayers.... That had been excellent. Worth laughing over, if the circumstances had been different.

Dropping the clothing packs she carried, Mailan moved over by the firepit and stretched out on the cushioned bench. It gave her an excellent view of the other woman. *I cannot sleep.* Jumping up, she opened the door to the gardens. "Crow, come in here and sleep. I might as well watch."

No protesting her giving orders—he was that tired. Well, then, he should sleep. Flopping down in a corner, Crow immediately curled up and closed his eyes. Locking the outer door as well as the corridor entrance, Mailan settled herself back on the bench, but this time she sat straight. No need to stand at attention for *this* one.

Why had Sheel kept her? He had questioned Crow intensely about her session at *guaard* hall—a rather inadequate session, from Mailan's point of view. Sheel also had requested the report on Darame's employer, a man called Halsey. Had anyone at the embassies been questioned yet? Not yet? Sheel was interested in everything, suddenly—all the politics he had pointedly ignored in the nine months since his return to Nuala.

"Keep her close . . . and watch her," was all he said. Did he think her part of this thing? Then why risk keeping her under his own roof? Could he be so interested in the woman he had lost all caution?

If she was dangerous, why had she not already tried to kill him?

Something had been bothering Mailan for several hours, but it took a few minutes of peace to bring it to mind. "How did you know the cat had died?" she said abruptly in Caesarean.

It took the woman several moments to realize she was being addressed. She stared oddly at the *guaard* until Mailan repeated her question.

"Crow told me."

"No," Mailan said patiently. "Crow told you only after you asked him what kind of animal was killed. We were speaking Nualan except when we addressed you. How did you know?" Mailan tried to keep any threat out of her voice. It was extremely unlikely the woman had learned Nualan off-planet—only scholars exported the language tapes. Most people would never anticipate the need.

"You looked in the pouch, after he removed the third creature. You obviously expected something else," the woman said in a reasonable tone.

And I thought you were reading the pill package, Mailan thought wryly. Possible . . . and observant. This one was very clever—she would indeed bear watching.

A noise at the lock heralded the return of others. Mailan leapt to her feet and moved to the peephole. Ayers's shaggy blond countenance blocked her view. Hmmm . . . The plan had been to leave Ayers with Leah, and Ayers's sister Sheri with Avis. What had gone wrong? Pulling a knife from her arm sheaf, Mailan hid the weapon in her hand. Glancing once over her shoulder to make sure the woman had not moved, she opened the door.

They trooped in like a procession: Ayers, Sheel, and Jude. Two others followed; seasoned *guaard,* both of them, but Mailan was close to neither. She stopped them with an upraised hand.

"One on this door and one on the courtyard entrances," Sheel said quietly, moving to the tiny bottles arranged on a shelf near the firepit.

They needed no other orders; one of the men promptly took up a position outside the door, while the other walked through the room, unlocked the courtyard entrance, and continued out, pulling the door shut behind him.

Turning to her, a glass of bottled water in his hand, Sheel said: "Dirk insisted that I take them. But I will choose what we do with them."

He looked unbearably tired. Mailan started to speak, and then thought better of it. What matter if he tried to sleep? Would sleep come to him?

"My mother has been told, and will arrive early in the morning. All has been prepared for the services." Seeing Mailan's eye on Ayers, he added: "Leah does not care what Iver claimed he saw—she will not 'insult' Dirk's choices for her. We left Sheri with Avis. . . . Do you think Sheri can select other *guaard* to rotate the shift?"

"I was going to ask Fion . . . about it," Mailan finally said, swallowing her surprise. She had expected Sheel to be closeted with Dirk until starrise, at least.

Again, he almost seemed to read her mind. . . . "I mentioned Iver's words to Dirk. . . . Not, of course, telling him how the message was sent. He was livid at the thought, and rather sceptical." Sheel took a long drink of water. "I did not pursue it at the time, but I told him I wanted to see the permanent rotation sheets first thing tomorrow." The glass paused in midair as he lowered it, and the sudden expression on his face made Mailan long for some way to comfort him. "Mailan, I do not even know which of Cort's advisors currently holds the most power. How am I to do this? I never imagined . . ." The words trailed off as he focused on the off-world woman.

Mailan consoled herself with the thought that no one was throwing the name of Sheel reb Riva Atare around in connection with a conspiracy. The very idea would provoke laughter: the preoccupied healer, concerned with politics? Now that lifelong disinterest could be dangerous. . . . Mailan's gaze floated past Ayers's upright form, over Jude's slumped figure, and finally settled on Sheel.

He had moved over near the— Darame. Steadily sipping her drink, the woman had not acknowledged the new arrivals or their conversation. Now, she seemed to notice the lull in speech, for she looked up. Mailan was at the wrong angle; she could not see the look that passed between them. Her shrewd eye did detect the slightest tightening in the woman's arm as Sheel reached for her drink.

"It will not help," Sheel said softly in Caesarean, "and it is unlike you. Sleep would be better." He tossed the contents of the glass into the firepit. Flames leapt from the last pressed stick, devouring the alcohol and tingeing the room with a sweet smell. Lifting the bottle, Sheel moved back to the ledge and placed both glass and whiskey next to the carbonated water. Refilling his water glass, he wandered into the bedroom with scarcely a lifted hand in farewell.

Darame remained on the sofa, idly stroking the kitten in her lap. She seemed hypnotized by the fire, unaware that Mailan was studying her. The *guaard* could not control the annoyance building within—it was obvious something was wrong. Did the woman fear being accused of the murders? She had the best alibi on the planet. Or did she fear the Atare line? But Atare did not rule with the heavy hand of Dielaan. Iver's death? She had been silent since then. . . . Could she fear Sheel personally? An absurd idea; the man had his choice of women, he had no need to bully any— Mailan paused with the thought, twisted it slightly. . . . The healing. Damn. Mailan had forgotten about it. Most off-worlders were extremely nervous about that talent. . . . *You fear him because he is a healer?* Impatiently Mailan stood and paced the room, checking the doors to be sure they were locked, listening as Sheel re-checked the door to the terrace.

Then why do you stay? Tempted to ask, Mailan controlled her curiosity. *Do you see in him what I see, despite your fear? Or is it something else?*

"You may return to the hostel, if you wish," Mailan chose to say, her tone formal.

"No. I cannot," was the low response. Shifting the kitten to the sofa cushions, Darame stood and stretched. "I must stay here."

Walking up to the woman, towering over her, Mailan chose to speak—for reasons she herself could not isolate. "He is not a man to force his attention where it is not wanted," she said calmly, studying the off-worlder's black eyes.

Something stirred in those black eyes. So—part of it. Not all, but a part. Why stay if you fear him? Moving to the niche by the sleeping room doorway, Mailan considered the question. Only two reasons immediately sprung to mind, and they were not comforting.

Because someone—or something—had told Darame to stay

with him . . . or because the woman feared something more than Sheel.

THIRTYEIGHTDAY · TIERCE

It was the incense that brought Sheel back to the moment; sweet and heavy, the burning sticks outnumbered the sweep of candles covering the transept walls. Soft plainchant had been echoing in the vaults above for hours. The splendor of the light ceremony had sent him drifting into some vision—of what, he could not say. Sleep had followed, even as he remained upright upon his knees, and either no one had noticed, or no one had had the heart to wake him. He had been dreaming when the incense intruded—the beginning of a nightmare, he suspected. All Sheel could remember of it was shadow and light, the repetition of shadow and light, and then sudden pain across his chest, like the flick of a whip—

Long, pale fingers reached into his line of sight, touching his wrist; flinching, Sheel regained full consciousness. Delicate, porcelain features turned slightly, offering him a profile view, and one clear, light-filled eye of pale green studied him. Sheel was fascinated by the control in that face: this woman had just lost her only surviving sibling and five of her six sons, yet her expression was serene. *What strength you have, my mother. What a ruler you could have been, had you chosen to accept the power. . . .*

"Are you well?" she asked, her delicate tones chiming like a cast bell.

"Tired," he admitted, wishing he were holding up as well as she. Service had begun at starrise, and fourth bell, tierce, had just rung. Kee was halfway to her zenith, blazing with a strength rare in the second month. Leah and Avis were in no better shape. Although Avis still huddled on Riva's far side, Leah had seemed in danger of fainting, and several priestesses had escorted her back to the palace not long after the service had begun.

Tobias remained at Sheel's left side. He stirred rarely, unusually still for a child his age, his expression somber. Reaching out, Sheel impulsively gripped the boy's arm, and Tobias responded with a swift, secret smile. Instantly smooth, remote . . . Did Tobias understand everything that had happened? He was certainly maintaining a calm outer face; only the tightness of his embrace upon greeting Sheel that morning gave any hint of his unrest.

Why did they kill Cort Atare? the boy had finally asked. By then the procession was moving from the narthex into the nave, and Sheel was spared an answer.

Why—simply to confuse the government? To attempt a power grab during the reorganization? An old grudge . . . even a renewal of hostilities with Dielaan? It made his head spin. *My brothers, what have you left me to? I will be no better a guardian of Atare than Iver feared himself to be. . . .*

Bells tolling broke into his reverie even as Riva folded her small hand around his wrist. Finally, an end to things, a chance to discuss the autopsies with Capashan. Tobias took hold of his left hand and tugged him toward the aisle, where Crow waited with other *guaard* at his heel. No sign of Dirk; still offended over the request for copies of *guaard* positions the past few days. Still unwilling to consider a traitor in their ranks. *Sweet Mendulay, what does the man need to inspire caution: to catch a* guaard *trying to stab Leah or Avis?* Perhaps he had other theories, or other evidence he was not yet ready to reveal. He had seemed reticent last night, when Sheel presented the problem to him. Always proud, was Dirk, and prone to offense when his judgment was questioned. *Why did you not take the captain's seat, Fion? Why trust all to this one, admittedly an excellent* guaard, *but with more pride than years?* Necessary to make some sort of peace with Dirk as soon as possible. . . .

Along the aisle, out the north door and into the colonnade, the path back into the temple quarters arched over by a roof. Riva Ragaree followed slowly, arm in arm with her youngest, Avis. Sheel hesitated halfway down the walk, waiting for them to catch up. After all, Riva was . . . Dear Ones, was she really almost one hundred eight years Terran? Incredible how she kept both her wits and her vigor. It had been several moons since Sheel had checked her health; perhaps later in the day. . . .

Bringing up the rear was the second row, now passing him as he stepped aside. A multitude of children and wives, the survivors of this massacre, as well as the women who waited on his mother and sisters, various dignitaries and ambassadors, and— yes, Darame was among them, as Mailan had been instructed. Flicking him a long glance, her silver eyebrows raised in question, the woman moved past him like a whiff of spice, Second Ambassador Brant not far behind.

"Lovely, is she not?" said a soft, feminine voice, and Sheel turned his head, looking down to meet his mother's eyes.

"Yes, most would agree with you," Sheel answered tranquilly.

"But not you?"

Did he imagine it, or did Riva sound disappointed? "I find her quite attractive," he said seriously. "Unfortunately, she witnessed a healing yesterday."

"Ah." Riva set her hand on his arm, touching Avis's cheek in farewell as the maiden moved to embrace her remaining brother.

"Get yourself some hot saffra and then send for Stephen," he whispered into his sister's ear. The response was half chuckle, half sob. "Avis, what is done is done: our brothers took their pleasure too gladly to begrudge you what comfort you have to support you through the next days."

That seemed to make sense to her. Straightening, Avis gripped his hand momentarily and then took hold of Tobias, who seemed willing to return to the palace now that his grandmother had assured him she was coming to see him. Neither Sheel nor his mother spoke until the two had turned into the cloister and disappeared around the side of the temple quarters, a troop of *guaard* in tow.

"Indeed . . . Well, perhaps she is strong enough to come to terms with it, someday. Only the best can accept it," Riva said gently. It took Sheel several moments to realize she was speaking of Darame. Riva Ragaree leaned on his arm, her eyes scanning the courtyard and the host of people beyond it. The throng was flowing out the west door of the temple and into an already crowded street, for even the Mendularion S Atare was not large enough to hold the multitude which sought to show their respect to their departed Atare and heirs.

"You have acquired a few more *guaard* since I last saw you," his mother continued, drawing him along the colonnade.

"In a hurry," Sheel agreed, fighting an undignified urge to smile, or worse, laugh hysterically.

"A good boy, Crow, if a bit young for such responsibility. . . . And Jude always struck me as very dependable. But Ayers . . . This is a hard time for him as well," Riva said vaguely, turning her head to cast a curious look out her eye.

Sheel met that undisguised gaze of watered topaz with a lifted eyebrow and a hint of a smile. "I offered Ayers to Leah and Sheri to Avis. Leah felt Dirk would be offended, however, and assured me of her confidence in her regular staff."

"Avis accepted?"

"Avis is gracious when it comes to humoring me," Sheel admitted. Sweet Mendulay, enough stalling—he would have to tell her something. "I had to be sure of the loyalty of the people around me. . . . Right now I am concerned about Leah and Avis, but I was told last night that as best as Dirk can determine, no attempt was made on their lives. I, on the other hand . . ."

"Must be very careful." Riva stopped walking and turned to face him, her smooth, pale face at sharp contrast with the heavy wrinkles of her neck.

How much alike we are, he thought, not for the first time, and tried to picture himself reaching her age, his flesh drawn tight over sharp cheekbones, the betraying skin of neck and arms marring whatever looks he had. *If I live through the next moon . . .*

"Iver apparently saw who stabbed him," Sheel whispered. His mother's fine white brows lifted, even as Sheel glanced over her shoulder to see who accompanied her. Their names escaped him, but both *guaard* had been with her for at last fifteen years, if memory served him. . . . Surely Fion had said fifteen years? Well, the rumor would spread through the *guaard* soon enough. Even their normal reticence could not withstand this information.

"And?" Riva prompted, drawing Sheel's attention back to her face.

"It was someone dressed as a *guaard,* mother. I suspect it actually *was* a *guaard.*" Sheel waited for a reaction, hoping Riva was still as strong as she looked, reaching for her hand to be ready for any undesirable physical response.

Silence. As Sheel watched, something flitted across her eyes —an inward vision, a private horror she did not share aloud— and then all was the same, amber bubbles of iridescence floating in hazel waters. Her eyes abruptly mimicked his own: one light, one dark, then both pale as early morning. Only her pulse increased, a slight racing. . . . Nothing to cause him alarm.

"The temple has taught me well," she murmured. "Control is everything, when it is needed. Do you have proof?"

"Of tampering with the *guaard?* Yes. That it was truly *guaard,* or a name—no. Not yet. First I must convince Dirk the theory has merit. Now that Iver is dead, it will be harder. . . . His words were ambiguous at best." Quietly Sheel repeated Iver's last message to his brother, marking his mood and expressions even as Mailan saw them. His mother was quite literate—she would grasp the inference quickly.

Riva's face was vague, her mind far away, as he spoke. He feared her concentration was wavering until she said: "Yes. I see your dilemma. If it was no one Iver recognized, he would have immediately sent for the Captain and *guaard* trainers, to ferret out the impostor. Iver did not have your brains or cunning— Yes, cunning," she continued, her voice sharp as he began to shake his head. "Though you have used it little in the past. But he was no coward, and he knew his duty. He would have turned the place inside out looking for such a creature . . . unless he recognized the person." Riva's face softened. "I understand how he could be paralyzed by the realization. The very suggestion makes my blood run chill."

"Leah will not even discuss the possibility. I have not told Avis yet," Sheel continued.

"You must. Do not make the mistake Cort did with me: Leah and Avis are not women to take kindly to being shunted into the background." The woman began moving toward the temple quarters even as her voice roughened. "The balance of power must return."

A lifetime of delusion flashed before Sheel's eyes, and he reached for his mother's arm. "Mother . . . are you saying Cort forced you out?" The idea was too shocking for words. "Why? Why did you not demand your rights?"

Smiling slightly, Riva slipped her arm beneath his and continued toward the cloister, forcing Sheel to accompany her. "You forget, my son; I was quite active as a judge until shortly after Leah was born. You forget that everything changed in the year following her birth. When news came that *First Frost* was lost in transit, something in your uncle . . . hardened. Troubles with Dielaan started up then, too, probably brought on by news of the loss. Suddenly I was the only possible ragaree, with but two living sons and one daughter. I knew my duty and I did it. Five more children in the next twenty years."

"You have lost almost everything," Sheel murmured, his hand tightening on her knuckles.

"No, dear. True, I lost three siblings in one sweep of Mendulay's hand, and little James at birth. And now, this . . . I am thankful my mother did not live to see her line murdered in their beds. I praise Mendulay your father did not see it, just as I say thanks day and night that we had so much time together. But, to answer your original question . . . By the time you, Avis, and Iver left for Emerson, and my duty to the line was complete, your uncle had grown used to absolute rule. We would have badly shaken the house and the nation, if we had battled the issue." She smiled faintly. "I am not without influence, Sheel, nor without power."

Sheel felt a dimple twitch. The information network his mother had amassed was legendary, and the tendrils of her authority had crept to the highest levels. "Will you pull strings behind my back, mother?"

Riva actually chuckled. "No. Sheel. You are too shrewd, and more intelligent than Cort. Which is saying quite a bit, for Cort was no fool, and a good ruler. But he lessened what his reign could be, by failing to use my talents within the government. Learn from his mistakes, Sheel. You must have an immediate coronation—I would not even wait until the period of mourning is past." She slowed to let the *guaard* open the gates. "Although I would not actively start seeking a bride until we cease the black and white—"

"Mother . . ."

"I have been very polite, child of mine," Riva said quietly, steel in her voice. "I have not asked what happened to scar you, on Emerson, or why Avis purposely chose to return without a mate. . . . So as to accompany you to Caesarea, so you would not be alone? But you no longer have the luxury of carelessness with a legal line." The woman gracefully lowered herself to a bench inside the cloister gates, and lifted her eyes to meet Sheel's.

"Surely I have done my part for the gene pool, Mother," was all Sheel trusted himself to say.

"Indeed." A smile touched her lips. "But unless the next generation of named descendants is to be composed of nothing but outkin, you will have to continue to do your part—even marrying one of your brothers' widows, if no one else will suffice." She folded her hands and leaned back against the stone wall. "A new council must be convened, and Leah named ragaree—"

"Nothing should be done in haste." Sheel was almost as surprised as Riva by the tone of his words—there was no room for argument within them. He did not want to tread this ground, not until he spoke with Leah. Before, he was an underling brother, forced to be satisfied with struggling for her trust. Now . . . Now he would be Sheel Atare, and when he told her she *would* allow him to examine her, it would be a private fight of equals—a fight he would win. Blackmail was a dirty business, but when she discovered he knew her secret, perhaps she would let him help.

The fewer people involved, the better. Riva did not need this grief to add to her burdens. She was a tough old woman, but to find out the house depended on one unmarried, untried girl was more than Riva needed to hear.

"I must talk with Leah about many things before a council is called, or a conferral made. You forget that an assassin still stalks our family." Sheel forced his voice to soften, to modulate to a model of consensus.

Glancing around the cloister—fully ten *guaard* within sight, practically within arm's reach—Riva said: "I can forget no more than you." She seemed to drift again, her eyes seeing something beyond the cloister walls, beyond the courtyard and temple grounds. "It is against every law of nature for a mother to bury her children. . . . We have dedicated our existence to our children, we Atares. I believe it is why we prosper when other lines have failed." Suddenly sharp once more, Riva asked: "You will speak to Leah? Soon?"

"Soon." A flutter of cloth caught his eye, and he lifted his head. Several *guaard* moving around the corner, leaving—he had seen silver cloth, not black. "Who was it?" he asked Crow.

"The Serae Leah, my Atare," he said quietly. "She saw you in conference, and departed rather than disturb you."

"How long did she wait?" Sheel continued, wondering how much Leah had heard—and how much she had inferred.

"Not long, Atare. A few moments only."

Sheel stood silent, considering how much could be said in "a few moments." Without conscious thought he tensed . . . and finally relaxed. If she heard, she heard. . . . And so was warned of his suspicions—knowledge? That his talent could tell him such a thing was something she might not know. . . .

"I must speak with Capashan," he said aloud. "Can I see you back to your room, Mother, or do you prefer to rest here?"

Riva waved him off. "You have a great deal of work ahead of you. I shall content myself with visiting my grandchildren and trying to cheer Avis." She gave him a long look before closing her eyes. "If you need me, Sheel, you have only to ask."

"Thank you, Mother." Turning away, Sheel started down the cloister, fighting a smile. Such spirit in that woman! To think he had never bothered to connect her information network with the power it represented. He had been blind too long—it would cost him. He would have to work doubly hard to make up for his ignorance. But there was nothing for it but to try.

His racing thoughts translated into movement, and Sheel realized he was walking so swiftly it might as well be a run. The arches of the cloister whipped by like leaves in a tempest: now shadow, now light, now shadow—

The image brought him to a sudden halt, so abruptly the *guaard* behind him peeled off to either side to avoid trampling him.

They were not the only ones fooled. Later Sheel remembered it as a hiss, as if the air could not part quickly enough. Burning lashed across his chest, even as Crow threw him back and sideways into the wall of the outbuilding. Bright sparks shattered his vision as the slap of leather against cobblestone told him the hunt was up. An image melted in and out of his line of sight: Crow, his face ghastly pale, reaching to lift him into the light at the edge of the row.

Had his own thoughts—a teasing vision of stippled light, a memory of pain—saved him? Or had Crow's action? His eye caught a reflection, near his head—more than one blade. So the youth deserved some thanks, except . . .

"Well done," Sheel managed to whisper, though only Crow heard him through the shouts for a healer, for a doctor for The Ragaree. Damn! Had the woman suffered a stroke, seeing this? "Of course you may have done more damage than the assassin . . ." There was more he wanted to say, but the darkness swarmed in like starspot, and he lost his grip on consciousness.

SHEEL'S HOME   THIRTYEIGHTDAY   TIERCE

"May I watch?" The words came out very soft; Darame had no idea what possessed her to speak.

"Watch?" the healer repeated, his swift, competent hands stilling their movements.

"Watch," Darame repeated, stepping slowly into the sleeping room. Crow, his face even now white and still, made no move to stop her. Continuing her walk, leaving her empty hands loose and free, Darame did not halt until she reached the other side of Sheel's bed. A quick glance out the window showed a *guaard*'s back. *The place is probably crawling with them,* she decided, and then finally forced herself to look at Sheel.

It had been a shock, being seized without warning and thrust into a dark vehicle packed with *guaard.* Worse to find Sheel out cold on the floor, even worse to realize the large, dark stain across his chest was blood. No one had volunteered any information, but Darame could make a few educated guesses. The hospice was no longer considered secure; the temple also, although why they had changed their minds she did not know. This house was certainly large enough to provide several means of entry to an assassin. It smelled faintly of paint. . . . Sheel's home, the evidence of violence erased by skilled hands?

The doctor had kept busy since they carried his patient through the doorway. Cleaning the wound had taken a few minutes. It no longer looked as severe as Darame had feared: long and shallow, bleeding copiously, certainly, but nothing vital was punctured. The blow to the head looked worse—could the skull be cracked? And a few bruises on face and shoulder were beginning to show. *Who would have thought they would try so quickly?*

Whatever the healer read in her face, he was apparently satisfied. Reaching, he carefully brought in the edges of the wound, tracing smooth arcs from either end, and then began his seal from the center radiating out.

Much slower than Darame had imagined. Had it taken that long . . . when, yesterday? Two days ago? Or was Sheel faster with slashes? She forced herself to watch, to keep her eyes fixed on the injury, to think of it as an abstract problem, a demonstration, a cold torch sealing a wound. Someone entered the room; there was an intake of breath, a soft comment in Nualan. Spot touches to attend to a few nicks in the muscle and fascia, and then continuing, returning to the center to move in the opposite direction, across the sternum and breast, just under the nipple, the edge of the chest wall—finished.

Her stomach remained under control. It *was* fascinating to watch. . . . Had she imagined a faint glow around his hands? If only she could let it go, blank it out when it wasn't necessary. . . .

"Does it frighten you?" she asked bluntly.

Studying the result of his efforts, his hand checking beneath Sheel's jaw for a pulse rate, the healer did not answer at first. Then he glanced up at Darame. "His condition? There is no danger. A slight concussion, blood loss, but the blade was not poisoned."

"I mean the healing. . . . That you can do such a thing."

Thick eyebrows twitched, although his expression did not change. A pause, and then he said: "Not anymore." His Caesarean was precise, clearly a second language, unlike Sheel's fluency. "When I first used my talent, in my youth . . . yes, it frightened me. Now it fills me with awe, that Mendulay gave me such a gift." He looked down at the unconscious man. "The Atare's skill is greater than mine, as if the gene gains strength each generation. He can even predict the sex of a child while it is still in the womb—quite a feat, since instruments cannot penetrate a Nualan uterus without miscarriage."

Moving toward the windows, Darame asked: "Why is healing preferable? Or are you simply more portable than a cold torch?"

The Nualan actually chuckled. "More than that. A cold torch freezes the skin layers, killing them. That is why an instant scar forms. With hot healing, the traumatized cells are soothed and encouraged to knit together. When this finally heals, only a thin white scar will remain, if anything. And of course Sheel will mend quickly, since he is a healer."

"Capashan?" The physician turned his head, and then moved over to Mailan, who had entered the room sometime during the healing. A quick, whispered conversation ensued, all in Nualan. Darame's eyes flicked over the walls of the sparsely furnished room, her mind drifting as she tried to guess their location.

"Lady Darame?" Surprised by the honorific, Darame turned and faced the speaker. Mailan, still in uniform, but without the stiffness of duty—not her shift, then. "Your employer is in the friendship parlor." The woman—for she *was* a woman, despite her neutral dress and manner—gestured through the doorway, and then turned back to the healer.

Darame did not think twice about the invitation. Gliding through the doorway, absently noticing that Mailan had brought her things, she asked: "Where are we, by the way—if that is not privileged information?"

It was Crow who answered. "The Atare's home, lady."

The old Atare, or do you mean Sheel? Entirely too many Atares the last few days.... Darame hastened down the corridor to the living area.

He was standing over by the glass doors, his huge frame blocking a great deal of light. The thin, curly hair seemed sparser by filtered natural light, but the blazing, confident smile was the same. Halsey started to open his arms wide, paused—thinking better of it—and then shrugged, continuing the sweep of his hands.

He's right. Does it make any difference, after what we've been through? I told them I'd worked for the man twelve years, of course we're friends! Darame reached around the huge torso as far as she could, muttering, "Old Bear."

"Ha! And how is my precious gem?" boomed the tenor voice. "I understand you had a narrow escape, that first night."

Of course, Brant had volunteered information. Darame loosened her grip, meeting his eyes. "How are you getting along without me to chaperon? Did you remember to tip?" *Tipping* was always the same: a code for "Are you involved with this scam?" In this case, the assassinations.

Smiling, Halsey shook his head. "Of course not. Obviously I

need you close by." *Close by—damn. Worse and worse.* That meant multiple unknown factors, and the possibility that bailout would be necessary, blowing off the job and fleeing the area.

"I'm not sure that's possible right now. They told me where I am—they may not want me anywhere I can be asked about it." *Yes, old one, I am being watched, and probably monitored as we speak, although you expected that.* She glanced down at the face of her roman. . . . Still white.

"Well, it can't go on forever. Surely with both the Atare family's private *guaard* and the local people on it, some leads will turn up soon. Can't have a murderer on the loose." *Saints, it can't get any worse—so sources (probably Brant's) can't turn up anything, either, and multiple groups are looking. Very smooth, very professional, this job.*

"The ambassador I spoke with told me to sit tight and he'd contact all citizens when there was news," Darame went on, turning and moving toward a low couch. *Did you get that one, Halsey? Brant wants me right where I am, in the bedroom of a mutated human someone is trying to kill. A good lawyer could pull a charge of "Localized Treason" out of this, and I'm not ready to die!*

"I know no more than you," Halsey said gently, strolling down the wall of glass, his light step at odds with his appearance. *Hell's bells! What do you mean we don't have enough vocabulary to discuss the situation? By Sebastian's Arrows, we'd better come up with the vocabulary!*

"Perhaps they'll let you start making some limited presentations in town," Darame suggested, carefully slowing her breathing. No sense in panicking—probably a delayed reaction to what had happened to Sheel, to the knowledge that she herself had missed an ugly death. She could see the length of the corridor from where she sat: Crow had a plain view of both she and Halsey, and could probably hear them as well—the air circulation system was very quiet. *Not the best time to start up a new set of codes, but we may not get another chance.*

"I was also told to wait on the embassy," Halsey replied, idly shaking his head.

So . . . Brant doesn't want either of us to move. I feared it was serious, but I didn't want to think . . . The last time she saw Brant, in the cloister corridor, came vividly to mind. He was bidding Darame and several other Caesareans a polite farewell when the Serae Leah had rushed up to him, her eyes blazing. The troop of *guaard* surrounding her did not encourage them to stay, so the citizens started out into the courtyard toward the streets. Darame had heard only one thing, almost a hiss, pass between the two: *He will place her before me.* Leah spoke in Caesarean. . . . Brant had never been quick at learning languages. *He's had over three hundred days. I could learn almost anything in that much time. . . .*

"This is going to be a long day," Darame muttered, rising and moving away from the sofa, her fingers gently trailing across a fine piece of glazed pottery displayed on a pedestal.

"Watch your step," Halsey said suddenly, reaching out as if to steady her. Glancing down as she took his hand, looking for a cat, Darame saw nothing. Code? Uh-huh . . . Not good. *Stay close but not too close to Sheel? That may call for more skill than even I can muster.*

SHEEL'S HOME   THIRTYNINEDAY   NONE

A brisk gust of wind buffeted Darame as she stepped out onto the balcony. Bouncing after a leaf, the kitten's behavior made it plain she approved of the weather. Settling down on a stone bench next to the building, Darame spoke to her reprovingly: "You don't need to be so happy about it. Pretty soon it will be *cold* up here!" She pulled the flaps of her cape closed, grateful Sheel had offered her the use of it. Not necessary to throw one strip over her shoulder—it was not a bitter wind, not yet. But they were far to the north; Atare was the most northern of the great cities.

I will have to send to the ship for cold weather gear, she thought idly, lifting her arm slightly to pull her tassels away from the cat. Instantly recognizing a new game, the creature pounced on the dragging tips of the garment. "Stop that, Nyani," she murmured, lifting the kitten by the scruff and placing it in her lap. The creature sulked for a few moments, trying to bite Darame's hand; a piece of string dangled for Nyani's benefit quickly mollified her ruffled feelings.

It was like the calm before a storm . . . both within and without the house. The *guaard* had kept both messages and company away from Sheel, jealously protecting his rest. Only his sisters had visited, and his mother—briefly, for the previous day's events had been quite a shock to her.

Expecting to be tossed into a guest room, Darame was astonished at her freedom of movement. *Suspicious, rather . . .* Why was she still present? Granted, any one of these *guaard* could probably restrain her with one hand while disemboweling a shadowy enemy with the other, but why take the chance? Sheel had desired neither conversation nor . . . anything else of her, though he did seem to be mending quickly. A rattle at the doors told her he was coming out, and she glanced up, forcing her gestures to look natural.

Too drawn, too tried . . . He was not sleeping well. *Is that surprising?* she admonished herself, tugging vigorously at the kitten's string. *He needs a confidant . . . damn.* She had forgotten the young man who had died in this very house, scarce nights ago. His only close friend? Possibly—Sheel seemed reserved by nature, and there were thirty-four years of Sleep Transit between himself and his childhood companions. Numerous court acquaintances had inquired after his health, but the messages had been ringed with formal courtesy. *No time since returning to make any close friends, especially if you thought you were going to Caesarea. What now—do they ship potential brides to you?*

Although he did not speak of inner distress, Darame had remained curled on her side of the master bed, and she saw his face upon rising. Tears left their mark on the cleanest countenance. . . .

Sheel was carelessly dressed in faded trousers and a sweater of muted grays; Darame was startled to see that he was barefoot. Eyes widening, she opened her mouth to speak and was stopped by the look of resignation on his face.

"Not you as well, please. I am quite used to the cooler months here, before the snow flies. And the sun has warmed the tiles." Seating himself on the opposite bench, Sheel crossed his legs, tucking his feet beneath. Gazing out over the wind-tossed treetops below, he absently rubbed at the back of his right hand, as if seeking something.

"Do we need to get you a substitute?" Darame asked pointedly, her glance taking in his gesture.

Smiling faintly, Sheel shook his head. "I miss the weight," he replied. "I am not always playing with it, I assure you. It will be back soon . . . perhaps tomorrow." He unconsciously looked down as he spoke, to the white stripe of flesh which marked where his signet ring usually rested.

Darame had never paid any attention to the ring, after her first examination of it. It was made of trine gold, and to stare at it seemed rude. The personal crest meant nothing to her, although she understood the importance of signets to rulers: a seal for major declarations, or some such rot. Now it was to be bordered with the sign of The Atare's seat, a chain of office circling the personal emblem. More important than a coronation. . . . Of course, he would work as ruler before the ceremony. . . .

"Any leads?" she asked abruptly.

Sheel did not pretend to misunderstand. "Nothing yet."

Not enough. Darame would not play games with herself. The situation was serious, and grew more so by the hour. Uneasiness within the town could explode into trouble, and off-worlders were obvious scapegoats. Halsey had been confined to his room at the hostel; no doubt if Sheel dismissed her, she would join him there. No real time to set up new code words, and no chance at all for an audience with Brant. Information might protect both Halsey and her, but getting that information . . . Where to start? . . . Her mind looped, returning to the difficulty of seeing Brant; returning to his office, and Leah's unannounced arrival. Just how close was he to the eldest daughter of the ruling house?

"It is so quiet," she murmured, hardly certain of where her words were going. "The very sky is still. I have never been in a monarchy at the death of a ruler."

Tapping a finger on the railing, Sheel did not speak. *So, hints will not be enough.* As she considered another tack, the man finally answered her unspoken question.

"Those who loved him mourn; those who disliked him wait to see if the next reign suits them better." After a slight pause, Sheel added: "I imagine those who hated him celebrate."

"I suppose your entire house will come into town for your coronation," Darame went on. "Even those who missed the funeral."

He was not really paying attention; it took several moments for the finger to stop tapping. "No one missed the funeral . . . except a cousin who was ill."

"I understood that your older sister is married?" Darame said easily, wrestling the kitten for the string.

"Richard was present. . . . Merely elusive. He is something of a recluse," Sheel told her.

"Fortunate your sister has so many friends among the embassies," was the careful response. "They can be supportive without breaking down under any grief of their own."

She waited several moments before lifting her head, and when she did, her eyes focused on Jude's back. How did the *guaard* decide on their shifts? Puzzled, she turned back to Sheel, and found him studying her. Darame met the gaze, even as she controlled a tendril of fear. That look went right down to her marrow. *Idiot, he is an absolute monarch! Halsey may be trying to help you in a few moments!*

"I did not know my sister had so many friends among the embassy personnel," Sheel said easily, still studying her.

"She seems to be very good friends with Second Ambassador Brant. When he spoke to me after my interview with the *guaard,* she walked in on us. And after the funeral yesterday, when he was speaking to a group of Caesareans . . . she broke in on it." Darame met his gaze, watching for some sort of reaction.

"I would not have thought Brant to be so sympathetic," Sheel murmured. "Interesting."

She did not follow up—if he wanted any more, he would have to ask for it.

"How was she then? I did not have time to speak to her before my . . . accident."

Darame shrugged expressively "Agitated. The *guaard* sent us all away. All I heard her say was 'He will place her before me.'" *Coin from a woman who has nothing, coin for a man who can buy little. Is it worth anything to you?* That was as far as she would go. Any further might place her partners in jeopardy—and she would never know how or why.

A high-pitched yell off in the trees interrupted their discussion, and Darame jumped straight up into the air. Jude was at Sheel's side immediately, her blades drawn, even as the man rolled off the bench and under it. Footsteps echoed on the stone walkways, and Darame heard someone calling for Sheel.

It was Mailan. She came up the balcony steps two at a time, her face flushed. "Atare! He is here!" Seeing Sheel and Darame on the ground, she immediately drew her blades and threw herself against the wall.

A soft, low voice reached Darame's ears, speaking Nualan with a light burr. From her vantage point on the tiled balcony, Darame could see no body to go with the voice. But in a few moments, a head and shoulders rose into her line of sight, followed by a short, compact male body. He was wearing the day uniform of a *guaard.* Although gray streaked his hair and short beard, this man's physique would rival many a youngster's. The height surprised Darame: she had expected a *guaard* to be taller, but the man reached barely past Mailan's shoulder, a good head shorter than Sheel.

That his arrival was a happy occurrence, there was no doubt. Whatever he said, it was appreciated: Mailan flushed and sheathed her blades, even as Sheel started laughing. Darame slowly pulled herself back up to the bench.

"We must be formal, we have a guest," Sheel said easily in Caesarean. "I will not deny I will sleep better now that you are here. How was your journey?"

"Mostly uneventful," the man replied in the same tongue, his burr still pronounced. "But all of you have better tales to tell than I do. Please."

Looking to Sheel for permission, Mailan immediately burst into a swift description of the past few days. She interspersed her story with Darame's name, and paused to identify the newcomer as Trainer Fion, another of Sheel's *guaard*. Why Darame was still present was not voiced. The older man, now leaning against a portion of railing, questioned neither omissions nor choice of presentation.

I understood some Nualan, Darame finally realized: Mailan's first words, "He is here." Not much, but something. As she set the wiggling kitten down on the tiles, she understood something even more important: they were speaking Caesarean. Was this her reward?

No. No secrets here: it was a straightforward account, told as a journalist might report it. But when Fion started speaking, she sharpened her hearing.

"The outlying areas are calm, Atare," he was saying. "I saw nothing out of the ordinary, except . . . perhaps one thing. There seemed to be several off-worlders on the side roads. Traveling alone, riding rugged-looking horses. Speaking to no one, starting early, arriving late. I saw two of them at separate times."

"Where were they heading?" Sheel asked, leaning his head back against the bench and folding into a lotus position upon the warm tiles.

"One was on the northern track toward Dielaan. The other I saw just as I left town on vacation. He was boarding a ship heading south, taking a horse with him. I spoke with the *guaard* watching the port, but apparently the fellow's travel permits were in order. A camper . . ." Fion frowned slightly. "There was no reason to question it, then. . . . But something about the man's gear, his preparations . . . It seemed the same as the off-worlder heading east."

"No doubt there is an explanation," Sheel said softly, a vague, unfocused expression crossing his face.

Something in that look told Darame that the conversation was about to become intense. Time to leave before she was asked to disappear. Glancing around for the kitten, she was amused to see the animal had crawled into Sheel's lap. He was stroking her lightly, seemingly unaware the squirming Nyani was trying to reach his toes.

"I suspect you have business to attend to," Darame said without preamble, standing and reaching for the door handle. A mere touch unsettled it, and the door burst open, the three adult cats swarming out onto the balcony. No one appeared worried about this exodus so Darame ignored them and, with a nod to Sheel and the others, went inside.

It was stuffy in the house after the wind on the balcony; could the windows be opened? Moving into what Mailan called the friendship parlor, Darame glanced around for an outside vent. No vents, but the windows... locked. *By Barbara's Tower, I must open a window!* It was hot in the house as well. But that was to be expected; she was used to the coolness outside. Removing the cape, she tossed it on a low sofa and started for the hallway.

Like walking through a pool of honey, dragging at her feet... Shaking her head, Darame paused, wondering if she had managed to contract a native illness already. *Haven't been this dopey since coming out of Freeze—* The thought stopped her movement. Leaning back against the sill of the entranceway, she tried to remember what she'd had to eat upon rising. Could someone ... But it had been hours! A light meal at noon—sext, they called it—and fluids later, but...

So much like coming out of Freeze—no, like going into *Freeze—*

The air. Not the food—something was wrong with the air in the room. Darame reached for the front door, a languid movement, as though time had slowed. She banged on the door— Did she? Several times? No response. Could a *guaard* hear through the thick door? How hard was she striking the wood?

Out. Must get out. To the balcony, open doors... Can no longer walk steadily—use wall, furniture.... Balance gone, falling, grabbing a pedestal, what kind of gas worked so...

MENDULARION S ATARE   THIRTYNINEDAY   COMPLINE

"Atare?"

Sheel stopped rearranging the blankets on the cot and slowly turned toward the door. It was Mailan, loaded with various backpacks and duffels, her arms supporting a reflective foodpac.

Dangling from the curl of an extended little finger was his signet ring. After staring blankly at it a moment, Sheel reached for the trinium circle.

"How did the jeweler finish so quickly?" It was not what he had intended to say, but surprise drove the original question from his head.

"Superstitious," she murmured, settling her burdens on the sofa.

"What?" The healing must have drained him; his wits were dull.

Mailan turned around, her expression closed. "He is superstitious. Apparently he went to work on it immediately. I think he thought you would disappear or something if he did not finish it quickly."

A crooked smile pulled at Sheel's lips as he slipped on the ring. "I am still going to disappear."

"You are determined to follow this course of action?" came a soft murmur from near the wall.

Sheel sat down on the edge of the cot, careful of Darame's feet, and faced the speaker. The Archpriest Ward, immaculately dressed as always, was leaning against one of his bookcases, arms folded and ankles crossed. He looked . . . not actually annoyed . . . but close to it. Recessed lighting made his features harsh.

"Do you have a better suggestion?" Sheel asked politely.

Ward waved abruptly in impatience, his hand a diagonal slash, and turned his body so he could see the old man sitting quietly in the corner. "What say you, Jonas?"

The high priest studied them both, his gentle face serene. "I can tell that no matter what I say, one of you is going to be angry with me," he said reproachfully.

"You could barricade yourself into the temple," Ward said quickly, his dark eyes returning to his ruler's face.

"I did that. The moment I set foot outside it, someone tried to kill me—twice." Glancing back, he continued: "If she had not pulled down that pedestal when she fell, I would have still another life on my soul." A tendril of weariness threaded his mood, marking his body with a tender imprint. "Going in circles tires me, seri. Let us face the facts. Someone wants me dead. This someone is powerful, and can even arrange to attach a cylinder of poisonous gas to the circulation pump of my home. Can you protect against that?" No one returned an answer. "Even my *guaard* have not been able to protect me." Shaking his head,

Sheel slowly rose to his feet. "No—the best solution I can see is to hide. I will take with me only those I can trust without question. You will hear from me at regular intervals. I feel it will look better than having the entire seaboard find out that the ruler of Atare is living in the Archpriest's library."

"You will take the boy?" Jonas asked. His words fell into a sudden silence.

"Yes, Seri," Sheel answered, moving to kneel at the priest's feet. "Do you disapprove?"

"How can I?" Jonas whispered. "After the last few days . . . it is logical to assume that the child is in danger, just as it seems your sisters are safe—at least for the moment." Lifting a withered hand, he touched Sheel's shoulder. "But are you strong enough for such a journey? Your injury, and now healing this woman . . ."

Sheel shook his head, denying the man's concern. "I can rest at our destination," he stated, reaching over toward Jude. The *guaard* was busy with a rasp, filing away at a broken piece of pottery. Examining her handiwork with a hard eye, the woman handed the fragment to Sheel. Muted grays and reds, a slash of scarlet across one edge—Darame had been clutching it when Mailan found her. Healing the cut in her hand had taken more energy than pumping her lungs, but the damaged pot had proved useful.

"But what *is* your destination?" Jonas looked worried as he asked the question.

"What you do not know you cannot have forced out of you, friend," Sheel said quietly, gripping the old man's hand. "You will see that Leah and Avis get the messages?"

"You will not tell Leah before you take the boy?" Ward asked abruptly.

"And give her time to assure me that Dirk can protect us?" Now was not the time to tell Ward that Dirk's interest in Leah might be more than professional. Ah—what did it matter? He would at least keep her safe. "And the frage for Darame." Standing once again, Sheel moved back to the cot.

You would have been a good shield, if things had been different. That was his original plan: keeping her under his roof would warn off other women, plus give him time to observe her closely and decide if she was somehow involved in all this mess. Now . . . Now he could not wait for her to heal, and it would take many days. *I am not sure I trust you enough to take you. . . . Not with Tobias in my wake. But with Ayers and his sister Sheri hov-*

ering over Avis, and Dirk with Leah, I can trust you with my sisters.

The message he left was simple: take care of my sisters, and take care of yourself. Whatever she was, she was more than a simple protocol specialist. Too blunt for that, yet skilled enough to make it work for her . . . *What are you, ice princess?* The pale face returned no answer.

Sheel placed the pottery piece back into her hand. This woman might be clever enough to figure out the message within it, if she had need. As for the frage . . . He reached to the nearby table, and realized Mailan had placed it into a small pouch. Catching the woman's eye, he lifted the soft bag, no bigger than his hand. Within was the frage . . . and a packet of *rav* pills. Fascinating . . . He looked back at Mailan, but she was examining the sight of her mag gun. *We have gotten as far as requisitioning hand-guns. . . .* He set the pouch back on the end table.

"Well, Jonas?" Sheel heard himself say. "Are you ready?"

"Are you?" the man countered gently.

"As ready as . . ." he hesitated. "Do it." He moved back to the priest and knelt before him. At his back Sheel heard the clanking of metal, and shivered. Ward came up beside him, carrying in his hands the chain of office, the trinium links glittering in the soft light. A ruby sent forth red reflections, patterning Sheel's pale shirt. *This thing I think I will hide.*

Lifting a beaker of warm oil, Jonas slowly began to speak. "And in the Year of Our Coming Three Hundred Eighty-Seven, he who would be Neal Atare Nightrider said to his followers, 'I will end both strife and dissension.' And his sister Naomi asked him how he would do this thing. Nightrider told her: 'We will stand at the source of the Summer River; and all that we can see shall be our responsibility and our joy, ours and our heirs, for-ever. . . .'"

Chapter Six

Fumbling in a state of semi-consciousness, aware that the left side of her face was warm and the right side cold, Darame forced herself toward the surface of her mind. *Hard ... never this hard to come out of Freeze....* Her mouth was so parched she could not swallow.

"Darame?" The sweet voice belonged to a stranger. Gentle hands lifted her head and held a tube to her lips. "Drink this— slowly! Only a little ..."

Cool liquid trickled down her throat, bringing welcome relief. Her eyes finally obeyed, opening wide, but the room was hidden in shadows. Someone drew back the darkness against a wall, and cold, pale light flooded the room. Curtains ... They were curtains, against the walls, heavy and rich in color. A deep, deep blue ...

"Where ... where is this?" she asked in Caesarean. Nothing she had seen on Nuala looked like this room. Elegance out of an ancient past ...

"One of the guest rooms, of course! Where else would you be?" replied the delicate voice.

The sound came from somewhere to her left. Turning her head slightly, Darame saw a dark form outlined by a fire. Moving closer, the figure was caught by the light from the windows. A woman.... One she had seen somewhere.

Widely spaced eyes framed by long, thick lashes, a curly mane of blonde hair.... She had Atare eyes, in soft pastels, the right one tender green, the left a blue many shades paler than the curtains. Dressed in black ...

"Do you remember me?" Younger than Darame had first

estimated . . . or more innocent. Tucking the downy comforter close, the maiden continued: "I am Avis, Sheel's sister."

"Where is The Atare? Did he? . . . The air . . ." Darame began slowly, hampered by her hoarse throat.

"Sheel is fine, as far as I know. He left several days ago, after he healed you. Do you remember what happened?" Avis said quickly, her response opening up a myriad of questions. Darame managed a slight shake of her head. "Someone attached a cylinder of poisonous gas to the air ducts. The mix pushed the oxygen to the floor—that is why the cats were still alive, and why they left the house in such a hurry. Everyone on the porch heard the crash when you pulled over one of the pedestals, and then Mailan pulled you out."

Darame had become aware of something hard in her hand. Unfolding her fingers, she lifted the object to the light. A piece of pottery. . . . She stared at it until her arm began to tremble. Why was it familiar?

Avis reached for her hand and laid it back upon the bed. "All that is left of the pot that broke. I heard it was in a million pieces! You still must have been conscious after you hit the floor, because you were holding this when they rescued you." Avis picked up the fragment and examined it. "I think they smoothed the edges before they gave it back to you. Sheel had to mend a cut across your palm."

That revelation caused Darame to raise her hand. Avis had moved once again, and the firelight illuminated the smooth contours of her palm. *Heal* . . . She could see no scar at all. *A cold torch always leaves a scar.* . . . Darame realized her entire body was shaking. *I have been healed.*

"He left a message for you in this pouch," Avis continued, lifting a tiny bag from the table next to the bed. "I imagine it is a frage; that is what he left for Leah and me." Setting the bag down again, Avis reached to tuck the down quilt closer to Darame. "You should rest, now. You have been unconscious for several days."

"Why is it so cold?" Darame whispered.

"Ah, you can tell the difference? Many visitors cannot—between degrees of coldness, that is. A *norther* came through several days ago, and it snowed last night. More snow coming—the sky is heavy with it." Smoothing the coverlets restlessly, Avis promised her something hot to eat when she woke, and then left her alone.

Lying motionless in the soft bed, the crackle of the fire her only companion, Darame wondered what twist of fate had brought her to this place. Guest rooms. . . . They were nothing like the temple rooms. This must be the palace. The palace! How could she be in the palace? What had happened since she walked into that house and passed out? And where had Sheel disappeared to? Or had he been abducted? . . .

Do not borrow trouble. Oh, for the strength to reach for that bag! What kind of message did it contain? Later. . . . No one and nothing was going anywhere. . . .

"Ayers. . . . Can you find me a Nualan language probe? Sleep tapes would be fine. A primer, and then as many levels as you can access." Her voice still sounded incredibly hoarse, but Darame was certain the man understood. Why was he here? Surely he should be with Avis. . . . A thin tendril of cold twined around her shoulders, and Darame pulled the comforter close, shifting uneasily in the chair.

It was late. How late, she had no idea: no bells had rung since she'd woken and moved to the sitting area near the windows. Past compline, surely. Darame considered asking Ayers and then decided against it. *Am I guest or prisoner?* Maybe both. . . .

Her infirmities had not dulled her hearing. The pad of feet on the thick rug was almost soundless, but she noticed something. Turning her head, Darame faced the blond, hulking form of Ayers. Black eyes met blue ones, neither pair blinking.

"Serae Avis wanted you to rest," he stated formally.

"I am resting. I am sitting in a plush chair, my feet elevated, a blanket over my shoulders." He had not commented during her shaky passage from bed to alcove. . . . Why now? "Can you find me some language probes?"

"I can call down—"

"No." *By Magdalen's Hair, just what I need! I'll thank you not to announce my comings and goings to the world!* "I do not want any trouble. I thought you might be able to get them for me when you went off duty. Never mind." Turning away from him, she looked out the window, studying the swirling snow in the flood-lights mounted against the building. *Idiot. What difference does it make? You have no power here, and the only one who protected you is gone.* "Though why he let me stay is beyond knowing," she murmured aloud, her fingers tightening on the blanket across her lap.

"Who let you stay?" said a voice, as Darame heard the door hit the wall with a dull thump. It was Avis once again, a servant in tow carrying a tray of food.

A split second to decide, and then: "Your brother was very kind to me. I cannot imagine why," Darame said carefully. Ayers, she noted, had retreated to the other alcove.

"Well, you *are* very pretty," Avis pointed out cheerfully. "He has shown no interest in anyone since we came home. Mother was afraid—" She broke off suddenly, as if aware she had said too much. A rosy blush touched her cheeks.

"I think he is tired of . . . warding off advances?" Darame suggested.

Avis nodded, the excessive color beginning to fade. "Having an off-worlder under his roof would keep the native women away, at least. But he told me to take care of you—in his last message—and he would not do that casually. Sheel can be very absent-minded, even cold, when he wishes. But he can be very observant of . . . proper conventions?" She frowned as she arranged her dressing gown and then sat in the other chair of the tiny grouping. "That cannot be the right word. He always remembers my birthday, or knows when someone he cares about is upset—although he does not always comment. He knows when to speak and when to keep silent. At least around me!

"Oh! Tara, #*(#)//!" Nodding at the flow of Nualan words, the servant lifted the small pouch resting on the end table by the bed and handed it to her mistress. Avis promptly passed the article to Darame's lap. "Sheel left this for you. He left me a frage, is that not odd? As if sending his love would be thought a secret!" She lifted off a cover, examining the offering within. "I ordered a broth for you, vegetables with poultry stock. You are not an herbivore, are you?" This last was worried.

"When I'm hungry, I'll eat anything that doesn't try to eat me first," Darame assured her. "Do you think it's wise to eat?"

"You could sip something, or some hot tea, surely. Tara, #*//$ *(())# ***#. Is there anything else you would like?" Avis added in Caesarean, twisting her body back around to catch Darame's eye.

"I'd like to be able to speak Nualan as easily as you do," Darame said impulsively.

Avis tossed a hand in scorn. "I would not send you a servant who did not speak Caesarean!" As Darame started to protest, she went on: "Of course you did not think I would do that! But if you wish to learn some, that is no problem. There is a screen behind that panel. We can switch it to ROM, and with the earjack—" Avis paused in her rush, picking up a tiny cracker and nibbling on it. "Probably not in this room. . . . But I can get you an earjack! Sleep work is better for languages. You will be able to say thank you like an Atare in no time!" Leaping up, Avis waved the swerving woman out the door and followed her in a rush. Darame now saw another *guaard* hovering outside the doorway. "There is one in my quarters, I will get it for you!"

Darame could not help but smile. Avis did not seem used to her servants—or was the woman a kitchen worker only? The rhymes and reasons of this place would require exploring. Her eyes wandered back to the window as her fingers tugged on the pouch's lacings. The cord was sealed with wax, and as she examined the stamp, she recognized enough of it to know it was Sheel's sign.

The pouch contained two things: a frage and the pill packet. Darame stared at them a long moment, and then once again at the seal. Yes . . . it was Sheel's. So his hand had placed these things within, or he had ordered it. A sharp memory pierced her, of a clean, arced slash, and of heavy steps through air so thick— Shivering, Darame broke open the packet and placed one of the pills in her mouth, using the glass of pale wine sitting on the tray to wash it down. Years at her trade had given her immunity to many common poisons . . . but not rav poisoning. *You'll need steel next time; I'll be ready for anything else.*

Darame waited until her hands were perfectly calm before breaking the frage open. Fortunate that she was in a reading corner; she could see every word.

"Be very careful of yourself—you are on your third life. I have no fear for Leah, but if you would help me, watch Avis." Simple words, easy to memorize. . . . Darame let the frage crumple into dust, her eyes unfocused, pondering his meaning. Third life, eh? True, many would say she should have died that first night. *Then you are on at least your fourth, my Atare.* No fear for Leah—of course, the captain of the *guaard* shadowed her. Was that assignment or preference?

"Found it! You can flirt with the servants in no time," Avis laughed, bouncing back into the room.

Darame pushed the pouch under the lap blanket even as the frage pieces fluttered in the wind Avis had stirred. "I have no heart for it," she replied, smiling.

"Sheel is much more interesting, trust me," Avis assured her as she offered up the earjack. "Oh, you read it! Any words of wisdom?"

"Much like yours, I imagine," Darame said carelessly, reaching for the mug of broth. "To be careful of myself, and to keep an eye on you. How shall we go about keeping an eye on each other?"

Avis chuckled, momentarily older than her years. "I can think of a million things to do, if the snow will only stop! I have not been out since Sheel left. I am so glad you are here, it has been so lonely since everything went wrong!"

The words obviously came from the heart, and Darame did not have to ask what had gone wrong.

STARRISE MOUNTAINS   FORTYTWODAY   COMPLINE

In a perverse twist of nature, the cavern grew warmer the deeper Sheel walked. "Warm" was a variable word, however. Atlhough his breath no longer froze into great plumes of mist, a dry chill slipped into his bones. Long centuries ago slender torches set in irregular brackets had illuminated a winding path. Tonight "hot cans"—cylinders of fuel—substituted for both torchlight and modern power; the potters had closed down until the spring, locking up their emergency generator, and Crow still had not figured out how to start it. Of course the solar panels were buried under snow. . . .

It *was* warmer, especially as he climbed down into what the potters called the green cave. This part of the cavern was always dry and low in humidity, which was why the raw clay pottery was left here until it had dried into greenware. Row upon row of free-standing wooden shelves extended into darkness, the boards covered with neatly placed pots and plates. Sheel lifted a hand to trace the rim of a cup. Unglazed . . . unfired. The endless variety of clays and glazes had never failed to intrigue him, and his collection of stoneware was large and complex. Long ago, before he'd left for Emerson, Sheel had visited this quiet workshop. That this place would one day become a sanctuary had never crossed his thoughts.

He hoped the thought occurred to no one else. It was as unlikely a place to hide as any ruler had ever visited; that was why he had chosen it. Koi Klays was the best of all possible choices, isolated without advertising its remoteness, easy to defend, and close enough to several villages to allow supply runs within a few hours.

And we can stay warm here, Sheel admitted to himself. There were few places to choose from: most were either obvious or a place the *guaard* would eventually think of, and the others were open to every change of weather. For now, these caverns, nearly deserted until the thaw, would prove a safe hiding place.

"Sheel?" The soft voice came from somewhere above him. Glancing up, Sheel saw a familiar jacket of violent orange.

"Down here, Tobias."

The boy carefully made his way down the narrow path, flicking a tiny "pocket torch" from side to side. Sheel settled upon one of the boulders skirting the trail, loosening the scarf wrapped around his throat. Soon Tobias was seated beside him.

"I did not want to interrupt your thinking," Tobias explained gravely.

A smile threatened to slip out, but Sheel controlled his features admirably. The boy was always so serious. His way of phrasing things always made Sheel want to laugh. *Where do you get this serious streak from? I never thought your father long in the face.*

"There is something I wanted to ask you," Tobias went on, switching off his pocket torch and letting the hot cans above take over. "But I thought I would wait until we were settled in our hiding place."

"This is as far as we go," Sheel said easily. "What is it?"

"You said we had to hide because someone killed Cort Atare and your brothers and then tried to kill you. We are the last men left."

Allowing the slightest pull of a dimple, Sheel nodded his agreement. "We must be careful of ourselves. I was afraid someone might try to hurt you, if they could not hurt me."

"But why?" Tobias had asked this once before. A dozen answers, or none . . . This time the boy did not stop with his question. "Our line passes through mother and Avis. Why kill us?"

"I do not know, Tobias. That is why we are hiding. Mailan and Fion are going to try and find out why. I imagine it is one of two things, or perhaps both. . . . Someone has a grudge against our family, or someone hopes to acquire power during the reorganization of our government."

Tobias did not speak, but he looked thoughtful. "You would not give power to someone who hurt our family, would you?"

"Not knowingly. But that is a fact of life for a ruler, Tobias. People who pretend to be friends sometimes are not. . . . " Leaning back against the wall, Sheel considered the situation abstractly for a moment. No one had tried to curry favor. . . . There had been no time. The attacks had begun immediately. *I was meant to die the first night.* Had Iver also been meant to die? Or had someone intended for him to live? And then had a change of heart? *Because . . . why was Iver no longer useful?*

Because he could not be controlled. Someone mistook his simple honesty and lack of subtlety for spinelessness, or worse, disinterest. And then found out otherwise. . . .

"*I* would not give power to anyone," Tobias said confidently. "I would watch them all first."

"A good idea. Be sure and tell your mother I said so, if anything happens to me. She would be your regent until you reached your majority."

"Who would be regent if mother died?"

"Avis. And after Avis, your grandmother. . ." Idle words . . . which brought Tobias's words into focus. *Our line passes through mother and Avis.* . . . Through the women. Vendetta or power grab? . . . But there were corollaries. If it was a power grab, one of two things had happened. Either they had made a major mistake, or they knew exactly what they were doing. . . .

Cort's reign confused the issue. An outside observer, *even one Nualan-born*, might have misinterpreted Cort's ironfisted rule as the new norm. After all, Dielaan's ragaree only had power in the advent of The Dielaan's death. "They" might have thought that removing the men . . . would lead to Iver's inexperienced rule? A boy ruler, as on Emerson, or ancient Terra? A cousin taking the throne?

Riva and Cort's only sister had died when *First Frost* was lost in transit. So the Atare line would go back further. . . . Ilse Ragaree had . . . two sisters?

"Only if both Leah and Avis died," Sheel murmured aloud, trying to narrow his thoughts. He did not know right off who the current heirs to the line would be. But that they would murder a dozen people for it? He had thought his folk had grown beyond such scheming. . . .

No. Too fantastic a thought for now. Either it was vendetta, or someone who thought to gain from Iver's rule. But to eliminate him so quickly. . . . Was controlling the regency also a possible plan? How?

Leah had acquired a sizable power network in her short lifetime. As for those who influenced her, directly or indirectly . . . Dozens. She was insecure and needed the advice of many before she chose her own way. But it would be her own way! She would not give up any of the ragaree's power, once she had it in her hands. Avis? Still very young as far as politics was concerned. If something happened to Leah, Avis would be a frightened and uninformed regent, in worse shape than he himself currently sat.

Had the murderer thought that cousin—blast, what was his name?—would rule until he or Leah died? Had the murderer thought to control the fiery Leah?

Was the murderer controlling Leah?

Abruptly Sheel remembered the boy sitting next to him, and wondered what he had muttered aloud. Glancing sharply at the child, he saw a bleak, frightened visage.

"Grandmother would be regent only if mother and Avis both died?"

Sheel slipped an arm around Tobias's shoulders. "Do not worry, Tobias. Both your mother and Avis are healthy, and well guarded. I do not think they are in any danger."

Who had influence over Leah? Her husband Richard had some influence, when he chose to exert himself. But only because he rarely exerted himself. . . . She had easily a half-dozen lovers from the embassies. That was common knowledge, even Darame had heard of it. Brant, Lutae, Taylor, Gregg of Gavriel—even Dirk of the *guaard,* Sheel began to suspect. Not the first woman of the line to take a *guaard,* but her predecessors had waited until they had borne all their heirs. . . .

Damn! Why did Darame fall prey to that attempt? Sheel wished he had packed her up and brought her. *She knows something, she must know something.*

Or . . . she knew nothing, and was as expendable as Sheel Atare.

ATARE PALACE, ATARE   SEVENTYEIGHTDAY   VESPERS

"Ah, the cold!" Avis led the way into the huge entry hall of the palace, her entourage in tow. She was busy unwrapping the monstrous fur cape thrown over her black and white mourning clothes, and consequently dropped several small items as she made her way across an acre of pastel deep-pile carpet.

"You're littering, Avis," Darame commented as she scooped up a leather glove. Behind her came a few whispers and giggles as other attendants retrieved a delicate riding crop, a scarf, and a pair of snow goggles.

Avis paused, whirling, at the foot of the magnificent staircase which swept up and divided, framing a circular stained-glass window. The dragon of the Atare line peered over her shoulder in an incredible array of rose, lavender, royal purple, and violet. Her eyes lit up even as she reached for the glove.

"Do not pick up after me, Darame! If I cannot manage everything, I should travel with less equipment!" Taking the fine woolen scarf from one of her companions she shook her head at the other items. "Excess baggage, that whip, the way I ride. No wonder I always lose it! And the star was hidden again today, the goggles were a waste of time."

"If you had not used them, you would have missed them," Darame said placidly, taking the aforementioned tokens from the young woman who held them. "Are we early for the last meal?" This last, in Nualan, was directed carefully to a servant standing at the entry door.

"Serae Leah has requested a formal dinner," the man responded slowly and gravely. "Sherry will be served in the fire room shortly."

"Nothing until compline!" Avis laughed in Caesarean, waving off the others. "We should humor Leah. The first formal dinner in a month! Everyone get dressed, we will see you in the fire room." Bounding up the staircase, oblivious to the chaos in her wake, Avis led the way to the dressing rooms.

The *guaard* Sheri lightly matched her steps to her mistress's, Darame following at a more sedate pace. Passing the immense chandelier as she took the curve of the stairs, Darame noted idly in passing that the delicate crystal drops were still chiming in the breeze of the open hallway doors. The Nualan servant, closing the huge wood doors securely, nodded to Darame as he vanished off into a side room.

They are kind and helpful, Darame thought, loosening her short jacket's front panel. *With a bit of patience I may master this language.*

Dressing quickly in a floor-length, long-sleeved dress of black, and slipping on black evening shoes, Darame completed her toilette without assistance. Servants had been provided, which she gratefully allowed to clean her laundry and keep her clothes in order. The rest she preferred to handle herself. Wrapping a black lace shawl around her shoulders and securing it in front with a pear-shaped diamond stickpin, Darame flipped her hair free of confinement and started for the other end of the hall.

Ayers abandoned his post by her door and followed. She had despaired of shaking him: not hints but bold suggestions had been thrown his way, and in vain. He shadowed her without comment . . . unless a friend did the honors for him. Slowly other *guaard* had trickled into the insular group surrounding Avis. Darame suspected that Ayers and Sheri had selected them, and only after debate and long consideration. *Terrifying to examine everyone you see, wondering if they might be a murderer.* She had done some of that herself. . . .

Several people were already in the sitting room Avis used regularly. A sweet-faced older woman was sending her small children off to the wing reserved for all youngsters not yet presented at court. She wore traditional Nualan widow's garb, a white dress trimmed in black velvet with a black shawl thrown over all.

Darame felt better about her lace shawl. The bodice of this dress was cut too low for courtesy, at least during the Nualan three months of strict mourning, but there was no help for it. Every dressmaker in town had been deluged after the deaths, as the wealthy families paid tribute to their dead ruler and his heirs, so new clothing would be almost impossible to acquire. As an off-worlder, mourning garb was not required. As Avis's constant companion, however, Darame felt her usual peacock colors would not do. The palace seamstress had helped her with a compromise, providing accessories to mask and otherwise disguise her white and dark clothing into something appropriate for the occasion.

As the boy and girl departed the sitting room, the older woman looked up and saw Darame. The Nualan's face was drawn, even strained, her common expression since her husband's death. She forced a smile as she gestured to the chair at her left. "Well, did your ride calm Avis? She has been so restless today."

"It is always hard to tell, Serae," Darame responded, sitting and smoothing her skirts. "She fights her grief instead of letting it run its course. I hope you were not lonely."

"No," the woman said, turning toward the french windows. "Bette brought the baby up, and we spent a pleasant afternoon. I do not think she will join us for dinner; she still tires easily. But I will admit to missing Riva Ragaree. Surely she must be home by now."

"I understand the roads have been good the last few days," Darame agreed. "She will probably contact her daughters soon."

The woman nodded absently, her gaze still fixed out the window, and Darame wondered once again if Serae Camelle would be happier under Riva Ragaree's roof. The morganatic second wife of Fabe was a very distant cousin of the Atare line, a natural daughter of the ruler of Seedar, and Nualan to the core. By rights she should be an attendant to Leah, but that was not something either woman would choose.

In her forties, perhaps? Several generations younger than Riva's attendants, yet never quite fitting in with Leah's group. She had seemed more relaxed since Avis requested her company . . . until today. *Shrewd of Avis to see the problem*, Darame reminded herself. It would not do to think Avis flighty, despite her natural effervescence. Avis had not missed Leah's little tricks—it took the deaths of the men for the youngest daughter to have excuse enough to ask for Camelle's "support." Was Leah tired of baiting the older woman? Glad to have the only Nualan wife out from under her heel?

"Seri Fabe must have loved you very much," Darame suddenly said aloud, settling herself deeper in her chair. She had learned in a month among Nualans that blunt statements did not offend them.

Camelle finally turned away from the windows. A faint smile toyed with her lips. "To risk the censure of marrying me? Yes . . . I suppose he did." She shrugged, reaching for her needlework. "He did not care what others thought . . . which was why I lived with him, those last years before his wife died." Glancing up, Camelle added: "Unnamed children of power learn to ignore gossip."

Darame knew enough about Nualans to understand that oblique remark. Although the child of the current Seedar, Camelle's mother had been Nualan; hence, Camelle had her mother's status, not her father's clan name. *Though that is not quite true.* The pecking order was topped by the royal lines, but directly beneath them were the unnamed children. . . . Which was another reason women like Crystal reb Lesli pursued Atare men.

"They were happy enough in their youth," Camelle went on, threading a needle. "And they had six fine children. But Anna was too interested in the trappings of status, the parties, the social life of the city. Fabe was a simple man. . . . We preferred the country. After she died, why not suit himself? He had done his duty."

"It is not hard to see why he loved you," Darame said simply, watching as Camelle took a careful stitch.

"We were happy." Camelle glanced out the window, as if gauging the twilight. "Darame . . . I need to speak privately with Avis about something. It may take some time. We will probably be late to dinner. Could you smooth things over, if anyone comments? I will not keep her long."

"Of course." Darame took that as a cue to depart and stood to leave. "I'll play hostess in the fire room until the Serae arrives." *And we both know which one I mean.*

"Thank you."

The relief on her face aroused Darame's curiosity. Walking down the hall toward the front staircase, she wondered if it was worth investigating, and then dismissed the thought. Caution had been her watchword the past month; her position was placid on the surface, precarious beneath the waters. *I have been eliminated once already. Better not to ruffle any feathers.*

Expendable. With Sheel gone and Iver dead, she was a loose thread to the original scam. Brant had not contacted her since the funerals, and she had carefully avoided him, saving a visit for an emergency. The business community had loosened up, but nothing major was going on yet. And the government was still moving in loops; no new business was being conducted. Calls from Halsey had been few and general: "no change in status" was the only message wrapped in casual conversation. Darame suspected he was under the Nualan equivalent of "House Arrest," but had not been able to confirm it.

Clever, my Atare, she thought dryly as she entered the fire room. Sheel had been anointed before leaving the city. That officially made him Atare, and his word was now law. His orders? "Maintain the status quo until we solve this thing," was all Avis reported. At least that was what Leah claimed was in her frage. *Why do I always think of the word "claimed" when I think of Leah? I should be kinder. . . . Of course she is worried about her son.*

Several of Avis's companions were already in the formal room, sherry in hand. Accepting a glass from the young man tending the drinks, Darame chatted quietly with Stephanie reb Lena Atare, Cort Atare's youngest daughter and Avis's closest friend. She was a quiet, graceful woman, successful in her hunt to Emerson and rumored to be with child, although Nualan women usually did not speak of such things until they were well into the pregnancy. Remarkably free of envy, as well: Stephanie had shown no anger over Avis's growing friendship with Darame, unlike a few of the other attendants.

Darame had her back to the door when Leah entered, although the mirrors covering the fireplace wall enabled her to watch every person in the room. The heir apparent to the title Ragaree looked very good in white, with her dark complexion and brown hair. Black ribbons trimmed the formal gown, an elegant dress which was a bit too seductive for mourning attire. Several ambassadors dressed in black were in tow, the shadow that was Dirk last of all.

Brant was present, of course, and Gregg of Gavriel. Lady Tia Se'Hawkins, first ambassador from Garrison System, and her chief second, Stephen Se'Morval. . . . Many faces this evening. Officially they had visited only once since the funeral, but Darame knew that Brant and Gregg, at least, had seen Leah several times, and Stephen had been in constant attendance on Avis.

Although Leah did not introduce any of the ambassadors to Avis's attendants, all the dignitaries eventually made their way over to greet the women. *Especially me*. Interesting. . . . Why so attentive? Because she was a wild card in the deck, and no one wished to offend someone who might become a face card? Even Brant made brief small talk, asking if she was comfortable, saying that there was no change in her status— *Which is "non-trade" at the moment. When will you free us up, Brant?*

Her busy thoughts continued throughout dinner, which was announced at the ringing of the compline bell. Leah sat at one end of the long, polished table, with Lady Tia on her left and Gregg on her right. Victoria, young widow of Caleb and Leah's satellite, was to Gregg's right. Brant was placed to the right of Avis's chair, at the opposite end of the table, with Stephanie across from him. Darame found herself in the middle on the back side, looking through a large centerpiece for glimpses of Stephen Se'Morval. Neither of the people seated next to her was particularly interesting, so Darame bided her time and watched for Avis and Camelle.

The group had finished the first course when Avis and Camelle arrived. The youngest child of Riva Ragaree was flushed, her lovely curls tousled and shimmering in the formal candlelight. Upon being seated at the foot of the table she properly greeted Brant and began to engage him in conversation. Camelle, on her part, seemed relaxed once again and was attending to her dinner. She seemed unconcerned with Leah's awkward seating arrangements.

There was nothing in the behavior of either woman to give a clue to the topic of their discussion, but Darame noticed that every time she glanced in Avis's direction the young woman was looking her way. Not obviously, or enough to draw Brant or Stephanie's attention, but as if trying to catch her eye. Resolving to gain a seat near Avis during the sweets and brandy in the fire room, Darame applied herself to talking politely to a distant Atare relative.

Carrying out her decision was more difficult than anticipated. Stephen Se'Morval pounced on Avis the moment dinner was adjourned. As she had not seen him in at least three days, Avis was delighted, even as she once again caught Darame's eye. Pausing to acquire another glass of dry sherry, Darame smiled and nodded at Avis, trying to relay that she understood her friend's interest. *After we get rid of everyone. I'll be there.*

The rest of the social evening was enlivened with card games and conversation. Darame amused Ambassador Gregg with a rendition of her attempts to learn the fine art of riding hazelles as opposed to horses, and Avis did impersonations of various elderly dignitaries on the judicial bench. Serae Leah was bright and animated, contrasting sharply with the dour Captain of the *guaard,* even as she hinted at inner distress by bringing the discussion back to the topic of Sheel and her son. "We have not heard from them in a month," she kept saying. "What if they have been abducted? Or . . . killed?" The only other topic that interested Leah was everyone's theories on the murders.

Darame was surprised at the discussion, but it did not seem to disturb Leah. Stephanie, a bit pale, excused herself halfway through the evening and Avis, still a bit flushed, chose to accompany her. The two women left during a heated exchange comparing the merits of an off-world conspiracy versus an outclan attack, but Darame stayed until the first ambassador rose to leave.

Never draw unwarranted attention to entrances or departures, Darame reminded herself as she slipped into her own room. Peeling off the black dress and shoes she hastily donned a loose-fitting evening robe and slippers. Now, to find out what Avis was "up to". . . . If it was possible for innocent Avis to involve herself in any secrets. Guileless as clear water, Avis had quickly shown Darame that skulduggery was not her game.

Will Stephen stay the night? Even Stephen's visits were not really a secret; only enough of one to keep the fallen suitors at bay. One or two others had shared Avis's affections until just recently, Brant among them. *Romancing both Atare women, Brant? Interesting. Maybe dangerous.* Darame walked slowly down the carpeted hall, *guaard* Ayers still in tow, wondering about her last thought.

Not an exaggeration. Darame had done her own silent observing the last month, and she knew why Leah disturbed her so. Not Leah's need for men constantly in her circle, or her indifference to mourning (for her dislike of her late uncle was widely known), but because of her attitude toward Avis.

Officially, Leah was everything that was proper to a little sister: gracious, generous, instructive—even proud of the attention Avis drew without effort. But Darame had more than once done nothing but watch Leah for an entire evening . . . and a chilling undertow ran beneath the surface of Leah's concern. Leah hated Avis. Hated her, feared her, was jealous of her. Watched her, constantly. . . .

Had Sheel suspected the enmity between the two? Although Avis apparently did not hate her sister, she was no more than friendly in the vague manner one might use with a distant aunt. . . . Even with Cold Sleep, fifteen years separated the women. Avis liked people, however, and looked for the best in them. *I am not sure you know . . . or if you do, how seriously you take it. I am no longer sure who Sheel would have me protect you from. . . .*

Knocking at the oak double doors of the royal quarters, Darame was admitted by an unfamiliar *guaard*. Her first thought was that there were too many people present . . . and a number of them were in strange uniform.

Avis was seated in a circular grouping around a huge firepit. Darame could see her beyond the flames, dressed in a fiery coral caftan which floated from her shoulders like a cloud. Next to her on one side was Camelle, still in her widow's weeds, pouring hot saffra into delicate cups. The young woman to the left of Avis was unfamiliar.

Moving closer did not solve the mystery—Darame's puzzlement increased. The features were teasing, from her past. . . .

Gavriel? Not the height: Darame could tell from the sleek lines of her black syluan dress that this woman was dainty. But the eyes were the same, so pale a blue they might have been glacial, while the thick braid of hair was a blonde so fair it was almost white. Nualan clothing, however . . . and she was speaking Nualan to Avis. Oddly accented Nualan.

Noticing her entrance, Camelle stood and reached out a hand for her, a tense smile crossing her face. "Thank you for coming. The Serae was certain you could help." As always when Camelle helped her with the Nualan tongue, the words were slow and well formed.

"If I can, you know I will," Darame answered, her eyes flicking toward the stranger.

With perfect aplomb, Camelle said: "That is Quenby Ragaree."

For a moment Darame stared at her, confused, although aware that something ominous was threaded through those words. "But . . . Sheel has not—" Then she stopped, because she understood. Part of the mystery, at least. The woman was a ragaree . . . but not of the Atare clan. "Where is she from?"

"She is the Regent of Seedar. She has come for consultation."

Avis finally noticed her presence and leapt up, reaching to pull Darame close. "Oh, good, Praise Mendulay you have come! It is all a mess, and we need your tricky brain. Quenby, this is Seráe Darame Daviddottir, an off-worlder from Caesarea, and a friend of The Atare."

I wonder what Sheel would think of such an introduction. Darame chose not to volunteer her thoughts, but glanced at the roman on her wrist. No indication of surveillance. . . .

It was one of the strangest gatherings Darame had ever attended. Like a tea party gone mad, from the steaming red fluid they sipped from delicate china cups to the big, burly blond men arranged in a half-circle at the back of the suite. She could not laugh, however—not after seeing the two tiny children curled up on huge pillows in the corner. Apparently the guards would not let either Quenby or her children out of their sight. Wisely, no one took offense at their attitude.

Something was wrong in Seedar. "He has been weak for years, Avis, for many years, but the illness sapped his legs, nothing else," Quenby whispered, her voice shaking although her hands were steady. "They told me that he died in his sleep, that his heart stopped. He was but sixty-five Terran! As young as your brother Baldwin. Since I have both son and daughter, the line passes on, with my regency. But, Avis . . . things are wrong in the government. Someone was pressuring my brother, I am sure of it! Information is missing, and there have been deaths among the blackmarket traders. That much I am sure of—other things are more hazy. I did not know who to trust, and I feared my surviving brother as advisor, because some of his advice . . ." She shook her head, sipping at her cup of saffra. "I cannot tell even you. But he does not have the best interests of the state at heart."

"So you just packed up and left?" Darame prompted, grateful the woman spoke competent, if accented, Caesarean.

"Not exactly." Quenby smiled, her eyes suddenly glinting. "We thought it up together, my husband Rollin and I. I left him to act in my absence, handling the day to day things. He has no authority to change anything, so they cannot pester him. I am on a religious pilgrimage to visit the great temples of Mendulay!"

Avis began giggling. "That is wonderful! Even if they doubted you, they could not challenge it."

"I travel as the spirit leads me . . . and send back messages at regular intervals, all designed to keep them thinking I am a grief-stricken sister, atoning for the distance between my brothers and myself. It may allow mischief to brew at home, but Avis, I could not risk my son! And after I heard what had happened up here—" Tears surfaced in her huge, starry eyes, and Avis reached quickly to comfort her.

"Why did you choose to come to Atare, Ragaree?" Darame asked gently, pouring herself a fresh cup of saffra.

"Because Kilgore was at war with the Ciedarlien again," she answered, dabbing at her eyes with the hem of a priceless gown, "and it was easier to reach Atare than any of the other houses. Of course," she added, "Sheel is still alive, or so folk say. A man who can keep himself and his heir alive may be capable of other things as well. I wanted his advice."

"Why did you come to Avis?" Gently, probing the waters . . .

"I sent word to Camelle when I reached the limits of the city. She told me Sheel was not here, and suggested I talk to Avis, because Leah . . . does not care for other women." Quenby trailed off uncertainly, Darame's black gaze brushing her self-assurance.

"Has anyone threatened your children?" Darame said, leaning forward and seizing the handle of the poker extending from the flames.

"I am not positive. . . . I think so." The woman elaborated on her statement, explaining why she was hesitant to speak. A fire at the palace of Seedar, enveloping the children's wing. No real threat to the children, who were not in residence, but various courtiers had spoken to her in the following days . . . and in their words Quenby read threat. "They knew who set the fire, Serae, I am sure of it. But I have no proof, and we of Seedar have never needed a *guaard* to ferret out information. Each Seedar has had a group of people to do the private business."

"Why do your brother's followers not help you?" This was from Avis.

Quenby's expression hardened. "One died recently. . . . An accident while hunting. Another left court. He has a young family, and . . . I think he fears for them. Two others are now in the camp of the Prime Minister—my brother, who seems to think he can be Seedar in all but name." Straightening, the woman turned to

Avis, her expression defensive. "I know! There is so little to use for conclusions! But Camelle thought you would listen to me . . . and was not sure your sister would believe me. Avis, my brother had a strong heart! We have excellent physicians in Seedar, and a healer attached to the palace. Surely there would have been some sign. . . ."

"Not if he died as Iver did," Darame murmured. It had finally trickled out, the news surrounding Iver's death. A poison that faded rapidly in the body. . . . If those in Seedar had no reason to suspect murder, and the autopsy was not performed immediately . . .

"What should we do, Darame?" Avis fastened her bright gaze on Darame's face. "We cannot do anything officially; each state is sovereign. I cannot send a troop of *guaard* just to help out in the crisis. . . . Only Sheel would have that authority, since there is no anointed Ragaree and the official procedure would be involved." Frowning, Avis reached for her cup. "But surely *all* this cannot be Quenby's imagination."

"No . . . I do not think so. In fact, it is a pity you Nualans are all on such poor terms with each other. It might be interesting to talk with the other families and ask them how things fare." Darame's words caused Avis to continue frowning, but Darame pretended not to notice.

What to do with a frightened and threatened queen? That was what she was, in so many words, although the basis for her authority was different from anything Darame had ever imagined. The women had cut themselves off from Leah, which was probably just as well. True, Leah did not care for other women, a named ragaree especially, but the real reason Camelle had chosen Avis as a confidante over Leah was not personality. Camelle was more generous than that. No: it was because Leah still refused to believe that there was any danger to herself, to her son, or to Avis. Leah would have offered dozens of explanations for the happenings in Seedar. Now, having been passed over as the obvious authority in Atare, she would be even more likely to dismiss the Ragaree's vague fears as imaginings.

Quenby Ragaree did not need reassurances; she needed someplace to hide and breathe freely. Plans for the future could come later. . . . For now, where to hide the Ragaree of Seedar?

Not in Atare. The intrigues swirling in this palace meant that someone would surely discover her presence, if Quenby had not already been detected. Bursting in on Riva Ragaree unannounced would be poor manners, and the event would surely reach Leah's ears. Someplace unexpected . . .

"I think we need to hide you and your children, Ragaree," Darame said abruptly. "The best place would be with the heir of Atare . . . if we can find him. If not, I have a few other thoughts. We will continue to send your traveling notes by as devious a route as possible. But unless we drag others into this, such as the high priest of the local temple—" Avis immediately shook her head negatively. "Then we must deal with it ourselves." After giving Avis a long look, Darame faced the Seedar ragaree and said: "I imagine you know that the murderer—or murderers—of Cort Atare and his heirs have not been found. Anyone can be suspect. It is better not to turn to anyone outside this room."

"Darame, do you know where Sheel and Tobias are?" Avis's eyes widened noticeably.

"No. . . . But I suspect I know where to look for him."

CAESAREAN EMBASSY   SEVENTYNINEDAY   NONE

"You want to *what?*" Brant's incredulity was actually reflected in his face.

Controlling an inner smile, Darame sipped delicately at her wine. *Let him wait. . . . Sweet Saints, I've certainly waited long enough.* Settling back deeper in the cushioned chair, she said easily: "I want to go look for Sheel."

"Whatever for?"

That surprised her just a little bit; Brant was rarely so blunt. "Isn't it obvious, Brant? I'm going crazy cooling my heels at the palace. I don't have the slightest idea how things are going, and you and Halsey aren't telling me anything."

"There's not that much to tell," Brant said dryly, pouring himself a glass of the wine and lifting it from the mirrored tray in front of Darame.

Once again they were locked in Brant's office, sharing a fine imported wine—this time one selected and provided by Darame. The language was Caesarean, of course. It was unlikely Brant knew of her growing proficiency in Nualan, unless Avis had volunteered the information. Darame had been observant in her stay at the palace, taking note of who kept track of her comings and goings. The Caesareans only noticed when she contacted Halsey, called *The Gypsy Rover,* or used the encyclopedia bank. No one from Brant's personal group was tailing her. That a Nualan might be watching her *had* occurred to her—but there was nothing to be done about it. And who might that Nualan be working for? . . .

"Wouldn't it be convenient if we had an 'in' with Sheel Atare?" Darame went on. "It couldn't hurt the plan, and might help a great deal, if only by smoothing tariffs and the like. After all, Avis claims he healed me of the effects of the gas, and he let me stay in his household up until then. Maybe I can talk him into coming back to the palace."

"The government would probably start moving again if he returned," Brant acknowledged, leaning against the edge of his desk. He had his remote expression on his face, and was looking over her right shoulder.

"I could assure him of Caesarean help during this time of crisis," Darame suggested. "How far could I stretch such a statement?"

"Not very far. We're not allowed to meddle with planet politics, you know. Localized Treason Laws." He took a long draught of the wine. "But I could personally offer my friendship and support. Sheel always kept to himself, I didn't have much of a chance to get to know him."

"Perhaps I can change that." Would he push for more information? Was her reason good enough? Good enough for the kind of person Brant believed her to be?

"You're not starting up another job on the side, are you?" Brant asked, chuckling. Darame let her eyes settle on the mirrored tray at this, watching his expression. The change was so minute she would have missed it if she'd not been watching for it. A tightening at the mouth, a slight hardness of the eyes . . .

I've never taken two jobs simultaneously when working with this group. Halsey doesn't allow it. What makes you think I'd do it now? Because you would, if something tempting opened up? Just how close to Leah are you, Brant, and what good can she do you?

"You know me better than that, Brant. Halsey'd dock my bonus—and the bonus money promises to be good this time." Darame said it simply, almost flatly. Keep his mind on the money, let him think your mind is on the money. . . .

"How do you propose to find him?" Brant asked. "I have my people working on it from here to Dielaan and south to Kilgore. There's been no sign of him."

"Your people—off-worlders?" A simple, obvious question.

"Of course. Nualans are loyal to Nualans first, in almost every case."

"Precisely. I hope that if I send out some feelers and move into territory where he is known, word will reach him of my search. I thought I'd take the rail service as far as I could, and then just wait." She studied the light reflecting in her wine, swirling the remaining few sips. Not really a lie. Sitting in her room last night, half-listening to a Nualan reading of a favorite book, random facts had finally fallen into a pattern. Trust an old teaching device to instruct in more than one way. . . .

Solve the puzzle, Davi. It will teach you much. Halsey had always brought her puzzles as a child: intricate wooden ones, exotic woven ones, delicate paper ones. She had solved them all, and learned more than the art of assembly. There were ways to discover the picture without completing the puzzle.

That piece of pottery. Why leave it in her hand, unless it was to tell her something? And how to interpret the meaning without letting others know what she sought? Not the encyclopedia bank, then . . . the books in Sheel's library, real books, gloriously illustrated with examples of Nualan pottery.

And maps of where the clay was found.

"Halsey may be in trouble," Brant said suddenly. That brought her out of her thoughts. She looked directly at him, but his expression was an expected one, both thoughtful and slightly worried. "The local authorities are having no luck with their investigation, and the *guaard* apparently has nothing for them, or so my sources say. A sucker is needed."

"Why Halsey?" She kept emotion out of her voice.

"Why not?" He shrugged slightly.

Saint Elmo's Fire, man, you have always at least pretended to cover for your partners! What are you going to do about it? She repeated her last thought aloud.

"I'm doing what I can. The embassy has already put in an appearance, pointing out that he did not arrive until the night of the murders and that one man could not accomplish such a feat, his lack of contacts here, his ignorance of who it would be worthwhile to kill off . . ." Brant rattled off numerous arguments without looking up from his glass. "I don't think they can pin it on him. Nualans may wish for someone to take the blame, but they're not known for selecting innocent people for the post."

Darame controlled her anger, sharpening it like a dagger. And then an unworthy—and appropriate—thought crept to the surface of her mind. *You protest much, my man, but everything in Halsey's favor could point at you. Are you truly in all this, Brant? So much of it is messy, clumsy—you don't usually work*

that way. How much is you, and how much requires that I look
elsewhere? She poured a meager portion of wine into her glass.
Or was all of that merely to keep me in line, aware of Halsey's
peril . . . and my own?

"Should I use the money I had for my hostel?" she asked,
returning the conversation to her original proposal.

"Call Mona for what you need. And try to reassure her—don't
mention what I said about Halsey," he added briskly. "I trust you
can handle the details, and keep people from commenting. We've
talked long enough, you'd better leave."

Nodding, Darame rose from the chair, leaving the wine untouched. She had a general idea of where to begin—and was
afraid to ask for more specific information. But what if she was
totally wrong?

Sweet Saints, can I risk the royal line of Seedar on a hunch?

ATARE PALACE   SEVENTYNINEDAY   COMPLINE

"*What?*" Mona's voice held the same incredulity as Brant's,
but it was sharpened by alarm. "Going *where?*"

"Into the Starrise Mountains, Mona," Darame explained patiently, hitting the transmittal button and sending her list of clothing and supplies. "I need you to send these things immediately.
Can you make the next window?"

"Mountains? What are the mountains? Halsey sending you?"

"No, Halsey's still under house arrest. I'm running an errand
for one of the royal family," Darame added, hoping Mona was
waiting for the entire message before replying.

She definitely heard everything. "*What?*" Mona's voice went
up the scale. "Lost your mind?"

"I'm going to look for the ruler, he's in hiding since all the
attacks."

"Lost your mind!" Mona repeated over Darame's words. "Let
couriers run errands! Stay put in the city! Mess with local *poli-*
tics? Crazy!"

"She doesn't have any couriers, Mona," Darame rushed on,
feeling as if she were losing hold of the conversation. "She and
her brothers had been home only nine months when everyone was
murdered. Believe me, she's a babe in arms and has no one to
turn to!"

"Mothering eggs, eh?" This typically Emersonian sneer was

actually encouraging. "Idiot. Not your business. Getting senile—since when get involved with the natives?"

"Mona, they have no idea what they're doing!" This was sharp. "The new ruler was never trained for the job, the older sister's into power games, and the younger spends her time weeping over her uncle and brother and then pretending she's fine!"

"So the government will collapse. Why do you care?"

"Just send the clothes and freeze packs, will you? I am fine, Halsey is fine, Brant is fine. We'll keep you posted." Darame hurriedly clicked off the communicator before Mona could continue the argument. She was cautious during that talk, in case of taps, but the last few comments were far from discreet. Why had Mona upset her so?

Not intentionally. Why did her words upset you? Darame let her fingers toy with the dial a moment, contemplating that thought. Two images kept slipping into her mind. . . . One of Avis's heart-shaped face, worry and grief erased by Darame's offer to escort the Seedar ragaree. The other picture was misty: gray day, gray clothes, and gray mood blending like water droplets on a windowpane. Sheel was no more than an outline, folded neatly onto the window seat, two of the cats nesting in his lap. He had not spoken when she had entered the room, but the shadow of a smile that had suddenly appeared seemed a question for her alone.

You're getting soft, said a scornful voice in the back of her mind, but Darame did not have time to listen to it.

Chapter Seven

Rising wind that smelt of snow tickled Mailan's nose, but she ignored it. Nodding a greeting to Crow, who huddled just within the entrance, she wound her way through scattered boulders into the cavern, knocking ice pellets from her boots as she walked.

"How about a fire?" Crow suggested hopefully.

"Why not just stand at the opening and yell 'Here we are?'" Mailan responded, grinning.

The man sighed. "Not thinking today. Hot rods?"

"I will see what I can find," Mailan promised, pulling off her poncho of thick vatos wool. "Do you want a poncho, too?" She eyed his regulation black jacket with thinly disguised disapproval.

"Trying to get me to go native?" was the response.

Mailan shrugged and started into the cave. "So be cold."

"Mailan! I was kidding! Mailan!" Unable to leave his post, Crow hopped up and down to emphasize his plea, dislodging a puff of snow teetering above the entrance and sending it sliding onto his head.

Smiling at the echoing profanity, Mailan handed her poncho to a village youth on his way out the arch. "Give this to the *guaard*," she said, pointing toward the exit. Grinning back, the young man nodded and continued out the passage.

Considering how well Crow had been trained in mountain techniques, he was remarkably susceptible to cold. Jude was also lowland, and having difficulty with the novelties of mountain life. Fortunate for Sheel he had selected his *guaard* from every possible background.

Fion and I are home. Almost—Maroc was northwest of their position, and Mailan's own village a full day's hard ride, at the

133

least. Close enough for comfort . . . Pausing at the portable stove, Mailan poured a mug of saffra for herself.

"If you get a moment, take some saffra to Crow," she told the man watching over their bubbling dinner. *Make native jokes to me, will you, son of the plains? You can wait until old Harald has time for you.*

"How are the supplies?" came a voice behind her. Glancing up, Mailan met her mentor's sharp gaze.

"Secure. We have twentyday stored below, and I talked to Warner while I was in Portland—he will keep fresh materials coming every fiveday." Only a handful of people knew they were here, which was just as well. Although she trusted the loyalty of these sturdy mountain people, Mailan dreaded the thought of someone testing that loyalty.

Nodding, Fion bent over the stove and used his leather gloves as he carefully removed a pot from the warming ledge beneath. "Grab a few mugs." Carrying the hot crock carefully, Fion started down a side passage toward the meeting room.

"Where are Sheel and the boy?" Mailan asked, following him into the dim corridor.

"Out watching the star set into Summer Pass," he responded. "Jude is shadowing them." Setting the pot on a metal trivet, Fion took the mugs from Mailan and arranged them on the old table. "Here, join me." The pale, honeyed liquid filled one mug and half-filled the second. He shoved the partial portion toward her.

"I go on duty at compline," she said regretfully, shaking her head.

"A good three hours yet. Half a mug will relax you; you are too tense. Figured out what is bothering you yet?" Settling himself in a warped frame chair, Fion sipped cautiously at the hot brew.

Mailan gave him a long look and then toyed with the handle of the mug. "Can you always read my face?" It was more wistful than she had intended; Fion actually laughed out loud. Then his face sobered quickly.

"No, not always. But there is something about your silence that mirrors The Atare's. Too bad you are *guaard*, girl, and entirely too conscientious—I would be curious to see what strange talents a child of yours and Sheel's might have." He smiled faintly at the scowl which flashed across her face. "I know—too late, now. But you are unfair to him, to think he would never have looked at you. Your eyes have more life than a dozen Claire reb Guin's."

"His thoughts must walk the same path as mine," she agreed, leaving alone Fion's other comments. Lifting the mug, she carefully sipped a bit of the native mead, and then took a long draught of her saffra, for she was thirsty. Leaning back against the rough stone, Mailan studied the man's somber expression. They had explained the secrets of this venture to him that first night he'd returned. Fion had offered no new thoughts or theories, except one: he had narrowed their list of suspects. A trainer himself, he was familiar with the changing of the roster, and he knew its operation inside and out. Before their departure he had found a few moments to visit the *guaard* system.

"You are positive no one tampered with the computer?" she said again.

"The answer has not changed, girl," Fion replied, shaking his head. "If they tampered with the computer, they deleted all evidence of their entry. Such things leave traces. I would have found those traces. Either they have skills beyond imagining, or the entry into the computer was legal."

Silence. *Say the words, stupid, say them!* "I think it was legal entry," Mailan heard herself say.

Fion did not seem surprised. "Only eleven people have access to that screen," he said, "except for the 'current location' slots, and we can alter only our own slot, with our own voice- or thumbprint." Mailan nodded. "So," he continued. "Why do you think the entry was legal?"

"Because no one commented on it." Seeing his slight frown, she continued quickly. "There were only three trainers on duty in the city; you and Herb were on furlough, and the others were outland, training their groups. Surely one of three trainers, or Dirk, would have noticed the changes to the schedule."

"The Captain only approves the schedules, Mailan. He does not enter them, and he often approves changes after the fact," Fion pointed out.

"I know that. For all I know, Dirk has not looked at a screen in days. But you said it is possible for trainers to make changes without signing them, although they are *supposed* to sign them. One of the trainers must have done it, and done it at just the right time. The people who were changed *died*, for Mendulay's sake! You do not keep old rosters, do you?"

Fion shook his head, leaning forward to rest his elbows on the table. "Why keep them?"

"Exactly! If I had not been too busy to discard mine, who would notice that the bodies were in the wrong places? Only two

people were moved: Martin and Reese. And there was movement
only where two *guaard* were stationed. Why? Such a little thing
—would people not think that *they* requested the change?" As
Fion looked as if he would speak, she rushed on: "But they did
not take a different assignment, because I saw Martin with Cort
not long after compline, and Reese with Baldwin! The hospice
said they all died between matins and lauds—the next shift,
Fion. Why would they take another shift? Because someone with
seniority asked them to take it. Someone so senior they would not
call in and check."

"But if someone had noticed it . . . was to meet one of them
later . . ."

"The person would have the altered roster staring him in the
face, denying his memory. I would think Martin had made a
mistake, or something . . . not deliberate misdirection."

"But within the code banks . . ." Fion persisted.

"Oh, yes, I have heard that once saved, always there, even if
later deleted. But if the trainers all denied the previous schedule,
and it was all you had to go on . . ."

"They would assume it was something Martin and Reese had
done between them," Fion said quietly. "What other answer
could there be? Since the program was not tampered with . . ."

"Get someone to break into the code banks on such little evidence? Hardly! And who would take the next step—an accusation—on such a flimsy thought?"

"Your theory has merit, even if a few of your suppositions are
fragile," Fion agreed. "Before I break a few supports, tell me
why this makes sense to you. You are holding out on me," he
added.

Mailan flushed. "I just wanted to be sure you thought it had
merit before I sprung the next part on you."

"Yes?" Fion said dryly.

"I think . . . I think Seri Iver sent a literal message." Mailan
studied her mentor's expressionless face, waiting for an interruption. He nodded for her to continue. "It must have been the prov-
idence of Mendulay that he thought of that story, but he did. The
perfect message. And it explains why he would not speak to the
guaard in the room when he woke up. Irulen should have believed it possible that Alger would turn on him. Alger, *the albino*. He was white-skinned, Fion. White."

"You are suggesting—"

"I am suggesting that Iver did not speak because he knew who
stabbed him. And that person was in the room! Even if he feared

conspiracy, even if he did not know whom to trust, he could have whispered it to Serae Bette. I am sure he would have tried to tell her, somehow, if I had not come—perhaps in the same manner. But it answers the question, Fion! Why would he hesitate to tell a *guaard* he knew to be a trainer, among the most trusted of our troop? Can it be coincidence?"

"You are suggesting treason." Fion's voice was mild, probing.

"Someone has betrayed Atare. White fits. Why do you think I have waited so long to speak? You know we hate one another. I could not say anything until I was certain. I have weighed many possibilities, Fion, and this one seems to answer the most questions."

"Is Iver that smart?"

"His favorite childhood story, Fion. The albino turning on The Atare—at the least, it told us a traitor walked among us. But there is more. I saw Iver's face, Fion. I saw the fear grow in his face when he recognized White. Whether he consciously made the connection I do not know, but I know this: he feared White."

Fion sat in silence for several minutes, sipping his mead. Knowing better than to interrupt, Mailan waited without comment, slowly turning her mug of mead in circles between her fingers. Finally the man lifted his grizzled head, his dark eyes settling on her face.

"Have you spoken with The Atare?" Strange, how easily that title came to his lips. He remembered Sheel as a child, yet the word "Atare" did not feel foreign.

"No. Because something else occurred to me. I may hate the ground White treads, but I must admit he is a skilled warrior. Fion . . . If White intended to kill someone by stabbing him—"

"He would be dead," Fion finished for her. "No doubt about it." Fion took a long, slow sip, his eyes becoming unfocused with concentration. "Iver was not meant to die. At least not at first. I see why you hesitated, child, but you need to take it a step further. If Iver was part of a plot for the throne, it is unlikely he would have feared White. On the contrary, White would have been in his pocket, if you will. I never thought Iver wanted the rule, and would not believe it, without more evidence than what we have before us."

Mailan was warmed within. "We"—so he was in this with her, as always. It always felt better with a friend at your back.

"Then . . . what?" She offered him her palms in a gesture of despair. "I keep coming up against Iver, and I cannot believe he would murder his uncle and five brothers for a throne he was totally unprepared to sit upon. Was he so good an actor we were all fooled?"

"No," came a soft voice behind her. "Iver was a lousy actor."

Appalled, Mailan whirled. To be so wrapped up in a conversation she had not heard! But Fion was facing the irregular entrance to the small room. He had chosen not to tell her of Sheel's approach. Facing her Atare, Mailan tried to push her heart back down her throat. No saliva. How much had he heard? She did not want to hurt him with useless speculation. . . .

"Suppose you start at the beginning, Mailan." Sheel smiled briefly as he began to peel off his damp jacket. "And take your time; otherwise, we will have to eat whatever horror old Harald has prepared for us."

It was Fion who reiterated their discussion; Mailan was still too embarrassed to speak. The expression on Sheel's face as he listened was at once distant and yet calculating, as if he were trying to remember something.

He finally spoke, his tone soft and low: "Responsibility terrified Iver. He feared a judgeship—never mind about the possibility of inheriting the throne. You must step further, Mailan. There *is* a way for your theory to work . . . and it is the only theory we have right now, so we might as well explore it. It matches something I have been considering. Who would benefit in the confusion following the murders? What advantage is there to Iver's sitting the throne?"

"But to kill you just to make it look as if Iver should have died?" Mailan said, the horror of it rising anew within her chest.

Sheel shook his head. "No. If someone thought they could influence Iver, they would have to be absolutely certain I would never become prime minister. As a healer, I might refuse . . . but then again I might not. Even unofficially, Iver would probably have turned to me for advice with certain things. Those who wanted him as Atare could not allow that. They needed him as an easily controlled pawn." Absently Sheel reached for the dregs of Mailan's saffra. "What if he saw it was White who stabbed him? He may have died because someone panicked, and feared they could not turn his mind away from what he thought he saw. Even a whisper of such a possibility could not exist . . . or Iver might have had those code banks opened."

"What price to betray every oath you have ever sworn?" Fion said suddenly.

"That is what you need, Mailan," Sheel added, sipping the cold saffra. "Why would White do such a thing? I do not think he cares for me, but to kill Cort and the others . . . what was his price?"

"There is another question, Atare," Fion said, draining his mead and reaching for the remnants of Mailan's. "White is Dirk's man, ever pushing that youngling to power: star student, youngest trainer ever, youngest captain ever. Would White do something like that without Dirk's knowledge? Have they had a falling-out? And if they are still as tight as brothers, what could Dirk gain from this that he did not have before? I can think of only trivial things . . . and Dirk is not a trivial person."

"Dirk with his ramrod spine, always following orders to the last word," Mailan muttered. "He is one of the most powerful people in Atare. Why would he strike at the hand which gave him almost everything he has, save his family's wealth?"

"Especially since killing Iver would put him under my foot," Sheel said, "which he would not care for at all. I keep too close a counsel for him." A finger tapped lightly on the table. "If only we knew for certain how—by whose hand—and why Iver died. . . ."

"Atare?" The stooped form entered hesitantly, nodding his fealty. "Dinner is served."

Mailan felt immediate complaint from her stomach, but she said nothing. Sheel flashed her a wry smile, and thanked the man for his efforts. As Harald walked slowly back into the corridor, Sheel leaned over and whispered: "We chose him for his loyalty and closed mouth, not for his cooking."

"Mendulay preserve us," Fion murmured without a trace of humor, and the three rose from the table, Sheel leading the way toward the central fire and what passed for supper.

PORTLAND, ATARE TERRITORY EIGHTYFOURDAY VESPERS

Somewhere within the confines of the tiny mountain village of Portland the vespers bell was ringing. Settling herself at a table near the fireplace, Darame sourly decided it was time for a drink. She ordered a goblet of the house wine, along with some cheese, bread, and fruit, and then leaned back to study the small evening crowd.

They had reached a dead end. Unfolding her hand, Darame examined the pottery fragment she had toted for three long days. The clay came from this region, and a large retail shop faced the town square. It occurred to her that Sheel's party might have gone to ground in that closed hotel, but there was no way to find out. Not until word filtered out to Mailan and the other *guaard*.

Surely they are watching the local town. They have sent messages to Leah. Messages delivered by *guaard* in the dead of night, individuals who disappeared as silently as they came, forcing the reply to be announced in code by satellite. What had Leah told Sheel, in those messages? Avis said he always asked the same question: How did the investigation progress? Other than that, he was fine; Tobias was fine. They would send another message soon. . . .

You should not have left her to her own devices. Shivering in the cool room despite the fire at her elbow, Darame reached for the warm wine the server had delivered to her table. Leah was a puzzle. Firm, in control sometimes, but there were other times . . . Darame shrank into her jacket, wishing it were warmer. Visiting the monuments of the dead, with Avis in her silent grief and Camelle's constant, quiet tears. Nothing from Leah, except at the graves of Caleb and Iver . . . Then, she wept. *At least something touches you besides hate.*

Ayers waited at the bar across the room. Nothing Darame said could persuade him to remain with Avis. He had trailed the off-worlder to Sheel's home, watched her search his ruler's books and wall charts under the thoughtful eyes of the cats, refrained from comment—even when she'd confronted him, asked him if he really wanted to know what she was doing. Why did Ayers stay so close? He denied her nothing, made no attempt to steer her footsteps, much less inhibit her wishes. And he offered no explanations, not even when, exasperated, Darame had asked him to swap jobs with his sister, remaining to watch over Avis.

If I suggested to Sheri I could do her work better than she could, she would gut me, was Ayers' only comment. *I was told to stay with you until further notice.*

Even Avis in danger could not sway him . . . if he believed an off-worlder's suspicions. Reaching for the tiny loaf of bread, still warm to her touch, Darame began methodically ripping it apart. *Was I right to tell her to skirt the truth?*

Pregnant. Avis was pregnant, to her great joy. Only Darame, Camelle, and her cousin and attendant Stephanie knew, and none of them was talking. The obvious questions—who was the father, and when was it due?—were not easily answered on Nuala. The woman was positive Stephen Se'Morval was the father, unless Sheel had missed a new life in his hasty search the night of the party. When? She could count only from that date. Late spring or early summer...

Why did I tell her to mislead them? It had burst from Darame's lips without thought. *"Tell them it is Stephen or Brant—is there anyone else possible? No? Then tell them just that, will you, please? For me?"* Avis had promised she would, although the odd look she gave her new friend spoke volumes.

The guaard *will protect a pregnant daughter of the line, and if necessary, Brant will protect a child that might be his... a child who might rule Atare.* But the looks Leah sometimes gave Avis ...*I begin to doubt that woman's sanity, and I fear to leave you to her power.*

And Halsey. Her old friend's plight ran through her thoughts like counterpoint. *Brant has abandoned him, I know he has....* The thought made Darame angrier every time it crossed her mind. *Always guard your partner's back, always!* Blinded by trinium, Brant was— Enough. Halsey could look after himself, if necessary. She was not so sure about Sheel and Avis. *No choice but to hide in the mountains? Have you no allies?* A disturbing idea. *For what it's worth, I'll help you.* She still was not sure why.

Now, in a silent, snow-covered town in the shadow of Mount Habbukk, she waited. How long until word of her presence would reach Sheel? Who of these villagers would carry the message? Several of them had been studying her since she entered the village limits. Slogging through fresh powdery snow, from stores to hostels to taverns, with Nualan shadows dogging her heels. No, no one had heard anything.... If The Atare was in the region, he had not greeted the town elders.... Yes, if his people came through, they would pass along a message.

"Serae?" Darame lifted her head to face one of the shadows that had flitted in her wake all the long afternoon. Bright eyes peered at her from under shaggy brows. The man wore a long, hooded poncho over some type of skintight, insulated suit; his face was hidden.

"Yes?" she said in Nualan, wondering what this meant. She had not expected an approach so soon....

"You seek Sheel Atare in the Starrise Mountains?" the husky voice asked.

"I seek him," she answered, studying the man's stiff stance. He clung to a staff with his right hand, the left holding a mug which was supported by the fireplace mantel. The poncho was belted close to his body, and heavy gloves were tucked in that belt.

"Why does an off-worlder seek our Lord?" No change in expression or tone that she could see. It was that strange Nualan bluntness, at odds with their fetish for privacy.

She opened her palm to reveal the chip of pottery. "He left me a token of his passing, if I should have need of him. I have need of him."

Nodding once, his eyes devouring the fragment, the man turned his head to sip at his drink.

Uncertain of mountain protocol, Darame indicated with a gesture that he could join her table. Choosing instead to sit at the opposite end of the fireplace, the man propped up a foot on a box marked FIRE CRYSTAL STICKS and leaned his staff against the stone wall. Shrugging, he pushed back his hood.

Blond hair both long and graying, as thick and shaggy as the brows and beard. His eyes were unexpected. . . . They echoed the watered topaz of old Riva Ragaree's right eye, their color like polished amber. Darame liked his face; although solemn, the crinkles at his eyes and mouth promised humor, as well as time spent outdoors. His gaze was too steady to lie.

But Nualans did not lie—they only bent the truth. . . .

Placing the pottery piece on the table, Darame leaned back in her chair. "So. Were you merely curious, or have you come to grace my presence for some other reason?"

"'A woman of ice, with a heart of fire,'" the man said suddenly, and he spoke as if he quoted Holy Writ. "'And the grass that refuses to bend in the wind shall burn at her words.'" He nodded once again, as if satisfied with something, and then drained his mug in one breath. Darame studied the flash of firelight against his cup of beaten metal. A thin white scar etched from little finger to wrist momentarily caught her gaze.

Watching the man set his tankard on the table and signal to the attendant, Darame felt her eyebrows slowly draw together. This one reeked of some religious fringe. Wonderful. How to get rid of him without offending anyone? . . .

Settling back in his chair to await a fresh drink, the stranger suddenly said: "I am Fergus reb Fern, of Lebanon way. I have traveled these mountains some thirty years Terran, and I am no bad guide."

"What could you guide me to?" Darame asked carefully, indirectly.

Smiling wolfishly, Fergus said: "Many things." He paused,

watching the attendant carefully refill his mug with some sort of ale. "My tab," he told the youth, who nodded his understanding. Glancing over at the woman, he added: "The boy is deaf and mute, but reads lips quite well."

"You know what I seek?" she said, glancing at the bay window across the room. Darkness was falling fast—she would have to return to their small camp soon.

"Sanctuary," Fergus replied, his nod slower this time, and drawn out. "I think it can be arranged."

"Do you know where to find what I seek?"

"No." The man's expression did not change. "But I can make a very good guess."

Darame covered her annoyance. "I do not have time for riddles," she said gently. "Others more frail than I depend on your answer." She shivered as she spoke, for the outer door had opened, several snow-dusted figures entering.

"You will not find another guide," he told her simply. "The loyalty of this town is absolute." Rising to the balls of his feet, he leaned forward to seize his mug.

"And your loyalty is not?" Bland—no accusation, no threat, not even curiosity...

Fergus laughed softly in his throat. "My loyalty is to Mendulay. Loyalty to a god is not always the same thing as loyalty to one's ruler."

"You are a priest," she said carefully, uncertain of the noun.

"Very good. You learn our language quickly." At her lifted eyebrows, he said: "No, no accent... at all. Your speech is too precise. But one must know what to listen for...." He blew the foam of his drink into the fireplace, giving a sudden, yeasty smell to the room. "You need not fear the path I will lead you upon, woman. I owe the royal Atares a debt; one I am not sure I can repay. Leading you to Sheel Atare will not begin to settle the balance."

"How much?" That might be too blunt, but subtlety was not helping with this one.

"As I said, I owe a debt." He drained the tankard quickly, soundlessly, and then turned the mug over, the dregs dripping into the fireplace. "Are you ready?"

"Tonight?" She frowned, wondering what Ayers would say to this development. "Perhaps at dawn... Heavy snow is promised tonight. Where... can I find you?"

Fergus shook his head and stood, seizing his staff. "We will be snowbound by morning. If you do not move quickly, your camp will be buried." He grinned suddenly. "I noticed them before I sought you." The mug disappeared into the folds of his poncho, and he flipped up his hood. "Come."

Dropping several coins on the table, Darame pocketed her pottery fragment and followed.

EIGHTYFOURDAY   COMPLINE

Used to the higher noise level of the caverns, Sheel did not really notice Jude's arrival in the cave, nor Mailan stepping aside for conversation. The screen had absorbed him; they had power, now, and he *would* solve this mess. Somewhere in all of this was an answer to Cort's death, to all the deaths. Something they had not seen—

"Atare?" Mailan's voice was especially low tonight, cutting through his thoughts. "You have a visitor."

Lifting his head, Sheel fastened his gaze upon the *guaard*. "A visitor?"

"There are many outkin in the area, my Atare," she continued steadily. "It was inevitable that one of them would learn of your location." In her usually expressionless working tones Sheel detected both exasperation and amusement. "She says she has news for you."

"What is it?"

"As she is a serae, I did not presume to question her without your presence." Approaching the usual lack of expression, the mountain lilt invisible. . . .

Sheel sighed and ran his fingers through his hair. After two cups of mead, he was not at his sharpest. Who would have expected visitors? "Send her in," he said finally, suspecting that this game could go on all night. Why was Mailan suddenly so evasive?

Squishing snow was suddenly audible in the corridor; it was Fion who led in the visitor. A delicate, familiar fragrance floated in the air. Dressed in the browns and whites the locals preferred for outdoor wear, she was almost unrecognizable. Almost.

"Crystle?" Straightening in his seat, Sheel made no attempt to hide his amazement.

Removing her scarf and sodden hat, the woman smiled tentatively. It was an embarrassed smile, pasted on a tense form. "Atare." Although her snow gear was as casual as any could be, she made a formal courtesy to him. Half-rising, Sheel took her cold hand and pulled her toward one of the other packing crates they were using as seats.

"Welcome to the informal meeting room," he said easily, struggling to hold back his laughter. *Dear Mendulay, I surrender! This woman has defeated me!*

"You should have come to the hotel," she said without preamble. "It closes for the winter, you know. Avalanches are too common here for winter sports. Surely it would have been as private."

"The lights." At Crystle's blank expression, Sheel continued: "The lights of the hotel can be seen from the town. I could not arouse comment too soon. It seems we are already undone. Where is our weak link? Or have you come to finish me off?" He asked it lightly—Crystle might want to kill him for avoiding her, but that was another thing entirely—but the woman's face drained of color.

"She is unarmed, Atare," Fion said quietly, still waiting by the entrance arch.

"I am teasing you, woman," Sheel said quickly, afraid she might faint. "I know well your loyalty to our line."

"I have closed up your weak link," she started softly. "The men who bring your supplies, Warner and Joseph—they were talking in the stables, my uncle's stables. I had just come in, and overheard them. They have learned not to discuss even supply trips. They claim it is the first time they have spoken aloud. I hope so. . . ." Relaxing slightly, Crystle brightened as Crow appeared with mugs of hot wine. "I came to tell you that someone has asked for you in town."

"Indeed. When?" Sheel released her now-warm hand to allow her to take a drink from the tray.

"Just this day. I think I have seen her before, although in snow wraps it is hard to tell. The silver-haired woman your brother dumped a drink on at Seri Tobias's party. I think she is an offworlder—do you remember?" Crystle asked, her soft blue eyes lifting to meet his.

"Yes, I remember," Sheel said smoothly.

"Since I left town right after the party, I did not know she was still here. I suppose everyone is being detained until they find who murdered The Atare." Sipping at her mug, Crystle continued her story. "She asked everywhere for you, but she did not leave word of where she could be reached. She asked only that if you passed through, someone should tell you she had asked for you."

"So you do not know where she is?" Sheel said, his eyes shifting to Mailan's still form.

"Not exactly." Crystle's brow furled slightly. "Warner says he followed her to the tavern. She had a light dinner there, and began talking to one of the local holy ones. She left with him."

"Holy ones?" Crow asked.

"Yes, holy ones," Crystle went on. "Fergus reb Fern, one of those called a prophet by some of the wandering bands that winter in this area. He is from Lebanon—"

"A Sini?" This was abrupt; Sheel doubted if Darame would know how to recognize either a Sini or a mock-Sini, and that could be a problem. It would never occur to a sini that an off-worlder could get so far inland and not know the traditional signs.

"A mock-Sini. He has been in this area since before I was born. Everyone knows him. Warner could not hear all the conversation, but the holy one seemed to think he could find you, and offered to lead the woman and her group."

"Group?" This was from Fion.

"Yes. I am not sure what that meant, I saw no one except the off-worlder and one other man who shadowed her." Crystle turned to face Fion at this.

"What do you mean, 'shadowed'?" Fion asked gently.

"Followed her everywhere, like you follow The Atare." She glanced back at Sheel.

Nodding, Sheel looked over at Mailan. "Well?"

"The snow increases, Atare. We may be stranded by morning. I fear you are stuck here, Serae," she added, glancing at Crystle.

She shrugged. "I knew it was a possibility. I will not be missed, while Warner or Joseph might have been. Many people suspect you are in the area, and Warner will tell my uncle I went off with a message, should he ask. No one will search for me." She sipped her wine once again. "I brought some things to keep me busy: a few rings to listen to, if you have a spare machine, and some fine needlework. I will keep out of your way."

Smiling faintly, Sheel flicked his eyes toward the exit. "Bring her here." Without further comment Mailan vanished into the shadows of the corridor, Crow at her heels. Fion also backed out the irregularly shaped entrance, and leaned against a stalagmite of hard rock.

Sheel finally reached for the other mug and took a long drink. "How did you end up here? I thought your parents lived south of Atare, on Half-Moon Bay."

"They do," Crystle answered calmly, leaning back against the rock. "But I do not take to the sea well. I never have," she added ruefully, taking a longer sip of the cooling wine. "Much to my trader father's dismay. It is necessary for me to be able to return to Atare quickly, so we all decided that visiting up here would be a good idea. I must return to town after the Yule."

"A good fortyday yet," Sheel said, propping his feet up on another crate. "Are you warm enough?" he asked suddenly. It was something he often forgot, that others were cold when he was comfortable.

"Yes, Atare. Do not concern yourself." She concentrated on her wine once more.

At least she is not paralyzed by my position, he thought wryly. A few had been, since his sudden elevation. That Crystle could talk to him as they had before—before she became so desperate about a child—was a wonder.

"Thank you for bringing us word," Sheel went on quietly. "The off-worlder may have some important news for me."

"A strange messenger, an off-worlder," Crystle commented. "No one would think of her, that is certain."

At least not up here, Sheel agreed silently. Crystle's tone intrigued him. "You do not care for off-worlders?"

She straightened at that, coloring delicately across cheeks and throat. "I . . . do not know the woman, Atare. I meant nothing specific—"

"The question was a general one," Sheel interrupted, sparing her further explanations.

"Then . . . no, I do not. At least not for the men. And few of the women. They seem hard to me. . . . They come here to take, and do not care what they destroy in the meantime. I thought that would make me not care. . . . That I could come to the capital and succeed where my sister failed. But I cannot bear the thought of them, much less their touch." She looked down into her glass. "I know they bring needed trade to our home, but still . . ."

"Succeed where your sister failed? I did not know you had—" The wine had loosened his tongue; Sheel stopped abruptly, and then realized the pause had drawn even more attention to his words.

"I do not. Not any more." Crystle kept her eyes on the soft white light of the globe sitting in a wall niche. "She finally conceived late last year—either a trader or one of the younger ambassadors—and tried to carry the child full term. She lost it this spring, before Ascension Day. And her own life. . . . There was too much blood, and she was far from medical help when it happened. Careless, to assume things would continue to go so well." Her tone was very even, more controlling emotion than lacking it. "I am now the mother of my line. I must be careful of myself."

Just about the time you switched from pleasant scenery to haunting my footsteps, Sheel thought, but did not say aloud.

"Feeling as you do, I hope you do not intend to go to Caesarea," Sheel murmured, reaching carefully for the insulated pitcher sitting on the tray.

That surprised the woman, and the look she gave him spoke many words. "How could I? I am the last. My mother would never sleep again, or worry herself into her grave, if I took ship. And what if I failed even then? . . ." Shaking herself, she resolutely shook her head. "No. I am satisfied with my decision . . . at peace with it. I was not fertile during the Festival of Masks, unfortunately, but the lab thinks I may cycle close to the Yule. I will go back right after it, and try my luck then."

"You should have told me you were going to the lab," Sheel said simply. "I know all the people there, I could have made it . . . easier for you." *Defeat of any kind is a hard admission.*

"I would have asked you about it, but . . . I did not decide until after The Atare was killed," she finally said. "It did not seem like a good time to bother you with such small things. And then, after Seri Iver died—" That seemed to choke her.

Reaching for her mug, Sheel poured her another glass of wine. "I miss him, too," he said gently.

"He was always kind," she whispered, "and his wife was—is —a sweet woman. Were all the women on Emerson like Serae Bette?"

Crystle was wrapped in private thoughts, and did not see Sheel stiffen. "If they had been," he said quietly, "I would have brought someone home."

She was sensitive to nuance—her grip tightened on the handle of her mug. "I apologize, Atare. I did not think." She looked over at him, studying his face. Something she saw there made her ask: "Do you dislike them, too?"

"Remember I *have* to marry one," Sheel pointed out dryly as he settled his attention on his mug. "No . . . Dislike is not the word. I do not understand them, Crystle. I begin to despair of ever finding an off-worlder who can accept both Nuala . . . and me."

"Whatever could be unacceptable about you?" She sounded so shocked that Sheel started laughing.

When he finally got control of himself, he realized she was embarrassed. "I think I needed that," he whispered through chuckles. "That does put things into perspective. Healers do not frighten you?" The question was calm, but he watched her intently as he asked it.

"Of course they do," she responded, returning to her drink. "To be able to seal broken flesh with a touch! It must be like being an . . . an intermediary between man and Mendulay." There was so much reverence in her voice he could not find her words offensive. "I can see how it might frighten an off-worlder. Especially if they did not expect such a thing. Nowhere else have humans mutated so, have they?"

"No." It sounded abrupt, but Sheel had no words to expand it.

"You will find someone," she said, radiating an air of supreme confidence. "Someone will recognize your superior qualities, and they will come to terms with your talent."

"Curse." He took another drink. *What am I doing getting drunk with this child of the sea who smells of meadow flowers? I am not sure this is approved etiquette.*

"Surely . . ."

"Not to our people, of course. But to me, a curse. Do you know what it brought me after a year of searching Emerson? Two women I thought I could live with for the rest of my—theoretically—long life. One of them was too terrified of the planet and the Long Sleep . . . of waking and knowing her parents were probably dead. The other thought I was fine for minor pleasures, but the idea of actually carrying my child apparently turned her stomach." That brought him up straight in his chair. He had not meant to say that much, and hoped she did not try to see within the gaps.

"Last spring I would have killed for what she refused," Crystle murmured, snuggling back against the stone.

"Crystle, I am sorry—" He started, and then wondered what he was going to say to this woman. *You obviously have drunk too much today. . . .*

"Do not say it, Atare." She turned slightly so she was facing him, her soft blue eyes glowing in the dim light of the room. "You owe me no explanations. If Emerson was that bad for you, no wonder you had no thoughts for women in the spring. And the way I was acting a few months ago . . ." She frowned sourly. "It worked for Claire reb Guin. I had more dignity . . . until my sister died, and then . . ." She glanced away from him, her eyes moving from one globe to the next, trying to hide the bright unshed tears caught in her lashes.

"Why not Iver? Or Caleb?" *I do not believe you are asking this question.*

Crystle smiled a tight, wry little smile. "But I did not want Caleb or Iver, Atare. I wanted you. If I'd wanted good genes that badly, I suppose I should have swallowed my distaste for off-world men. They certainly find Nualan women attractive."

"All women."

His stress was not lost on her. "Perhaps that is it. They looked upon me as merely an extremely attractive woman. . . . Perhaps artificial for all they knew, but for what they wanted, it did not matter. As for your brothers . . . Caleb flitted from woman to woman. His new wife . . . She had the prestige and money, and his attention, occasionally. I did not want to be passage in the night. And Iver was sweet . . . indeed, persistent. I had decided at that party to give in, but he had noticed the silvery woman, so I planned to wait. Iver . . . He laughed at the wrong things. Not the things I found funny. You, however . . ." Sighing, she smiled at him. "You always had that sly laugh in your eyes, like you saw how funny everything was—all of us, the off-worlders—and yet you seemed to like things. Even that private sadness around you did not dampen the brilliance that clings to you, like polished trine." She set her empty mug on the table. "I wanted someone who wanted more than a night, someone whose child I would enjoy raising. Obviously not the right attitude for the head of a line. Mother would have hysterics if she knew I turned down Caleb and Iver for those reasons. She thought I settled on you because you were a healer."

"Healing protects only from the hot strain," Sheel reminded her quietly. "There is no guarantee about anything else, Crystle. Not even that you could carry a child of mine to term."

She shrugged. "I will try a general implant once. If I fail, back to the knife. But I will not keep trying, and kill my children."

It was so quiet Sheel could hear a drip of water falling in some remote cavern. He had not felt so peaceful since before Cort's death. Long before— No, this was a familiar feeling. . . . Darame had inspired a similar feeling. *Could you learn to live with my healing, silver lady?* Focusing on Crystle, an odd thought tickled his consciousness: *I always thought you a genuinely kind person, Crystle. How can I allow Claire reb Guin to succeed where you failed? If you had only shown up at the same time, there would have been no contest!* Without thinking he reached for her wrist.

Startled, Crystle stiffened and looked suspiciously at him. "Atare, are you drunk?"

"Shhhh." It was harder to run the checks through the alcohol he had absorbed, but not impossible. Not fertile, but not far from it, either. Yule was more than fortyday away, so . . .

"Fifteenday," he pronounced after several minutes, still holding her wrist.

"Atare?" She straightened and leaned toward him, puzzled.

"I think you may cycle within fifteenday. Yule may be too late. We will have to keep an eye on you." He set the mug carefully on the tray. "I think, Crystle, that if you have not changed your mind about me, perhaps you should come here in fifteenday. It bothers my sense of justice to know that Claire has a son because I wanted to get rid of her, and you are childless because your manners are kinder."

The woman simply stared at him, the color draining from her cheeks even as her pulse increased. "But . . . But Atare, you . . ."

"I only wish I could find an off-worlder like you. But you must marry someone in a high house, and do your part for your family. Even as I must." The thought was depressing. Bette was a nice woman, but her brains were scattered from Nuala to Emerson. *Is that my fate?* "I keep locals at a distance because I might get a jealous one like Caleb's wife. Then what?"

"Yes, that is another reason I refused him," Crystle agreed, that wry smile pulling at her lips. "I did not intend to hang around your neck like Cort's Nualan consort . . . but I hoped you thought of me as more than a body for the evening."

This startled Sheel out of his daze. "Have I not made that plain?"

She flinched from his intense gaze. "Yes, but Atare . . . you want me to leave and not come back for fifteen days?" There was something about her expression, and the tone of voice . . .

The hint finally soaked into Sheel's awareness. "My Serae, are you trying to tell me you would like to practice first?" *She is right, you are drunk.*

Crystle giggled, her amusement drawing his attention, and Sheel felt himself start to blush.

COMPLINE

Everything was black, except for the tiny light bobbing frantically in the distance. Darame had not expected it to be so dark.

The blinding brilliance of the day was swallowed up in night, buried deep in night, as if the snow had been imagined, and they were walking in a land of glazed basalt.

There had been surface melting during the day: a layer of rough ice made movement easier than it might have been. If only the wind would die down, the falling snow would be a minor nuisance. How could that man walk so quickly? The swirling pellets of ice and snow felt like blows from a scatter gun, and the gusts frequently blew her off her feet.

I am weak, was her hostile thought as she pulled herself up once again. *It has not occurred to him that this trek might be difficult. . . . He is in his element.* Whether she meant the snow or the mountains Darame was not certain. *What I wouldn't give for his poncho.* Her gear was meant for casual outings in sunny, snow-tossed scenes, not for heavy weather. Temperatures were well below freezing, although the snow still fell in a thick and heavy veil.

The light no longer bobbed—Fergus had halted. *Why am I following you? Because of a name?* It had not occurred to her until later that Fergus had been her father's father's name. She had met the old man only once, in the dim recesses of her childhood: a twinkling sprite of a man, with the same black eyes he had given his descendants. *You remind me a bit of that other Fergus. I hope fancy has not led me to my death.*

Somewhere far below, Ayers waited with their small group. The arrangements had displeased the *guaard,* but there had been little else to do. Someone had to lead the others to a specified meeting point—Foster's Breach—and at least Ayers could figure out where the priest meant. Darame was totally lost. *Ayers must trust him, or he would have objected more strenuously.*

Finally, the light— Fergus was leaning into a niche, using a slice of stone as a windbreak. She stepped into the still place; lifting shadowed eyes to meet his amber orbs. Only the man's eyes showed—everything else was hidden. The expression in his eyes was intense.

"Are you tired? How do you feel?" he asked softly, the wind carrying his voice away.

"A bit. I'll be all right," she answered, shifting her scarf toward the front.

Fergus abruptly whipped off a glove and pressed the back of his fingers to her cheek. "Can you feel that?"

"Not really. Just some pressure—" She broke off as the man

swore mildly. A flurry of garments, his own disarrayed in his haste, and Fergus was rearranging her huge scarf around neck and head, completely covering her face. A flap of material gave her a tiny area of vision.

"Put your hand under the scarf—without your glove!—and tell me when it starts to tingle." Uncertain, she did as he told her. Catching the look in the one eye that was still visible, he added: "You have a touch of frostbite. Not too serious, but we should not let it go. We will wait until you have feeling again."

"That may be a while," she muttered. "I am always cold."

"That is one problem I have never had," he replied, and that wolfish smile was back.

Standing in the darkness, looking beyond the tiny light toward heaps of snow, it was impossible not to consider her position. *Idiot. If you're lucky they'll find you when it thaws.* Under lashes caked with ice she studied the man's lean, unbending form. That staff was handy; she had seen him testing the path with it, seeking rock beneath powdered snow. True, she was cold, but she had no intention of mentioning it. There was nothing to do but turn back, and turning back would surely take as long as going forward.

He had used his right hand . . . with the scar. No, surely that scar had been on his left hand. They were too similar. . . . Something ceremonial? Even the robe seemed formal, unlike anything else in the mountains. It was a soft, muted gray with a bold ribbon of bright yellow striping the lower edge.

"Remember to keep your distance." Ayers's parting words came back to her. The holy man kept his distance; there was no need to tell her that some religions prohibited interaction between sexes. But Nualan clergy married. . . . She was sure she had seen that information somewhere.

"Nualan clergy marries?" she asked carefully.

Fergus turned at this and lifted the glass box he carried, bringing the light to her face. "Yes, they can marry if they desire, although this is hardly the time for a discussion on religious discipline." He looked almost amused.

"I mean . . ." She flipped a hand at him in disgust, and realized it was the one without a glove. Her face had started tingling—good. "Ayers told me to keep my distance from you. I do not mean to offend, but I do not know your customs—"

His snort surprised and silenced her. Pulling on her glove, she glanced up. "It is tingling, now, like pricks of heat."

"Good." The man studied her intently a moment, his expression unreadable. Then he secured his scarf once again, and led off into the snow.

There was no sense of time, little impression of distance. Darame felt her legs become wood, then stone, then nothing, as feeling drained from them. *Now I should say something*, came a thought, but she was too tired to shout. Fergus was closer than before, and stopped often, looking over his shoulder for her.

As if reading her thoughts, Fergus stopped abruptly. Staggering, she almost ran into him, but he extended an arm quickly and caught her. The light seemed feeble, now—either it was fading, or the snow was falling more thickly. She could see a sheer thrust of rock before them, fading into the blackness of the sky. Not much further...

"Here I leave you," Fergus announced, pulling a small metal device from his pocket and pressing on it. At the audible click, a brilliant red light flashed, pulsing. "Here is your beacon. If The Atare has *guaard* with him, they will spot the light, and investigate it."

"He has *guaard*," she whispered, too tired to argue with him. "How ... long ..."

"Not long," he said quickly, tugging at her jacket. "We should have stopped and bought you a poncho, this off-world issue is useless up here." He sounded disgusted. "Over here." He pulled her over to a boulder and settled her behind it, where little snow had blown. "If they do not come immediately, you must dig down, into this bank, and make a snow cave."

"But ... where—" Darame began.

"I will be nearby, I will not abandon you," he said roughly. "I did not bring you here to freeze, though you may doubt it now. Sweet Mendulay, woman, you have ice in your veins! You should have spoken. There are things we could have done."

"I ... cannot stop now," she said softly to the boulder. Fergus muttered something in reply, but the wind tore his words away. He wrapped her gloved hands around the base of the beacon, placing it to one side, away from her eyes. "Will ... they see? ..."

"This thing is lighting up the entire outcrop, woman, half the mountain can see. We cannot get closer or they might *not* come —it could give away their hiding spot. This is just right...." Standing, he seemed to scan the darkness beyond their few lights. Then he stooped beside her once again.

"Why not come with—"

"Oh, no. I am much more useful to Atare wandering these mountains than cooped up with potential jackals." He actually seemed amused. "Not yet do I confront that one. Not until he earns the name of Mindbender. But you must remember some things, woman. Where is your group?"

"Foster's Breach," she said promptly.

"Good. Now—what does the yellow stripe on my poncho mean?" She gave him a blank look. "It means I am a Sini, Child Eyes—a *mock-Sini*. Do you know what that is?"

"Hot . . ."

"Yes, hot, but not deadly, not prohibited. We move among the populace at will, but we do not stay long, because the danger is in length of contact. Do you understand? Whether in cities or wilderness, it always means a mock-Sini. A red stripe means Sini, just Sini. Keep your distance! You cannot be in their presence long without problems. . . . Dizziness, nausea, and even worse. A red stripe. And if you see a blue stripe with the red or yellow, that means *Sinishur*. Mind your manners, then. . . . What you see may not be what you expect, but it is human. Do you understand?"

Darame nodded once, sharply, at this speech, shocked out of her stupor. *By all the saints of my varied childhood*— She could form no coherent words. There was not even strength to grip her arms, to make sure she was whole.

"Take care, ice woman. You will not freeze, not here. You will thaw before the end." Smiling, Fergus re-adjusted his hood and scarves and then flitted into the wall of snow. Yellow light vanished with him, leaving only the eerie blink of stabbing red as company.

"Thank you," she said aloud, wondering if the wind would carry her words. She put off any other thought, afraid to think past the moment. *For a usually capable person, you have really set yourself up for this one*. Had there been another way? Not without leaving the Seedar ragaree to the intrigues of Atare city. Perhaps they should have descended upon old Riva. Surely the woman could have kept anyone from knowing . . . but there are spies everywhere. If only she could have confided in the *guaard*, asked his advice. . . . Damn this secretive world!

It was better than thinking about the cold. She was still trying to analyze the steps that had brought her to this snowdrift when a hand reached out of the darkness and clutched her wrist. Lifting her head, she peered out of her uncovered eye to see a figure cloaked in black with a lighter-colored garment thrown over all.

Goggles were lifted, revealing familiar eyes, tinged red in the irregular light and then gone, blackness, as the beacon was shut down.

"Foster's Breach," she whispered as Mailan bent over her. "Ayers is with the others at Foster's Breach."

"Foster's Breach? What others?" It was hard to tell with the wind, but Mailan sounded a bit annoyed.

"The Ragaree of Seedar." This statement brought exclamations from both the *guaard* and a shadowy form behind her, but Darame was folding into blackness, and heard only a whistle of wind.

Chapter Eight

STARRISE MOUNTAINS   EIGHTYFIVEDAY   LAUDS

Darame's first impressions were of warmth and noise. Instinctively she moved closer to the warmth, burrowing into it, while grimacing against the ringing in her ears. Gradually the sound dissolved into coherent voices, their words just beyond her understanding. *Inside . . . I am out of the storm.* Had she imagined the arrival of *guaard*? No, not likely. . . Who would have found her body, otherwise?

A blanket had been tossed over her back; she could feel the roughness of the weave against her skin. *Skin . . .* Darame did not have to use her hands to know she had been stripped to her linings, a whisper of silk between her and the vatos wool. And flesh against her cheek, warmth that belonged to another . . . Memory trickled into awareness like the rising tide, and her nose told her the scent was familiar. Sandalwood, and a touch of musk. In her fear, she had forgotten how comfortable . . . Lifting her head, Darame tried to focus her eyes.

The form she sprawled against stiffened—a tangible tightening of skin and muscle. Although conversation did not die, *his* words stopped abruptly. When light and dark finally melded into their proper forms, Darame realized she was curled into the hollow formed by Sheel Atare's right arm. In fact, she was using his chest as a pillow, his shirt peeled to either side. *Natural warmth for frostbite . . . I wonder if he had to heal me*.

His expression was unreadable—no, not quite; subtle. She saw resignation in that fair face, and expectation . . . a fragile form of pain she had never seen before.

A dozen quips filtered through her fogged brain, but the words that popped out were in Caesarean: "It's all right. I think I'm starting to get used to it." As she spoke, the nebulous others became aware she was conscious, and conversation died.

She waited for reaction; there was none, at least in his face. But she felt relaxation, the slightest release of clenched musculature, and wondered if he understood what she meant.

Finally Darame realized she was trembling, and fought to hold her head up. Sheel seemed to take in her condition at the same moment, because he shifted, his arm hard behind her back as he pulled her over to one side. A mug, filled with something steaming, materialized at his side, and he carefully took hold of the handle.

"You must drink some of this," he said quietly, bringing it to her lips. "Slowly."

"I am always waking up in strange places with people telling me to drink things," she muttered, extending shaking fingers to steady the mug.

"I hope you will not think me ungracious if I point out that if you were to simply avoid me, many of your problems would abate." Although his face was still immobile, Darame detected a glint of humor in his odd eyes.

"Would it were that easy," she replied, taking a sip of the fluid. It was saffra, and warm, not hot, so she took several long swallows, enjoying the sensation as it trickled down her parched throat. "I did not think you could get so dry, with all that snow about."

"Many people die of dehydration long before they can freeze to death," came a low, dry voice.

So it was Mailan. . . . Who else? Did you think she would leave him, unless he sent her away? The room began growing fuzzy, and her arms were very heavy. Again, Sheel seemed to know before she did; his arm tightened around her, and the mug was set aside.

"Rest. For now I will talk to the Ragaree. You need to get your strength back," Sheel told her, glancing to one side as if checking for blankets.

"You're the doctor," Darame murmured, relaxing against him.

"Healer." The word was a puff of wind curling past her ear as she wandered back into sleep.

NONE

This time Darame woke into silence. It was a type of quiet rarely experienced; after orienting herself, she realized she could detect sound from the heat disks glowing in the firepit. A cot had been prepared next to the grate, and blankets were heaped over her. Still she shivered. *Always cold, fool. And yet this planet is covered with desert.* With Sheel, she had not been cold. . . .

Straining, she listened for voices. Nothing, even at a distance. Somewhere in the darkness beyond the makeshift room she could hear a steady trickle of water, but there was no sign of life. The smell of clay made her nostrils twitch.

Fully awake, fully alert . . . Slowly, pulling a blanket close, Darame sat upright. Her dreams had been hazy, and troubled. Dreams of disaster, abandonment . . . death in a frozen waste. A warm touch had chased away the night tremors, but whether the hand had been phantom or real she had no idea.

"Finally, you stir," came a husky voice, the words Caesarean, and Darame turned her head in response. Mailan had appeared out of darkness, indicating where the entrance was located. "How do you feel?"

"Cold." Evasiveness might serve with Fergus the Sini, but not with this *guaard*. *She knows too much about me, at least on that score.*

"I was afraid you would say that." Mailan was carrying a basket. "I will see what I can do." Setting the basket on the foot of the cot, Mailan bent to sprinkle heat disks on the fire.

Smelling food, Darame rooted around in her bundles. The bread was not fresh, but was still soft, and the cheese was the smooth, pale variety sold at the tavern. The stew actually had meat in it.

"Go ahead, do not wait for me," came Mailan's voice.

She even notices pauses, when she chooses. Lifting the lid off the stoneware mug, she sampled the contents and almost gagged. The seasoning!

"I know." Mailan turned and sat on a low stool near the bed. "Bad."

"It has been well preserved," Darame said politically, starting on the bread.

"Slowly," Mailan advised, reaching for the basket. "Make sure your fingers will hold things. How do they feel?"

Wiggling her fingers and then her toes, Darame nodded her satisfaction. "Everything works."

Saffra appeared in a flat-bottomed pot with a slightly chipped spout. Mailan tilted her head toward Darame, raising an eyebrow in an excellent imitation of Sheel.

"Please," Darame told her, gesturing at the mugs.

"You have been with Avis—everyone starts pointing and flinging arms around after they have spent time with her," Mailan commented, pouring two cups of steaming brew.

"Sheel told me to keep an eye on her," Darame offered, one eye on the *guaard*. "It was the least I could do." She did not volunteer anything else. This was strange, at best; Mailan had never spoken to Darame while off-duty. *At least not in any extended manner,* she thought ruefully. That one night of drinking . . . had Mailan been on duty or not? Almost human, then. Granted, there had been no time, no place they could feel Sheel was even moderately safe. Of course Darame never had been one to encourage idle conversation. . . .

"I see you took the pills." Blandly spoken, but the *guaard* was watching her closely.

"Yes. It seemed prudent after the gas attack."

"We shall be interested to hear about your sojourn at the palace," Mailan went on. "A fresh eye is always valuable." She paused to sip her saffra.

Darame suddenly felt as sharp as ever. *Halsey, I think I've found us a route home!* They know nothing . . . or at least nothing they find valuable, even after all this time. And what if no one in Atare city is trying to find the murderers? . . . No one important, that is . . . An odd thought which had troubled her for many days returned to the surface of her mind. She decided to play devil's advocate.

"Well, how goes the investigation?" Darame started, reaching for the other mug of saffra. "Any leads on which *guaard* killed The Atare?" Although she was facing the fire, Darame could still see Mailan out of the corner of her left eye.

The woman stiffened—there was no other word for it. After a

long moment, she turned her head as regally as any queen, her intense gray eyes settling on Darame.

Stretching out her legs toward the fire, Darame arranged herself in a cascade from the cot to a crumpled cloth rug. Only after picking up a wedge of cheese did she glance at Mailan. "Shall we dispense with the games? You have no leads—or few you can use. You told Ayers to shadow me to protect Avis and Leah *from* me. But I didn't try to do anything to them because I never intended them any harm. Not now, not previously—not to any Atare. But I have eyes, Mailan, to see what can be seen, and I know how the guards are placed in that palace complex. Both regular forces and *guaard*, Mailan—the place is crawling with them. And was before the attacks. . . . Only the guards on the outer door have increased. Only the *guaard* on Leah and Avis has increased."

"Your point?" Mailan said tightly.

"It is obvious that only an insider could get close enough to Cort Atare to kill him. Staff would have noticed anyone moving around the palace at an odd time—anyone, even a member of the family. Except a *guaard* or a regular soldier. And the *guaard* would have questioned a regular soldier approaching Cort's private chambers. It had to be someone dressed as a *guaard*. And to actually kill *two* of your group without any noise at all? Another *guaard*, of course—who would catch them unaware, not expecting their own to turn." Darame felt her voice was a bit relentless, but she trusted it was having the proper effect.

"We do not think it happened quite that way," Mailan finally said, draining the saffra in one gulp, heedless of scalding.

"Almost."

There was a long pause. A stick on the fire shifted suddenly, sparks flying into the air. Mailan calmly reached for a poker and began rearranging the burning fragments. "Almost," she said finally. Glancing at Darame, she asked, "Just what are you, anyway?"

"I think you need to be a bit more specific," Darame temporized.

"No games, you said. I have seen people in your line of work before. You are . . . not like them. Close, but not like them. You are too good at what you do, and you do not use drugs to heighten your senses. I checked, when The Atare healed you, after the gas incident. No implants, either. Nothing to be cut off by trade embargoes, nothing to be blackmailed for. . . . You must be expensive, whatever you really do."

This turn in the conversation was unexpected; Darame had expected her records and her mind to be examined. It seemed the Nualans did not hesitate to check even mundane things, like medical implants. . . .

"Your machines do not check for that on arrival?"

Mailan shrugged. "Only illegal or dangerous implants. It is not illegal to be constantly alert . . . just draining. A natural must be solid trine gold to someone."

"And yet I have made more than my share of mistakes this trip," Darame responded, pulling the last of the bread out of the basket.

Mailan actually smiled. It looked good on her face. "You take chances, and use instinct. Sometimes it is clumsy, but ultimately you succeed, yes?" The strange inflection spoke of remote origins, beyond Atare city.

"That is part of it," Darame admitted. She was not sure about the rest of it. Risking the Ragaree on a hunch. . . . *Liar. Why did you come here?*

"So. You will help us?"

"I am not sure I can," Darame began.

Mailan shook her head, still smiling. "Perhaps not. But you have already done quite a bit for us. And I do not think you are seriously in danger. After all . . . questions are asked when a tourist vanishes."

That entire pronouncement was intriguing, but Darame doubted she would get anything more out of Mailan. Not without trading something else. But how to talk without revealing her own reason for coming to Nuala?

A sucker is needed. Brant's words came vividly to mind. She examined them, weighing every last nuance, questioning posture, expression, intonation. *He is going to let Halsey take the blame. Why?* And then a second thought—one which Darame allowed to squelch all other questions, all other reasons for taking risks. *If I help them, the reward could easily rival anything Halsey and I might have gotten otherwise. Better our skins and a little profit than a disaster.* Something nibbled at the corners of this thought, mocking her professed reasoning. . . .

Darame quickly leaned over toward Mailan. "I'll make a deal with you. You get The Atare to agree to immunity from prosecution, for myself and my partners, and I will tell you what I know and what I guess. I suspect you could use an outside perspective."

Mailan's face closed. "I cannot give you such a thing. Almost a dozen murders, our ruler dead, and—"

"Not that." Darame waved a hand irritably, this time recognizing the gesture as Avis's. "For anything else *except* murder. I don't know how tight your laws are, what you classify as Localized Treason. I can't tell you a thing without that guarantee. But I will tell you this: I had nothing to do with Cort's death. *Nothing*. It was unnecessary to why I came here. I can say the same for Halsey. As for anyone else in the extended network of working associates, well, if they were involved in the murders, they deserve whatever is coming to them." On other worlds she would have qualified that, using the word "humane" in some fashion. But the rulers of Atare were the judges, and she could not see Sheel sentencing anyone to a penalty that was less than humane.

The *guaard* stood, a clean, crisp gesture, and started gathering up the dishes. "Rest a bit. I will ask The Atare of this. I will bring you his reply before vespers." Basket in hand, she was gone.

Such abruptness puzzled Darame momentarily. What could they hope she knew? *Do I know it? And if I do, should I tell them?*

"I do not think we can trust her." Mailan spoke in a terse, controlled tone, her rigid stance revealing her irritation.

"Oh?" Sheel prompted, his gaze flicking back to where Tobias learned to throw a pot on a potter's wheel.

"She is withholding information."

Sheel felt one eyebrow lift as he turned to his chosen *guaard*. "Of course she is, Mailan. That is why she wants immunity."

A bit of exasperation slipped through Mailan's control. "I mean I do not think she will tell us what she knows even if you give her protection."

Stirring slightly in his seat, index finger tapping against the table, Sheel considered the problem. "If you mean that she may not tell us what she *suspects*, I believe you are correct. But if Darame knows anything that might help us, she will tell us. Consider your conversation as you related it to me. Darame controlled that talk, Mailan: she implied that she might know something useful to us, and then arranged for you to barter for something useful to her. Why did she do it?" If the woman recognized it as a genuine question, she had no answer. "Several possibilities come to mind. She wants information that only we can give her, for her own reasons, or for her employer. . . . Her official employer, or someone else who has a claim on her services. It is possible that she has observed enough the past moon to make her want to help us for its own sake. But I may be too trusting," he admitted, his elbow settling upon the table, his other hand reaching to support his cheekbone. "She may hope for a reward of some kind from us, or from someone else. . . . She may even be in some sort of trouble, and needs our protection." Holding Mailan's gaze with his own, Sheel added: "I do not think she intends to kill me, if that is what concerns you. She has had several opportunities. The people trying to remove me are in a hurry . . . or were. They would not have wasted an assassin in such a position . . . waiting until all other attempts failed."

"You will give her immunity?" Mailan asked, her face a bit resigned.

"I want you to ask her two questions. First, did she listen to the tape every new visitor is given upon arrival? Second, did she understand it? Tell her I cannot give her immunity from anything in that introductory tape. But anything else I can waive in return for her assistance." Sheel's finger stopped tapping and started migrating toward an empty cup, the motion tracing a sinuous path along the table.

"That is all I should say?" Mailan looked surprised.

The finger stopped moving. "Do not mention names, if you can help it. White's or anyone else's. Other than that, use the information as you see fit." Sheel glanced up at her once again. "I do not suggest you try standard questioning with her. She will talk rings around you. Just get her to join—" Straightening, Sheel seized the cup. "Crow!"

"Atare?" The youth appeared in the entrance to the room.

"Go with Mailan. Get something warm—saffra, cocoa if we have any—and take three mugs to the meeting room. Go over the information Mailan has collected, help her discuss it." Seeing the protest rising in the young man's eyes, Sheel added: "I will sit in the fire room. I can hear what goes on, but you will be close at hand. If you can round up Jude, all the better."

"Fion is on the door," Mailan inserted.

"You can tell him about it later, he knows what you know." Sheel waved it off. "Jude with Tobias, while Mailan escorts Dar-ame. Now." The last was not particularly emphatic, but the *guaard* disappeared.

VESPERS

They were going about it wrong, Darame decided. *No wonder you're not getting anywhere.* In their eagerness for information and their desire to avoid traditional questioning, Mailan and Crow had tried to direct the discussion along a half-dozen paths. Three had led nowhere, and the others left Darame completely lost, since they referred to snips of knowledge unknown to her. Crow had ended up placating and Mailan annoyed. How to turn the conversation in another direction without offending the two *guaard* . . .

"Maybe we should start with theories on who might have done it," Crow suggested, looking from one woman to the other. "Your news of Caesarea is more recent than ours, maybe you have ideas about motive that have not occurred to us." Mailan frowned at him, shaking her head negatively.

"Wrong." Darame took a long sip of the saffra and pulled her blanket closer. The room Mailan had brought her to was larger, hence colder—fortunately they had brought blankets with them. "Forget motive. It's not really important." Caesarean had served them for this discussion. Where was Ayers—with the Ragaree? Had he mentioned her talent for Nualan yet?

"What do you mean?" Now Mailan was frowning at her.

"Just what I said. Motive may be interesting, but it won't get us anywhere. People do things for obscure reasons, Mailan—even murder. Medical types say anyone is capable of murder under the right circumstances, but everyone has different pressure points. *How* it was done is the question. I think you'll find that only a few people could have done it. Eliminate those with alibis, and you've got your murderer." Her words were soft, memory taking over. The man who'd taught her that philosophy was an acquaintance of Halsey's, another old partner. After he and Darame were crossed on a job, he had patiently explained to her his theory of discovering the traitor. A few days later, the erstwhile third partner turned up, dead, and the gold was recovered. But there was no point in telling Mailan and Crow about the details. . . .

"Then where do we start?" This was Crow; he sounded interested.

"At the very beginning, of course. Do you have a screen here?" Darame sat up and reached to arrange a blanket closer to her feet. While she fiddled with her wraps, Mailan brought over a pressure pad and control box. Touching the box, she illuminated a screen, projecting the light onto a stack of wooden crates.

"Good. Now, correct me if my memory is wrong. There was no attack on Avis, Leah, Tobias, or any other member of the royal family except Cort and his immediate male heirs. Correct?" Using the light stick attached to the control box, she began to draw a graph on the pressure pad. Lines of light appeared on the pad, while black lines appeared on the screen projection.

"Seri Baldwin's wife and—" Crow began.

"Incidental. They died because they were with their husbands." Darame lifted her head, meeting his gaze. "Agreed? None of the other wives were attacked, only the ones with their husbands?" Crow nodded. "All right, then. To continue . . ."

She diagrammed the entire evening for them, down to each *guaard*'s position before the attack. "Then we eliminate the technical things."

"Technical?" Mailan said, her tone polite.

"You must have an alarm system. Did anyone check it? Was it operable?" Knowing Mailan had been with Sheel, Darame turned to Crow.

"Yes. I checked it myself at Seri Baldwin's home. It worked."

"No one could have disconnected it earlier, and reconnected it before the deed was discovered?" Darame looked from one *guaard* to the other.

"It is part of the wiring to the house, and has its own back-up system. It was untouched, I checked the historical record on the house." Crow was emphatic, and Darame made a note in Caesarean under the graph. *No tampering with alarm*.

"You understand where that leaves us? I take it the alarm is only a jump away from a *guaard*?"

"The system has multiple end points," Mailan said smoothly. "At least two in each room of the house."

"Worse and worse. It has to be a *guaard*. Did you tell Crow why I thought that?" She glanced at Crow.

"No one else could get close enough." His voice sounded flat, discouraged.

"Yes. Now we get to the strange part. Two *guaard* took a second shift at another station. Why?"

"There is no way to know." Now it was Mailan's turn to sound discouraged.

"No way? How often do you change shifts among yourselves?"

"Never."

"Never? No exceptions?" Darame wasn't sure she believed this statement.

"We are assigned to stations by a trainer, acting under the Captain's direction. The Captain decides who guards which Atare, or is on door watch, hall watch—that sort of thing," Mailan explained. "If an Atare requests a second *guaard*, I could call in and request one in his name—but a trainer would check later to be sure the change or addition was requested by that Atare."

"You checked to see if Cort or Baldwin requested a change, of course?"

Crow nodded. "No record of a request made."

Darame began drawing diagonal lines inside each box of the graph. "All right, we know where everyone was before the shift changed. Then it was—what's after compline, matins?—and the *guaard* changed." She paused at that, her fingernail trailing over the pressure pad, sparks flickering under her finger. Glancing up at Mailan, she asked: "How many *guaard* are usually on The Atare?"

"Two. Also on the heir."

"And everyone else has one, under normal circumstances?" Darame persisted.

"Yes. Although what 'normal' is, I no longer know," Mailan admitted. "Why?"

"Because only one dead *guaard* was found at Cort Atare's side."

Leaping up from her chair, Mailan glided over to the projection, studying it intently. "I do not— Stupid, stupid!" The *guaard*'s hand came up swiftly, and the smack against her forehead was audible.

Crow was too bewildered to speak; he kept looking at the pad under Darame's hand. She did not prompt him; she was still not certain what the information meant.

Mailan finally turned back to face the others, raising a hand to them as if to seize their attention. "We were so busy trying to figure out why Martin and Reese were in the wrong places—" She stopped there, her face frozen, her thoughts far away. "I need a drink." She moved woodenly to a small keg resting on wooden pylons, reaching to the shelf above for a stone mug.

"It all happened so quickly, and *kept* happening," Darame offered quickly. "It's no wonder you have had no time to think clearly. Whoever did this knew that speed was essential . . . and probably intended no survivors."

"We were dupes," Crow said suddenly, his eyes riveted to the dregs of his saffra. "We move as one unit, and think only as ordered. . . . The perfect weapon of war." He looked up at Darame, and the expression in his eyes made her shiver. "Our strength has become our greatest weakness."

Darame nodded. "Someone saw this, and exploited it. Either a *guaard,* or someone controlling a *guaard."*

Crow gestured abruptly, negatively at this statement. "No one controls a *guaard."* As Darame tried to continue, he rushed on, his face set and stubborn. "No. Someone may think they control a *guaard,* but no. Not totally. We act alone when an Atare's life is at stake. We *can* decide for ourselves, if the crisis is upon us. If we have a traitor, he has re-attached his loyalties improperly, that is all."

Darame felt the puzzled look creep across her face. It was Mailan who clarified Crow's impassioned speech, wandering over with her mug of ale. "He means there are shades of loyalty among the *guaard.* It is inevitable, I suppose." Sitting once again, she hunched over her mug. "For example, I am Sheel's *guaard.* He chose me—just as he chose Crow, but in a more dramatic manner. So my primary loyalty would be to him—even if Cort had suddenly decided he should be killed. I would have had to make the decision for myself whom to support in such a case."

"How would you decide?" Darame was fascinated, and the subject of the conversation hushed her voice.

"The only way we can decide: through the body of our oaths. There is a contradiction in the oath a *guaard* swears to The Atare.... I suspect the contradiction is intentional, or at least providential. You did not understand Nualan then, did you?" At this, a gleam lit in the *guaard*'s eyes.

"Not then, no," Darame said, smiling.

"You are good with languages, too." It was a statement of fact. "But the oath . . . It is completed with the line 'for so long as they hold to their charge.' The Atare and Ragaree's response ends in a similar manner: 'holding your trust as I hold to my charge: head, hand, and heart of the heirs, now and forever.'" Mailan's expression grew intent. "Do you understand what I am trying to say?"

"You're saying . . . that killing the heirs is forbidden?" Darame started slowly.

"No. I am saying that the proper raising and protecting of the heirs is The Atare's primary concern—The Ragaree's primary concern. The health of the land hinges on the heirs. They are the symbol of our renewal; our survival. If Cort felt Sheel was a danger to himself, he might have him watched, or restrained— but not killed. Not without absolute proof of treachery, and intent to kill—even if Sheel wanted his throne. Unless Cort could prove Sheel intended to kill him for it, he could not order his death. As you saw in the tape, we take death seriously. Few people actually die, even when we are at war."

"So if one of the heirs wanted the throne, and tried to get it, but failed, The Atare could only banish him?"

"Exactly," Mailan said, nodding. "Unless intent to kill was proved. So Crow is saying that *our* primary loyalty, as *guaard*, is to the throneline of Atare. A ruler is a passing thing, but Atare is forever."

"And someone no longer has the throneline's best interest at heart?" Darame continued, smiling wryly.

"So it would seem."

Darame considered this idea for a while. How could she help these people? They might have actually evolved beyond the rest of the Seven Systems, at least in some respects, but they were lambs surrounded by wolves in other ways. She felt alien among them. Although she had killed only in self-defense, Darame had been angry enough once to plot someone's death. It had been a person who had violated the private code of the free-traders, which was what displaced persons like Darame called themselves. *If Hank hadn't killed him first, I might have.... All because I felt he had betrayed me. I didn't even care that much about the gold. Hank got rid of him and found the gold as well.* A point of honor, that. Different from the methods of other free-traders, like Brant, who she suspected would kill with little provocation.

"Can people who avoid killing succeed against people willing to kill?" Darame murmured the words over her mug, polishing off the last of the saffra. Then an incongruity in Mailan's explanation occurred to her. "Why did Crow have to give Sheel the oath? Didn't he give that oath to Cort when he became a *guaard?*"

Crow nodded in the affirmative to her question, while Mailan looked uncomfortable.

"You did not know then that a *guaard* had turned traitor?" Darame persisted.

"No. But Sheel . . ." She seemed reluctant to speak.

"I had had a nightmare; and my nightmares are the raw stuff of reality," came Sheel's voice from the entranceway leading into the room. "The fire room is smaller, but warmer. Perhaps you all should join me there?" The question held a note of command; the two *guaard* were instantly on their feet.

Rising slowly, Darame pulled one of the blankets closer around her shoulders. Leaning against the support dividing the rooms,

Sheel watched as she reached to pick up the shawl covering her feet while Crow gathered up the screen, control box, and pressure pad. Mailan was busy gathering mugs and a plate; Sheel stopped her with a gesture.

"I have warmed some wine." Gesturing politely for Darame to precede him, Sheel followed her into the adjoining enclosure. "Even Atares are allowed occasional moments of paranoia," he added, sitting near the fire burning in the center of the room.

Was that an explanation or a smoke screen? To draw my attention from your statement about dreams? It was said her father's mother had something his people called The Sight. . . . Something like that? She shivered, only partially from the draft creeping past her bare feet. Of course there would be a draft, how else to draw the little bit of smoke from the room? . . .

"Shall we return to the very obvious point Darame has brought home to us? Only one body was found at Cort's side—in Cort's quarters. Where was the other *guaard?*" Reaching for the mugs Mailan was carrying, Sheel poured hot wine into one and offered it to Darame.

She did not reach for it. "You did not have to hide. I have nothing to say to Mailan that I would not say to you."

"Protecting me distracts them from watching you," Sheel explained patiently, smiling. The mug was still extended.

"I'll take the next one." But she smiled back.

Sighing, shaking his head in mild amusement, Sheel passed the mug to Crow and continued filling containers. He lined up the remaining three and let Darame choose at random, which she did quickly. Crow had set up the screen in the meantime, setting the pressure pad on the table next to Darame.

"What happened to the other *guaard?*" Crow asked as if she were telling a story, and he waiting on the next installment.

"Good question. Let's figure it out. Do you have a copy of the assignment sheet, or whatever you call it?" Darame asked, her eyes quickly taking in the group.

"Roster." Mailan extracted several information rings from one of her myriad pockets. She reached for the control box and inserted first one and then the other. A command was tapped in and the pressure pad graph disappeared, replaced by a split screen showing two rosters. "This one I had when I went on duty that night . . . this one was in the machine the next day. Note that no changes are indicated between the time Jude gave me the first roster, and when she gave me the second. Yet changes have occurred."

"Tampering?"

Mailan shook her head. "Fion checked. The computer has not had its programming changed. The intrusion was legitimate . . . as far as the computer was concerned."

"So changes can be made without indicating who made the changes?"

"Quick," Crow said admiringly, reaching to point at the projection. "All that is required is for a trainer or the Captain to activate the change mode. If they forget to turn it off, anyone can make changes."

"And it would register in the name of the person who left the change mode on?" Darame asked. The two *guaard* nodded. "I imagine that rarely happens, then. It is too important. So the Captain or a trainer recorded the changes. Did you ask the Captain why Martin and Reese were in the wrong place?"

"There was no time for specifics," Sheel began.

"I asked him." Crow's words silenced the group. The others turned to him.

"Well?" Mailan prompted.

"He said he did not know, that he doubted we would ever know, unless we found the killer." Crow looked somber. "Fion says there is only one access code for both captain and trainers. . . ."

"I assume the trainers know each other's numbers?" Darame kept her eyes on her mug. "Why not? So the name on the entry is not necessarily the person who made the changes. Voices can be recorded for voice identification." She pointed to the projection screen. "Are those all the people who were scheduled originally to serve at matins?"

"Yes. All except Martin and Reese."

"The *guaard* found with Cort was not one of his regulars?" Darame kept talking, waiting for inspiration to come.

"No. But he was high enough up that Dirk or a trainer might have sent him there, if there was need." This was from Crow, who was clearly looking for a pattern to her thoughts.

"And no one questioned . . . of course. No one was left to question. . . ." She finally looked up. "I don't think your killer expected anyone to look at that schedule. . . . Even moving Martin and Reese was a last-moment thought. I think the killers—plural —expected to have someone to take the blame, and weren't worried about a proper investigation."

"But how—" Mailan started.

"Mob justice." Seeing their blank faces, she rushed on. "If all had gone as planned, Iver would still be in the hospice, in no condition for anything, Sheel dead, and the two senior *guaard* dead! Leah would be trying to establish some sort of order. Word leaks out that outsiders—off-worlders, or simply non-Atares—killed Cort and the others, and a few names are suggested. Might not a few people take the law into their hands, and see that these people were punished?"

"The constable's officers and the *guaard* would not—" Mailan began.

"But if someone in the *guaard* allowed them to get at the suspected people? Dead men usually don't tell their side of a story." No one tried to break in after that. Both Mailan and Crow looked a bit pale, while Sheel kept his gaze on the fire. "When you've dealt with conspiracies in the past, the *guaard* were all united to find the problem. This time, you have a divided house, and the best of your group actually working against you." She made a face, and decided not to soften her words. "To me it sounds crazy that you never considered such a possibility. But I begin to see why you didn't."

"We did." Sheel's words were very quiet. "As you say . . . it is difficult for us to believe. We may even have a name. But we have no proof."

"Can you highlight Martin and Reese's names somehow?" Darame turned to Crow for this, wanting to shake him out of his scattered thoughts. Reaching over, the young man tapped a few spots on the control membrane, and the names were washed with a pale blue. Darame studied the rosters, her mind still blank, waiting. . . .

"Of course," she whispered. "Stupid child, now who's being dense?" Darame turned to Mailan. "It takes a mag gun to stop one of you, doesn't it? That's why your criminals don't bother with weapons: they're useless against *guaard*."

"Weapons are a capital offense, if turned against a sentient creature. The various troops of the great clans do not need a weapon to immobilize someone, if that is what you are asking," Mailan told her. "Their training is similar to ours. Only we devote our lives to it."

"Even a *guaard* couldn't jump a *guaard*. Unless there was an element of surprise! Don't you see?" Untangling herself from her blanket, Darame moved beyond the firepit to the projection on the crate. "It's a variation of the old shell game! Look—the traitor, someone with authority, takes the kid with him to Cort's rooms. He gives Martin an excuse that Martin accepts, something that makes him go to Baldwin's home. I imagine it's just what it looks like—maybe they arrived before shift change, and he told Martin to take the next shift at Baldwin's and send Reese on down the line. That was a mistake, see—he should have had Reese come back to Cort's, and killed him there, so the body count would be right! But a killer was already waiting for Reese at the other brother's; he had already killed the new shift!" Darame had no idea if they were following her gesturing, but she was sure what she was suggesting was close to the truth. Still . . . "But . . . but that means the killer must have been waiting for Martin, and how—"

"Yes!" Mailan leaped to her feet. "The hospice said they died between matins and lauds, but lauds is canonical for healers! That means it could have been the end of compline, because matins is late this time of year!" She moved to the projection, the others invisible to her. "Baldwin's home is the only place to do it. They come at shift change, someone senior enough that Martin feels it is all right to leave Cort Atare. Martin walks to Baldwin's home—"

"But why not just have Martin tell the next shift to go back to barracks?" Crow protested, slamming his fist on the table. "They killed them for no reason!"

"They could have no witnesses, Crow," Sheel said mildly. "And Baldwin's house is where the search was concentrated . . . after the evidence was removed. Martin arrives at shift change, gives Reese the message, and settles in. The second *guaard* going off duty returns to barracks. But what of the *guaard* actually scheduled for matins?"

"On his way to his death. The second *guaard* was found on the path outside the house, off to the side," Crow said quickly. "Martin gave the message, and then went into the house—"

"No! Don't you see? They didn't have enough time, or enough conspirators!" Mailan's shriek stopped all conversation. "I have watched at Seri Baldwin's, and I know the procedure. One at the outer door, one in the bedroom. If Martin dismissed Reese and his second, he would have waited at the door for the second *guaard*. Who came. With intent to kill. The traitor killed the scheduled person on the way, just as you said, Crow. But somehow a killer took the place of the originally scheduled *guaard*. He must have told— Who was it?" She broke off to examine the projection again. "Dex! The killer told Dex that there had been a change, and he—or she—was on duty with him at Baldwin's. Someone reasonable, possible. So Dex never suspected, never questioned—" She whirled to Crow. "If I came up to you in barracks and told you I was taking a shift with you, would you question it?"

Crow shook his head. "But Mailan...that is so cold-blooded!"

"Isn't it," Darame muttered, studying the screen. "Go on, Mailan, this interests me."

"The killer takes care of Dex just out of earshot, and then comes up to Martin. Even if there was blood, Martin would not see it in the dark."

"Smell it?" Darame asked quickly.

Mailan paused. "Possibly. I do not know."

"No blood," Crow said, gulping some wine. "Dex's neck was broken."

"So, no reason to be suspicious. Except we are always nervous at shift change! And Martin is alert. So Martin, as senior, goes inside, while the other pretends to set up outside. Only he follows Martin inside, and—" Mailan's gesture was graphic; even Darame winced.

"And kills Seri Baldwin and his wife at his leisure, since they probably slept through it," came another voice. The group looked up to see Fion leaning against the opening to the fire room. "I left Ayers on the entrance when I heard the shriek. You are getting noisy in your maturity, Mailan. I take it you are getting somewhere."

Both Mailan and Crow started talking swiftly in Nualan while Darame reclaimed her seat. Seeing the expression on Sheel's face made her feel old and tired. She studied him, ignoring the storm of voices raging above her head. Now he was wooden, no trace of emotion on his face, but during Mailan's speech she could have read him like that projection. Withdrawal was the only word for that delicate pain.... As if Mailan's words had been weapons. As if the betrayal of *guaard* by *guaard* was even worse than what he already knew. *I find I wish I could spare you this....*

The voices had ceased. Looking up, Darame saw that Fion was studying the projection intently. "It works," he said finally. "Unfortunately, it works. Reese is sent to the house farthest from Seri Baldwin's, and meets his death there. I talked to the woman who was supposed to be at Seri Baldwin's.... Dex grabbed her and told her the schedule had been changed, and she was not needed. She did not question him—she had a gentleman to visit, if she was off duty."

"That could have been a loose end," Darame offered. "If Dex had only mentioned a name!"

"No name." There was anger under Fion's regret.

"But that does tell us something," came Sheel's voice. "Whoever left with Dex must have been authorized to watch Baldwin." He did not look up from the fire.

"It's a place to start," Crow said quickly.

"There are other things I wish to know. When I was in the computer, I saw the death toll of *guaard* for that day. It listed nine."

"So? Two bodies at Baldwin's and Caleb's, one everywhere else—" Mailan began, and then stopped, her face suddenly flushed.

"Not everywhere. You were with Sheel. Who else died that day, Mailan? Was anyone sick?" Fion's voice was mild, but his expression was taut as he settled onto a crate, loosening his scarf.

"No illness or accident that I heard about." Crow's words dropped like stones into the pool of silence.

"So . . . who was authorized to watch Seri Baldwin? How are the alibis? And why did an extra *guaard* die?" Mailan spoke softly, pacing away from the projection. When she paused, it seemed almost natural. "And the blood . . . We must check the blood tests."

The group as one turned to her. "I keep forgetting. . . . There has been so little time. Rob reb Dorian of Drake died that night, but not in Seri Sheel's bed. He was on the floor, in the front room. . . . Jude said there was blood all over the bedroom, hallway, parlor— But the woman died from a single blow." Mailan focused on Fion. "He was well trained, that one, to accompany the Seri on his trip?"

Fion nodded slowly. "He could have been one of us, if he was not so high in his house."

"I want to know how that ninth *guaard* died," Mailan said softly. "Once we know how he died . . . we may know where he died. Could one of the conspirators be cold already?"

"That may be too much to hope for," came Sheel's voice. "But you will investigate the possibility."

"But it gives us nothing concrete!" Crow exclaimed, turning to Fion. "Who sent Martin to the heir's home, and how many of these killers do we have to deal with?"

"A half-dozen or so?" Darame suggested. "It is best to keep the numbers low in conspiracies. Somehow I think that one of the *guaard* here would have heard something, if it was a widespread rebellion."

"But how will we find out who is behind this?" Crow turned back to Darame as he reiterated his demand.

Carefully refolding herself into the blanket, Darame sighed. "It is still 'How,' Crow, that we deal with. You say the youth at Cort's was improbable, but not impossible. Who would Martin leave with him, and not question it?"

"Martin?" Crow laughed. "He thought he was the only one who watched Cort Atare properly! That was why he was always on public duty with him: parties, crowd appearances . . ."

"He was an extremely careful man," Fion admitted. A slight frown crossed the *guaard*'s furrowed face, and his eyes flicked up to the projection. "Where were the trainers?"

"Only one on duty," Mailan said, after a moment. "She was with Seri Fabe's wife, on country duty—he would not have brought Serae Camelle into the city for a party thrown by Serae Leah. . . ." Her voice trailed off, and she glanced at Fion, puzzled.

"Edan had just gone off duty, from watching Tobias. He could have made it to Cort Atare's door in time," Crow started, and then jerked, as if struck. "Edan? But Cort—"

"Cort Atare never used Edan—said he was too young to shadow an old man. Martin definitely would have wondered about that, although if Edan told him it was an emergency . . . I do not know." Fion looked grave. "And White—"

"Martin would have called to find out the nature of the emergency," Mailan said swiftly. "He was that way—and he had time, if we are correct, and it was before the shift ended. It had to be, or else Reese would have already left! A call to stop him would have told Reese's second there was a problem . . . and given alarm too soon." She sat down next to Fion on the packing crate, her face very still. "Why keep spinning around the truth? Only one person could have dismissed someone of Martin's seniority without his questioning it, and that is Dirk."

A long silence followed Mailan's whisper. Into the quiet Crow breathed the word "No," even as Darame offered up a rhetorical question. "Why doesn't that surprise me?"

Chapter Nine

Another sleepless night drove Sheel from his bedchamber. Crystle had left him long before, already accustomed to his nocturnal stirrings, so no one except Jude marked his silent padding down to the fire room. His dreams had been uneasy, full of feverish wanderings and disjointed fragments of conversations. The visual images had been vague and shadowed, or complete fabrication. One in particular haunted him: Dirk, tankard in hand, in a jovial mood, uttering words Sheel had never heard him speak: "Our primary loyalty is to the throneline of Atare, you know. A ruler is a passing thing, but Atare is forever."

Mailan or Crow had said those words, trying to explain *guaard* loyalty to Darame. *She did not understand.* How could she? How could anyone not born here understand such a thing? A year on Emerson had shown him numerous governments in action; none of them had anything close to the Atare line and its *guaard*. *Has anyone ever built half their rule on genetic cleanness?*

Entering the fire room, Sheel was surprised to find Darame seated by the pit, tossing on a mixture of heat disks and fire crystal sticks. What was the time? Surely still well-centered in lauds. Much too early to start breakfast.

A smile pulled at his lips as he said aloud in Nualan: "Surely breakfast does not require such early rising." After several pointed comments about the food, Darame had spent her first few days in the cavern delicately weaning old Harald from his cooking pot. The man's wife had sent ample and varied stores, but her husband's talents had little to do with meal preparation. Sheel suspected the old trader secretly had been happy to turn things over to the newcomer.

She looked up at the sound of his words, and Sheel stopped a good meter from the pit, startled by her appearance. The hollows under her eyes were black, accented by firelight. Exhaustion had pulled thin lines at her mouth and nose.

"You are sleeping worse than I am," he said tersely, shocked into bluntness.

Darame smiled wanly. "I seem to have a faulty thermostat. Either I am cold, or I sweat from the mound of blankets Mailan tosses over me." Her answer was in careful, unaccented Nualan, but the sheer attempt always amazed him. Few people tried to speak Nualan, far fewer succeeded at it; its marked formality was foreign to any language used in the Seven Systems. He had learned that Darame could converse in so many tongues she could not list them all without thought. . . .

Sitting down on a low stool, Sheel noted she had moved the stove into the fire room and was heating some cherry apple cider in a pan. "Cold sensitivity can be caused by many things. Perhaps I can help."

Sprinkling some cinnamon into the bubbling liquid, she smiled slowly. "I am not Nualan." The planet's name was usually the hardest thing for foreign mouths to form, but she did it handily.

"Planet origin has nothing to do with it," he answered, standing to seek some mugs. "My speciality is human anatomy . . . with a little 'cat work' thrown in."

"I miss the cats," she admitted. "Their warmth, their funny ways, their inquisitive little faces peering out at me from odd places. Too bad we had to leave them at your house."

He had found the mugs and returned to the fire. An image caught him as he set the ceramic tankards before her, the memory as sharp as smoke. A cold, windswept day, with them seated on his deck, this woman wrapped in one of his capes, her hands busy with the kitten. What was she saying? "All I heard her say was 'He will place her before me.'" What had brought that thought to him? His dream involving Dirk?

"Atare?" He heard the word at a distance, its meaning barely registering. "Sheel?" She reached for him, delicate fingers touching the back of his wrist. He glanced up and realized he had paused in mid-movement. Flushing slightly, he let go of the mugs and sat down.

"Something you said brought back another image. . . ." His words trailed off as he considered what she had described. Why would Leah say such a thing to an ambassador—Brant, was it not? Probably she used several of them as confidants, but why did he suddenly picture her telling Dirk those words? For the memory had twisted on him, and she was speaking to Dirk, not Brant.

"The cats?" she said, pouring them each some cider.

He shrugged and accepted a mug. "Possibly. Actually, there is something else seeing you brings to mind." He sipped carefully at the warm fluid. "For more days than I would like to count, Mailan and Fion have argued about the conclusions reached by your little discussion group." The irony in his voice did not pass unnoticed; she gave him a quick grin. "The storm aided us, there: they would have thundered off to Atare, bursting with theories, and likely provoked many things I would rather let lie. But this flurry of voices has kept me from returning to a remark you made . . . a remark I have wondered about. Darame, why, when signs pointed to Dirk as being part of a conspiracy, did you say you were not surprised?"

At first she did not speak. Careful with the hot cider, her boot shoving at what Sheel recognized as a cast-iron bread mold half-buried in heat disks, Darame seemed to ignore the question. Then she cast her black gaze at him, eyes slit with concentration. "Same rules apply?"

That took a moment. Then he remembered her request for immunity from prosecution. He nodded.

"You are not going to like the"—she lapsed momentarily into Caesarean—"implications of this."

"Probably not," he agreed. "But I suspect I should hear it."

"The palace suited my present situation quite well," she started, setting the mug down by her side. "I enjoyed getting to know your younger sister, and palaces are notorious hotbeds of gossip and innuendo. But there is always a grain of truth in such information, if one knows how to sift it. And, as I told Mailan, I have eyes to see." She turned slightly, looking at him directly. "Dirk is one of Leah's current lovers," Darame said calmly. "The preeminent one, I would say, although one ambassador seems to be giving him a run for it. She has not lived with her husband Richard for several years, although Tobias does, often—and Richard would have her back any time she chose to join him. Dirk is always with your sister, Sheel—always. They are usually shadowed by another *guaard*, so it does not seem to be duty, exactly. Deepest rumor says he is crazy about her, and would do anything for her. I suspect that is part of the reason people seem to fear Leah: through Dirk she has access to a lot of privileged information, if he chose to give it to her." She reached once again for her mug. "But that was a hard tidbit to dig up; apparently

Dirk does not like the rumor that he is being led about at her skirts, and his hand falls heavily on those who repeat it."

"She has a way with men, my sister. They cannot resist her," Sheel supplied, tacitly encouraging her to continue.

"Just how strong is she, Sheel? Would a man do anything for her? Anything? Even something . . . she may not have actually requested?" Darame's expression was strange, intent.

"I do not know. Leah does not affect me that way. But she controlled Caleb and Iver with that charm," he admitted.

Darame stared down into her drink. "I know I told Mailan and Crow that motive was unimportant when looking at murder, but it can often back up a theory. I like to . . . play games in my mind. Puzzle games, word games, number games. People often figure into my games. . . . Sometimes that keeps me alive. I notice things about people, things others take for granted or miss completely. And, most importantly"—she lifted her head as she said this, facing him again—"I connect things other people do not. Or perhaps fear to connect."

"That was certainly enough preparation for the ruler of the wealthiest clan on Nuala," Sheel said gently. "I think you should tell me what is bothering you."

"How much does Dirk hate off-worlders?"

That surprised him—echoing Crystle's words of days before . . . He had not thought of that angle. "I . . . No more than any other Nualan. I think Dirk is a proud man, proud of himself and his line, which is well-off and breeding well. But I do not remember any incident that . . . would lead me to believe he *hated* off-worlders." This was truth; he did not see what she was leading him toward.

"Before we start arguing fine points, let me tell you some specific things I have picked up while living in the palace. Not why I believe them, just the basic information. All right?" The mug returned to the floor of the cave.

Nodding, Sheel leaned back against a crate, feeling it slide until it touched a fissure in the rock.

"To begin with, your sister Leah is an incredibly insecure woman. She has no confidence in herself or her position, and is jealous of anything she regards as infringing on her province. I suspect she was enraged that you took Tobias—not worried, although she put on a good act, talking about it a lot—enraged. She will not forgive you for it. She hated Cort Atare, partly because he did not name her ragaree, and partly for other reasons. She was fond of Caleb and Iver. . . . Whether because she

had them under her finger, as you suggest, or simply because
their characters and hers matched well. She does not trust you, or
so hints lead me to believe. I suspect she thinks you favor Avis
over her—" She held out her hand as Sheel started to speak. "I
know, Cold Sleep divides your family into obvious blocks, of
course you would be closer to Avis. I said 'favored,' which was
what I meant. And she hates Avis."

Something about the way Darame said "hate" sent a shiver up
Sheel's spine. It was emphatic.

"Not that Avis is ever discourteous, or condescending, or any
such thing to Leah. In fact, she is very careful to keep from
offending Leah. But it is understandable, considering the age
difference, that they would not be close. At any rate, Leah hates
Avis, is jealous of her, watches her constantly. She certainly
thought Cort Atare preferred Avis—which, as a person, he probably did."

"Dirk?" Sheel asked.

"I shall return to Dirk. Another question for you. What could
helping Leah get someone?" As Sheel started to frown, Darame
continued: "I mean, what exactly does her power base consist of?
What can she give for services rendered?"

Sheel sighed and reached for the pan of cider. "Leah has what
any member of the royal family has, I suppose. Large amounts of
mining stock and influence. She has quite a bit of control in the
trading industry, I understand, and, as you suggested, I have
heard rumors that she will use blackmail when nothing else will
serve her ends. Although be careful whom you tell that to: there
is no proof that I know of, and as blackmail is illegal, that could
be libelous." He lifted an eyebrow at her. "Her lovely body, of
course, has often gotten her what she wanted. A vast network of
embassy friends and informants of the highest level—"

"Is it because of Leah that Dirk is captain?"

Sheel considered the question while he poured some more
cider for himself. "She could not have arranged it . . . but she had
Caleb's ear, and Baldwin listened to Caleb. Cort, of course,
would at least give Baldwin courtesy hearings. Dirk has had a
very distinguished career, Darame. He was the popular choice for
the position."

"The Atare and the trainers select the captain. If several
trainers were offered inducements to make him captain? If he was
already in the running, anyway?" She looked intent once again.

"No. I doubt that. But if careful maneuvering made Dirk Cort's
main choice, they might take it as a sign to follow his lead. Cort

respected strength, and preferred to deal with a strong captain, rather than a board of trainers." *One on one*, Sheel added to himself.

"Yet I understand Dirk did not approve of Cort's handling of the Dielaan incident." She seemed to choose her words carefully.

Smiling, Sheel paused to sip some hot cider. "No. Dirk *does* hate Dielaaners. Our rivalry extends back more than a thousand years. I think Dirk would have liked to use the strength of the extended *guaard* to crush the Dielaan trade routes, crippling them for generations. Cort did not feel that was a wise move, and made a truce with them, after extracting reparation for the damages they inflicted on the mines." He stretched his legs off to one side. "Dirk wants to be a warlord, I think. But Cort had no mind to destroy another of the great houses."

Darame studied him several moments, and then said: "Here is the big question: Can anyone control Leah?"

This time Sheel looked over at her. "I have been asking myself the same question. Did whoever arranged all this realize that Leah would be Tobias's regent, and did he—she, they—think he could control her? I do not think Leah can be controlled." He folded his legs up, wrapping long fingers around his knees. "I never knew her first husband, I was in transit when they returned. They had little over a year before he died in that accident, but I understand they were happy. He was a strong man, it is said, and she preferred him to lead. She lost their only child shortly after— a girl. Leah had to take ship for Caesarea almost immediately, and was still back nine years before we returned from Emerson. I suspect her controlling urges started the second trip—Richard being so pliant reflects that. She fears loss of control, and so she tries to dominate everything, or something like that." Sheel felt a frown creeping across his face. "I tried to let her know she could confide in me. . . ."

"I think it was too late, Sheel. Whatever triggered this behavior in her was entrenched before you returned." It was Darame's turn to frown. Taking a deep breath, she rushed on. "Do you begin to see what I am hinting at? You have a neurotic, jealous woman, terrified of losing anything she has declared is hers. A proud, arrogant man controlling the *guaard*, a man who openly disapproved of his Atare's policies concerning the *guaard*. Suddenly there is a string of assassinations, and Iver is Atare. And do not try to tell me Iver could stand up to Leah's strength, especially with Dirk backing her."

"Iver is dead." It sounded more flat than he'd intended. "And I would have helped him stand up to her."

"But *you* were supposed to be dead, Sheel. Then what? Would Iver have named her ragaree?"

"No. It has been done, but it would be bad form to do it before she had a daughter. But he would have *treated* her as The Ragaree." This was treading on dangerous ground; Darame was entirely too quick. It could be disastrous for her to start thinking about Leah's fertility, and speak of it aloud.

"Something you would not have done, since for all you know Leah might have nothing but sons the rest of her life, or no more children at all." It was Darame's turn to stretch. "So, perhaps Dirk would have gotten a lot of things out of Cort's death. But why not stop at Caleb? Why use Iver?"

"Caleb was a selfish personality," Sheel admitted. "Assuming the chain of office might have changed his prior loyalties considerably."

"So—Iver. But then Iver died. . . . You think because he knew the *guaard* was behind this?"

"At least a few *guaard*," Sheel corrected. "He would have told Dirk and Leah, just as he told me, but how he did so, I do not know—" He broke off at the look on her face. The woman was suddenly quite pale. "Darame?"

A jerk of her body, and she was leaning forward, reaching for thick pads to shield her hands. "I forgot about the bread, I hope it is not burned."

Sheel closed his reaching fingers, stopping short of her shoulder. "What else?"

"Have you noticed how similar the situations are in Atare and in Seedar?" she said quickly, pulling the enclosed bread pan from the fire. "I have trouble thinking it is coincidence."

"I cannot believe it is coincidence," Sheel answered, sitting back on his heels. "But I cannot connect Dirk to Seedar. Can you?" This last was very soft; Darame's musings were too close to his own, and threatened to bring up something he did not want to face.

Breaking open the hinged mold, Darame removed a long roll of bread. "Crusty but not burned; excellent. I thought I saw some honey around here somewhere."

Sheel stood up. "It is in the next room. I will bring it in here." He moved quickly into the corridor. Jude remained in place, like a bas-relief carved from the wall, while Sheel retrieved the honey pot and carried it into the fire room. The break in conversation had given him time to compose his face. *Do not think about it. At least not yet.*

Crossing his legs, Sheel folded down beside her, handing her the honey. As their hands brushed, Darame actually jumped, as if touched by static electricity. Guiltily she lifted her face, meeting his gaze.

"I . . . I am not ready to theorize past this point. Everything else is still very confused." It sounded rather weak, but at least she was admitting the cause for her distress.

"More confused than seeking motives for Dirk being a traitor?" Sheel regretted the words before they'd finished leaving his mouth.

She shook her head as she broke off a piece of bread. "Motives are always a mess to deal with. But, Atare—"

"By now I would think you could use 'Sheel' comfortably."

Silence. A few more deep breaths. Then: "I agree that connecting Dirk to Seedar is difficult. I imagine he dislikes the other clans almost as much as Dielaan."

"Almost—not quite as much." Sheel felt his dimples fighting to break out. When she fixed her dark eyes on him, however, he lost all desire to laugh.

"To a certain extent, Dirk could be a single threat, acting on his own to get something for himself and the woman he seems to adore. Or . . ."

"He could be working with Leah to actively place official power into her hands." Amazing how steady his voice sounded saying the words, beating her to them. They were not surprising words; something within had been thinking along those lines for a long time. *Can you not protest, not even the slightest? She is accusing your sister of condoning murder!*

"It is worse than that, Sheel. If Atare and Seedar are truly linked, then there must be someone else involved. Someone who unites the others, and pulls their needs and desires together. Someone who recognized both your sister and the *guaard* as weak links in the Atare chain . . . and is exploiting those weaknesses." Her voice was barely audible over the crackle of the fire.

"And you think you know the identity of the third person." He said the words as fact.

Darame nodded.

"Will you tell me the name of that person?"

The woman shook her head slightly. "Not yet."

A feeling of disquiet crept into Sheel's stomach. He recognized it as disappointment.

"I wish you would stop rationalizing!" The volume surprised even Fion; his mouth closed abruptly and he reddened.

Mailan had always felt that the best defense was silence; she did not respond. Her hands did hesitate, however, as she sorted through her belongings, deciding what she would leave and what she would need in the foothills below. Fion's hand shot into her line of vision, seizing her left wrist.

"Look at me." It was an order. He had been her trainer; old habits died hard. She turned her head, looking down at him. "There is no more to be said. It never could have been anyone except Dirk—you see that, now? Unless one of the line has indeed betrayed us all. Do you think Iver went and supervised Cort's death before engineering his own attack?"

"Of course not." She turned back to her packing.

"Then stop torturing your conscience! I know well that however much you dislike Dirk and his inner circle, you would never accuse them of such a thing without proof." Fion leaned toward her, his lips almost brushing her shoulder. "So find the proof."

That stopped her. She turned and dropped to the cot with a thump, giving the *guaard* a steely look. "Do you think a *guaard* would leave proof of his passing?"

"Dirk? Unlikely. I doubt he switched Martin and Reese's names. But his followers are clumsier. Iver saw that a *guaard* stabbed him—perhaps even saw who stabbed him. Somehow an extra body showed up on the count that day, a body that no one was supposed to notice. Such mistakes may lead to the proof we need!"

"And if they do not?" There. She had said it; the fear of her heart. If they *could not* prove it—then what? Return to Atare and spend the rest of their lives looking over their shoulders? Ring Sheel's home with trainees? Take others into their confidence? Jude and Ayers were shaken by the news, true, but Crow's shock still had not completely abated, which was one reason he would accompany her on her mission. How would other *guaard* respond to the reality of a traitor in their midst?

Fion smiled faintly. "Maybe we will hire our own assassins." He chuckled as he said it, but his eyes were very dark.

"Fion . . ." Mailan reached for a stack of socks. "You mentioned once that you could only think of trivial reasons for Dirk to turn on Atare. What were you thinking about?"

Frowning slightly, the man seated himself next to her on her cot. "They are things only a petty man would use to keep score. I have never thought of Dirk as petty."

Mailan smiled, a twist to her lips. "Yet I have always thought him petty." She turned to look at him. "Fion... you are not of Dirk's generation, and I doubt he sees you as a threat. He is too arrogant to see threat in a man close to retiring from the field." Grinning at her friend's lifted eyebrows, she continued: "I do not wish to sound conceited, but... if there had been an older choice for captain willing to take it, who do you think the successor would be? Dirk? Or would he be back running his family's wealth by then, and someone else be chosen?"

Fion reached to tug on one of her curls. "Troublemaker. You would be right up there in line, as you well know. And that is a good point: Is Dirk willing to give up the prestige and wealth of his family position to continue as a *guaard*? Many think not, which is why some gave the captainship to him now. They expect him to retire in a few years."

"At any rate, he has always gone out of his way to make things hard for me... as if it hurt his pride that an ignorant mountain girl was as strong a *guaard* as he." She waved off his interruption. "I am telling this from Dirk's point of view, remember. To me, pettiness is his middle name, and White nothing but a sneak. But those trivial things?" she prompted finally.

"Two things keep coming to the surface of my mind," Fion confessed. "Have you noticed Dirk has not married? Others of his rank either chose an off-worlder who came here to marry, or left for Caesarea. Dirk loved a native, apparently... but her family forbade the match. They wanted 'clean, outside genes.' I know Dirk resented that. He started competing for active work in the *guaard* not long afterward. And then... did you know that Dirk is an Atare?" Fion looked at her sharply as he spoke.

"So are we— You mean he is throneline?" Mailan realized the volume level of the discussion had increased, and lowered her voice. "Are you sure? He does not have the eyes."

Fion smiled. "'Are you sure?' Dirk's eyes are corrected. Even I have never been around when he cleans the lenses, every month or so. Besides, you know as well as I that the eyes do not breed true from the men. When the trait is present, it appears, but when it is not—none of that line ever show it. It is a strong trait, but while it always overcomes off-world genes, Nualan genes are stronger. That is why so few of the unnamed have the eyes."

"His father?"

Fion shook his head. "Further back than that. But Dirk's family was entwined with Atare long before he became a *guaard*. That is all I know."

"Have you noticed how closely Dirk attends to the Serae Leah?" she asked, suddenly changing the subject.

"She seems to prefer him to other *guaard*, and The Atare apparently did not object to surrendering Dirk's talents to her." Fion's expression was carefully neutral, implying he did not speculate on that situation.

Mailan felt a smooth, narrow smile settle over her features. Sparks of The Path: certainly Fion had wondered as much as she had, although naturally she had forgotten about it in the hysteria surrounding the deaths of Cort and his heirs. One of the latest rumors to surface was that Dirk, too, had access to Leah's bed. Did that change any theories their little group had dissected? Well, she was not going to point *that* one out to Sheel, if the rumor had not yet reached his ears. But she and Crow would have to investigate it. "I think I will ask The Atare what he and the Caesarean spoke of this morning." Glancing at Fion, she added: "That woman knows more than she tells, and I will not tread these paths until I know what she hides. Too much rides on it."

"She will not volunteer information until it serves her purpose." Fion sounded neutral, usually a sign of disapproval. But then his devotion to the line was absolute. Mailan freely admitted she was Sheel's *guaard* first . . . and for some reason Sheel seemed to want—no, need—that woman in his shadow.

"I think I can force it from her," Mailan murmured, thinking furiously. It had occurred to her last night. . . . Something Darame had said, or not said, in her talks. Not much about Avis. The off-worlder had liked Avis—a chink in her shield. *Anything Darame knows that we do not endangers Avis. We will be like stampeding tazelles without the complete story.* She was on her feet and heading toward Sheel's sleeping area, her last words echoing in the corridor: "To defeat that one, you must tell her the truth."

Darame shifted once again before the firepit, trying to find a position that was both warm and comfortable. Such a blessing that these heat disks and sticks—fire crystals, wasn't it?—gave off so little smoke. At least the wind was from the right direction; the natural flue which rose within the cavern was carrying most of the smoke outside. A murmur of soft voices was harmony to her thoughts, the clink of breakfast dishes reminding her that the meal was not long past. Cooking had occupied her mind, keeping it from facts she dreaded facing. Now, there was no place to hide.

Well . . . she would face the nightmare, even if it was not of her making. So, Sheel was certain Iver had told Leah and Dirk about seeing a *guaard* stab him. How much had he seen? A slip of uniform? A face? Several faces? Words she had nearly forgotten now haunted her—words that had meant little when she overheard them. As clearly as the moment it happened, the scene rose up before her: the pale blue light of Brant's office and the swift entrance of Serae Leah framing the words.

"Brant, you must speak to Iver, he is raving on about last night and demanding an inquiry—" No more; Leah had then noticed Brant's company, and stopped speaking.

Did you ever explain to her our unique relationship? Darame wondered, nodding approval as Quenby Ragaree's little girl brought her stitching for the silver lady's inspection. Probably not, judging by Leah's treatment of the off-worlder. Then again . . . Leah perceived all women as competition, in all things. Maybe Brant *had* mentioned his companions. . . . *I hope not.*

Sheel had his link. Serae Leah had said "you." As if Brant had some influence with Iver, and could somehow sway his thoughts, his line of thinking. Brant had claimed inroads with both Iver and Caleb, of course, but . . . that Leah should ask Brant to intervene . . .

Darame realized she was shaking. *Are you a kingmaker, man who would be king in all but name?* It had been years since she had played chess, or even found anyone else who knew the game, her father's favorite puzzle. *And you—blinded by your own involvement, worried about knights and missing the bishops! Are you pawn, blindly following the path Brant has set your feet to, or will you be a queen, and cover the board with your schemes?* Pawn or queen—the eternal question, the question her father had always asked her when things got tough. But then he had treated his child like an adult, always. . . .

Leah and Dirk . . . and Brant. Of course Sheel would not see it—he had no knowledge of how the free-traders arranged their games. But Darame knew what part was Brant's, and now understood that he had played his hand too well. Find the weak links, and exploit them: the age-old rule. To an outsider's eye, Leah was an obvious weak link. She had to be, or else Brant would not have bothered with her. Sex, like everything else, was merely a corollary of power for Brant. Avis? An ace up the sleeve, as the old card-skimmers would say. Iver? Gulled, she was sure. Iver was not subtle enough to be trusted with details, even if he had agreed to any schemes, which she doubted. Darame suspected that Iver was a fifth suit: a dupe used to deceive opponents as to the real depth of one's game.

The Serae was obvious, but how did Dirk fit into things? As a necessary power piece, yes—but what bait was Brant using? Blackmail was his least favorite form of inducement. What could Brant offer Dirk that would make the *guaard* turn on his ruler and peers?

And Seedar. Again Darame cursed the tribes as a whole, wishing for some form of friendly communication. Only trickles of information passed from one city-state to another, unless it concerned gene recombination. Not until a ragaree had both feared for the lives of her heirs *and* was unable to trust her near kin had a dialogue been established. And if there had been no Avis—no sympathetic, patient ear free of judgment? What would Quenby Ragaree have done? What was happening in Dielaan . . . in Kilgore, Andersen, and the other great cities? Brant knew how to set up black market undergrounds; Darame had helped him do it in one city on Caesarea. That scam was still pouring money into Brant's accounts. Now that she concentrated, she remembered Fion saying something about off-worlders traveling on the great roads. . . .

A scam with Leah and Dirk, and a scam without them . . . and courting the unmarried daughter of the line on the side. Darame straightened as potential presented itself to her. *Sweet Saints, Brant! Get rid of that neurotic woman and Avis's young man, and you could be running the entire coast within five years!* It was a kingmaker play in more ways than one. . . . Was Brant willing to follow through? To risk everything and anything for the goal he sought? *Even your own skin?*

"Darame?" The word broke into her disconcerting thoughts. Glancing up, instinctively drawing her poncho closer, Darame realized that Sheel and Mailan were standing next to her.

"Did you bring saffra?" she asked them, and was rewarded with one of Sheel's increasingly rare smiles. That smile struck her like a blow, cutting into the depths of her musings. *This is what you came for, foolish child. You followed the memory of a smile. . . .*

"I will get some for all of us," came Crystle's voice from somewhere off in the dimness of the area. A rustling of material was followed by soft footsteps as the woman departed the room, the Quenby Ragaree's little girl close at her heels, if the echoes were any indication.

"I have told Mailan about our talk early this morning," Sheel said without preamble. "She would like to pursue several points with you. Any help you can give my retinue would be appreciated." The man settled himself upon one of the peeled bark chairs the potters had left; Mailan remained standing.

Retinue. I suppose they are your retinue at that. Strange to see a monarch cut off from his advisors.... Afraid of his advisors? Could the web of treachery stretch further into the royal sphere? But Brant liked to keep his conspiracies small....

"What do you need to know?" Darame asked carefully.

Mailan drew herself up and took a few thoughtful steps away from the firepit. Keeping her back to the pair, she said: "Thank you for speaking of what we all feared to mention—that the Serae could be involved in this somehow. I still find it hard to believe that she would agree to a dozen deaths to reinforce her power base, but"—Mailan shook herself abruptly—"we may never know the entire truth. Better to concentrate on weeding out the sandburs in our compound." She turned back to Darame. "I suspect you know I dislike my captain."

"The possibility had occurred to me," Darame said gently, a smile drawing in one corner of her mouth.

"Still, with a charge so serious, I feel I must have total proof of the deed." Mailan allowed herself a brief smile in return. "Just knowing Dirk's personality, I could believe he would kill what he saw as a useless old man. But why choose Iver over Caleb, who had a grudge against Dielaan? . . ." She shrugged.

"How much do you know about Dirk's personality?" Darame asked, watching the woman's delicate face. Not pretty, precisely, but those huge eyes would draw attention from any healthy man.

"He is . . . a man of extremes. Devoted to his family, to his friends, to those who serve him well."

"And those who do not?" This time Darame spoke in Nualan.

"He . . . 'leans' on those who displease him. His hates are as vigorous as his loves." Mailan lost her guarded look, and spoke earnestly. "He could be shadowing Serae Leah because he is honestly worried about her. Even if he did kill the others, or arranged it—what if someone else decided to pick up where he stopped?"

"True," Darame agreed. "That is a problem. I suspect that there are several things going on, and several people involved. One hand may not know what the other is doing. Could any of the outclans be involved?"

Mailan frowned. "Dielaan was hit hard when we retaliated, and other clans would mostly heed their example. Always possible . . . but I still doubt it. Dirk is well known to be totally loyal to Atare, and merciless with outsiders. Or was..." Her face tightened.

"Including off-worlders? All outclans? Even sinis?"

"Oh, yes. Dirk resents off-worlders tremendously. I am always surprised when he makes a . . . friend . . . of one, and it never lasts long. He will not go out for a wife, and he resents being told he is less than any of these foolish men who come here looking for wealthy brides—" Mailan smiled at the look on Darame's face. "It works both ways, Serae. Men come here as well, trading on a pretty face and good health, hoping for a rich marriage with a woman who does not demand fidelity or hard work."

"Resents all but Atare. . . . Then why turn on Atare?" Darame said it softly, considering Mailan's words and trying to make them fit into previous talks. A new pattern emerging. . . .

"I do not understand it, either," Mailan admitted, "unless he thought he could convince Iver to attack Dielaan. Fion tells me he is even a descendant of the royal line, somehow. It would be like turning on your own family—"

Darame straightened, the rest of the sentence lost to her. Could that? . . . But that would be impossible, unless Leah could control the labs as well. . . . Could she? *If he loves her, and does not want her to lose her position . . . a position two off-world husbands have not been able to secure—* "Does Dirk have any children?"

Mailan had broken off when she saw Darame become preoccupied. Now she frowned again. "I think so, but not named children of his house. He has no wife."

"So he is a 20."

"Yes—heir to his house's industry. He will have to resign eventually, and take over the family business. A common excuse for his push into authority at a young age." There was a neutrality in her last words which Darame recognized as veiling irony.

Find the weak links, and exploit them. It clicked in her head as cleanly as a clasp on a chain. "What a mess." Darame bowed her head over her hands, pushing back loose strands of hair. The grit under her fingernails could not distract her from the words echoing in her head. *Weak links. Weak links.*

A familiar fragrance floated to her nostrils, of delicate flowers. "Darame?" Saffra was pushed at her.

"Thank you, Crystle." She actually managed a smile for the woman, which seemed to startle her. *Do you think I resent you? How can I resent you when I rejected what you so ardently desired? Weak link, weak link . . .*

It must have been only moments, for Sheel and Mailan still waited attentively. Sipping at her drink, Darame allowed herself to meet their intent expressions. "Sh— Atare, we—" She paused. It was sometimes hard to call Sheel by name, especially when the *guaard* were present. As if it were an intimacy which could draw them closer together. . . . "We have Dirk's weak link. More than one of them, in fact." As Mailan scowled and started to speak, Darame continued quickly in clipped Caesarean: "I didn't say it would make complete sense. We're not dealing with totally rational people. We've got an insecure woman trying to solidify a power base. What she really needs is more children to do it, and for some reason her husband isn't giving them to her, which is why I suspect she's stopped sleeping with him. Can people become sterile after coming here? If their systems can't take it?"

"It has happened," Sheel admitted slowly.

"Anyway, then there is Dirk, who looks down on and resents these weak off-world men, none apparently capable of giving the woman he adores what she wants."

"But . . . the Seedar situation coming on the heels of Atare," Mailan began.

"Or too late? Or maybe Cort Atare died too soon? What Dirk, Leah, and their partners want may be very different than what they tell each other they want!" That made even better sense, when Darame thought about those off-worlders heading off to other city-states. Why would Dirk panic . . . or not panic, but act before Brant intended?

Her gaze flicked from Mailan to Sheel, and then an odd feeling began to grow within her stomach. How could she tell him any of this without looking like an accessory . . . or, worse for her pride, a dupe? *Can I afford pride? Can I convince him I'm not a murderer?* The rest made no difference—she was not ashamed of how she lived. Predators always made a herd stronger. . . .

"I think you should be very careful around Dirk, Mailan, if you intend to speak with him. He has already killed *guaard*. A few more bodies may not concern him. It is just as you feared." Unfortunately, Mailan's face showed she clearly did not make the connection. Darame tried again. "He has changed his priorities. His loyalty is now to Leah and Leah's line, I suspect. Tobias is in no danger . . . but Sheel certainly is."

"And Avis." Mailan said it as a fact, and something tightened around Darame's heart.

"Of course." Sheel's whisper drew both their attentions. Turning sharply to Mailan, he said: "I want you to trace Dirk's family tree, his education—anything you can find out about him."

"Sheel . . ." Darame purposely chose to use his name; as she hoped, she immediately had his attention. "I think there is a much bigger game going on, one Dirk probably isn't sure of, even if he's smart enough to suspect it." Taking a slow, deep breath, Darame chose. "Do not allow the Caesarean Embassy to monitor your movements, Mailan. Do not trust any of them, because I suspect one of their superiors is involved in this, and any underling might report to him." Swiftly she told them of being in Brant's office when Leah and Dirk entered.

"Not good," Mailan agreed when she'd finished. "But it could be innocent—that Iver made friends with this ambassador and—"

"No. Brant has no friends who are not useful to him. Believe me, Mailan, the man does nothing without potential profit in it. He grew up from poverty and abuse to take what he wanted when he wanted it. In fact, I have seen him infiltrate the underground of a city and take it over. I do not know what kind of black market you have on Nuala—"

"Nebulous. We keep identifying the potential leaders and pushing them off unsteady pedestals," Mailan supplied.

"In that case, it is ripe for takeover. And Brant specializes in finding weak links and exploiting them. He will have a united underground in a year's time, if that is what he is up to, and I doubt you will be able to locate him, much less stop him."

"You speak from experience?" Sheel's voice was very quiet.

Darame considered her position. *Peter's Keys! Why does it matter if he thinks badly of me? Idiot.* "I have worked with Brant in the past. I came here to help in a 'Mirror Game,' which is when you locate someone you can cheat with their own greed and dishonesty. Brant was supposed to do the groundwork and find the weak links: people who could help us get the contracts we wanted. Caleb and Iver were considered weak links, as was Leah. But I have seen this man betray his partners before, and I don't trust him—I came here partly because I did not want my mentor working with him alone. Now I think Brant figured out an even better deal, a deal that cuts all of us out and sets him up for life. He will have the underground, and whatever influence he has with Leah, an inroad with the *guaard*—"

"No. Dirk would not allow himself to be controlled, and I doubt he could be blackmailed without the ambassador giving himself away. Surely Brant would keep his post as long as he could?" Mailan said.

"I would think so—" All of a sudden light broke into her thoughts, and Darame jumped so sharply her saffra spilled. "Sebastian's Arrows! And *I* gave him still another possibility, although he must have already—" Rising to her feet, she seized Mailan's shoulders. "Get back to Atare immediately! You have to get some more people you trust on Avis! And...maybe on Leah." Releasing the woman, Darame bent with trembling fingers to recover her saffra. The enormity of what she had done made her momentarily weak.

Hands reached into her line of vision, righting the mug and pouring more of the liquid into the container, even as they guided her back to her seat. Sheel's voice asked smoothly: "What have you done?"

"I tried to protect Avis from Leah," she whispered. "I was thinking that Dirk and Leah was a momentary thing, or even a convenience, but that Leah's resentment of Avis was long-term, and..." She finally met his odd eyes. "Avis is pregnant."

His response made no sense. First a gleam of pleasure, followed by a stillness that seemed to deepen into quiet unease. *I knew it, I never should have told her to say that—* "It is probably Stephen Se'Morval's child, but I told her to say it might be Brant's," Darame continued. "I thought that if Brant knew it, he might protect her from Leah even if Leah decided a little poison or something might take care of *that* problem—" Darame raised her hands in entreaty. "I think of the picture as having *you* in it! It never occurred to me— I mean, without you Leah is Regent, but without Leah, is Tobias still Atare?"

"Until Avis would bear a daughter and a son, yes. Then her son would become first in line for the throne. Power passes though one woman," Sheel whispered, his thoughts clearly elsewhere.

"Brant is perfectly capable of discarding Dirk and Leah after they play their part, although he might take his time about it. Too many bodies can cause comment." Her words fell into total silence. Quenby Ragaree had taken her children from the room, Darame noted finally, and even Crystle had fled. *Things are getting too hot in here....*

"If Dirk could kill his Atare, he is capable of anything," Mailan said. "Especially arranging the death of an off-worlder who has served his purpose."

"Sweet Saints, are you going to find a pile of bodies?" Darame felt herself growing numb at the intricacies of what was developing.

"Ayers!" They all jumped at the volume of Sheel's voice, echoing throughout the cavern. In a moment footsteps ran down stone corridors, a rush of sound battering like a dozen *guaard*. The husky young man threw himself into the room, both blades drawn, although Mailan's total ease stopped him in his tracks.

"If only we could harness all this energy," Sheel said wryly. "I want you to pack your things. Leave with Mailan and Crow, but do not travel together. Be careful: I do not think Dirk will start killing off more *guaard*, but it would be foolish to assume we have uncovered the depths of this thing. Go to the palace. I want you or your sister on Avis at all times, unless there is someone you can trust with her life as you would trust with your own. It is a burden; it will wear you away like water against a stone. But she may be in grave danger. Wartime *guaard;* do not let her enter a sanitation unless you have first inspected it."

Ayers's nod of fealty was deeper than usual. "Sheri already has three with her that can be trusted, my Atare."

"Good. A five shift will keep you rested." Sheel paused, taking a long, deep breath, and Darame detected the slightest trembling of his body. "Can you leave today?"

Even Mailan turned her head to stare at him. At breakfast there had been talk of spending the night in Portland and leaving tomorrow. . . .

"I can be ready to leave by tierce," Ayers responded.

"Then may Mendulay shadow your steps."

The two *guaard* took his blessing as dismissal, and abruptly Darame and Sheel were alone.

Staring deep into the firepit, unable to face the woman across from him, Sheel surreptitiously looked to see if his hands were shaking. Black against the flames, they seemed calm. . . . But then if his entire body trembled, would it appear calm to his own eye? Pulse racing, increased heartbeat—he tried to direct his thoughts toward calm.

"Are you all right?" Darame's low voice was rougher than usual, and remote. Embarrassed? Not likely: this woman did not waste time with either regrets or conventions.

I am the one who is embarrassed. She can scan me like a ROM. "Yes. Just realizing the dangers to my house. It is one thing to fear for your own life; it is another thing entirely to fear for not only your siblings, but the future of a ruling line." It was as much as he could give her—the chasm which had opened before him was still too shocking for words.

So she was a thief. . . . Not just a thief—the best of thieves. What did they call themselves? He had heard the word. . . . Free-traders. Not bound by any laws of trade, any planet restrictions. Some were very careful, fleecing only those who dared themselves to skirt the legal lines. It sounded as if Darame fell into that category.

It did not matter to him; he wanted her here. A long time since he had wanted a woman decorating the scene. *Emerson is past; find what you need.* How cynical, Atare. . . .

Then there were other types of free-traders. . . . It was his luck that Brant was one of the most dangerous. A perfect legal facade, and beneath it completely amoral.

Was it time to take someone, *anyone*, into his confidence? Now that one of the deepest levels of this nightmare had been plumbed? *If Leah definitely knows she is sterile, would she tell anyone?* Her idiot doctor, perhaps, but anyone else? Dirk could not know. Brant? That one might suspect, which was part of the reason he had tried hedging his plans with Avis.

His hands were shaking visibly, now. Surely Darame could see them; she was not blinded by firelight. All Sheel could see was Leah's face; contemplative, furious as she studied Cort Atare; hungry, predatory as she watched Avis; pallid, frightened, at the hospice after Iver was murdered. What did it all mean? That Iver's death was unexpected? Was Iver but one of many unexpected things that had happened in the past moons—unexpected even to Leah? *You hated Cort, sister—I know you did. And I was afraid you hated Avis.*

Burying his face in his hands, Sheel scarcely felt the delicate, cold hand which folded around his wrist.

Too late. Too late for everything. Sheel had glimpsed beyond the veil, blue sky torn to reveal the void. Whether Leah already could see her way, or had yet to find the path, Sheel knew what was coming. Avis was finally pregnant. *Dear sweet Mendulay, if you truly watch our path, let it be a boy.* A boy, and Avis would live. But a girl, guaranteeing the succession . . .

Avis would probably "die" of the birth . . . and Leah become the uncontested regent, accumulating a power block to remain unbroken within her lifetime. After all . . . what was one more death?

Chapter Ten

"No, no, Tobias, you are not paying attention," Darame said quickly, shaking her head as she reached to lift the cup.

"It was under the left one!" Tobias was clearly dismayed.

"No, it was not. You let me red herring you." She set the small pebble of fired clay in front of the three small domes. "I was exaggerating the movement of my right hand so you would pay close attention to it. While you watched the right hand, the left moved the ball."

"Is that not cheating?" The formality of the Nualan words did not disguise the pout of a small boy.

"I would say it is not," she replied in the same language. "That is what a traditional shell game is all about: misdirection. On the surface, it is simple; I hide the position of the ball by moving the cups around, while you try to keep track of it. In reality, I must try to make you *think* the ball is somewhere it is not."

"Why?"

Darame sighed. "Because a good shell player should be able to use any kind of cup or ball, and with a lot of types of materials you cannot rely on speed. Therefore, guile is necessary. To win, I must fool you. If I cannot do it by bewildering you with sheer speed, I must do it another way. Only a clumsy player cheats. If I am good enough, I do not have to cheat. If I am not good enough, I have no business starting a game. If we were playing for money," she added, lifting a small chocolate drop from his pitiful pile, "you would be very poor right now."

Unconvinced, Tobias turned back to the cups and stared at them with great concentration. "I will never learn this game. It is called 'red herringing' someone when you use your right hand to fool them?"

That made Darame laugh. "I am not trying to turn you into a free-trader! It is more general than that. On Caesarea, a red herring is a diversion meant to distract your attention from what is really happening. Sometimes it is something physical, like the movement of my hands. Other times, it is a flaw in a story I do not want you to notice, or maybe a piece of information meant to mislead you."

"Funny words," Tobias told her, reaching to slide the cups over the surface of the worn table. "These *are* hard to move. Do the funny words you use mean whatever you want them to mean?"

"Yes and no." Darame reached for her mug of saffra, but found it was cold. Sweet Magdalen, what she wouldn't give for a cup of tea. Saffra was tasty, but she was tired of it. "Those words mean basically the same thing all over the Seven Systems. You can change the definition, but at least one person must be told your new version, to understand exactly what you mean. Do you know why?"

"You tell me." There was a sparkle in the boy's eyes, and Darame wondered for the hundredth time if Sheel approved of these impromptu classes.

"Because all those funny words stand for complex thoughts; and a code is just as useless if no one knows it, as it is when everyone knows it. We could decide that . . . to 'Tobias' something would mean to take it apart and analyze it. But if I decided that, and did not tell anyone else, how would anyone know what I meant when I said I was going to 'Tobias' something? The word would fail to communicate its meaning."

This caused the heir to dissolve into giggles, and Darame took the opportunity to move to the stove and pour herself some fresh saffra. Sheel, who was hunched over a drawing of a chart, caught her eye as she rose from her squatting position.

"I think I might kill for a cup of tea," Sheel said blandly, his face just as smooth.

It was Darame's turn to let a laugh escape. "My sentiments exactly! Perhaps we should return to cocoa for a day or so?"

Sheel shook his head. "Too rich for me, but as you will."

"My Uncle Caleb told me that a shell game was a . . . an illegal game played to cheat someone," Tobias said suddenly.

Pausing, Darame looked over at Sheel for a clue. His face was still impassive, although the odd eyes were now studying her. "How do you answer that?" he asked finally.

Moving slowly back toward the table, Darame said: "I imagine your uncle said that because many, many people cannot play the shell game properly, and it is an easy game to cheat at. So easy that among outsiders it has become a synonym for something dishonest. Among free-traders, however, the shell concept is used either for a 'Mirror Game' or a 'Bunco Game.' "

Tobias let out a shout of laughter. "Bunco! What is that?"

Darame smiled as she reclaimed her seat. "My father told me it was once a card game. You would encourage someone who did not know the rules to play, and then win through their inexperience. A mirror is the oldest game of all: to know that someone is dishonest and would cheat you if they could, and to cheat them *first*. It is the hardest form of free-trading, because to cheat an honest person these days is easy; the laws are complex, and vary from planet to planet. Since no one can know everything, one must buy the services of others to do business. A good climate for bunco. But to cheat a dishonest person . . . that takes skill, since a crook is always watching for another crook."

Still sliding the cups around on the table, Tobias kept his eyes on the fired clay pebble he was avoiding. "My Uncle Caleb probably knew a lot about all those things. He always needed credit. I suppose that sometimes, when he suddenly became wealthy before the next installment from the trust . . . he did some bunco to get the increase."

"Possibly," was all Darame allowed herself to say. "But we should not speak ill of the dead."

"Why not? It was true. Everyone knew that you could not trust him—even in little things." This was rather bitter; Darame wondered what Caleb had done to teach a child to be wary of him. The boy piled up the cups and moved them to one side. "How about a crib game? You know, I miss Crystle. She would let me win at crib."

"That is not good for you," Darame told him, pulling the crib board out of a pile of debris. "No one will *let* you win in real life. Why form bad habits? At least when you play with me, you know when you have really won."

"True," Tobias agreed, grinning wickedly. "Spot me a crib?"

"Incorrigible."

"We will hope for your redemption," came Sheel's voice. "Tobias, have you finished all your studies? It will be dinnertime soon."

Massive sigh, slumping of shoulders, heartfelt shuffling of feet. . . . "Can I work in here?"

"I think the meeting room would be better for your concentration." Sheel lifted his head, his gaze resting on the boy. Recognizing defeat, Tobias thanked Darame for playing and moved off down the corridor.

Darame rose and turned to the shelving, looking for the honey pot. It *was* quiet without Crystle. . . . With luck, her journey had been uneventful. She had her child, it seemed. Whether she could carry it to term was something else, something the Nualans apparently did not try to control except with rest and diet. *If it is meant to survive, it will survive,* she had placidly told Darame. And no curiosity about the sex of the child. . . . Darame could not see herself asking Sheel, when Crystle had resisted the temptation.

Glancing over her shoulder, Darame saw that Sheel was still staring at the opening to the fire room. "Thank you for cheering him," the man said abruptly. "The Ragaree's children are too young for him, and the silence makes him . . . remember."

"The father he misses, the mother he idolizes, the friends far away . . . the family gone beyond," Darame agreed, finishing his thoughts and lifting the honey pot from the shelf. "Grief is a mysterious thing in children. Like trust . . ." She paused, wanting to ask Sheel if he thought the boy would ever trust *guaard,* after this all came out— The sound of a rolling pebble caught her ear. Lifting her voice, Darame went on: "I am looking forward to seeing your essay, Tobias, when you have finished it."

"Okay." Caught, the boy gave up and continued toward the back rooms. Darame heard Jude greet him as he approached. At the table, already back at work, Sheel managed a chuckle.

"Good. Any normal child would be dying to know what was going on," was his quiet comment. "I hope someday he can be a normal child again."

Darame had already put it out of her mind. Walking over to Sheel's work table, nudging a fire crystal stick closer to the fire-pit as she passed, Darame sat down across from him. *What does he think about when Tobias and I talk about the Seven Systems? Does he hear us at all? Does he mind what I tell the boy?*

As if he had heard her thoughts, Sheel looked up again, smiling faintly at the sight of the honey pot. Leaning back in the peeled bark chair, he stretched luxuriously. "If he will communicate, he must understand that language is a living thing," Sheel said suddenly.

Is that his way of telling me he trusts my judgment? Her eyes drifted to his hands, now resting on the paper chart. The hands of a healer . . . She had watched him heal with those hands—when? Yesterday? The day before? Old Harald's youngest grandson had cut himself badly while chopping a bolt-hole through an ancient wall of timber which previously had sealed a crevice to the outside. Fortunately Sheel had been nearby, for the boy had lost a great deal of blood. Working quickly yet appearing unruffled, Sheel had stopped the bleeding and arranged to move the youth into the caves. The healing had taken longer than the last one Darame witnessed—because it was a deeper wound, she wondered? Asking about it still felt too personal. What had startled her was the gentleness in the man. There was no abstraction, no physician's distance: Sheel was absorbed with the problem and the pain, pushing the latter aside to deal with the former, perhaps, but not denying its existence.

He had slept long after mending the injury, half-curled beneath one blanket in his own small sleeping area. For once Darame had followed him to bed, for he did not wake for the evening meal. The thought brought a grin to her face. Sheel's way of finally solving her sleepless nights was still amusing. What she needed, he had explained with little introduction, was body heat. As he was naturally a warm sleeper, all healing talents aside, he was the perfect person for her to curl up next to. "Rather like a large . . . hot water bottle," he had suggested, promptly folding down upon her blanketed floor and wrapping himself in a sheet. By the time Darame had stopped laughing and prepared a few questions, Sheel was asleep.

And in the fifteen days since Crystle's departure that was all they had done nights . . . slept. Half-amused, half-chagrined, Darame honestly did not know what to do . . . what she wanted to do. Whatever had caused Sheel's interlude with Crystle, it was settled and over with the day Sheel realized she was pregnant. Darame would have loved to ask why he had changed his mind about the woman, but the words simply would not come. It was quite odd, sleeping next to a man simply for warmth. *Apparently you are not too old for new experiences.* Sheel had attracted her from the beginning. Now that there was something forbidden about him, the attraction had actually increased. *Are you ready to push the issue a bit?*

Leaning forward, she glanced at the chart. "A new one. You have another theory?"

Shrugging, Sheel slid the wide sheet over toward her. "It worries me, that we have heard nothing from Mailan and Crow since they reached Atare. I thought I might look to see if I could find the connection to my line that Dirk claims, but the basic encyclopedia lists only name children."

Darame studied the names and dates, marveling at the span of time covered. "The Sleep stretches your generations into infinity."

"I hope not that far." His voice was dry and distant, as if reflecting his thoughts.

"Seven sons and two daughters over thirty years! I get tired just thinking about it." Her finger paused at a name. "James... died at birth. So you were the seventh son. They have many superstitions on Gavriel about seventh sons and daughters." Darame looked up; Sheel was still staring off into space.

"As they do here. Also about third sons and daughters." It was almost musing. Darame wondered if he had heard her, much less realized his own response.

"Healers and prophets—"

"No." The word sliced into her sentence like a knife, silencing the woman.

He was rarely strident; Darame was uncertain what to say. They sat quietly for several moments. Finally: "Then why do your dreams frighten you?"

Tension; absence of tension, as the knotted muscles ran out of him like flowing water. Sheel closed his eyes, his head tipping back out of sight. "Because my nightmares have a talent for coming true. Not the good dreams, just the bad ones. Sometimes there is no warning at all; the dream—insight—comes almost simultaneously with the incident. One happened during the funeral service. A few minutes later, someone tried to knife me." Raising his head back to its normal position, he glanced at her shrewdly. "I had that dream your first night on the planet.... I knew that Cort was dead, although I did not want to face it. I saw it happen through the killer's eyes... and the killer wore the uniform of a *guaard*. *Guaard* present, but at the wrong angle, dead or killing..."

"Have you had any more nightmares lately?" Her voice sounded very quiet to her own ears.

"No. Just an uneasiness, like a storm cloud shadowing my pyre." Tension edged his words, and Darame wondered what was bothering him.

"Almost a personal warning system, yet... to see what you cannot help." Darame chose her words carefully. "I do not think I would care for that talent, Sheel. It also runs in my family, or so tradition says, and I am grateful I have never felt its presence."

Sheel turned slightly toward her, the right eye of pale green thoughtful. "I only hope Ayers did not frighten Avis with any half-formed warnings. She will cooperate with him simply to humor me. I would rather tell her myself about Leah." The man relaxed again, in his infinitesimal way, a weary peacefulness trickling out of him.

Content that the problem had passed, Darame bent over the chart once again.

"Such large families," Darame murmured after a while, pulling Sheel back from his thoughts. "And yet eighty percent of the population is sterile. Why? With your skill in genetics, why the problem?"

Sheel gave her a mellow look, trying to decide what she was asking. Such a feeling of calm, that he could not remember feeling. . . . He had never told anyone about his nightmares. Telling her had been spontaneous, almost belligerent, although he thought he had controlled his anger well. The mere idea did not seem to upset her—that an off-worlder could accept something with more grace than one of the flock! Hard to understand, to believe . . . but then she had not heard him recount a tale moments before its reality, either. Few had—Sheel had no intention of allowing someone to decide that his dreams were something to aim for genetically, and nipping material from the labs.

"Human genetic material is very . . . malleable. It mutates constantly. Most of the time it results in spontaneous abortion: a miscarriage long before the woman knows she is pregnant. But here on Nuala, things have been different. Our genes seem to be trying to adapt to the planet, despite grave problems. Human life has been born that, before Nuala, we would not have thought could survive."

"Like Fergus, the Sini who brought me here?" she asked, intent.

"I find mock-Sinis the oddest of our adaptations to the planet . . . next to my own talent. How can something become slightly radioactive? Why does the organism not die? Or not become totally Sini, a truly radioactive human? Why do Sinis live?"

"You mean a person can *become* a mock-Sini when they were previously normal?" Alarm registered in her face.

"No, not at all," Sheel said hastily. "The potential to become Sini is there at birth. In some cases it merely delays in blossoming to fruition. We shield our visitors from what could hurt them —the water, native-grown food, excessive starlight, the bad areas—unless they choose to take the pill series. You no longer need fear any Nualan water or food. Did the pills make you queasy?" he asked suddenly.

"Not that I noticed . . . but I was still weak from the gas, then."

"At any rate, Homo sapiens continues to attempt this adaptation. Those who become fertile have adapted completely to Nuala. Only an extremely high dosage of radiation—of any type, apparently—can affect them." A smile touched his lips. "Do not test your new immunity," he warned her. "An acquired immunity is good only for Dielaan radiation, unlike those of us who are born here."

"So sometimes an organism overcomes the planet and breeds . . . but not all the children may be fertile?" She frowned as she spoke.

Sheel nodded. "Some lines are more healthy than others. We are all Atares around here: descendants of the crew and passengers of *The Atare*, one of the three ships stranded on Nuala so long ago. Some lines adapted more quickly, and became sought after, fought over—ultimately, even powerful. They became the royal lines of their tribes, or clans if you prefer. People will eventually fight among themselves politically . . . so the schisms began. Once there were as many as twelve houses of tremendous authority, and many smaller ones."

"Once? . . . No longer?" She leaned forward on her elbow as she spoke, propping it on the worn table. Studying the firelight reflecting off a stray hair caught on her dark sleeve, Sheel tried to frame an answer.

"About a thousand Nualan years ago," he began slowly, "some of our people made a mistake. Our numbers remained small, and we could see little indication that our breeding attempts were working. The Nualan concept has been the same since it began: remove genetic material damaged by radiation, and breed toward our ancestors who were abandoned here, but with the vigor to withstand the planet's heat. Abruptly, several pockets of people deviated from this plan. They tried to improve the stock while removing defective genes. Unfortunately, such tampering has monstrous side effects." Sheel let his gaze wander toward the firepit, which was slowly collapsing into embers. "Breeding selectively for traits presumed by humans to be desirable —intelligence, beauty, creativity, physical and emotional strength—carries a darker side. It can be done, but it breaks down in the next few generations, causing medical problems: stillbirths, miscarriage, children born with diseases we had not seen in centuries and thought were eradicated. And of course, there is always the problem of who decides what is desirable in children . . . and what will be done with the undesirables." He sighed.

"Eugenics does not work without constant lab reinforcement," Darame said dryly. "So history tells us."

"It was Nuala which proved that once and for all. The two clans which were most heavily into controlled breeding began showing signs of deterioration. Live births became rare, and other problems cropped up. Some of the planned children, desirable in some ways but warped by other standards, finally assumed power and tried to solidify their control of their clans. One clan went to war and basically annihilated itself through treachery and the retaliation of its neighbors. The other tried to remedy its problem another way . . . by stealing fertiles from strong tribes."

"Atare?" Darame prompted.

"Atare, Seedar, and Kilgore. They did not take kindly to the future ragarees being stolen. Kilgore has always had a hot-tempered streak, and The Atare during that period was perfectly willing to prove that he was superior to any so-called human constructed piecemeal. By the time it was over, the royal lines of Cantrel and Saunder had been destroyed."

"But the labs today—" Darame began.

"Completely random, after known defectives have been spliced out. We learned a hard lesson. There are some who have tampered, slightly, since then. . . . I suspect Crystle's line has controlled some of the physical features of their clan. But as you have seen, it has weakened them." He let his thoughts drift. "It does not do to say we would not have made the same mistake. We of Atare just have never been that desperate." *Until now.*

"Like a bunch of squabbling children," Darame said, a slight smile crossing her face. "You need a nursemaid, the lot of you. Why not form a council or something to establish some planet-wide rules? I would think mutual distrust would make you willing to concede to some sort of general controls."

"It has been tried, several times. All attempts have failed, for various reasons. Sudden war, deterioration, simple paralysis due to suspicions and gerrymandering—even scientific arguments. All have defeated us." The simple recitation depressed Sheel even more.

"I take it that force has failed?"

Straightening in his seat, Sheel reached for his empty mug. "Those with delusions of grandeur have been defeated by several tribes uniting to stop them. No one has ever succeeded in meld-ing several groups with intent to conquer. Most tribes have internal controls to prevent it: the *guaard*, for example, serves that purpose here. It was partially created to keep the minds of the rulers on improving the lot of their people—especially the genetic situation. So far, the *guaard* has never been convinced that war improved our lines."

"Not unless you were breeding warriors," Darame agreed thoughtfully. Standing, she moved gracefully to the firepit and knelt to throw on several more sticks, the dusky maroon robe she wore spreading like shadow at her feet. "Or . . . if war were the lesser of two evils." She looked thoughtful as she stirred the fragments into life.

"I cannot accept that, Darame. I am a healer. It is my place to protect life; even more, perhaps, than the average Nualan does. And now it is part of my oath. War cannot be a choice, because it endangers fertile lives." His hands, suddenly restless, toyed with the mug before him.

"If the choice is between someone like Brant and war?" Sheel glanced up at her words. A fire was burning brightly once again, the woman outlined against it. Darame had retrieved the pot of saffra from the stove and was pouring herself a refill. "I am cold," she said with dignity, answering the amused look he gave her. Walking back to the table, she emptied the pot into Sheel's mug. "Be serious, Sheel. Even if you stop Brant, there are dozens like him at Caesarea Station and beyond. Some of them are even better at what they do." Sitting down, she gave him a hard look as she reached for the honeypot. "This will happen again."

"Probably," Sheel said, his voice bleak. "I admit to little talent for intrigue. No one ever dreamed I might rule, or even Iver—neither of us were really trained for it. And now it appears that I will spend the rest of my life watching for just such characters, in an infinite variety of schemes, all directed at the wealth of our planet." He met her gaze. "Or at its hidden wealth—I suppose they could try building an underground first, and then infiltrating legitimate business."

Darame smiled. "No talent for intrigue? You have imagination, Sheel—that is all it takes. Otherwise this news would have you as shell-shocked as Crow. You can imagine all we have discussed as possible . . . even theorize about other ways it might be done. You are learning quickly." Stirring her saffra, the woman chuckled. "Your straight face will be handy, too. It is hard sometimes to tell what you are thinking."

"What I am wondering is what we can do to prevent this from happening again," Sheel admitted. "I am also wondering where to hide next. We have paused here too long. It is time to move."

"Huh," was her response. Her eyes remained on her saffra for a long moment. "Do you really want to stop it from happening again?"

This brought Sheel out of his thoughts. "What kind of question is that?"

"An honest one. Because there are really only two ways to do it, and you are not going to like either one." At his nod for her to continue, Darame said: "You can safeguard your people in two ways: you can curtail their freedom, or you can increase their responsibility. Or something in between, if you can work it out." As Sheel started to speak, Darame said quickly: "You have to be able to watch people and situations much more closely, Sheel, if you want to anticipate something like this. A dictator with an army could do it; an elected council and a strong policing agency could do it; a ruler with a council could to it. But someone has to watch. And the more people watching, the better. And someone has to keep all the information coming into a central authority, because several different spy networks will only create more hostility. I personally think you need to consider someone doing exactly what Brant is doing—someone Nualan."

"'And all the peoples shall bow like winter wheat before the rising wind of Atare . . .'" Sheel whispered aloud, her words triggering an old memory. But he did not finish the quote. "No."

"Brant and Dirk certainly would not expect it," she offered, clearly amused.

"You do not know what you ask." History, religion, and politics reared up like a hydra, many-headed and venomous. Sheel felt a shiver rush through him, and wondered what Archpriest Ward would say to her.

"So explain to me what I ask." Darame settled in her chair, pulling up her feet to sit on them.

"Do you know the term . . . *jihad?*" Darame shook her head. "It means a holy war. What I think you are suggesting—that I should duplicate Brant's trick and unite the city-states—might touch off just such a conflict." This was uneasy ground. Sheel was not particularly religious, although he had read widely concerning theology and spirituality. But to talk about such things, even if he personally had no use for them, was awkward. "There are dozens of books of prophecy that have come down to us over the last thousandyear. Several of them contain hints that the day

will come when the other clans will bow to Atare. It is one reason
the other clans distrust us so much: no matter how often they
attack us or scheme against us, we just get stronger."

"Another reason not to let them know what has happened,"
Darame said wryly. "Well, you have enough trouble, Sheel—do
not borrow any. But if you played your hand cleverly enough, no
one would have time to think about religion. This is economics
and security, not gods and angels. A planet has more bargaining
power than a city."

"And as we have told you before: to attack this conspiracy
without proof could lose me all my support." At her puzzled
expression, he said: "Leah. To attack the one who would be regent is indirectly a threat to Tobias. I need proof of the conspiracy, a witness—something. Or I could lose the *guaard*."

His admission startled her, as he'd thought it might, but she
immediately grew thoughtful, as if slotting his words into her
store of information about the planet. "Do you ever talk to people
without an ulterior motive in mind?" Sheel asked impulsively.
Immediately realizing he had phrased the words badly, he added:
"I mean simply talk for the pleasure of conversation, or being
with the people."

Darame did not take offense, as he'd feared she might. That
thoughtful look remained on her face. "Do you know," she
started slowly, "that the only friends I have are that fat old man
who raised me and his navigator? People I can depend on, I
mean—people who would casually violate free-trader convention for me.
There are those I casually refer to as friends, from jobs or
vacations . . . mostly planetbound, and probably dead by now,
what with the passing of time. . . . But you are correct. I do not
converse with people . . . usually. Until recently." She smiled
faintly. "Your sister has a way of making those around her forget
their worries, even as she is crushed by problems. She is deep,
under her bubbling facade. Avis might have made a good free-
trader," Darame added impassively.

Sheel had to chuckle. "Please do not try to recruit her! I need
her right here, plying her protocol skills for Atare."

"There is much to understand here, before playing that game. I
am lucky I did not broadcast my intentions with every word."

"We knew you were not what you pretended to be," Sheel said.
"But then who is?"

That made Darame laugh out loud. "You are entirely too . . .
easy to listen to," she told him, a wicked smile curving her lips.
"I tried not to like you so much, you know. One night of play,

and then to work, if all this madness had not occurred. You could have taken my mind off my job, if you had desired. I would have had to bargain with Halsey to include you in the scam, so I would have an excuse to see you."

Was there a question in that statement? He studied her without comment, his inclination to smile struggling against caution. *I like you, woman. I had not planned on it, either, but I like you. I like your tricky brain, and the natural kindness you try to harness, and that wicked smile. I could want that smile for me alone. A woman like you is champagne in the blood . . . is almost obsession.* Sheel realized he was becoming tense, and abruptly changed the subject. Now was as good a time as any to act on his concerns. . . . "Speaking of bargaining . . . I have something for you."

The woman's delicate silver brows lifted, and she tilted her head appealingly to one side. "I suspected you were up to something. Old Harald and that package from town? I forgot about it when the boy was injured."

"So did I." Sheel smiled faintly as he rose from his seat, reaching for the shelving above his head. Were her mannerisms simply a part of her, or was there nothing she did without calculation? Did it matter at this point? "You will need this. It is a thank-you . . . and perhaps all the security I can give you. Personally, I would keep it secret, unless you must speak of it." Unfolding the piece of cloth, Sheel carefully lifted the glittering chain. The gasp behind him was his reward, although he kept his expression serene. Turning back to her, he sat once again, the decorative necklace dangling from several fingers.

"Sheel . . . Why? . . ." Darame began, and then stopped, clearly confused.

"I have succeeded in striking you speechless. I shall enjoy my momentary victory." Then the humor slid from his face. "I told you. It is a thank-you gift. The business with Leah and Dirk we would have eventually discovered, I think, once we forced ourselves to examine the worst-case possibilities. But Brant? There are a dozen ambassadors and aides I could choose from, if I wanted to find an outside confederate. Brant might have eluded me completely." It was hard to control his smile; he had never seen Darame so startled. She was looking everywhere except at him. . . . Shifting in her chair, she finally glued her gaze to the firepit.

Flame dangled from his fingers. The pale trinium links were studded every five centimeters with tiny faceted rubies, reflecting and magnifying the light beyond belief, throwing pale pink high-lights into Darame's silver hair. "The other reason," Sheel went on conversationally, looking away from her, "is that I have no idea how this will end. It may be that I will be dead . . . and there is no guarantee that Leah is your friend. Either you are with them, or they decide they cannot trust you. . . . Then you are an unwanted witness. Your credit and exit visa may be frozen. Take this to Marc reb Dor, in Amura By the Sea. For a few links of this chain, you will be able to buy Cold Sleep to Caesarea. Tell him that the mermaids are still singing. It is a childhood joke; he will know I send you, and will help as he can. I am afraid it is all I can offer. I have been back less than a year. . . . Finding people to trust takes time."

"In every line of business. Thank you, Sheel. Oh . . . and thank you for this, too." She reached, her fingers brushing his as she took the chain from him.

Was she blushing, or was it the firelight? Thank you for what, a bolt-hole? Then he realized what she meant. *Perhaps I am not subtle enough, but everything you have tried to talk me into runs counter to their plans. If this is a way of controlling me, it is rather interesting.* Physical sensation distracted him; he realized she had not flinched when their hands touched. Amazing. . . . Progress.

"So where are we going?" The question startled him, coming out of sequence. "From here."

"The ciedar, most likely. We have tents and equipment enough. There is little snow on the northern desert—the winds sweep it to the mountains, or sublimate it. But the north winds are wicked." Sheel shivered in spite of the fire. Although he could not re-member ever having been cold, the tales of ciedar winters were chilling in themselves. A frown traced his lips. "I told Tobias to sleep in back with Quenby Ragaree and her children, starting tonight. I still feel 'wrong' about something, and I do not want him in my shadow. It might be a dangerous place to be. If you wish to join them, feel free."

Darame smiled faintly. "It is cold back there."

Sheel considered the area, which was reached only through a narrow, half-height corridor. "A bit, perhaps. The fire is smaller, at least. There is a draft from our bolt-hole that cannot be closed off."

Another reason for Darame's comment suddenly occurred to him, and Sheel wondered just how quickly he could finish his reading.

ONEHUNDRED TWENTYFOURDAY   MATINS

Dinner and a quiet evening with Quenby Ragaree were worlds away from her dream; it was vague, disturbing, and filled with people wearing masks. Rather, they were wearing dominoes— ornate beyond belief, and stark in their colors. She kept seeing the same masked figure flitting just out of view, but the person within was changing: first Brant, then Leah, then Halsey, of all people. How much had Halsey surmised by now? Had Brant decided to let him in on things? Were her fears correct: was Halsey being set up?

The noise entered the dream as thunder, as voices crying tidings of ruin and war. That in itself was odd enough to half-rouse her; Sheel was quiet about slipping in, he never woke her. Although tonight she had hoped . . . Ah, he was a reticent man by nature, and her treatment of him the past moon had been fearful. It would be surprising if he could forgive it quickly—

Screaming and gunfire in the hall caused her to sit upright, her hands fumbling for the blanket. She had started searching for a pocket torch when bright light appeared further on down the corridor. It approached warily. . . . Darame stilled her movements.

The individual's pace was measured and soundless, the walk of one uncertain of what lay beyond each turn. There was something like fog outside the sleeping berth, casting a diffused glow over the rocky path. It was so unreal Darame pinched herself hard to make sure she was awake.

He stopped at the twin openings, turning his head slightly from one side to the other, as if trying to peer beyond the beam. Darame felt her eyes widen as she recognized from her sojourn in the palace the *guaard*'s pale hair and bulky shoulders. Was there any chance he would continue down the hall?

Then White raised his other arm, apparently to wipe his eyes, and she saw the mag gun. Who? . . .

Darame realized she no longer cared whether White continued down the hall.

Chapter Eleven

Pale green candles scented with brightbay filled the parlor with a heady fragrance, while garlands of spirit's breath, holly, and everlife hung above the firepit mantel. Fire crystal stick flames danced blue and green as well as gold, but Darame ignored the anomaly. It was exactly nine strides from the triple bay window facing the street to the only door, and she had lost count of how many times she'd completed the circuit.

A gust of wind struck the thermal panes on her next pass, causing a thrum of vibration. Darame paused, then, staring past her gaunt reflection into the swirling snow. Her left arm remained folded tightly across her waist, the fingers cemented to an ornamental dagger, even as her free hand alternated between the necklace hidden under her shirt and the softness of the collar itself. A pallid ghost of a woman faced her, shimmering in the heat waves rising from the fire, the eyes dark pits without expression.

Three days without sleep . . . afraid to sleep. Sleep could mean dreaming, or it could mean slumber too heavy to hear footsteps approaching. . . . At first she was infuriated when the fresh-faced *guaard* had escorted her back to the hostel. White's orders, they said, clearly embarrassed when she pointed out that her possessions were still at the palace . . . when the man at the desk indicated there were no vacancies. No rooms to be found in town, for it was the evening of the Yulc, and Atare City was packed to the rafters.

Frantic was a better word than infuriated. It was good that this had happened; she finally had time to think.

Wrong, all wrong, and no way to know what to do. *It's time to run.* Memory swept through her, of stumbling into the fire room and nearly falling over Fion's lifeless body, riddled with bullet holes. And Sheel as still as death, though she could see no injury. The scene provoked her one comment to White, the safest and most nebulous thing she could utter: "I only needed a few more days."

What else could I have said? Who knew what had happened in her absence? Were Dirk and Brant still working together? Who sent White, and how had he found them? He volunteered nothing, and Darame decided not to ask. What she was not supposed to know, she could not question. *I want your life, White. Your life depends on his. . . .*

They had not found the bolt-hole. . . . She was almost positive about that. The two young men from the village were dead, but she had not seen old Harald or his grandson lying anywhere. Standing silent in a corridor, her things hastily tied into a bundle, Darame had felt something from the darkness beyond nudged into her hand. It was a form of ring, the tiny transmittals used by the Nualans. Later, after an exhausting struggle through snow to the rail line, she had had a moment to use her pendant, a disguised enlarger, to examine the message. Who would have thought that Harald could write? In Nualan, unfortunately. It was too dangerous to carry; memorizing every stroke on the flexible film, she had cut the ring into slivers. If she ever found Mailan or Ayers, she would reconstruct the note.

How long would it take Avis to respond to her message? *Would* she respond? The Sweet Saints alone knew if she was still safe and well. *And Ayers with her . . . I must find Ayers.* Originally Darame had planned on going straight to Avis with her tale. A cooler head now prevailed. She was not sure she could tell her tale without including Leah in it; even if she succeeded, Avis would then surely go straight to Leah. Men dressed as *guaard,* taking her brother. No, not merely dressed as *guaard,* but surely *guaard.*

Three lousy days to get back to Atare, two of them spent on the train. Several avalanches had buried portions of track, which meant eating and sleeping on board. And a message . . . slipped into the food basket brought to her the second day. *Do not worry —you are covered.* She knew the odd symbol at the end of the Caesarean letters: Brant's private signature.

Sweet Mary, what is going on? This was crazy and totally unexpected. Killing Sheel and grabbing Tobias she could understand; wooing Sheel into returning with Tobias she could understand . . . but taking Sheel? *He was alive, damn it!* Why, why, it made no . . . sense.

Her steps slowed. Unless . . . unless there had been a major falling-out among the conspirators. *Every pawn has a value.* Sheel is one, Tobias is one, Avis. . . . Have even I been promoted to pawn? And do our values vary, and depend on who does the valuation?

White took Sheel, came looking for Tobias . . . yet Brant knew about it. *No one ever really sounded out whether they could use Sheel.* A quiet, apolitical physician. . . . Had someone decided to ask him? *Or . . . tell him.* She felt very uneasy. *Why* knock him out? Why kill Fion and the others?

None of those *guaard* who attacked had returned to Atare. The three young men, mere children, who had brought her back were as silent as any *guaard,* but Darame had overheard two of them conversing, rueful about an avalanche their air vehicle had probably caused. *In such a hurry they took to the air.* . . . A failed mission: no Atare, no heir. They were ignorant of what had happened within the mountain. Or were they? A trap for her? Better to keep silent for now. If White thought she knew something, surely he would have her followed, or questioned. Followed? Shadowed—she did not know the young man watching the parlor door.

"Where in Seven Hells is Halsey?" Darame muttered, wishing her stomach would stop churning so she could eat. He had not returned to his room in sixday, the clerk had reported, but his ship was still paying for his board. Possible, but not probable; Halsey was known to disappear on jobs, but not when things were so uncertain. No message to Mona on shipboard, no message to Darame. Offering to pay for his room had quickly shown her that her credit was still good, if unnecessary. For how long . . . *Time to run, time to run,* the silent voice mocked her, a voice she had always heeded.

Brant was not taking calls. Gone for the holiday, the embassy told her. Yes, they would take a message. *I will carve out your tripes when I find you, Brant!* Worse than what she had feared. . . . They were merely unnecessary, she and Halsey. Brant probably did not care what happened to them, as long as it did not fall back on him. Which could mean anything from stalling to elimination of details. *Details like Halsey and me.* Then why get her out of the cavern alive? . . . Because she had become too visible?

"Serae?" The word startled Darame out of her thoughts, her fingertips tightening on the dagger hidden at her side. Not merely a piece of jewelry, it had saved her life more than once. A *guaard* stepped into the room. "Serae Avis has requested that you join her at the palace for Yule."

Turning back to her pack to hide her face, suddenly fearful she had lost her masking talent, Darame reached for her jacket. "Do we have transportation?" Her voice did not tremble; good.

"An ice sled awaits."

ATARE PALACE

"Darame!" The delicate, sweet voice of Avis chimed like a bell, tossing the word into the chandelier as she rushed into the upper hall.

Reaching the top of the stairs, Darame suddenly realized how glad she was to see Avis—and how tired she felt. *Dear Peter, help me stay awake!* Two more steps and she was enveloped in swathes of bright coral silk.

"You did not send word of your coming! How long have you been waiting at that hostel? Did they hide you in a parlor or something? Camelle!" Tugging at her friend's hands, Avis turned to call for her attendants as she led Darame through the huge oak portal at the end of the hallway.

Realizing that Avis did not expect any answers right away, Darame quickly looked around for Ayers. If he was not on duty, should she call for him? Other royal ladies gathered to greet the long-absent off-worlder, and Darame forced her attention back to them.

"Did you accomplish all that you set out to do?" Avis asked, leading a servant with a tray back into the room. Something in the bright eyes of Sheel's sister warned Darame as she bent to remove her wet boots.

"I accomplished a great deal. We will have much to discuss." That was surely accurate. *She does not want me to speak in front of the others.* It was almost a relief. Rising up, examining several options for conversation, Darame spotted Ayers. "You are undoubtedly preparing for the Yule. Just how does one go about preparing for it?" Raising her eyebrows slightly at Ayers, she winked at him and tilted her head slightly in the direction of her old room. Ayers's head lowered a few millimeters in apparent understanding.

"Of course! You do not know about our celebrations! Sit down,

I have cheese and warmed brandy for you." Sitting herself, she added ruefully: "But not for me, of course!"

Chuckling, Darame said, "How do you feel?"

"Too queasy for alcohol, even if Capashan would let me have it! He says it is not good for the baby," she confided, offering Darame a basket of warm rolls. "The discomfort usually vanishes after a few months. I certainly hope so!" Her exasperation was so heartfelt, her pleasure in the pregnancy so evident, Darame felt a pang of conscience.

Time to run? Idiot! How can you leave now? Bending over to sip the brandy, Darame formed a resolve. *Forgive me, my young friend, but I will keep silent as I can. Until I know what has happened to Sheel, I can tell you only bare bones of news, and in bones there is no nourishment.*

ONEHUNDRED TWENTYSEVENDAY   MATINS

Darame was still struggling to push the tall window back on its runner when she heard her door open. Glancing over her shoulder she saw Ayers hesitating at the threshold. Turning back to the sill, gasping as a curl of wind lifted her hair, Darame leaned once more on the window, lifting up harder on the rail.

"Do not stand there gaping, come help me," she grumbled, aware that she was losing sensation in her hands. The snick of a closing door reached her ears.

Ayers's strong hand reached past her, lifting the hook on the rail. "Open or closed?" he inquired.

"Open." Rubbing her fingers to call blood back to them, she reached for the knife she had taken from her dinner tray. When she turned back to the window, she found that Ayers had thrown it wide. Scowling at him, she moved to the sill. "I was afraid to use any of the pads, in case they were monitored. What does this mean?" Carefully, trying to give her gestures definition, she carved Nualan symbols into the packed snow of the ledge. Ayers inhaled sharply while she wrote, but did not speak. "It is from old Harald, is it not?"

"Yes," he said after a few moments. "What happened up there?"

"The message—I want to destroy it," she stated, tapping the windowpane above the last word.

"It says that Jude will try and take Tobias and the Seedar woman to Riva Ragaree. It also says that the other servants are hidden, as well as the signet," Ayers said slowly. "Where is my Atare?"

"Ah, I almost forgot about that—he was missing the signet when I last saw him. Fast of Harald, to grab it while White searched for Tobias." Sighing, Darame obliterated the message with slashes and then pushed the loose snow off the ledge for good measure, sweeping the stones bare. "Last I saw him, he was alive, Ayers, though not in the best of shape. We must assume he is still alive; otherwise, everyone in that cave should have died, as witnesses to what happened."

"Old Harald said they did die—all who were found, except you." His voice was carefully neutral.

"Yes, that fact did not escape me. Why? Because I am off-world, and my disappearance would cause comment? Because someone told them not to harm me?" She moved away from the flakes of snow drifting in through the window and sat near the firepit. "Those children who brought me back to Atare did not know that Sheel and Tobias were within the caverns—or they pretended not to know. I never saw them enter. . . . They may be honest. Or they may have hoped I would trust them, and speak of things better left unsaid." She looked up at Ayers. "Suggestions?"

The *guaard* was off duty, she could tell; his face showed obvious concern. He pulled the window shut and then followed her to the firepit. "I do not know," he admitted, his voice soft. "Mailan and Crow left town several days ago; they gave no orders, other than to watch Avis ceaselessly. Have you any suggestions?"

"Perhaps it is time to talk to Riva Ragaree," she murmured, fingering the chain around her neck. It was no longer a secret, at least around Avis and Ayers. Darame suspected that they exaggerated its meaning, but she did not volunteer the truth—Avis did not need to know how serious Sheel thought the situation. Besides, their interpretation might make Avis more willing to trust her, if an emergency arose. *Take her to the ship? How could you get her there undetected?*

"How will you talk to The Ragaree without anyone overhearing?" Ayers asked. "Any palace line can be tapped, except the ones in The Atare's quarters, and it would be noticed if we tried to use them."

"Huh. I was thinking of face to face, but getting out of Atare unnoticed could be very difficult. They must be watching me!" This last was fierce.

"They are watching you."

Darame glanced over, but Ayers's expression was remote. "Listening?" She had checked for surveillance, but found nothing.

"The bedrooms are safe. Watch yourself everywhere else. I do not wish to make Dirk suspicious of me." Ayers frowned as he spoke. "He has not countered my orders to watch Serae Avis, but he has added *guaard* to her rooms. One of those?..." He shrugged.

Nodding, she continued searching her brains for an option. Thinking furiously as the minutes passed, Darame finally said aloud: "Tobias and Quenby Ragaree should be fine if they reached Riva, even if someone finds out where they are. I doubt the men can touch them there ... and Leah cannot protest without looking suspicious. I would rather wait on Mailan. Surely she will contact them through the village before she actually returns to the caverns?"

"If she can," Ayers agreed, temporizing.

"But how long..." She gave Ayers a hard look. "Since The Atare is a healer, does that ... give him any extra strengths? To resist bad conditions, or..."

"Torture?" Ayers said it easily, although Darame noticed a tic in his forehead. "Healers are very healthy: it takes a great deal to crack their facades. And The Atare has studied Elkita, the philosophy which is also self-defense, of mind as well as body. I would think he might hold out a long time in such a case, unless they used drugs."

"What do they want, and what will they do when they have it?" she whispered.

"They will kill him," Ayers said quietly.

"You do not know that." She straightened, her voice challenging.

"They must, Serae. I think I know enough of him to know one thing: they cannot control him. And if they cannot control him, he must die."

If he dies, Brant, I think I will have more than your tripes.

ONEHUNDRED   THIRTYSEVENDAY   NONE

It had to be late afternoon, by the angle of pale starlight filtering through the cave opening. Could he have lost track? Not likely. ... A day by air to this place, and thirteen nights since then. Had anyone shown up with water? Ridiculous—they would have awakened him. Sheel smiled at the thought, knowing the wakening would not have been easy. Working his shoulders once again, his ears listening for the slightest sound of movement, Sheel gingerly sought a comfortable position.

None was left: every part of his body ached with a dull pain he had never imagined. Bruises could not kill him, but they certainly had made a mess of his condition. Was there any area left untouched, except his face and hands? That interested him, that they were so careful to avoid marking his head. *Perhaps I am not dead. Perhaps you have another part for me to play. If so, when do we get to it? I am tired of secrets.*

A pebble rolled somewhere near the entrance, and Sheel tensed, ready to flip the heavy rope binding his hands back over the hook. Silence . . . Some small creature in search of seed? Not *guaard*. Fortunate he had learned how to remove the loop which held his arms above his head. Otherwise his shoulders would be in bad shape. Praise Mendulay the afternoon *guaard* was so indecisive about his post. *If this goes on much longer, you may be my pass to freedom.* Called Varden by his companions, the youth clearly was troubled by the activities of the past days. Not enough to turn on White, not yet; but enough to ignore the slipped rope and to signal with movement when others approached.

Is this how it ends? I begin to understand why people under travail come to a new understanding about themselves and their place in the universe. That was as much as he was ready to admit to himself. Sheel had never had much use for religion, and was not certain he had much use for Mendulay. The healing talent which his people prayed for certainly had saved many lives, but it had made his own difficult. *Just as I come to terms with it, all this begins. Now I must rule to keep my life—but what of those who need healing?*

So tired, and White was sure to show up soon. The polite question-and-answer sessions had deteriorated rapidly into practices civilized people abhorred. *How civilized are we Atares?* They had only tied him up about five days ago. *It finally occurred to you I might just disappear one night. . . .* Many days of "questioning," and no answers. Sheel was astonished that his gaolers were so unprepared. Had they really expected him to agree to their terms . . . or, failing that, fold so quickly? What could they have been thinking? *The luck should be running out soon. . . .*

They had brought no chemicals—none at all, not even the simplest of them, which merely weakened a subject's will. Laws strictly circumscribed when such serums could be used, but that would not stop this crew. White had had so little faith in the line of Atare, it was really not surprising he underestimated the teachings of the temple. Between the study of Elkita and long lessons with healers Capashan and Xena, Sheel found himself more than capable of dealing with short rations and minor abuse.

Minor abuse . . . His luck simply could not hold. So far they wanted him alive and basically undamaged, but for how long? White certainly had brought a RAM tie-in, and could request a delivery . . . if he had anyone to deliver. White and two others here: Dirk back in Atare, and the dead *guaard,* if Fion's suspicions had been correct. How many others? Would he recognize any of them?

Where is Tobias? The same question, phrased differently, even conversationally, a countless number of times. Sheel had freely told them: he did not know. White had not accepted that answer . . . and made his demand insistent. Finally Sheel had shrugged (literally, to White's obvious annoyance) and stopped talking. For ten days he had said nothing, not even during a two-day period when they stopped bringing food or water. What would be next?

Earlier that day his mind had flitted back to the clay caverns, wondering what had happened after the blow that knocked him senseless. Until now he had been unable to get past the moment of Fion's death. The old *guaard* would probably have been surprised at his reaction, since Sheel had faced death before—lost to death, when a patient was snatched from beneath his fingers, a candidate for The Last Path. Sheel could not let it go.

All this time I have known the purpose of the guaard. *Why does a man fulfilling his vow shake me more than even Dirk's treason?* Considering it, watching the star creep deeper across the cave floor, Sheel decided it was not the act, but the reason behind the act. *Not your death, friend, which you were always prepared for, nor even your death at the hands of another* guaard, *but the fact that you died for me.* Was anyone worthy of that sacrifice?

Had Jude also died, trying to protect her charge? Was this some sort of game on White's part? A game, possibly, but a serious one: whether Jude had lived or died, Tobias must have escaped, or the questions would have been different. Ridiculous —Leah knew the boy was safe. Which could mean only one thing: a schism in the ranks of the traitors. So . . . who is after Tobias, and why? Is Dirk telling Leah—and Brant—everything? White would not work for Brant, but for Leah alone. . . . *Is Leah afraid of Brant? And wants Tobias where Dirk can protect him?* Fruitless to speculate.

What of Darame? If White had not killed her outright, surely she had landed on her feet. *Watch over my heedless sister, if you can. I am not sure anyone can convince her of what we know, if Mailan finds no proof.* Ah, Mailan, she would take Fion's death hard, very hard. . . .

Too bad about Darame. That last night, he had sensed a calm in her not seen since they'd first met. *Not seen since she found out your curse.* Was a woman who had come to terms with his talent all he could hope for? And for how long? That one was not the type of person to become a dutiful spouse, even if more than casual interest grew between them. . . . There was a slight pull at his cheek as a smile threatened. *Your interest is more than casual. You are still a coward, because of Emerson. Mother is right. If you cannot find what you want, find something acceptable. Something . . . Such an attitude! But if you cannot find a lover, surely you can find a friend.* Too bad he could not take Iver's attitude, and find a Nualan consort of choice. . . .

"It has been a long time since I have wanted a woman." Scarcely a whisper; better to admit it out loud. He could have passed her off to Baldwin that first night. *I fell into your eyes, woman, and I did not want to climb back out. Nothing I have learned since then has changed my mind. Can you be a friend? Do you want friends?*

The image of Darame's wicked smile veiled by thick silver hair blurred, becoming White's broad, bronzed features, the eyes darker than ever in the dim light of the cave. Sheel started, afraid he had slipped into dreams once too often, but it was only that, a memory. Rising to his knees, Sheel stretched to flip the rope over the hook they had bored into stone. Better not to be caught unawares. . . .

Do you begin to fear him? It was a disturbing thought. Sheel already knew what worried him about White: his methods of questioning. Varden clearly found the entire situation distasteful, and the one called Teague was often sent from the area—why, Sheel was not certain. But White, for all his impassive demeanor, *enjoyed* beating people. *He hates me. I do not know why, but I can feel his hate. Fortunately something still restrains him. . . . Maybe Dirk and Leah do not know how he is trying to get cooperation. . . .* His thoughts swirled and dissipated like dust devils as, at a distance, he heard rolling pebbles and the scuffing of feet.

Several deep breaths, a touch of the trance state filming his mind— Sheel watched through half-lidded eyes as the trio entered the cave. Varden looked more distressed than ever, though he hung back, out of White's line of sight. Teague, on the other hand, looked . . . Optimistic was the only word. Glancing down, Sheel saw a gel in his hand. *At last, we get to the drugs*. His mind felt curiously light. The questioning had not varied throughout the ordeal, and Sheel doubted it would change. There were things he would prefer they not discover he knew, but it was unlikely he would betray Mailan. White would have to ask specifically for what he wanted to know. *I begin to think you do not care what I know. Are you that confident of your control?*

"Now you will tell us the truth," Teague declared, his extended hand revealing the gel, his youthful manner bordering on arrogance. White looked annoyed, but Sheel anticipated his speech.

"Would you know truth if you heard it, Teague?" Sheel asked, the faintest of smiles touching his face.

Something had happened, somewhere in the camp—something Sheel had not heard. Blood draining from his face, the youth leapt for him.

"Teague!"

Sheel heard White's commanding tone through a haze of twinkling lights, his head still spinning from the blow. Numbness spread along the edge of his jaw. . . . *The gel. He must have crushed it in hitting me*. No matter; it was absorbed through the skin. But it would work very quickly this way, and Sheel felt his own blood activity increase in response to it. Too much to hope for, that he could counteract the effects. . . .

"Leave us, Teague. You do not have the . . . delicacy . . . for this work." The repressed anger in White's voice drained the youth's color still further, robbing him of energy. Quickly the youngster backed out of the cave. "We must talk. After we find the boy, steps must be taken to calm the city. You will do this. There are things we require, and these will also be arranged."

"Unlikely." This haze was not from the pain. . . . Fascinating. *I should have tried one of these once, to know the effects*. It amused him that White never named him, never used any title for him. *I have become something less than human*.

"I do not think you would like the alternative." White's voice never had any emotion. . . . Why was he so sure the man liked beating people up?

"Too many corpses, White. Another death would ignite the outkin, Riva Ragaree leading their ranks. You would spend what is left of your life fighting your own people . . . until the outclans descended to finish you off." Sheel could have added that three *guaard* did not a conspiracy make, but he had no desire to be punched in the face again. Right on the bone, it would form an impressive bruise. . . .

"Then we will have to convince you to cooperate. After all," White added almost pleasantly, "we have convinced you to talk."

Sheel chuckled softly and wondered if he would remember what he said.

FLOODPLAIN   ONEHUNDRED FORTYDAY   VESPERS

Heavy, wet snow had become an enemy, slashing them in the face as they passed through undergrowth, dropping from tree limbs above. Mailan was too preoccupied to notice. Threatening clouds above matched her mood, and this trip promised little improvement.

"We have found nothing!" Scarcely a whisper, but with an intensity that hurt her teeth. She could not keep it within; the pain had become too great.

"How can you say that?" Crow asked easily, pulling a branch out of her way and letting her pass by. "We have found Dirk's connection to the Atare line. And we found the body, *with* enough irregularities to satisfy any judge!" He whispered the last; their guide was uncle to the youth, and they had been careful not to tell the old farmer why they had come.

"Here is the place," came the worn voice ahead of them. The lean, taciturn man came to a halt beside a family crypt and pointed to a plaque within the stone wall. "His trainer, White, brought him to us in an urn. I was surprised; usually they send back the body for rites, and then we burn it. But with all the confusion in the city, I figured there was little time for formalities," the man said quietly.

"Things are still confused," Crow offered. "No doubt that explains it."

"Not even a *guaard* homage," was the reflective reply. "Must have been pretty slashed up to send him back in an urn. And in vain. Nothing from The Atare, either, though I hear someone still wants *his* blood. Better he tend to staying alive—the dead will keep." He looked over at the pair. "Is this all you wanted to see?"

"Yes, sir. It confirms our records." Mailan's response was gentle. How had this child ended up in such a predicament? Scarcely twenty Terran when he died; how could White have convinced him to join such treachery? *Dirk, maybe. He can be persuasive when he wants.* No point in burdening the uncle. . . . He might never know.

Nodding once at the two *guaard*, the farmer started back down the path the way they had come. Mailan stood watching him until he vanished into the brush.

"Beastly, flat land," she murmured. "How could you stand it with no mountains to protect you?"

"How could you stand all that rock hovering over you?" Crow responded, smiling faintly. "I did not have to stand it: I was born around here, but raised on Half-Moon Bay, when my mother remarried a shipmaster. The cliffs of the coast are beautiful, if rugged."

"Yes, we have found a few things," Mailan said suddenly, starting back down the path toward the road. "We know White changed the roster—"

"At least that the roster was changed with White's code used for entry," Crow clarified.

Mailan waved off the difference. "That is why I think he did it: he could use that excuse if he was caught. But I do not think he considered being caught, Crow. I think they thought their plan could not fail. Everything went wrong for them when Sheel and I survived that night." She kicked at a chunk of snow, watching it break into fragments. "I suppose that is why all the following attacks have been so swift, so vicious. . . . We were dead from the first, as far as they were concerned."

"Maybe." Crow shifted the pack on his back, a frown crossing his usually placid features. Things had changed, during their trip together. Mailan no longer had the strength to lead, but since Crow no longer needed a leader, it was no problem. Recent events had settled and clarified Crow's personality: he no longer leapt into the fray at every opportunity. "So, where shall we sleep, and do you want to change out of our uniforms now or later?" They had spent most of their time out of uniform, for fear of being recognized. It had been hard to remember to avoid *guaard*—Mailan feared that a few moments of carelessness might have given them away. So far, however, there was no sign of pursuit.

"Time to report, I think," she said, glancing over at Crow. "What do you think? I think we should get back to town and hop the rail for Portland."

"I think our luck just ran out," he whispered, his gaze fixed on something up ahead. Mailan narrowed her eyes, trying to see what disturbed him. "In the trees up there, at least two of them. I am sure I saw someone hide."

"Huh. There may be an explanation—such as children shy of *guaard* or something—but I think we had better change direction." Quickly Mailan surveyed the immediate area. Long strides over packed snow took her to the edge of the road and across a ditch filled with frozen water. Crow followed without comment.

Mysterious shapes loomed up against the wooden fences rimming the road, blanketed in layers of snow and ice. Jumping through a hollow, Mailan led the way along the back of the artificial ridge, her ears trained on the road. Just what they needed, another kink in the chain. She had no desire to confront anyone on this trip, especially *guaard*. How would she know if they were part of Dirk's conspiracy or merely pawns? *We are surely pawns, Crow. You spoke truly.*

Thankful she was not alone, Mailan paused in mid-step, listening for movement. A touch at her wrist seized her attention; Crow gestured with his chin, indicating that at least one had swung behind them. Then he pointed past a shriveled bush. Fixing her gaze on the frozen leaves, she could see darkness beyond it. *Guaard.*

Crow moved purposefully behind her to stand back to back, his pack brushing against hers, his hand hovering close to his wrist knife. Mailan tensed, wishing she had duplicated the information rings she carried and left copies with Ayers. A brief wish—if these chose to interfere with her assignment, she would count the game lost. What chance, if not few but many embraced Dirk's schemes?

Several dark shapes materialized out of the twilight, moving slowly up to the fence a few paces beyond. Too far to jump, too close to try and scale—checkmate. Setting her fingers on her belt knife, she maintained her balanced, wary pose, her eyes on the leaders. At least four, perhaps others, faceless as always in uniform. . . . She vaguely recognized the man on the right. Goguen was the name of the woman at his side, a tenyear *guaard*. Behind them . . . Berry and Carolan? Who was Crow facing? Eyes narrowed, Mailan realized they wore fieldpacks.

The newcomers wasted no time. "So it is true," their leader said softly, his face suddenly weary. "*Guaard* have turned. Do you have names?"

Mailan felt her eyebrows lift. None of those facing her had

moved toward their weapons. They stood quietly, watching her, waiting for some sign.

There was a snort of impatience from behind her, out of her line of sight. "Come on, Mailan, you must know something. Sparks, Leen, and I get dragged into the Starrise Mountains by White solely to escort one off-worlder to Atare? When she obviously does not want to leave Portland? And is obviously afraid of us—of *us*, by Sweet Mendulay!" The speaker was moving around to the front, still another *guaard* in tow . . . Sparks? Yes, and she recognized this youngster, too, *guaard* less than a year. Mailan could feel Crow's arm as he swung to track them, tension tracing his muscles.

"Why did you go into the Starrise Mountains?" Mailan said softly.

"We heard that The Atare and his heir were being held there. We found nothing." Making a face, the youth—Frost?—continued: "White took the others and continued into the mountains. We escorted the off-worlder back to Atare by rail."

"Off-worlder?" Crow's smooth, bronzed face was still impassive.

"The silvery woman with the black eyes. White says nothing about questioning her, or staying with her, only that we are to take her to her hostel. Which has no room for her! Serae Avis sent for her before the day was out." Frost looked disgusted. "Foul weather no matter how you look at it! So, tell us: what is going on?"

Mailan hazarded a quick glance at Crow, who was still watching the two young men. They had floundered near the fence drifts, but were leery of approaching further. "For now," she said softly to Crow, and straightened, relaxing. The group relaxed with her, not knowing the code she and Crow had devised: "for now" meant we accept this situation for now, but stay alert. "It is as you have guessed, I know not how: there are *guaard* who have turned on Atare."

"It was the only answer left," the older man—Haven?—offered quickly. "Why else would The Atare leave in such a hurry, and not take full *guaard* honors? That speaks of fear . . . fear in high places."

Mailan nodded. "We have been seeking the proof. It was so unbelievable, we could not trust anyone—only those who were present when we discovered there was still danger."

"You and Fion are chosen," Goguen pointed out. "How did you contrive to win his trust, Crow?"

Her friend was actually embarrassed. "Not for my good looks or winning manner. I gave him oath, and he accepted it."

Several caught breaths and disconcerted looks followed. "It has gone that far," Haven murmured, his expression distant.

Mailan gave him another short nod. "Standing in a snowbank is not the best place to discuss this. What say we—"

"Company," Carolan hissed suddenly, turning sharply to face down the road. The others scrambled over the pole fence, bunching up behind her.

A dark slash of a figure was coming into view. The newcomer wore a throw that was as gray as the sky above them, a bold streak of yellow woven near the border of the poncho. A huge staff shod with metal slapped through the ditch ice with precise rhythm; it was this sound which had alerted Carolan. That the stranger was heading toward them could not be doubted: he showed not the slightest bit of perturbation at a knot of *guaard* blocking the road.

"Mock-Sini," Crow murmured, glancing quickly at Mailan.

She did not comment; her eyes were on the arriving visitor. Sinis were rare this far from the mountains—this far north, in fact. Could it be . . . surely not. *I only half-believed that story when she told it. Ayers did say there was a Sini, though. . . .*

Reaching the group, the unknown stopped and threw back his hood. It was indeed a male, the gray in the long blond hair and beard hinting that he was older than he looked. Penetrating amber eyes bordered by impressive crow's-feet studied the gathering, lighting longest on Mailan.

"You have set me a merry chase, Chosen," he said in a dry, husky voice. "It was almost Yule when I set out on your trail, and now the end of the month grows near."

"Who are you, and why do you follow?" Mailan said quietly, her fingers resting casually on her belt knife.

"Fergus reb Fern, of Lebanon Way," he answered, chuckling. "I do not follow, I seek—and now I have found what I sought. I have not yet discharged my debt to Atare. Soon." His gaze encompassed the *guaard* surrounding her. "Can these be trusted?"

Mailan felt the others stiffen as one at the insult, and then Haven's hand shot out, grabbing Frost before the youth could begin to move. "I think you should explain how you come to ask that question," Haven said smoothly.

Fergus smiled, and Mailan remembered something Darame had said: it *was* a wolfish grin. "Because I was shadowing your group, youngster, in the Starrise Mountains. These children I suspect may be trusted," he added to Mailan, gesturing to Frost and Sparks. "The white-haired one had them escort the ice woman downriver to Atare. Three *guaard*, there were, who took the Mindbender east toward Ciedar. True *guaard*, if these be *guaard*."

"Mindbender? Do you mean The Atare?" Mailan said sharply.

"You lie." It was a whisper; Frost looked more bewildered than accusing. Turning to Mailan, he said: "The Atare was not there! White said they found nothing! He sent us back with the off-worlder while he continued on east to seek both Atare and heir!"

Mailan closed her eyes wearily, fighting a rage she feared would burst her blood vessels. "Mailan?" Crow's voice was careful as he touched her arm.

"We should not have left him. I knew it!" She snarled the last as she stepped toward the sini. "What is your part in this, you secretive old man? Why did you let it happen?"

Fergus's shaggy eyebrows indicated surprise. "The white-haired one carried a mag gun and killed three with it, including the grizzled *guaard*, who was surely my superior at Elkita. Should I spill my blood uselessly? The one called Jude held to her duty—so the heirs of Atare and Seedar are safe."

"Where?"

Fergus shrugged. "One place, if all went as planned. Elsewhere, if not. She is competent, that one—she will watch over them. It is the Mindbender who is in danger. A man who would strike his Atare might kill his Atare." The Sini abruptly stepped up to Frost, staring into his eyes. Startled, the youth stared back. "And the other one," Fergus said, gesturing to Sparks. Glancing at Mailan and Crow for a cue, the *guaard* moved forward at their simultaneous nod. Studying the pair a moment, Fergus smiled. "They will do." Giving Frost a hard look, he added: "I am a priest, boy. I do not have the habit of lying."

"Fion is dead?" Mailan was amazed at how even her voice sounded.

"We have him on ice. Harald saw it happen, and can identify the man who killed him, whether *guaard* or merely dressed as *guaard*. I thought you might need his words." Something in Fergus slumped a bit. "The Mindbender lived when they took him away. Now? We must trust to Mendulay. Somehow I do not see immediate death as his destiny. I still do not understand why he was taken. . . . Too many people are making their own plans." This was addressed to Mailan, and his voice was low. "I sought my people first; they follow the white-haired one to the eastern face. On foot, I fear. Will you come now? Since the caverns were breached I have searched for you, and we must pick up a trail surely grown cold."

"Frost." Mailan turned to face him. "Where did you leave the off-worlder?"

"The hostel she originally checked into," he replied promptly. "Serae Avis called her to the palace before the day was old. When we left, fourday ago, she was still there." Frost looked a bit surprised, but did not question the authority of a Chosen one.

Mailan thought quickly, rubbing at her neck to relieve the tension. So, the off-worlder had yet to run. Interesting. Send her word? Why bother? Darame knew as much as she needed to know. Better to leave her with Avis; her sly brain would keep them both out of trouble, no doubt.

"Why do you call him Mindbender?" she asked aloud.

Fergus acted as if called out of a trance. "He has a way of bringing people around to his will, whether *they* will it or no." He chuckled once more, his eyes on something they could not see. "I think he will prove the strongest." A glance at Mailan was both question and challenge.

"Yes. We will follow." With a jerk of her chin Mailan indicated they would move out.

"Not follow. Seek."

CAESAREAN EMBASSY ONEHUNDRED FORTYSEVENDAY COMPLINE

Darame was in a white heat when she finally crashed past Brant's assistant and into his office. One look at her expression caused the young man to back hastily away from the doorway. Brant's eyebrows rose almost to his hairline at the sight of her, but her words forestalled whatever he'd been planning on saying.

"Twenty-one days, Brant. Don't you think your book is a bit crowded not to have ten spare minutes in twenty-one days?" The words were very soft and gentle, but the look in her eyes promised mayhem in the near future. Darame made a point of leaning over his desk as she spoke, taking every advantage of his sitting position.

After a long moment of silence, Brant indicated with a jerk of his head that his assistant should leave. A languid hand, and the pale blue light began radiating from the corners of the room.

"Where in Seven Hells is Halsey, you bloodless son of a Devian wombat?" she snapped, stomping over to his bar and ransacking the containers for a chilled spritzer. It was the only opening left.

Brant started laughing. "I didn't know your vocabulary was so extensive! Since it is unlikely you know the full meaning of that, I'll overlook it this time." He managed the slightest pause between "it" and "this" without breaking his stride or his smile. Darame let her lips thin as she listened to the rewarding hiss of carbonation and sipped directly from the tube.

Are you really that unobservant? If he wanted to think she underestimated the insult, fine—she was not ready to cut his throat. Not yet. Besides, Brant always smuggled a mag gun onto each world he visited, and Sweet Peter alone knew where it was hidden in this room.

Pouring a drink for himself, Brant wandered back over toward his desk. "In answer to both your questions, I haven't answered your messages because I knew what you wanted and I didn't know where Halsey was . . . then."

A new game. Delightful. "I hope things have been running more smoothly here. I had Sheel trusting me and listening to me, and then White shows up like a rotting corpse, ruining the scenery." She kept her tone petulant, wanting him to think her work had been compromised. "I could smell him in my sleep."

Brant frowned at that. "I had nothing to do with White. I think he's a bit strange in the head—and he dislikes Sheel, that I'm sure about. What happened up there?"

A short laugh escaped Darame's lips. "You tell me. When I woke, I had Sheel unconscious and the *guaard* dead, plus Tobias missing. If we're not careful, the authorities will have our skins for this entire mess."

Seating himself on the edge of the desk, Brant shook his head at her. "I have the two of us covered thoroughly. Atare taking a fancy to you helped: they can't do much to you when it's obvious their ruler trusted you. It's Halsey I'm concerned about." His expression became grave. "He's been missing for almost a month. I must admit I'm worried about him."

"He said nothing to you about leaving?"

"Nothing." Brant was both emphatic and annoyed. It was a good performance; Darame found herself almost tempted to rethink her theories. Almost.

"Not like him to leave for this long," she pointed out, leaning against the bar and studying an area just to the right of Brant's head. "Any theories?"

Brant tapped his nails across the polished wood of his desk, a slight frown pulling at his face. He apparently had not noticed Darame using his own tricks against him, but he clearly felt them—he was becoming irritable. "I don't think he's dead," Brant said at last. "I've kept a watch for loose corpses—murder draws attention in this town, it's rare." He chuckled at that. "They don't know how to deal with it." Glancing up, he added: "I think the *guaard* may be looking for a scapegoat, as incredible as that seems. That's the other reason I'm worried about Halsey. I think . . . I think that someone in the *guaard* may have been involved with Cort Atare's death."

Darame raised her eyebrows. How much was he going to volunteer?

"Seriously," Brant continued, misinterpreting her expression. "I told you, I think that *guaard* called White isn't playing with a full deck. He may be our best lead to Halsey, and I know he has Sheel Atare as well."

"Why?" No need to pretend puzzlement; the real question was, what would Brant say in return?

"Maybe to find out where Leah's boy is, maybe for some other reason. It occurred to me that a faction of the *guaard* might be trying to force some changes, even gain some control in the government. They may be trying to get Sheel to agree to some terms. Once I figured out where you all were, I kept an eye on things. When I decided the *guaard* knew, I dropped a hint that we—the embassy—wanted to know where you were and were concerned about you. So I knew you'd be fine."

"And sent an observer?"

"Of course."

Darame controlled a chuckle, allowing her smile to show. So . . . as usual, you know almost everything. A cold thought touched her stomach . . . If Brant had plans for Avis, Tobias was no longer needed, either . . . "I could have done a better job," she finally said. "Where do you think they are?"

"East of here, in the mountains—beyond them, even." It was too casual.

Darame had had enough of caution. "I think you know. What are you going to do about it?"

"What's it to you?"

Her eyes widened in feigned outrage, even as Brant added: "Not Halsey. The Nualan."

Her tube of wine crashed to the bar as she started for him, grabbing the first excuse that came to mind. "How are we going to salvage anything from this job if you—"

"Forget the job." Brant's calm expression did not change. "It's blown, forget it. I have a bit going on the side, and if you're smart, you'll start something up, too. I'm not sure Avis will be worth your while, though: she's a younger daughter, and they're as worthless as younger sons." The last was almost too casual, causing Darame's ears to sharpen. So, Avis *was* under his eye. Worse and worse . . . Then his expression altered, and amusement creased his features. "Of course. I should have seen it sooner. Brilliant, my dear! And with care and a bit of smuggling, you can even avoid children. It won't matter: his children have nothing to do with the succession."

"I don't follow," she said slowly, thrown off-balance in the conversation for the first time. Turning, she reached for what was left of her drink.

"Come, come, Darame, have you been too busy with short-term credit-shuffling to see a larger picture? That trinket around your neck is a toy compared to what you would have as Atarae." He played with the strange word, stretching its three syllables. Seeing Darame's frown, he laughed. "Is the word unknown to you? The wife of the ruler, sweet Gavrielian. He has to marry someone, and he certainly won't be blasting off for Caesarea to find her. Why not you?"

"I doubt the people of this city would appreciate a free-trader as their ruler's consort," Darame said wryly. "And I have this aversion to marriage. I'll take my trinium and a ticket for Cold Sleep, thanks." It took all her training to remain calm. *Don't mock me, you bastard, I know my place! Or do you know it looks like he's lost interest? Good God, was even old Harald in your pay?*

Brant shook his head. "Don't be crazy. More wealth than you could spend in a lifetime—probably as petty cash! I'll even give you a hint: the trade routes are closed this time of year, but my informants tell me that seven days east of here, a few hours off the road to the south, lies a small camp, unregistered as a wintering caravan. I'd look for Sheel Atare there. You can take my Arab, he's as tough as they come and fast." Brant reached lazily over his head to touch his communication board. "Irving, arrange for my Lightning to be taken to the palace for Darame Daviddott-tir's use. Immediately." Glancing at her, he added: "I'd take rail to Portland and save yourself some time."

"You're serious." She studied him quietly, controlling her elation, wondering just what was behind this offer.

"Very." The smile disappeared from his face. "Some odd things are going on right now, and I don't have my finger on them as I'd like.... You can move where I cannot. The act of returning you as he did—without any damage—shows that White thinks you no threat. So, pay him a visit. You can even tell him that it was authorized by me." That seemed to amuse him greatly. "Make Atare see reason. He can counterplot all he wants, once he gets back here alive. I'll even help him, at this point."

"Brant the kingmaker?"

He smiled at her turn of words. "Just don't forget who your friends are, my dear, when you ascend the bloody throne."

Reaching languidly to touch the necklace pressed against her skin, wondering how he knew, for it was hidden beneath her shirt, Darame allowed an answering smile. How smooth it all sounded—if one did not know how power worked in this place. *Ah, Sheel, this is not how you intended me to use this chain, but it has certainly come in handy!* As her smile faded, her thoughts took a savage turn. *He had better be just fine, Brant ... or between us we'll show these children what a real blood feud is.*

Chapter Twelve

Darkness was a better state of mind ... of being. Sheel suspected that it was actually past starset, but he could not be sure; the drugs blurred all distinctions, including day and night. It had been a long time since he had seen anyone ... Two days? Surely he had seen the star's light twice. *Losing your grip, fool,* he thought idly, contemplating the spur of rock his feet rested against. This new position was more comfortable ... comparatively. It was closer to lying down, at least, although the wire binding his wrists was infinitely more painful than rope. Wiggling fingers, wiggling toes, insuring circulation . . .

You had one chance, and it is gone, he reminded himself. But what other choice had there been? Grinding the ropes to threads a few days back, he had managed to slip away into the netherworld of dusk. Odd that their ignoring him for a few days should work to his advantage. He had walked until there was no strength to continue, and even found a trickle of a thermal stream, which had both bathed and filled his body. *What chance to evade* guaard? *They can track anything, anywhere* . . . Sleep was necessary, and of course they found him. Now the drugs which had caused his will to deteriorate were being used to make sure no further escapes would be made. The beating had merely released White's frustration.

Dead man. Names were being mentioned . . . Dirk's, even Leah's. The lines of choice were being drawn: assist them, or spend his last days wired to this bolt in the wall. Sheel had given up on Varden; the youth was simply too frightened of White. *What has he done to these children, to frighten them so?* That avenue had been explored before the ill-fated escape attempt. Sheel had chosen his time and his words carefully: *It is still not too late.* The boy had actually blanched, his voice trembling as he answered. *Not too late? It was too late the moment I said "You are right."* He would not explain this cryptic remark, nor volunteer any other information.

Not much time left. As Sheel had hoped, his training and healing abilities had enabled him to fight the erosion of his body and will, but things had changed abruptly in the last few days. Now White used the drugs to keep him from escaping, and he was not careful in dosage or mixture. Sheel understood a great deal about his own talents, and the chemical and electrical procedures he used to heal—but all stamina had a limit. White's current actions had the potential of damaging the mind; all Sheel's remaining strength went toward protecting his brain. Nothing was left for his immune system. Given sparse food, meager water, and temperature fluctuations, infection was inevitable.

Outside the cave was a crunching sound, infiltrating the steady trickle of water that lulled his senses.

The intruder paused at the entrance to activate a lantern. Pale yellow light wavered into the cave, illuminating the far end of it. Sheel quickly focused on the light source, knowing that a beacon might suddenly flare on. A large, unfamiliar form walked slowly up to his feet.

Totally unfamiliar. The man was not even dressed as a *guaard*.
Sheel studied his boots, wondering where White's game was
leading. *Who are you, and should I know you?* Now *that* thought
was almost frightening. He was so tired. . . .

Squatting near the flat rock White often sat upon, the stranger
placed his lantern upon the stone and settled his large body into
the sand. A big man, who once had been bigger: his clothes
seemed slightly loose. Several objects were laid beside the lantern, including a water bottle. That was interesting to Sheel: he
knew he was dehydrated, and that his body could not continue to
feed on itself. Most of the day had been spent trying not to think
about thirst.

"Do you remember me, Atare?" the man asked softly in Caesarean, his pleasant tenor voice rolling through the sound of
water falling.

"Should I remember you?" Sheel chose to say, the whisper
barely penetrating the silence that followed the stranger's words.

"Not necessarily. We met only once, for but a few moments:
the night of your heir's birthday celebration. I am called Halsey
in this time and place. My company was here to arrange some
trade agreements—we arrived the night of the party."

"And everything fell apart—for you as well as my family.
Why are you here?" There was no harm in asking. Either he
would explain or he would not; Sheel was fairly certain he could
tell if the man was lying. Pain seemed to make him sensitive to
nuance.

"I suspect I am here to kill you . . . in a manner of speaking."
Halsey reached for the soft water bottle. "You are called a healer.
I understand that part of your skill lies in recognizing chemical
imbalances. Can you do it with water?"

Sheel shifted slightly, trying to get a good look at the man. It
was awkward, what with his hands anchored past his head. Parting his arms at the elbows, he studied the off-worlder. Dark eyes
flecked with gold stared back, as if weighing, analyzing . . . "I am
not sure," Sheel began. "I can detect bad water, if that is what
you are asking. But water intentionally altered . . . poisoned? I am
not at my best," he added wryly.

Halsey's eyes moved to the water bottle. "I do not trust it.
Why would they have me deliver your food and water, unless
there was something behind the deed? What do you want me to
do?"

"Pour some of the water . . . No, not against your skin—"
Sheel changed his mind abruptly.

"I have lined gloves." Pulling them on, Halsey poured a tiny amount of water into his cupped palm. "And now?"

"I am afraid I must stick an appendage into it," was the dry response. "Unfortunately, it had better be my tongue. A finger would take a long time."

"What if it is highly concentrated?"

"It will probably give me the dry heaves," Sheel told him. "It has been a day or so since they have bothered bringing me water." Cautiously Sheel lifted his head as Halsey brought his hand closer. *And if you poison yourself?* The idea that he had a choice amused him, and he managed a grin before turning to the man's palm.

The effect was immediate. If anything, his mouth felt drier, and sparks which had no basis in reality danced before his eyes. He could hear Halsey move quickly, and the sound of water splashing on rocks.

"This, Atare." It was the man's other hand. Blind to his intentions, Sheel accepted the water. Tepid, brackish, but free of anything dangerous.

"What?" Sheel managed when his mouth was moist enough to spit.

"The basin of water in the cave. Heavy on minerals, but apparently *they* have not bothered to foul it." Wheezing slightly, Halsey bent to seize the bottle. "Can I rinse this out, do you think?"

"Several rinses: pour the water on the floor each time," Sheel instructed. His head felt clear for the first time in several days. Was dehydration disorienting his mind, or was he simply becoming ill? *You are confused, dead man.* "Then you might pour a bit on me. My bath is wearing off."

"You are not eating enough to pass wastes," Halsey pointed out. "Not good, Atare. You do not smell unwashed, you smell sick." Carefully refilling the bottle with the cave water, the offworlder brought it back and sat down next to Sheel.

"Quite likely," Sheel said, the faint grin returning. "I have the choice of protecting various portions of my body. Hot healing can only do so much, and lack of food and water weakens the ability." Slowly he drank some of the offered fluid.

"How about the food?"

Still sipping, Sheel considered it. "No," he said finally. "Better not to risk it." His pale right eye gave Halsey a sharp look. "It has only been two days since I ate. I can last quite a while without solids."

"Not good," Halsey told him.

"No." Sheel kept it simple.

"You were slender to begin with, and I can see by your face that you have lost weight. What else?" There was patience in the question.

Sheel did not pretend to misunderstand. "A few cracked ribs. . . . And my back has seen better days—do not bother looking! There is nothing you can do for it. Just cuts and bruises," he added quickly.

"I could wash away the blood." Into the quiet Halsey added: "But they will probably be back, won't they?"

"It seems that our usefulness draws to an end," Sheel agreed. "Pretend that you gave me the water and food. Few outside my field of study know just what a healer can do; perhaps they will think it must build in my system."

"Do you really believe that?" Halsey's expression was tired.

"Of course not. But short of lighting a flare to announce our location, I am out of ideas. You?" Sheel watched his face, trying to remember something about this man, something once known. . . . "You are Caesarean?" Why was thinking so difficult? Surely that meant something, something political. . . . It was taking everything just to concentrate on this man's face.

"My godchild has a bad habit of taking matters into her own hands. If there is a way to find me, she will. Can we stay alive until then?" Sheel gave Halsey a questioning look, and the man clarified his statement by saying: "Darame."

Ah. Was it worth mentioning that she might be dead? He did not want to think about the possibility . . . it increased the pain. *If you do not say the words aloud*. . . ."More water," Sheel said finally. Right now, life was enough. He would not bring death into it.

Night was far advanced. . . . Past midnight, for certain, and approaching lauds, moonset for Nuala's largest natural satellite. Darame leaned against her mount, sipping at the tube attached to her water bottle and watching the path for loose stones and shards of ice. A handsome black nose turned slightly, reaching to shove against her.

"I know, your turn," she told him affectionately, squeezing some tepid water into the shallow, soft bag Nualans used for watering their horses. Only a squirt, since they were still walking; no chances could be taken with her riding animal. Praise all the saints for concentrated food, or she would not be this far into the mountains. No pack hazelle could match this animal's speed, and few horses could equal his endurance. "You are much too good to be Brant's riding toy," she told the stallion, patting his neck. "I think I'll have to blight my Nualan record with a bit of horse theft." Snorting, the Arab tossed his head and extended his walk. "Ready to speed up again? Very well." Slowing the horse with a firm grip on his rein, Darame tightened the girth and then jumped into the saddle, wincing as she landed. "We have been blessed with a waxing moon—let's take advantage of it."

Lightning moved into his fluid trot. Darame let her mind settle into the stallion's gait, trying not to anticipate, trying not to worry. *There must be faster ways to get into the mountains . . . unless the mountains are the protective device the Atares use to guard against invading tribes.* Speed was of the essence. Darame felt as driven as she had the evening she spoke to Brant. The food supplies from the ship, untouched her last venture, were coming in handy. Ayers had sketched her a map and Avis herself had packed Darame's clothing. *I'll bet I was exiting through the town gates before matins.*

Do not strain your horse. You will need him to return. This was a nine- or ten-day ride from Portland, or so Ayers had said. Darame had discovered otherwise, at least on Brant's excellent stallion. No more than eight days, if the animal could keep up his current pace—and he showed no signs of flagging. *If my seat and legs hold out.* Darame was in much worse shape than the horse, and knew it. *Out of practice . . .*

"How would you like to be part of my new breeding project?" she asked the stallion, who flicked his ears at the echoes of her voice. "I understand that rulers here often reward partisans with land grants. I could start a program to create you beauties for export." Lightning did not respond, of course, but it took her mind off her legs. He was an intelligent animal, a mixture of the best of his ancient breed and the newer traits that Nualan scientists had added to his strain. . . . But even he had limits, limits she feared they might reach. "You would do very well out of the deal, you know: ladies galore, and exclusive visiting privileges."

The trail veered southwest, and moonlight flooded the pass. Crystallizing vapor made plumes about their heads and created haloes between the last moon and their path. Huge shaggy trees half-shrouded in snow hunched above them, climbing the sides of the gorge up into wispy cloud. The slightest sound echoed for miles—Darame had no fear of ambush, and no doubt she was announcing her passage to every animal within a ten-minute ride. She kept her hand on the mag gun Ayers had found for her, however—no sense in being careless. *Monkey's Paw, at best. Fire this thing and bring down the pass. What I would not give for air transportation—anything in the air!* Brant had discouraged it. He did not want the *guaard* to know she had gone east . . . not yet. *And Dirk knows when any air vehicle leaves or enters Atare.*

May you find what you seek. Avis, miraculously, had not pressed for details. When told that Sheel was thought to have gone east, sending Tobias to still another place of safety, she had seemed satisfied. This trip was officially to find Halsey. *Too trusting, my friend. Unless Ayers added to my tale? Some information which gave you reason to trust me? Or was it that stupid necklace, again? If Sheel's interested in me, he has a strange way of showing it.*

Did warmth ever come to this land? Lingering puffs of warm air had deceived her, the first few days on Nuala. *We are locked in ice, and shall never free ourselves* . . . Ayers had promised her little snow on the high desert plain to the east. But the winds— that part she dreaded. Fingering the poncho Avis had insisted she wear over her jacket, Darame wondered if even Sheel was cold tonight. *If he still lives.* That thought she avoided—could not face. *And if he is dead?* Her mind slowed with the stallion's gait as the footing became more treacherous. No—it could not be faced. She simply was not ready to deal with it. *Avis I would take to Riva Ragaree. That tough old woman has no intention of ending up like her brother, and she can protect Avis. If I can get Avis to her safely.* Then, she would purge herself of whatever Sheel's death left her. Anger, futility, bitterness, numbness . . .

"Why should it do anything to you?" Darame considered her whispered words. *You would miss him, woman. Admit it, damn it! Something is not right when you are more than a glance away.* Not good, not healthy, this feeling . . . And when this is settled, one way or another? *When you leave him behind as the wanderlust takes you?*

She was grateful when they reached dry, hard rock, and the Arab stretched into a trot.

STARRISE MOUNTAINS ONEHUNDRED FIFTYFIVEDAY SEXT

A puff of icy wind pushed Darame up the stone pathway. She kept her eyes on the tents below. Still sleeping, for the most part—White had been on night shift, awake when she rode in during the wee hours of the morning. Fortunately she was used to working long hours on little sleep; now a chance had arisen she had not consciously hoped for. A few more steps, around the bend, and there it was—the equipment stash. She paused, the lack of wind at her back an odd feeling, and then hailed the dark hole.

"He is asleep," came a voice at her ear.

Darame forced herself not to jump. Damn these *guaard,* and their soft tread! Turning her head, she studied the young man at her elbow. Tall, confident—a bit of White around the eyes. Kin of his? No matter. "I came here to try talking to Sheel Atare," she started, since he had not been present when she arrived the previous night. "White said we would discuss it in the morning." *I am rested, the horse rests, and I assume White must be close to rising. So get him.*

"I imagine he will be awake soon. Wait in here." Nodding toward the opening, which was catching the last pale rays of the morning light, the young man continued down the broken path and toward the slice in the hills.

Better and better. *Told* to wait inside! The saints were with her on this venture. Shifting her pack to the other shoulder, Darame entered, her hand moving to the roman strapped to her wrist. A pretty thing, keeping excellent time despite its decorative face and design . . . designed for a free-trader. Her eyes raked the small, irregular scrape, noting its lack of depth, the one slash leading into darkness. The roman's luminous dial did not change color: no surveillance equipment. She had expected none. Working the long, thin wire out of the stiff band, she moved to the portable RAM.

Everyone kept their box of rings near the screen. Sure enough, under a pile of rope and a jacket . . . Moving the items without disrupting them, Darame sat down next to the lockbox. Praise Peter it was familiar . . . and a nasty one. She had only one chance with this style. If she correctly interrupted the guardian field, she could remove the rings without anyone ever knowing how she had entered the box. White might not even notice their disappearance, if he had no reason to enter it during her stay. *And I'm not staying long.* . . . But if she missed, the contents would immediately char to ash.

The far right groove, as she remembered it. A while since she'd done this type of work. . . . A tiny flash, and the box popped open. Now, if Ayers's crash course in words had sunk into her brain. . . .

Names and dates. That was all Darame had tried to learn in Nualan. Names like Leah, and Dirk, and Brant, or anything without names, but in the right time period. And this looked promising; there were only four rings in the box, and they were all dated since the raid in the clay caverns. Tucking the rings into one of the near-invisible pockets in the jump suit she was wearing, Darame carefully shut the box and waited for the . . . click. Active once again. *Bless you, Halsey, for many lessons.* Carefully replacing the jacket and rope, Darame paused to jam the wire into the back of the RAM, shorting out the communications system. Now, anything else she should attend to? . . .

A quick sweep of the room reassured her. Nothing worth bothering with, except a packet of medical supplies. She rummaged in the container while she re-threaded her lockpick, finding a few things she planned on confiscating and a few things that were disquieting. The lip balm was a godsend—the wind had ravaged her delicate tissues—and she took some peroxide, gauze, and pads for caution's sake. White had plenty, he probably would not notice. But these bottles and capsules . . . Darame lifted one of the tubes of gels, studying it. Why so familiar? . . . Unless . . . Gavriel. She had seen someone use them on Gavriel, to get information out of a sneak. Also the red capsules. Controlling the tightening sensation in her stomach, Darame carefully set the tubes back into the kit and secured the lid.

Her timing was impeccable. No sooner had she smeared her lips with balm, stuffed the chosen medical supplies into her pack, and settled herself into the chair near the entrance than she heard the sound of falling rocks. Light angling into the cave was abruptly cut off, and White's snowy head popped around the cave's supporting wall. Darame promptly lifted her eyebrows at him.

"Go ahead," he said briefly. "Down the path and across the gap. The cave opening faces more toward the west. Teague is on watch." As always the dark eyes flicked over her without expression, and then White disappeared once again.

On watch, she mused to herself as she started down the narrow trail. For what? So you admit it? She realized that White probably did not know what Brant had told her. *What do you think I am here to convince him to do?*

Raspy breathing brought her to a halt. Some sort of dangerous animal—Darame turned her head slightly, her eyes traveling on ahead to another slash in the rocks. Not even to the ravine. Would White leave any threat in the area? . . . Deciding he would not, wishing she had left her mag gun strapped to her side instead of stowing it in her bag (at White's request), Darame ducked into the cave.

Thin, filtered light gave a ghostly aura to the small cave. It was no more than a closet in size, and was empty except for a pallet of cloth at one side. The unknown animal was over by the pile— Darame froze in place for a long moment. Then she moved over to the blankets and knelt.

Finally—suspicions confirmed, and all too late. Halsey— plump and jolly no longer, shivering as if in a stiff breeze, wandering in some delirium. Reaching for his neck, she checked his pulse. Erratic . . . Moving her hand slightly, Darame was appalled to see a bruise forming. What in Seven Hells—radiation? Here? For a moment she was terrified, and then she understood. *They gave you tainted food or water. The effect is not immediate, not to this degree—but it would start to damage you from the inside out. If I had not eaten concentrates this morning, they would know I am immune. . . .*

Something hard angled its way into her throat, but she held herself in check, biting her lower lip until it bled. *Grief is only for when you can bear no more.* Nothing in that box for radiation poisoning, not that she recognized from her limited experience on Gavriel. Nuclear weapons were among the messiest known arsenal . . . *What kind of barbarians would do this to another human being*— Barbarians. That was it. Beneath the polished Nualan veneer was the barbarian, and each person varied in how close it hovered near the surface. . . .

So this is how we fail. Have I ever told you what you are to me, old man? She knew what he would say in reply, if he could hear that question: *Why are you wasting time? Find that infernal ruler and take care of things! And remember: always have options.* No options left, Halsey. Somewhere I gave them all away.

Would this have happened if she had stayed in Atarc, had never gone to the caverns? Darame pulled one of her two canteens from her side and carefully lifted Halsey's head. Still conscious, barely—he took several sips of the water. Would it be more merciful to— No; where there was life there was hope. And Sheel was a healer. When she found him, she would ask him what to do.

Capping the canteen and re-attaching it to her bag, she rose to her feet and blindly started out of the cavern. No planning to be done, no anticipation— *Dear sweet Magdalen, if Halsey looks like this, then Sheel....*

Darame forced herself to walk, not run, down the sloping trail.

There was no greeting, no warning in Teague's stance. The *guaard* stood outside and to one side of Sheel's quarters, seemingly oblivious to her presence. Glancing at the plains as an excuse to check distances and angles, Darame saw that Teague could not have seen her enter Halsey's cave. *Good.* Would this man accompany her, or not? She started past him, shifting her pack to her other shoulder.

"I should warn you that The Atare has been ill," the young man said suddenly. "We have notified the nearest base that we need a doctor." He did not even turn his head in her direction.

Darame scarcely paused. *Do not bother—I know that the nearest base is in Atare.* The other words sobered her. *Doctor? For a healer?* Stiffening her spine, she walked slowly into the cave.

It seemed bright at the opening, where starlight poured in, with nothing but shadows beyond. Darkness increased her unease, despite the warmth of the cave. A strong stream of water trickled somewhere out of sight. To her right Darame saw several candle stubs on a ledge of rock. *Candles?* She remembered she had only one pocket torch, already on low charge.... Taking the largest, she lifted a strike from the small waterproof container provided and flicked it against the stones.

Candlelight was grossly inefficient to see the arrangement of the inner cave. Taking several other squat candles and long, singed strikes, Darame started into the gloom. Walking forward she could do. Call his name? Her nerve failed her.

A glint of metal called her toward the water. A basin, a tiny waterfall hollowing its sides ... and just beyond it, the object of her search. Stepping up to the crumpled form, she stood silent and still long enough for the wax to grow warm in her hand. Then she swooped to the flat rock by her left toe, scrabbling for the other candle stubs. Light! She had to see!

Feel, hear... *Sweet Mary, is he breathing?* One hand reached over to feel for his chest while the other rested against his throat. Yes, breathing, if a bit shallow ... pulse rapid, skin warm and shivering. Removing her hands, she watched carefully for bruising. Moments ticked by.... Nothing. Relief passed through her, an actual weakness. Sheel was covered with bruises, which had initially terrified her. Now she could see that the one on his face seemed to be old.... Candlelight was a poor substitute for starlight, but the pattern of the bruise spoke of greens and purples, not fresh reds and blacks. *And I thought you were thin when I first met you....* It took every ounce of self-control she had to keep from screaming "What have they done to you?"

Darame merely whispered it. There was a slight stirring in response, and she realized he was conscious. "Sheel?" Leaning over, she repeated his name. Glinting metal . . . Her fingers found wire wrapped around his wrists. "Wire?" The word was husky in her ears. *As if you were going anywhere....* It had cut into flesh in several places, prompting her to fumble in her pack for the peroxide. Bubbling foam caused Sheel to catch his breath, inhaling sharply.

On her feet without memory of the action, Darame turned to call Teague—and hesitated, thinking. Thinking . . . *This is intentional. They know very well how sick you are . . . they want you sick. And only your god knows how long they will let me stay in here.* Already facing Sheel again, Darame folded to her knees. *Fever. What do I do for fever?* Once more she was digging in her bag.

Salicin, she had recognized the symbol for salicin, a natural herb with much the same effects as laboratory aspirin. If she could get him to swallow it— *Surely Nualans can use it, Ayers would not have put it in my pack otherwise.* Her fingers closed on the vial. Pulling out her drinking cup as well, she moved over to the basin, testing the water. No, as tepid as her canteen. Better he drink what she was sure of.

It was not an easy procedure. Darame never claimed to be a good nurse, and Sheel was so confused he certainly did not recognize his attendant. From the smell Darame knew the concoction tasted foul. Somehow she got most of the mixture inside of him. Next . . . Compresses of water?

Rooting around in her supplies, Darame found the towel and washrag Avis had packed for use on the trail. Moving to the basin, she dipped the smaller cloth into the tepid water and rung it limp. Crawling back to Sheel's side, she blotted lightly at his face and laid the damp cloth over his neck and breastbone. Next, the towel . . .

Darame lost track of time as the pale streaks of daylight stretching into the cave lengthened. Seeking a more efficient means of transporting fluid, she filled the container she used to water Lightning and set it at Sheel's head. This helped with the washrag, but the towel required the full size of the basin. How long should she keep it up? When should she try to give him more salicin? She paused only long enough to dig out the lip balm. Sheel's flesh was more chapped than her own—enough so that she dreaded touching it with the ointment. As she feared, he flinched slightly, but was too weak for other forms of protest.

The starlight began to fail, to climb the wall facing the entrance. Outside she could hear snatches of conversation, even as the wind began to rise. Once she thought someone had looked in, but no one addressed her, no one stopped her. *Because you think my task is hopeless?* The thought was bitter, but anger rose to nudge it aside. *He is too strong for you scum! And I'll rot in hell myself before I let something this foolish carry him off.* Slapping the wet towel onto his chest, Darame paused to stretch her raw, sore fingers, shivering as a curl of wind tickled the back of her neck. *Coming from the northwest again. No wonder he caught something, with the temperature in here fluctuating so much.*

Shaking more of the salicin into her cup, she dissolved it in water and reached to lift Sheel's head. The awkwardness defied description. The wires were next: somehow, some way. *And a blanket out of the pack—the gusts of wind will lower his skin temperature faster than anything I'm doing.* Slipping a hand behind Sheel's neck, she tried to lift and turn him simultaneously. And noticed . . . Was it wishful thinking, or did his color seem better? Raising a candle stub, she looked closely.

Definitely more color. Touching his face, she realized he was not quite as warm. Tensing all over, refusing to think about it, she set the candle down and gave him the salicin, which he drank obediently. Less like a drugged man, though . . . more like a sleepy one. *Don't waste time hoping!* Wincing as her clothing brushed her chapped hands, Darame pulled out a lightweight thermal blanket and arranged it over his legs. Moving to his head, she seated herself and bent to examine the wires.

Unable to control the smile that spread across her face, Darame turned her face away from the entrance. No one must see, no one. . . . *Forgive me, Nameless One, for doubting. Surely there is a chance.* It was a single line of metal, looped and then twisted and heavily wrapped back up the main line, out of reach of his fingers. If they kept him drugged, of course it would have been enough to hold him. . . . Intent on her work, she began to unwind the coil of metal, concentrating on Sheel's steady breathing as accompaniment to her work.

She had forgotten how dark a cave was. . . . The moons approached full, and rose well in the eastern sky, except for . . . the smallest, which would shed little light. *Tougher than I thought, these wires. Rest easily, child, and I will do what I can—*

"Are you tightening those or loosening them?" came a whisper, and Darame jumped enough to bump her knees into Sheel's head. "Ouch!"

"Shhhh!" The sound was barely audible. "They have ignored my Nightingale attempts, but if you sing out, they will come running," she whispered. Leaning over for the cup, she refilled it from the horse bag. "Drink this—slowly!"

"Of course. I suspect you have spent a great deal of time telling me to drink things." Low, even raspy . . . Genuinely weary, his usual pose nonexistent.

As if we had time for games. . . . "You could simply avoid me. Your problems might decrease," Darame offered, feeling her throat tighten.

A long pause, as he savored the water in his mouth. Then the gaze flicked in her direction, and it was more alert than she could have hoped. "Would it were that easy." The barest hint of a smile, the dimples distorted through weight loss. . . .

Damn you, Sheel Atare. Damn you for remembering, and for knowing before I knew, and probably for not caring anymore! She could control her face, despite the turmoil within, but his next words brought tears to her eyes.

"Fortunately healers mend quickly," Sheel added, sipping from the offered cup.

So calm, now that his fever was decreasing . . . Yes, decreasing, he was beginning to sweat. . . . *What is your source of strength?* Swallowing her tears, Darame whispered: "Well, thank all the gods for that."

Darame's words so startled him that if Sheel had been holding the cup he would have dropped it. He twisted his head back around to see her face, but she had turned away. In a few moments she looked back at him, her face as wintry as ever; but her dark eyes glittered. "Keep drinking. We have to get out of here somehow."

"How long have you been here?" he managed to ask. "Are you a prisoner?" Such a shock, to open his eyes and see her here . . . really here.

"About a day," she answered, continuing to unwrap wire with one hand. "And no, I am not a prisoner, not yet. But if White catches me at this, it may stretch even my great talent for dissembling. Or if he notices I swiped his communication rings." A strong gust of wind swept into the cave, drawing shivers from both of them. "The wind is in our favor, but I think we should keep whispering."

"Why have they left you alone?" He knew why they had left Halsey with him, but this was different. How many con games was Darame running?

"The *guaard* looked in once, before nightfall."

"See who is on duty—you need more candles, anyway." A touch of strength threaded his voice, giving it authority. Obediently—well, with a semblance of obedience—Darame rose to fetch candles. She returned with several new ones, her face pulled in a slight frown.

"A young one I have not seen before, not quite as tall as Teague. Sheel, I think he can hear us in here, but—"

"I know." Fascinating. *Are you the dead man, Varden? Not me; you?* "If you can loosen one of these wires—" He left his comment dangling as he pulled his legs up to his stomach.

"You look terrible," she snapped suddenly. "They could at least have let you bathe."

"The odor was worse a few days ago," Sheel told her, giddily amused by her terse concern. *I need food.* "I was allowed outdoor elimination privileges when White could no longer stand the smell."

"That bastard," she hissed, falling into Caesarean. "I will—"

"Not yet." His calm, unspecified promise stopped her cold. "You will have to think of another epithet. That one does not translate into Nualan."

The woman stared at him for several moments, surprise registering in her eyes. Finally perceiving that he was trying to tease her, Darame dissolved into silent laughter, burying her face in her poncho to muffle her amusement.

Sheel could not join her; laughing hurt too much. He contented himself with thinking up other slurs against White's character, heritage, and general person.

Straightening, mopping the tears from her eyes, Darame said softly: "I do not think you should move around much."

"On the contrary, I had better make sure I can move. As you pointed out, we must leave this place. I had better be able to walk when we do." He stretched his legs again experimentally.

"I have a horse. He will not be as swift on the return, but better his exhaustion than yours." She flinched as one wire popped free. "Drink some more water."

"As you wish, doctor," he murmured in reply, stretching his fingers as he reached for the cup. All his idle finger- and toe-wiggling had had its benefits; he could grip the container. Slowly draining the water, he set the cup down carefully and then reached to pull up the blanket. "A few nights I would have killed for this. I am not going back with you, Darame."

Her hands jerked, causing him to hiss involuntarily.

"What do you mean you are not going back with me?" Darame whispered fiercely. "Are you still delirious? They are trying to kill you—as indirectly as possible!" The last was almost a snarl.

"Not quite. I think they were going to blame it on your employer," Sheel said steadily. She winced at his words, and he knew that somehow she had found Halsey before reaching this cave. "Does he still live?"

"I do not know." Her words were colorless. "He did at sext, but . . . I think they gave him tainted water."

Sheel shivered, and not from the wind. "I am sorry." *A terrible, lingering way to die, but I will not add to your pain . . .* "Even I could do little for rav poisoning, without certain medicines."

"Why not return with me?"

Interesting—she was not going to argue. At least not yet. "Because you must move quickly, and I cannot." Sheel slowly sat up, and then reached for her support. Seizing his arm firmly, Darame tugged him back toward the wall of the cave a foot or so behind them. He had to lean at an angle, but it was better than remaining on the floor. "You must get to Avis." The thought had tortured his delirium, that something had happened to Avis. . . . Had White actually threatened Avis?

"She was still at the palace when I left. Ayers and his group are watching her," Darame said promptly, handing Sheel a heavy canteen and starting to unwrap the other wire.

"You must convince her to leave Atare. Did you find my signet when you searched White's office? I wanted to send her a message." Sheel frowned, trying to think clearly. *I must explain this properly. . . .*

"Old Harald has your signet. At least he was the one who palmed it. I do not think White found those hiding in the back. The plan was for them to try and reach your mother. We have heard nothing else. I have not burdened Avis with any of this, since . . . you wanted to tell her yourself." Darame sounded uneasy as she spoke.

"Good. But I have no way to prove your words came from me." Now that his thirst began to fade, he was conscious of incredible aching, as if his body had been trampled. *In a sense it has been.* . . . At least the pain from his wrists made the cuts on his back minor in comparison. The last few days . . . Where did reality end and nightmare begin? He took another long swallow of water.

"Tell me something that only you and Avis would know," she suggested, flipping a handful of wire over his arm.

"Let Ayers decide on your destination. It will allay his fears. Remind Avis . . . Remind Avis of the time on Emerson when Rob was caught in the bedroom of that under-age heiress. We kept that a dead secret . . . He was terribly embarrassed . . . at getting caught, I think." Dear Mendulay he was tired . . . and he needed food. "Do you have anything I could eat?"

"What have you been eating?" was her response.

"Eh . . . to be honest, I do not remember what I had last. It has been several days. . . ."

"The only thing I have that you could eat is a hot spot. Keep working on the wire." She reached for her bag. Pulling out a silver-colored pouch, she seized the tape dividing the packet and quickly whipped it out. Immediately turbulence began within the container. "Remember to wait a few moments. It is bouillon, and has salt in it. Drink it slowly." Handing him the squirming envelope, Darame returned to the wire. "Sheel, the palace is practically a fortress, at least in the living area. Why not leave Avis there? Surely five *guaard* can protect her in such an environment. I doubt anyone would try to hurt her while she is in such an obvious place . . . at least while you live."

"No. She must leave Atare. Immediately." Sheel discovered he could not open the pouch with only one hand, and craned his neck to check her progress with the other wire. "She is in a great deal of danger . . . or will be, soon."

"Who would—"

"How far along is the child?"

His change of subject silenced the woman. "Perhaps halfway into the pregnancy." Darame had a great deal of wire in her hands, and it was slowing her work. "Sheel, you do not think they would hurt the child? Leah is still elder daughter, even if Avis has a healthy baby."

"Darame, do not try to be gentle with me." The harshness in his voice made her look up. "If it is a manchild, there is little concern. But a womanchild? Do you not see, my scheming free-trader? They arrange for Avis to 'die' of the birth, and Leah is regent for her lifetime!"

The look on the off-worlder's face was incredulous. "Surely she is not that desperate! Especially with Brant and Dirk willing to devote themselves to her bed." Darame suddenly stifled a laugh. "Leah may love her power, but I never thought she loved the bloodshed!"

"Darame . . ." The wire slipped as she spoke, and he fell back against the stone outcrop. Quickly the woman moved closer, lifting the blanket to wrap it around him and opening the hot spot. Sheel lifted one hand, his long fingers curling around her wrist. "Listen. Please listen." The faint words had her attention; she sat silently, watching him. "Leah is sterile, Darame. Perhaps permanently, I do not know—she will not allow me to examine her. She suspects her condition; I know. We are the only ones who have any understanding beyond gossip. Do you see? I think she honestly believes that I would be forced to keep her as ragaree, should Avis die. In a sense, that is our only edge. . . . If she knew that I would call in our eldest cousin to replace her, she would want my head as well." Darame did not move, her dark eyes studying him. "I am not making sense, am I?"

"You mean if Avis has a girl, Leah would assume she was . . . 'home-free,' as the traders say it." Darame's voice was very even.

"Yes, that is it. I think all this has started to unhinge her—I would confine her and have her observed. But she does not know that! Her paranoia does not look past her own control. She will solidify her rule. . . . Beyond that . . ." Darame brought the hot spot to his lips, and he reveled in the warmth that began to trickle into his stomach.

"Drink it slowly, please." Darame frowned at him. "Brant and Dirk are too smart to try and rule through a crazy woman."

"Your Brant plays both sides. That may protect Avis for a time . . . has protected her. Until they discover I have escaped. For I *am* going to escape this time. No mistakes. And Dirk may be as crazy as Leah, in his own way."

"He is not my Brant." She was offended, visibly stiffening.

"Of course. Bad choice of words," Sheel said hastily. "You must get to Avis. Please. I know how much you have done for us. Can you do this one last thing? Or everything else will be useless. As long as Avis lives, my house lives. But if she dies, I fear the outkin will explode into a clan war, trying to control the throne . . . and the mines. If the outclans see it as an excuse to attack—"

"Your cousins, whichever succeed in taking over, would have

no time to entrench," Darame murmured, offering him the canteen. "And since the *guaard* cannot be trusted—"

"Please. I do not want to think about the *guaard* just yet. One crisis at a time." He felt his eyes narrow. "First I must stay alive; then I will deal with the Rule." Nodding slightly, he accepted her offer of the canteen.

"I rather think you will." Her smile seemed to flicker in the candlelight, as she reached to light one of the new wicks. "I will be first in line with a treaty."

"You will have earned it. If you can figure out what in hell is going on, you can name your price. I withhold only the chain and heir . . . they are not mine to give." Closing his eyes, he sagged onto the rock. *Done. She can take care of this part. Now how will I get out of here?*

"Careful. You do not know what I might ask for. . . ." Her tone was wry, almost teasing. Sheel opened his eyes swiftly, but her expression was still and enigmatic. "Do not concern yourself; I will go. But what of you?"

Her agreement made his entire body relax. His grip on her wrist loosened, curled down her hand to entwine around her fingers. "I will run once more. And I will pick a direction they do not expect . . . into the mountains or the ciedar."

"But . . . you can scarcely stand up! Damn it, Sheel, if you die on me—"

He actually started chuckling; a soft, whispery sound, with no diaphragm behind it. "No chance of that. You haunted my delirium, serae, with your black eyes and mocking smile, calling me weak and leaving me behind. I have no intention of letting you harass me again." His lids slipped closed of their own accord as he added: "I feared you were dead. I could not face that. . . . I could not think of it."

Silence greeted his words. He wanted to see her face, to see what effect his statement had had upon her, but he simply could not open his eyes. Rustling sounds indicated she was stuffing things into her pack.

"Do not worry: I destroyed White's RAM, and I will take a shot at damaging that plane before I leave. I do not think it is watched. I will leave this canteen and blanket for you," she told him. "And some—"

"Keep everything else. I have nothing to carry it in. There are several villages, small ones, just north of here. Two days walking, I think. If only you are not too late." His eyes opened, seeking moonlight beyond the burning candles. "Take care of my cherished and pampered sister . . . please."

"Overly pampered. You will not protect her so in the future, Sheel, I will not stand for it. Be at ease. If your guess is right, they will not hurt her until the baby is due." Slinging the pack onto her shoulders, Darame cupped a hand and blew out the candles. Darkness descended like a cloak thrown over their heads. Slowly light welled into the cave entrance—the moons were moving into the western sky. Nearly full . . .

As Sheel tried to think of something to say, hands reached for him, seized his shoulders in a grip that made him wince. Delicate fingers traveled up to lightly touch his face, and soft hair brushed his cheek as Darame leaned forward to gently kiss his forehead. *Be safe,* he thought, and opened his mouth to speak the words. She anticipated him.

"*Live,*" Darame said simply, and her tone was an order, not a request.

The hands vanished; stones rattled across the rock and sand floor, and the full force of the curling gusts of wind struck Sheel. He was alone.

Only the moons knew how long he sat there until the sound of shouting and gunfire reached his ears. As if a mob had descended upon the camp. . . . Pressing his back against the wall, Sheel pushed himself to his feet. There was a stalagmite just beyond the water basin, he had stared at it many a day. . . . Wrapping the blanket around himself and clutching his canteen, conscious of the cold—*but I am never cold*—Sheel moved to hide behind the stone pillar.

Mere moments later a bright light burst into the cave, searching frantically for its occupant. Voices grew close, yelling in Nualan, and suddenly several figures crashed into the cave, seizing the figure with the light and dragging it outside.

I will trust you left, serae, Sheel told himself, holding to his spot until the sounds of close activity faded. Shaking his canteen to be sure it was full, Sheel crept toward the cave's entrance. By the light of the moons . . . They could also see by the moons.

Slow going, agonizingly slow, and he could not take deep breaths. Wind knifed into him, colder than he had ever imagined. The cave had sheltered him more than he had thought. *So this is what it is like to be cold.* . . . He hoped Darame had taken one of White's blankets—

"Here, here!" someone above him shrieked. "He is here!"

By the worn ruts of The Last Path, was Sheel's first thought as he contemplated his next move.

A scarecrowlike figure dressed in floppy garments rose up before him, easily half a head taller than he and far more robust. "We have found you, Atare, we have finally found you!" it screeched, descending upon him with glee.

Several retorts rose in Sheel's throat, but they tangled within, finally resembling nothing so much as a croak. *Not even a blade to my name,* Sheel thought ruefully, tossing his blanket at the apparition and attempting to sprint for the path. Stumbling, Sheel's fall was broken by several boulders and one surprisingly strong hand, which seemed to appear from the depths of the thrashing blanket.

A blinding light flashed into his eyes, and the entire scene began to fade away. As his mind dove for protective depths, a trickle of humor followed him down into blackness. Sheel was positive he heard a worried voice say: "He does not look so good, does he?"

Chapter Thirteen

ATARE CITY   ONEHUNDRED SIXTYTWODAY   SEXT

She moved slowly, keeping hold of her hood with a gloved hand, her cloak pinned by a brooch decorated with the royal crest of Atare. It was imperative Darame keep her features hidden: one look at her face and no one would believe she was Stephanie reb Lena Atare. Sitting in that dark cave pondering their fate, Darame had hoped for divine intervention. But first thinking of impersonating Avis's cousin Stephanie, and then actually finding her at home! That was a spark of supreme power—of omnipotence.

If you must be caught looting a closet, at least be caught by someone with brains, Darame decided, watching her footing as she glided along the side street. Almost to the palace, almost . . . as long as the *guaard* at her heels did not seize her elbow to assist her steps. Over halfway through her pregnancy, Stephanie was walking oddly, to be sure, but Darame's bony elbow would give away the entire ruse.

I must get into the palace, and I am not sure I can, Darame had told her without preamble. Hearing a rustle, Stephanie had pulled aside her rack of dresses and found an off-worlder leaning against the back wall. Unfortunately (ominously?) Stephanie did not seem to think either the situation or the statement odd. But then Darame had suspected there was a good deal of common sense behind Stephanie's calm.

Avis does not know you are back? was her only comment.

Not yet. I must see her, and I cannot risk anyone . . . questioning my movements. Panic was ungluing her mouth; why had she said that to the young woman?

Leah has asked to speak with you. Stephanie's expression told freely what she thought of that development. A long pause . . . *Your thought was well taken; no one would question me. I will get you a pillow.* With that, Stephanie had dropped the dresses back over Darame and moved off into her cavernous bedroom, telling her maid she would need no more assistance before her nap.

Setting her free hand on her soft, fluffy false belly, Darame checked the belt for the hundredth time. No slippage . . . And people avoided pregnant women in the streets, for fear of unsettling them. If no one hailed her, stopped her . . . This was Stephanie's usual day cloak, a heavy black wool, without adornment. *If I can only reach the grounds of the palace!*

Her "own" *guaard* left her at the gateway to the castle, knowing she would be safe within. *Hardly . . . But you cannot know that.* Darame prayed for strength and invisibility. Brant's Arab was about to drop from weariness, and she was little better. *If I survive all this, I will earn a pilot's license if it kills me!* Such a waste, to damage White's vehicle instead of taking it. *First the message; then, maybe, sleep.* And a bath; Sweet Saints, she'd kill for a bath. *Sheel would be amused at your weakness.*

No . . . But he thought she would be amused at his supposed weakness. *Damn you, Sheel! We should have stayed together, there is safety in numbers! If you know how to fly one of those things, I will kill you.* Had he escaped from the cave? Could she have forced him to accompany her? *Not that light, child; you would have had to drag him.* Damn her numb brain, that she had run out of schemes, out of suggestions. *And if I've left him to die?*

It was Avis he was concerned about, not himself. Avis, and the effect her injury would have upon his people. Well, no one was waiting at the rail depot to take her into custody, so White was apparently still far from communication lines—she hoped. *Has Sheel thought once about this mess unseating him?* Ah, he's not a fool, give him some credit. Fretting won't help....

Pausing at the entrance, she leaned against the great door, steadying herself. Her thoughts had become staccato, her father's crisp accent ringing in her ears as it had not in decades. *You would always be less to him than his duty, no matter what comes of this. Can your pride bear it?* Then, another thought: *He asks for nothing he would not do himself. Are you strong enough to bear the burden?* Damn you, Sheel, for being stronger than I....

Opening the great door, which swung on well-oiled hinges into the gloom of the hall, Darame entered, leaving the servant to close it in her wake. She had seen Stephanie act with such impatience more than once; the two *guaard* on either side of the portal did not so much as shift in their place. Up the curving staircase, pale light illuminating the dragon of Atare coiled above her, the landing in sight ...

Somehow she reached the oaken doors. And if Avis has moved for some reason? *Damn my imagination.* Her curses were losing both power and potency....

Upon entering, Darame recognized immediate peril. No one would question her hood while entering the building; now, she would be expected to push it back, and that was a major problem. Stephanie and Camelle she trusted, but the others present ... Still considering, she moved toward the door to Avis's room.

A hand reached to touch her shoulder. "She is napping, Stephanie. She asked to be alone." Camelle's voice. Dare she try?...

Decisions are best when swiftly made. Turning slightly, Darame allowed Camelle to see into the hood even as she gave a minute shake of her head.

"Are you cold, dear?" Fortunately the woman had finished her sentence. Raising her eyebrows slightly, Camelle continued without pause. "Oh, you brought it, did you? Good, she was asking for it." Turning the brass knob, Camelle led the way into the back room and then firmly closed the door behind them.

Someone had drawn the blinds, but the fireplace gave considerable light to the room. Avis was on top of the bed, a quilt over her legs, a fire screen between her and the flames. A woman in *guaard* uniform stood next to the door.

"We did not expect you so soon!" Camelle started, to be silenced by Darame's upturned hand. After checking her roman for surveillance, Darame nodded for her to continue. "Serae Leah has asked about you several times, and your ship has called. Did you find your friend?"

The questions were whispered, but Avis heard them. "Darame?" said a drowsy voice from the bed.

Loosening her hood, Darame fumbled with the brooch clasp. "In the flesh." Glancing over her shoulder, she studied the woman at the door. Who? Faith, that was her name. *How appropriate.* One of the five who watched Avis ceaselessly.

"Is all well?" Avis slowly sat up as she spoke, and Darame's heart almost stopped. But no, she was merely reaching the awkward stages of her condition. A small woman, and apparently a large baby...

"No, all is not well. Have you heard from your mother lately?"

"Not since you left. Why?" Rubbing her face, Avis peered at her friend. "Darame, you... you look terrible! What have you been doing?"

Up until now she had avoided her reflection...Darame quickly glanced at the mirror over the headboard. Her hair looked as bad as it felt, and she was bright from windburn, her lips many-colored and peeling. *So much for relying on your looks for anything right now.* "I look almost as bad as your brother."

"Sheel? You have seen him?" Swinging her legs off the bed, Avis reached for Darame's hands. "Tell me! Camelle, send for food, will you?"

"There is a great deal to tell." Slumping, Darame pulled a chair over near the bed. How to start?... "Avis...do you trust me?"

"Of course. Why do you ask?" She was puzzled, but alert; her words were not offered lightly.

"Because what I have to tell you will require a lot of belief. You have a lot of catching up to do. For starters, do you remember when Sheel's friend Rob was caught with that under-age heiress while you were on Emerson?"

"We promised never to talk about it!" Avis was both amazed and indignant.

"But I had to have something to tell you, so you would know Sheel sent me," Darame explained patiently. "I suppose it was the first thing that came to his mind." The tray of refreshment arrived then, an effective stall. *It only postpones things.* . . . "When I told you Sheel had gone east, I did not tell you everything. Actually he was *taken* east against his will."

"But . . . why . . ."

"The people who took him were *guaard*." Darame waited for some sort of reaction.

"Yes. I feared they were part of it." Seeing Darame's eyes widen, Avis added: "Did you think I would not notice that I always have the same five personal *guaard*? I have not Chosen —normally I do not repeat *guaard* for many days. And I could not think of any way for someone to get to Cort, unless they had inside help. My brothers, perhaps, but not within the palace." Her face remained calm, but there was the slightest tremor in her voice.

"You are correct. Sheel has been trying to identify everyone in this conspiracy, which is why he stayed away. You and Leah did not seem to be in danger, while he and Tobias surely were." Darame glanced over at Camelle, but the woman was absorbed with pouring hot water into cups and did not answer the look. "That has changed. Sheel wants you to leave the city. He thinks you are in danger."

"Leah as well?" So, no details needed yet. But how. . .

"No, not Leah. You. You carry an heir within you. Sheel wants you out of the power games of Atare city."

"Is Sheel all right?" This was very quiet.

"He lived when I last saw him." That was all she could offer. Darame prayed Avis would not pursue that point.

"Because I carry an heir," she mused. "Am I in danger from the same people who tried to kill him?"

"Yes." *Sweet Magdalen, can I get out of this without elaborating—*

"We must get help for Sheel! Let me call Leah—"

"No." The word dropped into the room like a stone into water. Avis gave her a puzzled frown.

"No?"

"Avis . . . somehow Leah is a part of all this. It is Leah who may be most dangerous to you. We must—"

"That is ridiculous!" Avis waved away the cup Camelle offered her, emotion flushing her cheeks. "Darame, Leah could never be a party to such things! Did Sheel tell you this?"

"Yes." That visibly disconcerted Avis. Exhaustion stole over Darame like a cloud covering the sun, slowly separating her from the source of her strength. "I do not think I can remember it all right now, I can hardly see straight. I made the trip back in less than eight days; a lesser horse would have died. You simply must believe me."

"That my sister is a murderer?" This was terse.

"No, no: that she was part of a plot to unseat Cort Atare. Sheel thinks things got out of hand. Too many people with too many schemes going on. He thinks it has gone beyond whatever Leah agreed to, gone beyond long ago. Wait, listen—" Avis was shaking her head negatively, and looked as if she would rise from the bed. "Martin was your uncle's most loyal *guaard*, right? He was on duty during the party, that night everything happened. But Martin was found at your brother's house the next morning. Why, Avis? Why would the roster suddenly read that Martin was on duty at your brother's house, when we saw him with Cort the night before?" Now Avis looked puzzled. "Who would have the authority to send Martin to another place, another shift—enough authority that Martin would not question it? Do you remember taciturn old Martin?" Darame was babbling, she knew she was, but Avis no longer attempted to pull away. "Only Dirk could do that, Avis. Only Dirk could tell a trainer something and not have it questioned. And it was White out in that desert, Avis. White who has been trying to break your brother into tiny pieces, for reasons I did not have time to fathom." Alarm was growing in the woman's face. "Maybe White who stabbed Iver, who definitely killed Fion, Sheel's *guaard*. We do not know exactly how they managed it, or why they are doing it, but Dirk has attempted to overthrow the legal line of Atare . . . and has very nearly succeeded." Out of breath and saliva, Darame stopped, trying to drag oxygen into her lungs.

A cup nudged her hands. "Drink some of this, you probably need fluids," Camelle said calmly. "And use some of this balm, for Mendulay's sake, before your lips fall off."

Numbly, Darame complied, grateful for wetness coursing down her throat. She kept her eyes on Avis. The young woman had grown pale, but did not seem in danger of passing out. . . . She was staring into the fire as her hands twisted in her quilt.

"Why do you think Leah is involved?" she whispered.

"Leah has power, Avis, and she wants to keep it. As regent, she can run the entire show. She must have figured out that Sheel would not name her ragaree until she had a daughter, so sharing the throne was impossible. And she needed someone strong, someone with good information sources, to help her run things. Like Dirk and the *guaard*. Or Brant, and Embassy Row."

Avis turned at this, studying Darame. "But why me? I am not a threat to her. I do not care about her scheming; a judgeship is enough for me. Why—"

Darame felt a hoarse chuckle erupt. "Do you think she can leave you at her back, like a weapon, blithely producing numerous progeny? You would become de facto ragaree without the words ever being pronounced." She coughed, and turned away, praying it was only dryness.

"Her children will rule, not mine." Avis looked confused, even as fear touched her; she was beginning to realize Darame was serious.

"What children?"

No one spoke. Finally Camelle said: "Nualan women often go years between pregnancies—"

"She is sterile, Avis. Sheel is positive of it. He does not know whether it can be reversed, because she will not let anyone examine her. And she knows she is sterile." Waiting quietly, leaning on one arm of her chair, Darame watched for reaction.

Avis was studying Camelle, as if looking for cues. The older woman made no sign. Wavering, but not convinced . . .

"Was she not always the rebel? The one to take chances? The one to actually slip past her guardians and run free on the Feast of Souls? Think of her behavior the past moons, the past year! Do not think how you would feel, what you would do if such a thing happened to you. Think about Leah." Darame tried to keep her voice soft and persuasive. It kept cracking, roughly betraying her at every word. "Avis, it can be so easy! If you bear a girl, someone merely makes sure you die of the delivery . . . and then Leah is regent for the future rulers." That was more brutal than she had planned, but. . . . *Sheel would not have spared you. I would not let him.*

Suddenly Avis's hand shot out, reaching for Darame. "Avis!" Camelle's cry was a command, freezing her action. Completing the young woman's motion, Camelle felt Darame's head for signs of fever and pulled down a lid. Only after inspecting her throat did she turn to Avis. "Exhausted, but healthy. And as sane as she ever was. . . . I think I will run you a tub of hot water."

"Bless you," Darame whispered, not caring if anyone thought her irreligious.

Color was returning to Avis's face. Remembering the baby, Darame suddenly wondered if she had gone too far, but Camelle did not seem concerned. Handing Avis a cup of saffra, Camelle stood and moved to the sanitation.

"I . . . cannot—" Swallowing painfully, Avis tried again. "It does not matter, either way. Sheel has asked me to leave." She smiled faintly. "He always gets his way in the end. No one can wear me down like Sheel." She sipped at her steaming saffra. "So . . . Where do we go—and how?"

Darame's relief was so intense that black spots actually swam before her eyes. Only someone's swift grab at her arm kept her from falling out of her seat. To her surprise, it was the *guaard* who held her. Silent and unobtrusive until now, Faith pulled Darame to her feet and courteously suggested that Avis take the chair.

"Just . . . very tired. Very glad to find you safe," Darame whispered, trying to summon up a protest. "I am just fine, I merely need sleep, and some protein—"

"I think you should let us decide what you need, Serae," the *guaard* responded, pushing her onto the bed and sweeping her legs out from under her. "This is the best place to hide you until the tub is full. Perhaps you should request . . . a cheese and fruit tray?" Faith's frown wavered above Darame's head. "A meal would cause comment."

"Need . . . Ayers. He will know where to hide." It took strength to speak; Darame had spent what was left. She drifted in and out of sleep, unaware a tray of food had arrived, and startled as Stephanie herself gave a knock and popped out of a sliding panel in the wall. Camelle was the most help, keeping Darame from falling asleep in the hot water, scrubbing her hair, trying to make her relax.

"But I left him, Camelle. He told me to come here, and I left him." The enormity of what she had done still haunted her.

"That is what obedience is, Darame," Camelle told her placidly, handing her a bar of soap. "A *guaard* may tell The Atare that an action is foolish, and risks his life—may even try to prevent the action. But the rest of us can only do as we are told." Her voice dropped in volume as she continued. "Even if you succeeded in getting him somewhere safe—what if Avis had been killed in the interim? A ruler must be able to ignore both personal pain and personal wants and needs. A pregnant female of the line, the only possible ragaree if his suspicions are correct, must come before his own situation. Granted, Avis would be terrified at the thought of becoming regent, but she is capable of it. She is much tougher than any of you seem to think."

"I keep telling Sheel that," Darame mumbled, shivering as hot water slid down her back.

"Indeed. Avis is very precious to Sheel, and not only because of her current position. Whatever abuse White has thrown his way, Sheel still feels that Avis in the palace is at greater risk than Sheel in the Ciedar—are they actually in the Ciedar?" This last was openly curious.

"The eastern face of the mountains," Darame replied. "I might be able to find it on a map."

"No matter now. Sleep, first, and then talk to Ayers about it. We will relay your message to him. Do not worry about Sheel. He has been well trained, I am sure. If he . . . I think the phrase is 'got the drop' on someone watching him, he could break the individual's neck. I think you should assume he is alive until it is proved otherwise."

This brisk sensibleness reminded Darame briefly of Mona. And what other choice did she have, really? Darame began to contemplate uninterrupted sleep.

COMPLINE

"Not The Ragaree's retreat," Ayers told them, shaking his head slowly. "Too many people are watching the road between Atare city and her home. To be honest, I am not certain where we should hide. We have gone to Portland once too often." There was an element of defeat in his voice that Darame could not like. It had spread to his face, drawing lines across his forehead.

Pulling the fur cloak Avis had loaned her closer around herself, Darame took a few steps down the cobbled floor of the stable. Clever of the Atares to have hidden outlets from their palace; of course Leah would know of them. . . . But Avis had retired early, pleading fatigue, and since the pregnancy often had her catching up on sleep, no one seemed to think anything of it. Glancing over at Sheel's sister, Darame saw hard-edged resolution in her face. *The rings*, Darame thought dully, still too drawn to feel pity. The forgotten rings, neatly pinched from White's box. Several of them mentioned Leah's name . . . Leah's consent. At least Avis now believed. . . .

"Ayers, would it be ridiculous to head south?" Darame asked suddenly. "Surely they would not expect it." Turning back to the *guaard*, she waited for response. That he paused before answering gave her hope.

"If I could think of a destination . . . even west to the sea! But I think you are right: it must be soon, and might as well be tonight." He was dressed, as were the other *guaard*, in civilian clothing.

Darame turned to Camelle, who was calmly pulling on her gloves. "Are you still determined to come with us?"

Camelle did not even look up. "Of course. I did not create that ring giving Stephanie watch over my children as an exercise." She did glance over at Darame and Stephanie as she spoke. "You should go on home now, my dear. Thank you for your offer, but two expecting mothers on my hands might make me a bit nervous—and your husband would be anxious. Leah is irritable enough as it is; we should not add to her paranoia."

Nodding at this truth, Stephanie gave Avis another hug. "I will have Stephen with me by this time tomorrow. He gets along well with Ting; they will discuss going backpacking in the spring and such things. No one will think twice about his visit," she told Avis, gripping her cousin's arms for emphasis.

"He will be furious when he finds out I have left without seeing him," Avis whispered. There was no remorse in her words, only affection. "Bad enough that he has had to share my presence with Brant." Avis turned to Darame. "Do you think that ruse helped any?"

"If nothing else, I am sure it weakened Brant's stand with Leah and Dirk," Darame said grimly.

"Good." Avis flipped her scarf over her shoulder with a certain satisfaction. "I am glad Stephen's sacrifice was valuable." She managed a saucy grin. "I will enjoy making it up to him!"

"You will be leaving me with a raving ambassador, Avis—unkind," Stephanie told her. "Maybe you should send for him, if you can!"

Both young women managed chuckles over this, and even Darame smiled. Good spirits would not hurt this trip, not at its beginning. Time enough for clouds of depression to grow—

A scraping sound seized her attention. "Ayers!" Darame whispered. He was already extinguishing the second lantern, leaving only the usual watch light burning. Darame backed into a vacant stall.

Muffled hoofbeats reached their ears, moving down the outside corridor and to the hidden lever. Someone pushed against the sliding panel, and cold air swept in from the sudden opening. Dark figures entered. . . . A black hazelle, its head drooping, and a *guaard*. The unknown walked like an exhausted man; fortunately the panel moved into place of its own accord. Something about him was familiar. . . . He slowed, as if sensing them—

"Crow?" Darame made hardly a sound, but the youth jumped, spinning in her direction, suddenly alert. "It *is* you!"

He stared at her for a long moment; Ayers stepped into the circle of light as well. Seeing the other *guaard,* Crow relaxed and leaned against his beast. "I need to rub this thing down," he said, indicating the hazelle with a hook of his thumb. "Let us talk over here—" Seeing Avis and the others behind Ayers, he stopped speaking. Slowly he turned to Darame. "How did you get here so quickly? You must have killed that horse! It took us six days to get that methplane running again—you would make a fine saboteur. I kicked this beast all the way in from the landing field." Pulling the hazelle into another empty stall, he clipped it to a ring and started removing the saddle. "So why did you leave the meth'?"

Darame took a deep breath. "Because I could not fly one to save my life! But if you brought us one—" Catching Ayers's eyes, she paused.

"I already investigated that possibility. No meths issued without the captain's express authorization. It happens occasionally . . . but I had thought we decided it was better they did not know we were leaving."

"It is better—how did you find that cave?" Darame said abruptly, Crow's words finally striking her. "Sheel—"

He understood. "We arrived shortly after you left. Fergus's people had tracked White there. Routed the place; it was quite a show! I was in the second group: Fergus's followers were a bit overzealous and did not wait for us to get through the ravine." He suddenly smiled. "I think that Mailan suspects you of supernatural powers!" Crow's face hardened as he started working on the hazelle. "At any rate, The Atare is going to be fine. White got away, although he left everything behind him. Fergus's fellows captured Varden, but we had to kill Teague: he slashed up a few people, badly. We think Sandal was the other one—White's younger son," he clarified for Darame, although Ayers was nodding grimly. "He also got away. But at this point I do not think I am supposed to mention it—to any authority, that is. The Atare still wants to handle this without scandal." Crow shook his head negatively. "How, I do not know. I was sent to bring you and Serae Avis to the new camp. But since we cannot take off again . . ." He paused.

"Another hole to be ambushed in?" Darame asked, studying him intently, fighting to keep the joy from her face. *Damn it,*

Sheel, you had better stay alive! I am too old for this kind of excitement. . . .

"Fergus said no—it is his regular winter quarters, whatever that means. I have the directions up here," he added, tapping his skull and returning to the hazelle's coat. "How much money have you got?"

"Quite a bit. We were about to flip a coin and choose a direction," Ayers told him, reaching for a curry brush.

"South," Crow announced, working his way down the hazelle's barrel. "Two days' worth."

"And?" Darame prompted, leaning against a pillar.

"My uncle has a methplane," Crow said vaguely, lost in thought. "Fuel is the problem, but I can think of two possible stops heading back northwest. Might take a while, going the long way. . . ." He looked at Ayers. "It seats ten." The two men stared at each other for a long time.

"In good condition?" Ayers sounded as if it was too much to hope for.

"It was last summer."

"Regular cabins heading south," Darame muttered, furiously making plans once again. "In three separate groups, I think. . . . Sweet Magdalen—Ayers, what do you think?"

"I think we should disappear, and quickly," Camelle said suddenly. "I am good friends with the housekeeper, and she hears all the latest gossip. I understand Leah is planning on going to Avis in a few days, and suggesting a move to a safer location."

Darame stared at the woman. "Why—" she began, and stopped. *Because we had already decided to leave.* Why mention it? It is perfectly innocent and sisterly. . . .

Sure it is.

"South," Darame reiterated, reaching to flick the second lantern back on.

CEDARPOINT, STARRISE MOUNTAINS   ONEHUNDRED   SIXTYTWODAY VESPERS

The sky above her was already flecked with stars, but Mailan knew that vespers had scarcely arrived. Deep in the cavern at her back, a handbell was tolling out the change of the watch. Who was taking her place—Haven? That was it. . . . *Sweet Mendulay, lift my exhaustion! How can I work when I can scarcely think?*

"I am here, Mailan. I think you should stay inside with The Atare for a while. . . . The priest is asking questions." Haven's soft voice was off to her left, and to her extreme embarrassment she had not heard him arrive. "Frost has dinner ready. Eat something hot and get some sleep." The man's voice was kind. . . . At least she did not detect any pity. A *guaard* too weak to hold up under stress was a pitiful thing. . . .

Moving stiffly, silently around a boulder, Mailan entered the cavern. Sheel was sprawled on a low couch which had been placed near the "social" firepit. Forcing herself not to stare, Mailan resolutely strolled to where young Frost was dishing up bowls of stew. Fishing several biscuits from the basket next to the pot of saffra, she accepted Frost's offer of dinner with as much grace as she could muster. Now if she could just get to the shadows without being noticed. . . .

"It is all right to look, Mailan," came Sheel's voice. Definitely amused; balancing her bread on the edge of the bowl, Mailan reached for a mug of saffra. Only when she had seated herself at the opposite edge of the firepit did Mailan look up at her Atare.

"I still do not think that I improve hour by hour," Sheel went on, tearing a biscuit in half. "But if it comforts you to check. . . ."

"Ha," was all Mailan could think of to say. Joke as he might, it had been too near a thing for the *guaard*. They numbered about twenty, now, and they took turns sleeping three deep at every entrance to this room. She had worried about picking up so many *guaard* along the way, but Haven and Crow both felt there was safety in numbers. Four *guaard* had been sent back to Atare, to start cautiously spreading the word that The Atare was ready to deal with Cort's murderers. . . . After tearing apart White's little camp, there had not been a soul among them unwilling to immediately repeat their oath. How many blood feuds had been sworn out that evening?

White is mine. She was Sheel's senior Chosen, now; she was Fion's favorite of all his students. *It is mine to avenge.*

"If you are going to look so fierce while you eat, Mailan, you will have to face the other way. It may not be upsetting your digestion, but it is annoying mine." Startled, she glanced up at this, and found Sheel's gaze on her. He wore that penetrating look he sometimes used, when he was dissecting something with his strange eyes. . . .

A hand clasped down on Mailan's shoulder, followed by a body plopping into the furs scattered near the firepit. "I will tinker with her," said a scratchy voice. "The choler will be squeezed from her in no time." Warmth trickled out of the hand, creeping through Mailan's shoulder down her arm and toward her chest, loosening the band which had inhibited deep breathing. Mailan turned to the third of Atare's healers, the eldest of the healers, the ancient woman Xena. As Capashan tended the coast, so Xena ministered to the highlands. Doctors and health workers the North had in plenty, but there was something comforting about a healer. . . .

"Thank you, Mother," Mailan said respectfully, in the way of the mountains. "Do you have strength to spare for such a little thing?"

"Not so little, that The Atare's right hand should be scraped so thin. Fill your stomach, youngling, and then partake of the wine. You are still tired in here," she added, tapping her smooth temple lightly. "At Cedarpoint there is time for rest." Grinning, her soft cheeks a mass of wrinkles in the flickering firelight, Xena released the woman's shoulder. "First we will eat; then we will work on those knots in your back."

Mailan decided not to argue. Crow had been gone but a day, and he was the only one who could soothe her frazzled nerves. *You take him for granted,* Mailan told herself, biting into a buttery biscuit. *He has been a loyal friend, and I begin to suspect a faithful lover. What have you given in return? Impatience.* Somehow, despite the crisis facing them, she would find a moment to speak with Crow, to tell him . . . What would she tell him? That time dragged when he was not there, and she had simply been too preoccupied, too worried to see it? *How do you tell a man you did not notice him until he was not there?*

As for not noticing . . . Her gaze traced the faces of others near the fire. Old Xena, with her delicate, wizened features, tiny and wrinkled beyond belief; and Sheel, already looking much better, at least to Mailan's eyes. Still horribly thin, but now it was more like someone who had exercised past health into obsession. Regular fluids had helped, along with soups, porridge, and now stew. Fortunate that Xena had been only a few hours away. . . . Even then it had almost been too late for the off-worlder. That one still could not sit up. At least Sheel's bruises were starting to fade; he still looked shadowed, as if someone had smudged his body with dirt. Dusty and scabbed, although the scabs were starting to fall off, leaving pale pink lines that looked unpleasantly like knife slices, and were something that Sheel would not discuss at all. . . .

We owe you a great deal, priest, Mailan thought wryly, afraid to say the words aloud. To turn Fergus's attention on oneself was not wise; he was apparently one of those who had "spells," when the dimensions were pulled askew and momentarily the future was now. *Guaard* avoided him; the immediate future did not look good, and they were in no hurry to meet it. Contenting herself with studying Fergus's handsome, weathered face, Mailan wondered how old the mock-Sini might be, and what he had been discussing that had upset Haven.

"Tansy," Fergus said abruptly, his gaze still lost in the fire. "It is said she was fair, Cort's consort, fair and sharp as a cat knife. Ambitious, too, which caused her downfall. So the Captain is a descendant of Tansy. . . ."

"Did you know her?" Mailan asked, suddenly quite daring.

Fergus laughed at this, a deep chuckle. "Do I look that old? Add the years of Sleep to Cort Atare, and you have her generation! A bit younger than Cort, but not much. Still a great beauty when he returned from Caesarea with his wife. Tansy lasted several more years at the court before her scheming pulled down her house. Bore him three sons, one of them after Cort returned. That last son had a son had a son . . . and the last was Dirk. Raised on poison, no doubt. Those boys never heard that Tansy fouled her own nest—only what the old woman chose to tell. The fortunes of their house are based on wealth she amassed while at court!" Still chuckling, Fergus shook his head, his face growing still. Biting into a biscuit, he reached for his familiar mug, rarely far from his side.

All sinis carried their own utensils. . . . Finishing the stew, Mailan set the bowl on a stack as it passed and accepted a glass of wine in return. A strange bunch, Fergus and his followers. Their expressed purpose was to move among the populace, decreasing fears about mock-Sinis by their very presence. Their private reasons included spying for The Atare, something Sheel had apparently not been aware of. . . . *Very unofficial*, Fergus had said with his wolfish grin. *Sometimes I or my own would hear things best dealt with by Cort Atare, and so it reached his ears*. Fascinating, that Sinis would choose to help any but their own. Only Atare was really tolerant of their presence, except for very restricted trade. After all, they refined the special metal which had returned Nuala to the ranks of spacefaring people. . . .

Settling lengthwise by the fire, Mailan allowed Xena to have her way, submitting to her pounding and rubbing with only a few groans as comment. It was pleasant, the flames throwing heat at her face and Fergus's husky voice droning on.

"So part of Dirk's deeds could be resentment, true. But you must not discount your sister, Atare, however painful it might be.

She is your sister, and you do not see her in that light, but I understand how a woman such as she could affect a man. She is a fiery claret, that one, on the edge of full maturity: a woman worth fighting over. . . ." Fergus's words were soft, and blended into the muzzy edges of dreams that Mailan did not remember.

Blazing fragments of fire crystals winked at her as she suddenly started awake. Somewhere beyond her dreams were the voices of Fergus and Sheel, but she could only make out a few words. Glancing around the cleared area, Mailan realized that the three of them were alone.

"So, can such radiation trauma be reversed?" Fergus was saying.

"I . . . do not know. It depends on the damage that has occurred. Scarring, or hormonal decrease—injections might counteract some of it. If it had been caught in time . . ." Sheel whispered.

"No chance of it, Mindbender. Leah took ship to Caesarea not long after our affair ended. Scarce months past that, my turnover occurred—a swift change. You can see why I suspect my foolishness was to blame."

"Leah was no child to be beguiled," Sheel said sharply, setting his mug down hard to make his point.

"She was suffering," Fergus responded, and his voice was very gentle. "She needed comfort. I can be a comforting person . . . and she knew I adored her. A simple mountain boy . . . It is said she was always one to flirt with danger, in her youth. Long before my birth; I was a child when she first left the planet. Never did she question the scars on my hands. Could she be so blind, that she did not know amputation when she saw it?"

"Unfortunate for you that you tend toward scarring," Sheel said, calmer now . . . only his fingers restless.

"I am the only one of five children who became mock-Sinis, yet several of my siblings had extra fingers and toes." Fergus had a distant look on his face. Mailan slowly sat up, trying to absorb what she had heard. "They shall bow to the rising wind of Atare, Mindbender, if you but choose. Can you stop reprisals against my people, once this tale is known?" The priest leaned forward on his elbows, hunching over his folded legs, his expression intent. "Do you want to stop the reprisals?"

Sheel's nonverbal reply was obscure, his face almost vulnerable. "So long ago. . . . And now my sister will be held up as an example for generations yet to be," he finally murmured. "If blame can be assigned, you have paid your debt twice over."

Fergus shook his head. "When you are safely on your throne, I will have made amends. Until then, you will simply have to accept my poor hospitality." The priest paused to drain his mug. "Enough of this: I have bent your ear backward, and you have been in my presence since vespers."

"A firepit between us," Sheel said, managing a faint smile.

"It should be fine, but I will take no chances with you, Mind-bender. You have children yet to sire that will be needed." Nodding in his abrupt manner, Fergus stood, shook his poncho into folds around his body, and stalked toward the outside.

"Atare?" Mailan said softly.

He glanced her way, the look piercing. "What did you hear?"

"He . . . Your sister is . . ."

"Yes. There is a good chance it happened just that way. Did you think it a boggie story, when your elders warned you against bedding Sinis for any length of time? Once or twice would not be a danger, but an affair of several moons . . ." Sheel actually started to chew on a ragged cuticle.

"Stop that," Mailan said idly, her thoughts elsewhere as she considered Fergus's words. "This could mean—" Her mind froze. The ramifications were too frightening.

"Yes. It is very serious. Now you know why I was losing weight long before White and his friends borrowed my person." Closing his eyes, Sheel leaned back against the bend of the couch. "There is a way to settle it without bloodshed . . . maybe even without scandal. There has to be a way." This last was scarcely audible.

Mailan waited until his breathing slowed before settling a fur over his knees and banking the fire for the night.

CEDARPOINT, STARRISE MOUNTAINS   ONEHUNDRED SEVENTYTWODAY   VESPERS

"We are here! We are here!" Avis went ahead of the group, her steps still light, indefatigable even after ten days of travel. The strange, swaying litter the *guaard* had strung between a team of horses was totally foreign to Darame, but it had made the last day or two of travel with a pregnant woman possible.

Darame dismounted slowly, glad to reach journey's end, uncertain of what she would find. Moving over to Camelle's horse, she held the stirrup while the older woman stepped down. Although Camelle had been silent much of the time, Darame knew it had been hard on her: she was not accustomed to heavy riding, and no amount of day jaunts could prepare the legs for a solid two days in a saddle. Smiling wanly, the woman accepted Darame's arm as support, and they started up the slope. Wind pushed at them, slicing like knives through their clothes, and Darame was relieved to note that the entrance was sheltered by a pile of boulders.

Bundles were scattered over the floor of the cave—another cave, Sweet Peter, is there no end of caves?—and *guaard* were everywhere. So many *guaard*, in fact, that Darame was suddenly nervous, her eyes taking in faces, looking for the young men who had watched Sheel so carefully.

"It is all right," came Crow's cheerful voice behind her. "They are on our side."

"How do you know?" she muttered to him as she helped Camelle over to the fire.

"You were the one who thought the conspiracy was small," he reminded her as he swept by, a saddle on each shoulder.

That was during my abstract period, she thought, but did not say aloud. *I am no longer an observer trying to stay out of the flood. I fell in—now I must keep my head above water.* "I would kill for a cup of tea," was all the reply she gave him. "Will you—" She cut off her question to Camelle as she realized how absurd it sounded.

"No, I will not sit down," Camelle said, managing a weak chuckle. "But if we can get enough hot water for a sponge bath, I will be asleep long before compline!"

"No murder will be necessary, either for tea or hot water," a low voice commented. Two mugs of steaming saffra were passed toward them. "Tea next time." Blinking swiftly to clear her eyelashes of ice, Darame recognized Mailan looming out of the firelight.

"More caves?"

Mailan started laughing. "This one is warmer, I promise. They cut it from stone themselves, and the passages and vents are well planned." Gesturing toward the stove against the wall, she continued: "You have timed it well: dinner is just being served." Under her breath Mailan added: "He is fine, just tired of the entire business. All the surface injuries have closed properly." With that, the *guaard* moved off to speak to the other new arrivals.

Relieved she did not have to ask, embarrassed that Mailan should think it important enough to seek her out—which Darame was certain she had done—Darame lowered herself stiffly to a backless sofa pulled sideways next to the fire. "I wonder who is doing the cooking," she said to Camelle, who was leaning on the high right side of the couch. "The last cook was a terror; I was almost poisoned."

"Frost has a high opinion of his biscuits and an exaggerated flair for spices, but things are edible." At that familiar, weary voice, Darame almost spilled her saffra, which she was clutching with two cold hands; old reflexes took over and spared her the indignity. Only after taking a sip did she look up.

Much, much better. Tired, perhaps—there were still dark circles under his eyes—but otherwise quite acceptable. "Welcome back to the land of the living," she said softly, offering a slight smile.

Lifting his mug almost in a salute, Sheel managed a pull of a dimple before Avis flounced back into the cave and seized him, eagerly asking where she was going to sleep.

I know that mood, Avis. You are determined to cheer all these worried faces, and I am not sure it can be done. Letting a sigh trickle out of her body, Darame ignored the entire scene—horses, *guaard*, dinner—and tried to relax. *He looks all right, you can stop telling yourself not to worry.* Dear God, two days on the rails, six either flying, waiting to fly, or refueling . . .

"Did Mailan send you in to see your surprise?" Sheel's voice was almost at her ear; this time she did jump, but the saffra mug was already half-empty. "The area behind the kitchen stove—"

"No, Atare, he insisted he was well enough to move to the general quarters," said an unknown *guaard*. "He felt you should have your room back."

Puzzled, Darame looked from one to the other . . . and then realized what they meant, the only thing they could have meant. Dropping the mug, she pushed past the *guaard* and into the corridor, looking from side to side, bewildered by a sweep of mock-Sini robes until . . . Yes, small piles of black uniforms by bed rolls—

"About time you returned! The Atare was getting moody," came a cheerful Caesarean call.

"Halsey!" Darame stopped herself just in time from leaping at him. Sitting up on a mat with a mug in his trembling hand, he was a ghost of himself. "You've finally lost some weight!"

The laugh was a bit weak, but with all the familiar tenor tones. "No bad jokes, now. I'm grateful for what's left!" Reaching out an arm to gently hug her, he whispered in her ear: "Did you gut the bastard, or did you leave him for me?"

"No time this trip," she told him, grinning slyly. "But I stole Avis. That is guaranteed to infuriate him."

Another laugh, which turned into a cough. "No, I'm fine! Nothing to laugh at for days, it feels good. Yes, I imagine that he's figured out the other one's too crazy to use. He will be very angry, Darame. . . . You must avoid him, unless you can get the drop on him." This last part was whispered, even though it was in Gavrielian.

"Oh, I'll get him for you, Halsey. It will be a pleasure." No one here but her old mentor knew her well enough to recognize the layers of threat in her purr. Glancing at the doorway as she spoke, she saw that Sheel was standing in the corridor, pointing out rooms to Avis. He caught Darame's eye as he moved by . . . and she wondered if he could now recognize threat in any language.

It turned out that Fergus and his followers had several large copper tins and a source of boiling water. Avis could not indulge, due to her condition, so it was agreed that Camelle would take the first bath, followed by Darame. The elderly healer in charge of the sick demanded the second tub for Halsey, which was how Darame found herself keeping Sheel company by the firepit, long after compline had been rung.

"So Jude made it to your mother's home with Quenby Ragaree and Tobias?" Darame confirmed, folding her hands around a fresh mug of hot cocoa. Something besides saffra to drink, praise Peter and Paul. . . .

"That was the report we received. It came by one of Fergus's followers who remained behind in Portland. There are others from the village who wish to join us here—Harald and his wife, for example—but they intended to wait until attention was drawn away from the river," Sheel answered, fumbling through several containers in search of the saffra.

"Then they could arrive any day."

Sheel's hands paused as he located the correct jar. "Yes, I imagine so." He settled comfortably on a pile of furs, stretching out his long legs and folding down on one elbow.

Comfortable speaking distance. On her part, Darame had no idea what to say. *How do we start over?* Not exactly over: intellectual curiosity and humor had led to desire, but that was so far in the past it was dust. *What do we have now?*

Respect . . . At least she respected him, even as she despaired over some of his tightly held ideas. He had imagination, he could still learn . . . Pebbles rolling, a flash of black out of the corner of her eye— The *guaard* did not know how to handle this situation. *I am related to the sick off-worlder, as they call Halsey, and to this plot. They know that much. Yet I travel with Avis and am a confidante of their ruler. No wonder they are confused.*

Gratitude. He had tried to express his thanks, just moments before, and she had turned it aside by asking about Tobias. *I don't want gratitude! I did it because I had no choice. You children were disturbing my sleep.* Patently absurd, but Darame had no strength to laugh at the voice within. *I will miss you and your bubbly sister, Sheel Atare, when this finally ends. Unless, of course, we fail, and then we're leaving together in a hurry. I wonder if your Last Path really appears as a path?*

And then there was . . . desire? What could she call it? Affection? That, too . . . *Be careful. It is dangerous in your business to care about people.* Where was that thought when she still had control over things? . . .

A breeze slipped into the area, strong enough to lift a strand of silver hair. Outside the cedars roared in the rising wind. Shivering, Darame reached for one of the furs and pulled it over her shoulders. Where had she laid that fur cloak?

"I begin to despair of your blood growing thicker," Sheel said quietly, watching her efforts.

"Does blood really thicken?"

That slight smile, a pull of dimple . . . "What really happens is that your system becomes used to certain extremes. If you are no longer cold when it is simply cool, it takes greater cold to penetrate your barriers." The abstract, clinical expression crossed his face, and he reached for her left wrist. "I wonder . . ."

Darame felt warmth trickle into her arm, spreading to her fingers. "Stop that," she said sharply. Before he had time to be startled she added: "You could have died less than twenty days ago. Do you think you are ready to do that yet?" Flexing her hands, she added: "It does help, but for how long? I just have a strange thermostat." Frustration flamed in her breast with every word. *The most important conversation I have ever tried to steer, and I am helpless before those eyes.*

At least there was no haste as he removed his hand from her wrist. A sudden grin blossomed over his face. "Between you and Mailan, I may be scolded to death. Xena, too . . ." His expression softened as he studied her, and Darame caught herself wishing that looks could replace words. "If I am boring you, or you are still annoyed at me for not coming back with you . . . I am sure Frost would be happy to teach you how to play Bones."

"Bones?" Her mind scampered after his train of thought.

"The sticks are carved of tazelle horns and bones."

"Whatever made you think I was bored? Unless that is a not-so-subtle hint that you are ready for bed and want me to get lost," she added, setting her empty mug down by her feet.

"No, no—I am not sleeping, as usual. Just not tired anymore." He looked away from her, then, toward the light in the back and the noise of several games. "I just thought . . . you might prefer livelier company."

"I am quite content here." *Not exactly, but close enough . . .*

"Frost was awed by your entrance this evening. I just thought—"

"No, you did not," Darame interrupted, her annoyance increasing. "You decided I am Frost's type or something? Whatever he may need, I do not need a man at my feet every hour of the day!" *I am not your sister.* "I have had enough problems the last few moons without having to deal with one of these children."

"They do seem like children." It was almost reflective, and made Darame look back at him. "I just do not want you to feel obligated . . . to . . ."

Something snapped. It had been too much, the many days since things went horribly wrong in Portland. Furs scattered everywhere, and Darame pulled back her fist and swung to make the blow count. Scuffling warned Sheel, who looked up in time to seize her wrist as she leaped at him.

Much of his strength had returned; he held her off with little effort as her flare of anger cooled, shaking his head at someone beyond her. *I suppose I am fortunate I did not get a knife in the back, but damn it, Sheel!* "Do you think I am some sort of court sycophant or something? Do you really think that is why I did what I did, when I could have stayed in Atare and dealt with whatever government survived?" Before she could stop herself, Darame whispered: "Sweet Saints, Sheel, who did this to you? If she is within reach I will take her apart myself!"

Wrong words. She could feel him tighten, through only his hand; releasing her, he reached for their mugs and stood to carry them to the washwater.

"Will you walk away from it forever?" *Idiot child, that's done it.* Darame cursed her earnest tone, wondering if it had revealed more than was wise.

"Darame, Camelle is finished with the tub!" came Avis's lilting voice from down the carved hallway. "Are you ready?"

"Coming, Avis." Darame watched Sheel adjust the temperature

on the kitchen stove, and then rose lightly to her feet. Dropping the fur, she paused, waiting for . . . what? Folding her arms at the sudden cold, Darame started for Avis's sitting area.

A wordless anger coursed through Sheel's thoughts for quite some time, lasting through another cup of saffra, a summons to a fresh tub of water, and well into scrubbing himself nearly raw. When his tension finally passed, the cessation left him emotionally drained, as if he had been in a shouting match. Slowly curling himself down into the tub so that the water tickled his chin, he tried to consider the matter.

Will you walk away from it forever? And what had she meant by "it," as if he could not guess. *Perhaps it is not imagination or wish-fulfillment. If there is something on her side as well . . .* "Coward." Barely whispered aloud, but there was no one to hear it.

So what if you were wrong not once but twice? Dig through the journals of your ancestors who kept writings: no doubt many of them had similar experiences. To bring Constance back here would have been a mistake. Cort and Riva's only surviving brother had made that mistake, bringing back a woman who had hesitated to leave her family, her planet—who had feared The Long Sleep. She had pined and died within two years of arriving on Nuala. No, Constance was right, and he was glad he'd seen the signs before becoming too enamored of her.

But Muriel . . . *Is it because I am a healer that it hurt so? Still hurts so?* Nothing in her behavior to indicate she'd feared him— everything had seemed fine. Until she became pregnant. *I never told you why I left. . . . Perhaps that was wrong of me.* Apparently the woman had not truly understood the range of his talent. He had not mentioned her condition to her, letting her discover it in her own time . . . but never thinking that— Sheel sat up abruptly, reaching for a kettle of boiling water, carefully pouring it into the foot of the tub. *To abort a healthy embryo and never tell me . . .* She had grown more distant, then, as if re-assessing whether to encourage him. . . . As if deciding whether the wealth and position were enough.

The entire container tipped into his bath, raising the temperature higher than necessary, but he did not step out. *If it was simple fear? If we had talked about it, could it have been dealt with, pushed into the past? I could not deal with it, and so I drifted away from her, never asked her about it, about marriage . . . about anything.* So many years, eighteen at least, on

Emerson; scarcely a Nualan year for him. . . . Why did he mourn
that child still? When he could see his line's strength so many
places—

No. Mere genetic selfishness was not the reason. *It was
healthy, and alive, and no danger to you. There are people on
Nuala who would have risked death for that child.* . . . *Sweet
Mendulay, woman, we could have removed it, placed it in Sleep
—given it to someone who wanted it!* The healer within raged at
the waste; the Nualan railed at the injustice. *Once, when we did
not have so many gifts of skill, I think I could have understood
such a decision.* But not now. Not with all that Mendulay had
given them.

You were wrong not to tell her why you stopped caring. Also
wrong to think she should understand, without words, how his
people felt about life. Her people decreed life began at birth;
there were others on Emerson foolish enough to think viable life
began at conception. *Not always.* He had been unprepared; it had
been a rude awakening.

So . . . what had his mother said, after the Light Ceremony?
Only the best can accept it. It seemed that Darame had come to
terms with his healing. That was certainly one of the strangest
things about Nuala. Very adaptable, that woman. . . . Enough to
stay here? To want to stay here? *You want her to understand
without talking about it. Unfair, Atare. As you must learn to play
politics with lives, surely she could learn equally valuable lessons from you.*

Standing, he let the heavily mineralized water stream from his
body. *She may not want to stay . . . may not be thinking beyond
the moment. So make her think beyond the moment.* Crystle had
wanted him, and not just for his genes. *You seemed interesting
and amusing and attractive.* . . . Darame's words, and he had responded in kind. Enough for a night . . . Surely enough to build
upon.

"So why did you do what you did, instead of remaining in
Atare?" Wrapping a thick towel around himself to protect from
chill, Sheel wondered if he had the courage to ask Darame that
question.

Walking back to the main room, Sheel found it deserted—except for Darame. She was seated near the fire, carefully combing
out her long, silver locks of hair. Furs were piled several deep
around her feet and legs, spilling over the back of the chair she
sat in. Somewhere she had found her bag, and slipped on a
sleeveless silk top. *It does nothing to conceal* . . . But then no one

was there to see. Pulling the huge towel tighter around his waist, Sheel moved over to her side and knelt by the firepit.

Silence has its own structure, if one knows what to listen for. . . . Sheel poked at a recent addition to the fire, artistically arranging the pressed sticks and increasing the flames. Finally, he reached through the quiet with the first words that occurred to him. "I think I owe you an apology."

"I have a terrible temper." She offered this quickly, not looking at him, still removing tangles from her damp strands. There was tension in the words—as if she were holding herself in check. "Usually I have it under control, but when I am this tired . . ."

"I do not know if I can explain this to you," Sheel started carefully, straightening and turning his head toward her. Her response was to drop her comb in her lap and twist toward him, delicate fingers reaching to rest against his lips.

"Does it have anything to do with prevailing inclinations?" she asked, her voice as low and vibrant as the first time they'd exchanged words.

"Which are?" Always surprising him . . . For the first time in many, many days, Sheel felt a genuine desire to smile.

"I cannot speak for others, but *I* have this overwhelming desire to touch you." She suited her action to her words, trailing the tips of her nails across his cheek and down the protruding muscle to the clavicle.

Unexpected behavior often swept him past the "What?" and to the "Why?" So he asked "Why?", regretting both the wariness in his voice and the increased thunder of his pulse, wishing her answer was not so important to him.

His reward was a rueful chuckle. "You do not know? It took me quite a while to understand it; but I think that, deep inside, I knew when I first saw you at that party—long before Iver's drink saturated us both." Darame's wicked grin popped out, and she added: "You were all the colors of the rainbow, while everything else blurred into gray." The elegant silver eyebrows lifted slightly, inquisitive.

There was no way to reply to that in words, so Sheel did not make the attempt. Instead he reached up and took several handfuls of silver hair, drawing her face closer to his. Only for a moment, filling his senses with spice . . . reminding him of what had filled his dreams. Then he rose to his feet, seizing her hands and drawing her up from the chair.

"Come . . . Too many eyes on this fire." His own voice was unusually husky.

"Since when does an Atare have privacy?" Darame whispered, still firmly holding onto his left hand and clutching a fur to her body with her free arm.

"You of all people should know that there is a way around every rule," he answered cryptically, kissing her palm and drawing her toward the niche he had reclaimed only that day.

Anger still threaded her thoughts, her body. He could feel it, a tension born of something other than need. Wrapped in the warmth of several furs and each other, Sheel doubted this was a good time to pursue it . . . except that this was not a woman to leave angry for long. Except that while pulling her into an entwined embrace, he discovered that her face was damp from tears. Letting fingers creep up to the form lying on top of him, he checked . . . Yes, tears. . . .

Are you angry at me or for me? And why do you weep? Puzzlement wove in and out of his thoughts, jumbled hopelessly with exhaustion and desire. Too tired, too preoccupied to analyze hormones, mineral levels. No more than warmth could trickle into a lover, not when he was this interested in what was happening. . . .

She pulled back suddenly, supporting herself on her hands, letting the cool air of the cave creep across their bellies. Not fair to leave her so . . . confused. . . . "Are you angry at me or for me?" he whispered suddenly, wondering if he should prepare for a blow.

Folding against him, the answer was half-chuckle, half-sob. It was all the answer he received, for a time, although the tension surrounding them dissipated. Determined to shake her from whatever troubled her thoughts, Sheel pulled them both upright against the stone wall backing the kitchen stove, adding the warmth to their pleasure. It did not take as long as he had feared to distract her. . . . She had wanted his touch as much as she'd wanted to touch him. And he had dreamed of her perfection. . . .

Later, buried under blankets and fur, with Darame tightly wound around him, Sheel gave himself to the exhaustion. So what if this had fed his tiredness; it had been worth it. . . .

"I do not care whether there is a Nualan word or not," Darame mumbled suddenly. "White is a 'bastard,' and I am going to cut his balls off."

Sheel choked back a laugh. "Mailan has designs on his balls. Will you settle for some other part?"

Fingers pinched the skin covering his ribs. "Beast. That he could do this to you, after swearing that oath to your house! And

Brant . . ." He could feel her fury increase even as she gently touched the vanishing bruise on his face.

"Are you going to snarl at me whenever you are mad at someone else?" Half-serious, half-teasing.

Surprised, Darame's building anger evaporated as she relaxed against him. "Ah . . . probably," she admitted weakly.

Pinning his laughter behind a broad set of dimples, Sheel reached with both arms to hug her tightly. *I am terrified—you will be a fiercer bodyguard than Mailan!* "I will get used to it," he whispered in her ear, nuzzling the elegant curve of her throat.

"Huh." Kissing the tip of his nose, she snuggled into the hollow of his shoulder. "Wise of you; it will save misunderstandings." In another moment she had surfaced again, responding to his laughter. "Are you always going to laugh at the way I say things?"

"Probably." It was faint, between chuckles.

"Do you know how to fly a methplane?" she asked crossly.

"What?"

"Do you—"

"No. Why?" He wished he could see her face.

"Good. I do not have to kill you after all." Kissing him lightly, she curled up against him, pointedly ignoring his laughter.

Chapter Fourteen

CEDARPOINT, STARRISE MOUNTAINS   TWOHUNDRED EIGHTYDAY   TIERCE

Finally, Darame understood what helped these Northerners survive the depths of their winters; deep in their hearts was buried the knowledge of spring. Now that she had watched it blossom for herself, she began to see how such a memory could breed endurance. Standing before the entrance to Fergus's cavern, letting the rising star warm her face, Darame felt a leap in her spirits.

Cedarpoint had experienced almost two moons of slowly warming temperatures—Avis claimed that to the south the process had started still another moon previous—but it had not touched Darame's soul. Too much threatening from the coast . . . Leaning against the rocks, Darame listened for familiar voices. Mailan was up, arguing about breakfast with young Frost; Crow's whistle echoed in the linked caves behind. Avis was insisting in a strident voice that she did not need her cloak outside, while Sheel . . . Yes, it was Sheel with whom she was arguing. A smile quirked Darame's lips; why did Avis bother? Sheel always won arguments. . . .Well, almost always; Darame had arranged the final word in a few disagreements. But Sheel always won when up against Avis.

Of course he only argues if it is really important, Darame admitted to herself. That was part of his deceptive strength: letting others have their way so often. With some rulers, that would breed arrogance in subordinates, but not with Sheel. What was it about him that exuded confidence?

Heating up, that argument, at least on Avis's part. Not good for her; arguments made her tired. . . . Darame strolled back into the meeting room.

Avis spied her first. "Darame! He is cosseting me!" Quite indignant, and close to tears—Avis with her hormones in flux was a weepy personality.

"Is he? Probably taking his revenge for all that coddling you gave him when you first got here," Darame suggested, taking the fur cloak from Camelle's hands and nodding her away. Sheel lifted his eyes to the stalactites above the artificially widened room, but said nothing.

This new tactic surprised Avis. "I did not!"

"You did not? Who was constantly trying to keep him lying down? Or with his feet up? Who kept asking Xena if there was anything he should be taking for his 'infirmities'?" Darame went on, shaking out the cloak.

"He was very ill!" Avis started to fold her arms and paused; she found the new ledge where her stomach used to be embarrassing, and avoided placing her hands on it.

"'Was' is the operative word. You know that healers mend quickly," Darame reminded her. "And you know that a healer always has a good reason why you should do something—even if it *sounds* stupid." This piece of reasoning left both Atares puzzled, since neither came out a clear winner. Bringing the cloak to Avis, Darame said softly: "You must think of compromises on these things, Avis. It *is* cold in the shade. So wear the cloak; but if you happen to find a bright spot shielded from the wind, and choose to pause a while, then of course you will remove it."

This reasoning immediately calmed Avis. "You think of everything!" Beaming, she let Darame help her with the cloak. "But he was supposed to be taking some things for his infirmities, you know. He was just stubborn."

Bringing her lips to Avis's ear, Darame murmured: "There is nothing infirm about him—trust me."

Giggling and blushing fiercely, Avis tugged the off-worlder's dragging feet toward the entrance. "You do that on purpose!" she accused the woman, finally releasing her and going out past the boulders.

"Yes," Darame admitted softly, crossing her arms over her ribs. "I find it hysterical how blunt you Nualans are about everything, including sex—except within your own family. Sweet Saints, Avis, he must have nearly two dozen children counting the mountain crew. And how do you think you got this way?"

Another serious giggling session, followed up by Camelle's smile. "Will you come?" the older woman asked as she passed by Darame.

"In a bit, perhaps. It . . . is still cold for me. I need more tea first." Waving cheerfully to them, Darame waited until they were on the trail to the cedar grove before she strolled back to the firepit.

Sheel had prudently withdrawn to the fire during the last moments of negotiation. When he finally looked up at her, his expression was pure mischief. "Just how did you talk her into wearing it?" he asked, handing her a mug of hot tea.

Her smile returned as she accepted the drink. "What, and give away all my secrets? I wondered if you'd heard that business."

"It was probably either something a healer would frown on, or something an older brother should not imagine his sister talks about," he replied quickly, settling by the flames.

"Both." As a vulpine grin crossed the man's face, she added: "I will give you pointers. Next time I will be the bad guy and you can rescue her."

Shaking his head, Sheel reached for a thick slice of cheese from the platter on the squat table between them. "She is tired of being pregnant, and I do not blame her. It is a great deal of weight for her small frame, and the womanchild will be large." He had told Avis the fetus's sex the day after their arrival.

"A daughter," Darame murmured, twitching a fur over her

lower legs and grateful she had packed her black pants. Camelle
had explained that daughters were hoped for first, since the line
went through the women. Laws even allowed intact inheritance
through one generation of solely female issue. But the preference
was for both daughter and son. . . . "It is more the psychological
pressure, Sheel. I think she fears . . ." Darame hated to say the
word aloud.

"Assassins?" Sheel did not continue.

As they sat in silence, a small group of *guaard* passed, heading
for the outside. Darame recognized none of them. There was the
problem—and the blessing, to be sure. In twos and threes, singly
and in groups, *guaard* kept showing up at Fergus's cave. It was
fascinating to Darame, this trickle effect. Mailan had tried to
explain it, when Darame had finally turned her attention away
from Sheel long enough to notice the increasing numbers of
troops.

We do not think for ourselves, remember? Mailan had said. *To
ask questions, to inquire into the state of affairs would not be
seemly. So they listened, and reasoned for themselves . . . and
started looking for us. We have people placed to intercept most of
them. . . .That they know the Atare is well and returning soon is
enough.* She did not elaborate further, except to offer Darame an
impressively fierce grin when asked how they were sifting out
potential enemies.

"But none of the assassins were real *guaard*," Darame said
aloud.

Sheel did not lift his head. "No, they were impostors, trying to
get close enough to inflict damage." It was as if he had known
what she was thinking. "I hope that means there are few true
guaard left in this conspiracy," His expression grew wooden. "I
will not forgive whoever sent the last one."

The last . . . ah. Meant for Avis, that one. Came within an
arm's length of succeeding. Only Crow's lightning reflexes had
stopped the intruder, pinning him to the rocks with one of those
monstrous knives the *guaard* carried. Not even a ruffled hair for
Avis, although she had quietly fainted after it was over. What had
Sheel told Crow? *Very nice, much smoother than last time.*
Something like that . . . The inner circle was still composed of
familiar faces.

"How many now?" she asked suddenly, refusing his offer of a
piece of yellow cheese. *Dear God, no food—and don't let him
notice.*

"At least half of them know that there are traitors in their ranks."

And there were only five hundred active *guaard*. Word was certainly spreading. . . . Some had conversed with Riva Ragaree's *guaard*, Mailan had said, but she had not named a figure.

"But that boy gave no number before he . . . died." The young man who had slit his wrists was not often discussed. Sheel had never had a chance to question him. Indeed, it was the news that Sheel was well enough to talk to him that apparently triggered his successful suicide attempt. Varden had started a confession of sorts before his life ran out. . . . Written on the stone wall in his own blood. White and Dirk were the only names mentioned. One disturbed youth—and why was he so upset? what had they used to threaten him?—was not enough evidence, at least to implicate Leah and Brant. *The rings I found were bad, but none of them ordered Sheel's death,* she thought dully. *We have so little. . . .*

If only Leah was not involved . . . or an off-worlder. Darame had almost lost her recent battle with her stomach when she'd discovered that Sheel could walk up to Dirk and slit his throat without giving much of a reason. Absolute monarchs had that right. They remained absolute by only doing it when it was both necessary and self-evident. Had Dirk finally become self-evident?

"No. No one knows how many conspirators are left." Leaning on one elbow, Sheel reached over and laid long fingers across her limp wrist. Excessive warmth, healing warmth passed into her arm.

"Now who is cosseting whom?" Darame moved away, but she smiled as she said it. Shouts outside interrupted her train of thought. Voices called for Mailan, to come and identify newcomers. "More *guaard?*"

"Most likely. I have despaired of anyone else." His expression did not change, but she knew he worried about several supporters who had simply vanished. Fergus had sent his people out on their spring rounds. Maybe they would learn something. . . .

"Atare!" It was Ayers, his long stride carrying him up to the firepit with ease. "The Portland group has finally arrived!" Ayers looked overjoyed, craning his neck to see how far away the new arrivals might be while trying to face Sheel with a modicum of dignity.

Off duty, Darame decided. A twinge from her queasy stomach momentarily terrified her. *They will know—* She chose to remain by the firepit while Sheel straightened, standing and moving to a high-backed chair Avis had declared a makeshift throne. *That is right, not at the door, Mailan would be appalled—* Her thoughts cut off at the familiar stooped figure entering the cavern.

Old Harald. By all the saints, he had finally arrived! The dame behind him . . . his wife, the famous cook of the tavern? *Mendulay, our stomachs are saved!* Frost had about six things he could cook well . . . everything else varied dramatically from day to day. *I bet you can evict him, old mother—I had no luck.*

Excited voices extended greetings and questions, but they lowered to a whisper as Harald walked deliberately over to Sheel. Slowly, with the air of a born courtier, Harald lowered himself to one knee. Carefully unfastening the cinch of a pocket, he withdrew a securing chain. Ah, the long-awaited signet. Bowing his head, Harald offered the ring to Sheel.

Leaning forward, Sheel removed the ring from the gold strand and slipped it on his finger. Wonder of wonders, it almost fit, only the slightest bit loose. Pausing, always uncertain how to respond, Sheel finally set one hand upon the old man's gray head and whispered something to him. Whatever the words conveyed, it was more than enough for Harald, who just as methodically climbed back to his feet and returned smiling to his family.

"Well, Mailan, it appears you have been appointed guide. Can you situate these people?" Sheel asked quietly.

"We are already making arrangements, Atare," she said simply.

"Then welcome, all of you. The food is not the best—although I suspect one among you will take care of that—and the quarters tend toward drafts when the wind is from the northeast. But it will not be for long."

Bright pink with pleasure, Harald's wife stepped forward and made a beautiful curtsy. "We have brought Serae Avis a present, Atare." Turning, she gestured to one of several forms wrapped in a poncho. It stepped forward, disentangling itself from several scarves, and revealed itself to be—

"Stephen!" Darame tightened as she realized she was interrupting procedure, but the young man turned eagerly toward her.

"Yer r' here! Stephanie said yer werd be. Where is Avis?" His dark, handsome face held a trace of anxiety, his Caesarean marred by more Garrison accent than usual. "Has she had the baby yet?"

"Not in the last few minutes," Sheel said, perfectly straight-faced. "Darame, perhaps you should escort Stephen to Avis? I would not have her tripping in her haste to get back up here."

"A pleasure," she said, laughing, and rose to her feet. "Let me grab my cloak and we'll be on our way." It was Frost who materialized behind her, clutching her fur cloak. "One of my children," she had called him, and treated him as such. Still, Sheel occasionally eyed Frost with that certain look he sometimes gave people. . . .

"You must have had quite a journey," Darame told Stephen as she led the way out of the cavern.

"Very circular, and the nights were cold," he agreed, loosening another scarf. "Things have tightened up in Atr'—questioning abert Avis's whereaber, herse sr'ches for signs of the heir—it's not a good place to be right now. So Ting and Stephanie decided to move me. We went to her family's summer home up nr' Portland oh, a half-moon back, and Hr'ald took over from there."

"Well, catch your breath and stop worrying, you sound like a woodsman today," she told him, chuckling. "House searches, eh? Sounds like some odd things going on in Atare." How much he knew she had no idea, so she chose not to volunteer information.

"Very odd. I have heard a few things that—well, I hope The Atare will explain as much as he can while I am here," Stephen finished carefully, in control of his 'burr' and his thoughts once more.

"I am certain he will." Avis would surely tell him. . . . Then again, maybe she would *not* tell him about the assassin. "There is your destination," Darame said quickly, stopping and pointing into the grove. "Say the right words, child, the lady is despondent!"

Darame waited while he dashed off, expecting Camelle momentarily. Sure enough, the woman rose and started out almost immediately, covering her smile as Darame heard Avis cry: "You cannot even hug me I am so big!"

"Sure I can, we'll just—" Realizing his error, Stephen continued with: "But this way I can hug both of you!"

"Overall, his arrival will be a success," Camelle said easily in Nualan as the two women started back up the trail. "Who came with him?" Darame's reply intrigued her; an abstracted expression crept across Camelle's face. "Someone was watching Portland, you may be sure, or Harald would have been here long since." A tiny sigh escaped as the Nualan glanced Darame's way "I . . . begin to doubt this can be solved without bloodshed."

"Of course not," Darame said steadily, not answering Camelle's curious look. "With all that is at stake? And it will happen again, if Sheel does not take steps to prevent it."

"I think he is is trying to deal with that." It was all Camelle said, an invitation if Darame chose, but the off-worlder pointedly ignored the hint.

Oh, yes, Camelle. He paces nightly, after the others retire and he hopes I am sleeping. To take power to avoid having someone else take power is not a solution Sheel would choose. Something curious flitted briefly across Darame's mind, leaving scarcely a trace. *Can you train your heirs to accept, but dislike the rule? What an interesting thought. . . .* A day of new information. How would Sheel react to Stephen's news?

Darame did not have time to question him, for by the time they were alone together, dusk was falling . . . and riders were approaching from the desert.

VESPERS

Every *guaard* in the place lined the narrow, winding trail leading up from the floor of the Ciedar. It was a hard path, too rocky for beasts, so the leader of the caravan dismounted from his champagne-pale hazelle and walked up even as Harald and his people had walked. His companions were not *guaard*, however.

Sheel knew what was coming from Mailan's careful description. Warriors, enforcers, and guardians, protecting the purity of their line—outkin of Dielaan clan. *Dielaan, by all that is holy! What has Dielaan to do with this place? And if they seek me, how did they know—* "Increase the *guaard* on Avis and Stephen, immediately," Sheel heard himself saying. "And get that crock of stew out of here. Leave some saffra, bread, and cheese."

Smoothing a hand down the fine wool tunic Stephen had brought for him, Sheel paced slowly in the enclosure. For the first time he wished for the chain of office. *Still hidden in the temple, if I have any luck at all.* Still, it would be nice to have it while facing down an emissary of the Ciedar clan. He glanced over at Darame, who appeared from the niche wearing a long skirt of dark red velvet, an over-tunic of black silk thrown over it and belted with dyed tazellehide. The trine necklace glinted like a strand of her hair.

"Have a seat. This could be interesting," Sheel suggested, turning and walking back toward the kitchen stove.

Gracefully seating herself on the couch by the firepit, reaching to grip the hand of Harald's wife in passing, Darame said: "Mailan said they come from Dielaan. How far is that?"

"Far. The other side of the Ciedar, next to the great inland sea. That is a lovely skirt, I do not remember seeing it," Sheel added, studying the graceful folds covering her delicate feet.

"That is because Merme brought us a few things," Darame said with a smile, releasing the old woman's hand. Holding pale fingers next to the deep velvet pile, she continued in her low voice: "I look like a vampire. You, on the other hand, look quite elegant."

"I thought you were not a court flatterer," Sheel reminded her, moving over next to the couch.

"Truth is not flattery," was the answer as her hand reached to touch his soft red tunic.

"How do you make truth sound so seductive?" he asked softly, bending to inhale of the spice that clung to her.

"Ha. I will explain later—in detail." She glanced past him to Harald's wife, but old Merme merely smiled and started for the inner caverns, a sack of grain under each arm. A faint Darame smile, releasing his clothing . . .

"Now to work," he murmured in her ear, straightening and strolling around the couch to the far side of the firepit. Even as he spoke a half-dozen *guaard* entered the cave, arranging themselves on either side of the high-backed chair. Mailan and Crow were openly wearing the mag guns with their ceremonial knives. Choosing to stand in hope that his height would make up for his gauntness, Sheel lifted his eyes from the fire to Darame, waiting until the brightness faded from his sight. A tilt of the head brought the Dielaan representative into his range of vision.

"So one of you survived," whispered a harsh voice. Sheel studied the speaker. Dusty of complexion, his hair and eyes black, the man was of average height and weight, but the fire in his eye was reflected in the brilliance of his clothing. Dielaaners dearly loved color, surrounded by Ciedar white, black and red as they were. A loose tunic and wide pants of turquoise silk were belted against his body for warmth; a long, heavy green robe was thrown over them, with some sort of multi-hued garment much like a northern poncho on top of that. Even wearing one of the hats they preferred, intricate and vivid, a thick slice from a ball with a brim to shield from Kee's glare on sand. The gauzy, colorful veils were tossed back, exposing his face. Interesting, that total exposure. The heavy trine ring on his finger denoted rank, and there was nothing respectful in his posture.

Typical Dielaan ambassador, Sheel decided, and nodded once without smiling. "So it seems. Shall we play courtiers for a bit, or would you like to get to the heart of your visit?"

Laughter like sandpaper on wood . . . Not a whisper, it was his normal voice. "Good, Atare. No games between you and I. Too much rides on this visit. We have a complaint to offer, first of your clan. It is your negligence that brings us here, and you who must repair the damage."

"Indeed?" Sheel moved away from the firepit. "Bring a chair for the ambassador." A low, backless chair appeared from the crowd of *guaard* as if by magic. Ayers placed it close to the firepit, but left the flames between the two men.

"You are first of your clan?" the Dielaaner went on, perching on the edge of the seat.

Lowering himself easily into the remaining chair, Sheel leaned casually on one armrest and said: "Yes, I speak for Atare." He did not offer his name, nor expect it of the Dielaaner: sometimes a Dielaan representative would be in Atare for years before anyone learned his name. And what other title was needed than "Atare"?

"The curse of the eyes does not mean you hold the reins of power."

My, we are blunt. "I fear we are at an impasse, then, since I hid the chain of office before I left Atare. Would you care for saffra?" Glancing over at the *guaard* on his far left, Sheel indicated his own desire to be served.

"There are other proofs. We heard of Ironhand's death, and that many of his heirs died as well. Only the pretty one and the healer survived. Which are you?" The black eyes narrowed slightly, their almond shape reminding Sheel of Crow.

A trick? If he knew about Cort, surely he knew about Iver. *"Pretty" does not quite describe me. . . .* "Does it matter?" Sheel asked, accepting one of the mugs of saffra and tilting his head toward the Dielaaner in inquiry. The man gestured for a mug.

"It does. We have had . . . communication problems since Ironhand's death."

Bending over the offering, the Dielaaner muttered a swift prayer and took a long drink of the steaming fluid.

"How can I reassure you? Will you believe me if I tell you I am a healer?"

In response the man purposefully pulled a dagger from his belt.

At Sheel's side Mailan stiffened, but did not move: the Dielaaner's movements were not immediately threatening. As the group watched, the man shrugged back his poncho and cloak, exposing a tight silk sleeve which was promptly peeled back. A flick of the knife, and a long, shallow stripe of blood wealed from his skin. "I will, if you heal this cut."

Sheel raised one eyebrow. The Dielaaner tilted his head back in response, as if weighing Sheel's controlled movement. Quite interesting. . . . Uncertain of where this was heading, but willing to be led, Sheel stood and gestured for the man to do the same. One of the *guaard* walked forward and took the ambassador's extended arm. Dielaan warriors stirred, but their leader stopped them with a glance. Still stiff—offended by the stranger's questions, Sheel was certain—the *guaard* drew the Dielaaner to the edge of the firepit.

A minor injury, easily healed, although Sheel had been careful about healing since his sojourn in the Ciedar. Pausing by the couch, his eyes flicking over Darame's impassive countenance, he reached over the edge of the pit, placing his hands on either side of the injury. Glancing up, Sheel let the slightest of smiles escape and said: "This will take longer if the blade was poisoned." Blood sizzled as it struck blazing fire crystal sticks.

An impatient movement. "No poison," the man replied.

The familiar surge of energy, and it was closed, as if an old injury. The thinnest of lines indicated where the skin had been violated. Examining the scar carefully, the Dielaaner nodded once in satisfaction.

"Good. *You* have a reputation for brains." He backed to his chair and dropped into it. "I am Tsuga reb Canade Dielaan, of the second tier." A major concession from a Dielaaner, announcing his name. So, he truly came as a supplicant. Second tier meant a second cousin to the current Dielaan and his sister, called ragaree but only a ruler if The Dielaan was incapacitated or dead.

Deciding to ignore the dig at his deceased brother's intellect, Sheel chose to answer the man in kind. "I am Sheel Atare." His mother's name was now only for genealogies. "What is your petition?"

"That is for my cousin to explain." Standing, he gestured toward the entrance. One of the warriors went to the opening and waved a large green scarf. "This was her idea." The last was almost muttered, and Sheel made the most of the distraction, returning to his seat.

"Another chair and mug, Mailan," Sheel said, catching Mailan's eye with his own. She knew that look meant: *careful*. Everything seemed smooth, but still, the war had ended only three years ago. . . . His circuitous thoughts ended when he saw who was walking into the room.

Crimson, violet, and sky-blue threads on green marked the long woolen dress as uniquely high-house Dielaan. Heavy trinium bracelets and necklaces adorned her person, as well as a peaked spear holding a thick twist of flaming red hair in place. Dark lace draped from her head, tumbling over her shoulders like a veil and patterning the white wool cloak which fell to her feet. Despite all this finery, it was her face that commanded Sheel's attention. Small she might be for a Dielaan woman, but her face was pure throneline, cheekbones high and jutting, eyebrows drawn by a master hand, nose straight and small, and those famous emerald eyes that often cropped up in the distaff line. Her flawless complexion was the color of tea and cream, paler than her cousin's. Before her walked other warriors of her line, behind her trailed a man whose features marked him as off-world, possibly Gavrielian. But he was of no consequence, if this woman was who Sheel suspected.

Standing at his seat, Sheel indicated the chair to Seri Tsuga's left. Lowering herself slightly first in the manner of Dielaan royalty, the woman took the offered place.

"The Ragaree will speak." Tsuga obviously expected no protest; scowling, he perched once again on the edge of his chair.

"I did not come to stare at him, cousin," the woman said crisply. There was a pause as she studied Sheel, who was gracefully retaking his throne. Angling her head in the manner of one considering a problem, she did not waste time in thought. "I am Livia reb Palmeri Dielaan, Regent to the Heirs." When Sheel did not interrupt, she continued: "My brother died at Yule—he was poisoned, along with our two brothers and younger sister. Fortunately we caught the assassin as he fled Dielaan." A faint smile touched her lips. "We persuaded him to tell us who hired him, and why. It was a Caesarean ambassador, Atare—one stationed not in Dielaan but in Atare. Our own embassy swears ignorance of this deed."

"Do you believe their innocence?" Sheel asked.

"We questioned the entire embassy—I am satisfied with their tale." She seemed amused by something, but did not add to her story.

Drugs with the embassy, probably torture with the assassin, thought Sheel, but he did not push the matter. Dielaan had never respected anyone's sovereignty but their own, and granted no diplomatic immunity. Despite this danger, the wealth of the desert still drew off-worlders like moisture-seeking krwb descending upon a pool of water.

"You understand Atare grants diplomatic immunity to its embassies?" Sheel reminded her.

"Even from murder?"

"Generally we make an exception in that case . . . but even then, the murderer can request to be judged by his own people. Caesarea does not have the death penalty."

Livia's lovely face pulled into a sneer. "I am aware of their laws. Personally I would prefer death to mind-tampering—I find it more merciful."

Answering her with a faint smile, Sheel said: "In the three previous cases of murder by a diplomat, all three have preferred Nualan justice. But the choice must be offered. You have proof?"

Now Tsuga spoke. "We have what is left of the assassin. He can still talk—I have promised him an easy death if we catch his employer," the Dielaaner added.

Spoken like a true clansman. Never mind the weapon—find the person who threw it. Aloud Sheel said: "Do you have a name?"

"He calls himself Brant, this ambassador." Livia's voice had no expression. "We have sworn blood feud."

Sheel's smile grew broader. "I think you will stand in line for your chance, Ragaree. Others are before you."

This seemed to confirm some private theory of Livia's, for she nodded at his words. "Your loss as well, Atare?"

"And Seedar's, we suspect."

Silence. Tsuga glanced at Livia out of the corner of his eye, but her gaze was on Sheel. "Tell me your claim, Atare, and I will tell you if it outweighs mine. I have lost not only brothers and sister. I left my city in flames!"

Both Sheel's eyebrows rose. He inclined his head toward Tsuga.

"There is a problem," Tsuga admitted, scowling his disapproval at Livia. "Splinter clans at the rim of Dielaan have made a bid for the throne. You knew about the plague—" Sheel nodded; a virulent plague had decimated the royal family of Dielaan years ago, forcing them into alliance with their outkin. "Since this outrage at Yule, Livia's two sons are the only clear choice to rule.

Therefore we have taken them from the city until order can be re-established. Air cars to Cardeaan, and caravan from there."

"In the meantime . . ." Sheel started.

"I want his head," Livia told them. "I will bring it back to Dielaan, to show what happens to those who would kill kings."

Glancing at Darame's impassive face, Sheel said: "I suspect he arranged the deaths of my uncle and my brothers, as well as those wives who were in residence and attendant *guaard*. He, or his accomplices, attempted to kill me three more times. They tried to kill the future ragaree. They have corrupted one of my house . . . even the head of my *guaard*."

Livia stirred at his last words. "Bad. I had hoped your *guaard* would prove useful in this case."

"They will . . . but it is more complicated than it seems. Not all the conspirators have been revealed." Sheel paused, uncertain what to say next. Livia took this to mean it was her turn to speak.

"These off-worlders are out of control, Atare. They are your off-worlders. You must deal with them, and make sure this never happens again."

My off-worlders. Dear sweet Mendulay, since when are they mine? It was not time to tell Livia of his theories, his plans. "You have your children with you?" he asked The Ragaree. At her cautious nod, he said: "I do not think we can fit your entire entourage within this cavern, but—"

"You have Sini here?" Tsuga said abruptly.

"A few mock-Sinis are living in the back, well away from our area."

"We will remain in our tents."

Sheel decided not to argue with this emphatic statement. "As you wish."

TWOHUNDRED EIGHTYONEDAY   MATINS

It was very late, the dark of the moons, and Sheel's energy was at its lowest ebb. Shadowy dreams had awakened him twice already—a silver-haired little girl with one black iris and one blue —and he had no desire to try again. Seated by the firepit in the front area, ignored by the *guaard* who occasionally passed through, he stared at the flames and fumbled for answers.

"Divide and conquer" were Halsey's exact words. . . . Sheel thought about waking the old man, and thought better of it. He

was greatly improved, but could ease into asleep in any position. Halsey was not ready to keep Sheel's hours. *And I do not wish to bother you with it anymore, lady.* Darame was probably awake, and would be glad to listen, he knew, but he suspected she was frustrated with him. *It is so obvious to you, and like sea fog to me. We must become one if we are to survive....Dielaan is going up in flames, and they did not even hint that they would appreciate help settling the problem. They need it—I know they do. Better for Atare that Livia rules, than some upstart distant seed of the line, untrained, unprepared....*

"How do I settle it with a minimum of bloodshed?" He whispered it aloud, hoping his ears had an answer his brain had overlooked. *There is an answer,* offered the voice within. *But it could destroy your house.*

"Who would rule instead?" He thought of other possibilities: the minor nobles seizing their own lands and making their own laws; merchants trying to set up some sort of order within Atare City itself; judges making the laws as well as ruling on them. A theocracy? No, that would never do, there had been enough trouble when the great Cied Schism occurred....

There is an answer.... He had thought of only one; one chance to do this without blood. Have an unquestioned champion of the Atare throneline stand up before a mass of witnesses and demand a fertility test for Leah. Whatever else Leah and Dirk had planned would surely collapse, and Brant... It would yank a support out from under Brant's house. How to keep him from getting away without a trace?...

If he returns to Caesarea, he is gone. Darame had no faith that the legal system could hold him. *He has too many friends—he will escape.* So instead we must plan his death? Have him slain before he opens his mouth? No—the evidence was piling up. If Leah broke, and he rather suspected such a challenge would break her, she might turn on Brant. But if word got out how Leah became sterile... The potential bloodbath of unsuspecting mock-Sinis—

Cold arms slipped around his neck. "You might pretend to sleep. They would worry less about you," Darame whispered in his ear.

"You would know."

"I might not tell."

A slow smile actually warmed him from within, and he leaned his cheek against her arm. "You would tell Xena, and she would start brewing her potions again." Straightening, he considered what he would tell her, explain to her. . . .

"Atare?"

Peering into darkness, Sheel saw a shadowy figure coming from the depths of the cavern, the light of a pocket torch flicking in front of her. Small, compact, deceptively delicate-looking—Ayers's sister, Sheri? "Sheri?"

Smiling that he remembered, she came forward. "Atare, I am monitoring the skies tonight with Fergus's RAM, and I finally detected a code with the prefix you asked us to search for. . . ." Starting for the back, she glanced over her shoulder at him.

Darame's grip loosened and Sheel stood up. "Come." He paused only a moment while she seized one of the furs and tossed it around her shoulders. Then they followed Sheri.

Fergus had a small communications room, scarcely large enough for one body. Squeezing sideways into the seat, Sheri showed him the pad. "I copied until the prefix repeated, Atare, but it is no code that I have ever seen."

Scanning it, Sheel nodded. "No reason for you to know it. I will take over—you have done well." He moved aside as Sheri crawled out, and then took her seat. Darame settled herself on the ledge at the entrance.

"Do you know it?" she asked.

"As a matter of fact, I think I do. Do you know that mothers remember incredible things about their children?" he said idly, taking up the light stick.

"I do not remember mine."

"That is sad—my mother has been a fascinating window on many worlds and thoughts. Damn, what is the break? . . ." With painstaking care, Sheel slowly began to decipher the code.

"Would Leah know it?"

"If she knew where to look for it. Unlikely, however. I doubt she knows I was interested in codes and ciphers as a youth. You forget I was only ten Terran when she took her first Sleep, and our lives never crossed again until this last year. There is no reason for her to know . . . and only a few places she could find this particular code."

Darame leaned over and examined the marks. "Pulses, varying in intensity. How would your mother guess this one out of all of them?"

Grinning, Sheel told her. "Because I used to send her messages in it, with the code enclosed. It was one of the special things we shared. A vestige of this system survives. Ships sometimes use it for distress."'

A squeak of a gasp came from Darame. "The dot-dash distress code!"

"Very good. I am glad you are on my side. Blast The Path, I cannot remember this letter. . . . Yes I do." His hand flowed along after the first line. "Just a few more key—" Sheel stopped abruptly, and when he did not begin again, Darame cleared her throat.

"Well?"

"Damn. Damn, damn, damn!" He pressed down so hard on the stick that the pad protested, throwing a crackle of energy.

"What? Have they found Tobias?" Reacting to the alarm in her voice, Sheel forced himself to grow calmer. ·

"No, no, not that. . . . I just cannot believe . . . And she told me she would not meddle in my reign!" A short laugh which was almost a snort bubbled out of him.

"Sheel . . ." Darame's tone was familiar, and rarely heard; it was the only warning he would receive.

Looking over at her, he smiled slightly and said: "I brought you here, so I owe you something." She nodded tranquilly in answer. "My mother and Quenby Ragaree have apparently been discussing recent events. They also knew about the deaths in Dielaan—do not ask me how, she uses magic or something. Being my mother, she is too smart to think such a wave of deaths could be the usual skulduggery of Dielaan politics. Riva and Quenby have decided that the only way to prevent such interference in the future is to have one family take care of off-world relations. They seem to think I am the perfect person to do it."

"Hmmmm . . ." It was a speculative sound, matching the expression on her face. In her black eyes Sheel thought he detected a sparkle of humor.

"If there was the slightest possibility that you could have communicated with them, I would accuse you of suggesting it." A touch of asperity laced his voice, but the entire situation was so ludicrous he was having trouble fighting laughter. Something in Darame's expression almost made him chuckle, until he realized how gaunt she appeared. Still losing weight? Without thinking he reached for her arm.

A stern eye pinned him to the table; he hastily withdrew his hand. "You have done enough of that today," she said severely. "Save it. I am just tired."

"If you are sure. . . ." He knew his mind was wandering back to the message even as he spoke. It could not help but return to such thoughts. And Quenby Ragaree agreed. . . . What news did Riva have from Seedar? Things must be much worse for Quenby to agree to such an idea, even if they just wanted him to act as a facade and mouthpiece.

"Livia is here." Casual, and very soft . . .

"Ridiculous. Dielaan cannot agree among themselves, do you think they would trust Atare with such a mission?" Irritation was rising; he started carefully framing an answer to the message.

"Not necessarily. But you might convince Livia to trust you."

Sheel started laughing; he could not help it. "How?" he finally got out between gasps.

Her face was thoughtful. "I will work on it. What will you tell your mother?"

"Not to do anything until she hears from me again. Sweet Mendulay, I will have to put some sort of harness on her. . . ." Busy translating his thoughts into code, he scarcely noticed Darame squeeze his shoulder and move off down the corridor toward the glow of the firepit.

TWOHUNDRED EIGHTYONEDAY   TIERCE

Somehow Mailan had ended up with the women. Normally she kept an eye on Sheel, but as he was still inside asleep, she left Crow standing over the fissure leading into his bed chamber and followed Darame, Avis, and Camelle outside. That they might end up sharing the grove with The Ragaree of Dielaan had not been expected. Mailan was grateful she had Haven and Faith as support.

Regal in fine black wool littered with multicolored threads, the Dielaan form of mourning, the woman had brought her children with her. She had three of them, the eldest an adolescent boy, his sister and brother a few years younger. They were occupying themselves climbing among the rocks and trees lining the grove, while The Ragaree paced, her eyes searching the whiteness of sand to the east.

Watching the tableau that was being played out before her, Mailan gained even greater respect for Darame's skills at manipulation. Introductions and greetings were a trifle stiff; it was difficult to be friendly when a half-dozen armed Dielaan warriors ringed the area. Yet Darame seemed oblivious to it, suggesting that morning saffra be brought to the grove, sharing old cook Merme's wonderful muffins, asking about their trip and leaving "holes" in her comments so the Dielaaners could volunteer what they wished about the situation in Dielaan. . . . In a way it was frightening how easy it seemed.

And if you were helping the others instead of us? That thought was troubling. Her interest in Sheel and Avis, at least, was genuine—Mailan had gone above normal interference levels to make it quite clear to arriving *guaard* just how much Sheel valued her.

In fact, what was *not* being said was almost more interesting than what was being said. Avis's pregnancy thawed The Ragaree's manner enough that she admitted she might be pregnant again—it was too soon to tell. Avis's volunteering that Sheel could not only tell her if it was so but could probably tell her the sex interested her greatly. The Ragaree approved of Camelle's presence, with such a young and inexperienced fledgling mother; she did not say so in words, but it was evident.

You know how to study your enemies, Mailan could not help but think. This woman was careful to include Avis and Camelle in the conversation as much as they wished, but it was obvious she was dealing with Darame. *The off-worlder is too clever to slip up and give something away, like Avis, but she might trade information, yes?* How Crow would enjoy this business. . . . Mailan's eyes flitted across the Dielaan warriors. Bored stiff—except for one, who seemed more concerned with eavesdropping than with the *guaard* across from him.

We must be careful to schedule those who especially dislike Dielaaners during the evening, away from the interlopers—Mailan stiffened suddenly as she realized what Darame was saying.

"You should have seen The Atare's face when he read that message! He never wanted the rule, anyway, and now two ragarees think he should start acting as an ambassador for Nuala as well!" Darame's face had a broad smile as she spoke, balancing her mug carefully on her fur-wrapped knee. A message had arrived last night, in code, and Sheel had yet to confide in his *guaard*—

"If we had a central clearing point for off-worlders, we could isolate the embassies," The Ragaree said thoughtfully, sipping her saffra. "My brother always thought uniting our trade would be a good idea, but our uncle was so—" She broke off suddenly, as if remembering whom she was addressing.

"Ah, yes, there is a bit of . . . competition . . . among the clans, I understand." Darame looked both innocent and interested.

Smiling, The Ragaree returned to her saffra. "Come now, surely you know some of our history."

"Actually, Ragaree, things have been so hectic, there has been little time for lessons!" The women both smiled over this, as Darame added a few words about the recent trials and tribulations of the Atare line. She told no lies, and was very careful what she did tell, but . . .

I had no idea we were that good. It took a great deal of will-power to keep from laughing tightly. So many lucky chances, smoothed into preplanned counterpoint by Darame's speech. *We sound like the Axis Guardians or something.* She glanced at Haven and found the man surreptitiously straightening. *Dear Mendulay, he believes it, too! Or wants to.* Either irritation or embarrassment—for she was the center of all this bravery and cleverness, at least in this version of the story—was about to betray Mailan, so she took a slow walk of the perimeter to calm herself.

One of The Ragaree's sons had returned and was now seated near his mother, heartily bored as well. Mailan found the second, and younger, as she walked; he was leaning against one of the cedars, his eyes on the horizon but his ears obviously soaking up everything. Nodding at him, Mailan kept moving.

"So Seedar came to you . . ." came the Ragaree's voice.

". . . if a man can keep himself and his heir alive, she reasoned, he might have ideas for the problems in Seedar. . . ."

"And you helped them. At least she did not go to Kilgore. . . ."

What could the Ragaree be thinking? Mailan weighed it as she walked, her eyes constantly counting the warriors and checking for unusual movements or tracks. Remembering the long enmity among the high houses, what could she possibly think but that an alliance was being formed—and without Dielaan? Any house joining up with one of the big three could change the balance of trade drastically. Darame could be sending them back into war, but then again . . . *What I would not give for your tricky brain. You paint Sheel as extremely intelligent, a strong potential ruler, allowing his enemies to make their own nooses—yet reluctant to use the power at his fingertips. Will you have Dielaan down our throats, thinking us weak?*

"I suspect he will kill this captain with his bare hands, though," came Darame's confiding voice.

"He is a healer," The Ragaree objected.

"He is a king," Darame corrected. "Who happens to be a healer. Humanity has a long tradition of kings as healers; but if they must bring war before healing, it is done. You would not believe it, Livia—he just looks at people and they dissolve. I wish I knew how he did it. The slightest change of inflection, and *guaard* come running! He . . ."

Mailan had moved out of earshot once again. When she finally completed the circuit, the conversation had shifted to Avis's expected daughter and possible names. Taking up her position across from Avis and Darame, Mailan studied the off-worlder. Wrapped tightly against cold despite the spring starlight streaming into the glade. . . . Warmer days had not really helped this woman; she looked a bit pale. Closer observation indicated she was still nursing along the same cup of saffra. Surely The Atare would have noticed if she were ill, yet he was so preoccupied lately. . . .

"I will see if The Atare is awake," The Ragaree said suddenly, setting down her cup. "This trade partnership must be discussed thoroughly, every limit and last iota. What a wonderful idea to keep the small clans in line! Tensar Dielaan would have been pleased." Without further comment The Ragaree rose and indicated she wished to walk to the cavern. *Guaard* stepped aside for her as she led her men and children from the grove.

Total silence was finally broken by a whimper from Avis. Glancing at the woman, Mailan was not certain if she was about to laugh or cry. Rising from the rock she sat upon, Avis turned to Darame.

"She thinks . . . I think she thinks this is all her idea! How did you *do* that?" Dropping to a whisper, Avis continued: "Darame, we have been fighting that tribe for a thousand years, and you have the mother of their heir thinking about a *treaty!*"

Smiling slightly, Darame said: "Do not become over-optimistic. We cannot trust her further than we could toss her . . . but right now that does not matter. Go quickly and be there to translate for Sheel when she starts spouting off. She is smart enough to keep twisting the vine."

Disconcerted, Avis began: "But you would be—"

"I will follow you. Hurry!" Her gesture was so convincing that both Haven and Faith obediently turned and escorted the women toward the cavern. Mailan was so intrigued that she did not notice Darame had moved until she heard a familiar and gut-wrenching sound: that of someone losing the contents of their stomach. She bounded over to the off-worlder.

Waving her off, Darame waited, poised, but the spasm seemed to have passed. Methodically using a napkin to wipe her lips, she gestured for the half-filled cup of saffra, which she used to rinse her mouth.

"I will find Xena—" Mailan began.

"No, you will not. You will wait until I have a little more color and then you will escort me to the caverns and put me where the light does not fall on my face," Darame said in a voice that allowed no contradiction. "Sheel is going to be both annoyed and bewildered when Livia descends on him, and I need to be there."

"But . . . he knows you are sick?"

Darame carefully wrapped the fur cloak around herself. "I hope not. He has enough to concern him without this little complication. I am not going to tell him for a while, and neither are you." That black gaze made Tsuga Dielaan's threats seem like child's play.

"You need—" Mailan broke off as a possibility occurred to her. No, off-worlders were careful about that. . . . How long had she *been* here, for Mendulay's sake?

"Yes," Darame agreed, watching her expression change. "I lost count. I am pregnant—lousy timing, eh? Except the mornings and my appetite shot to Seven Hells, I feel fine. Sheel does not notice anything these days unless it is pointed out to him—even about me," she hastened to add. "If you are preoccupied with a lover, you do not start checking mineral balance or hormone levels or any of those things that he uses to make diagnoses. There will be plenty of time to tell him later. . . . I suspect we will be returning to Atare soon. Help me keep it a secret for now."

Mailan studied her for several long moments, silent. *And then what? Will you tell him? Can you stay, a cipher to the guaard, to our people? We cannot let them know you are connected to this ambassador.* "I always wanted a few children," she said bluntly. "I was borderline. Fertile men do not bother with borderline women. So I started *guaard* training." *Now why did I tell her that?*

Extending a strong brown hand, Mailan carefully raised her to her feet.

"No, no, *no!*" Darame winced as Tsuga Dielaan's volume reached incredible proportions. Would the man ever run out of objections? Livia was starting to sound hoarse; Sheel had retreated to his chair, one hand over his face . . . and still Tsuga shrieked. Slowly rising from her seat, Darame moved to the stove and poured herself another cup of saffra. Lifting the full water kettle, she took it to Sheel's place, warming his tea. Seemingly oblivious to Tsuga, Sheel parted the fingers over his eyes and winked at her.

Feeling a bit better in general, Darame took the kettle back to the warming surface. Sheel had been visibly annoyed at the start of all this—at least to her; she knew that wooden expression— but had cooled considerably in the intervening hours. That irritation had relaxed, moved into amusement . . . even forgiveness? That last gesture seemed to indicate a good mood.

By the Lion of Saint Mark, will this never end? It had taken a day for them to hammer out exactly what Riva Ragaree meant by her comment (at least what Sheel intended to interpret it as . . .) and how they would put it to use. *It is the beginning of the end, Tsuga, and you cannot fight it.* Remaining standing, Darame watched from the shadows as the wall lights began to glow. This agreement could change this world forever, mean greater profits and security—and more? *We should not think beyond the moment. If only Livia is correct, and this ensures peace instead of triggering war. . . .*

"*Are you sure they will come?*" Darame had asked at one point.

"*They have no choice,*" was Livia's reply. "*Dielaan, Atare, and Seedar are easily half the population of Nuala. Our only competition, Kilgore and Andersen, are constantly at each other's throats. Without us to referee, they are in chaos, and they find working with the smaller clans distasteful. If they will not have their dreams of off-world trade wither in the face of our union, they must join us.*"

Down to the last, to the language in which the message would be sent. Whose name at the top? So petty, and yet she could see that even Quenby might question the presentation. With all the clans involved (except Atare—Sheel did not intend to tip his hand to Leah. . . .) everything had to be perfect.

"What do you think, Darame?" Livia's question jarred her out of her musings. Damn, where had the conversation traveled? The Dielaan Ragaree's face was controlled, despite her anger at her cousin.

My turn to draw fire? Darame had earned this question earlier, when she pointed out something—what was it?—that was clearly not in Atare's favor. Could Livia think her impartial? Or as merely giving the appearance of impartiality?

"The format, the names," Livia said quickly, before Tsuga started again.

"Well. . . . You said the structure of the message could be controlled?" At their nods, she continued: "Then I would have the message sent under Atare, since you have asked Atare to do this thing for all the clans. Then put all three clans at the bottom in the same type, with the members' codes beneath. You might as well give the appearance of being united behind this thing, or you are wasting your time." Darame sat at the end of this little speech, aware her legs were trembling. *Tired so easily . . . You should have taken a nap when Avis did. . . . How could you abandon Sheel to these vultures?* Flicking a glance in his direction, she saw his dimples pull. Then his face smoothed entirely.

"A good idea. Let us use it." Livia glared at her cousin as she spoke.

"About the beginning—" Tsuga started, ignoring this victory.

"Simple. Brutal," Sheel said succinctly. "We tell them that off-worlders almost seized power in Atare, Dielaan, and Seedar—and that we intend to band together to make certain it never happens again. We unite under the banner of Atare so that our trade and information are pooled, and Atare will speak for all three off-world. If others wish to join this venture and have Atare speak for them, so be it. Come to the palace in Atare—when?"

"Soon." Darame knew she sounded weary.

"Yes, soon. Come and make themselves known. We must pick a date, allow for our own travel . . ." Sheel's voice faded as his look of concentration grew.

"It will cause an uproar from Kilgore to Andersen! We will hear the shouting from here!" Tsuga said, actually looking nonplussed.

"It is calculated to cause an uproar. While they scream to the ceiling, we will pull the rug out from under them." Sheel fixed the Dielaaner with one of his most effective "looks," silencing him.

Darame was watching Livia. The Ragaree's eyes widened slightly as her face grew intent, but she was smiling.

Chapter Fifteen

On the far side of the Starrise Mountains the star was already visible, but here in the valley the cool gray of morning ruled. Sheel adjusted the closure strips on his borrowed jacket and wandered toward the nearest cooking fire. Heads nodded as he approached; they had long since given up on engaging him in early conversation. Scanning the area, his eyes took in the dawn regulars: Harald and his wife Merme; two of their grandsons; Stephen Se'Morval, dishing up a meal for two and retreating to a tent; even Crow was awake, although he had stood the early evening watch.

Wordlessly the *guaard* handed him a mug swathed in steam. Fragile, unfamiliar scents rose into his face, and Sheel inhaled slowly.

"Nice, isn't it? Merme found something blooming and added it to the tea." Halsey followed his own penetrating Caesarean words up to the fire, extending his cup for a refill. "I admit I might throttle someone for hot kona, though. Never thought I'd miss it so much." Smiling slightly, he accepted the tea from Crow and took a cautious sip.

"You are up early," Sheel said politely, his eyes toward the lowlands wrapped in fog. Fergus and his band ahead of them, the Dielaaners a kilometer back.

"I have not slept well lately, either," Halsey replied simply. He was staring in the same direction, his gaunt face thoughtful. Flicking a glance at him, Sheel decided he was finally starting to improve. The man had not volunteered how old he was, nor how many times he had been through Sleep, but Sheel suspected a long and varied career stretched behind him. Did that make it harder to recover from rav poisoning, the internal devastation wrought by Nualan food and water? Or was Halsey merely a severe case? Some people never completely recovered. . . .

"You need not worry until I tell you to," Sheel told him, finally taking a drink of tea. Like flowers, it had taste as well as odor, lingering on the tongue. What did flowers? . . . Crystle. Was she well, still carrying the child she wanted so badly? A daughter, though Sheel had respected her wishes and kept it to himself. *Her heir.* . . .

"I have worries of my own, Atare. I would not dream of shouldering any of yours." Halsey tried out a chuckle, but apparently found his tenor tones weak, for it faded quickly.

"Anything you need help with?"

"I doubt you can help. Our purposes are rather crossed." Sheel started at this comment, but Halsey continued: "I had planned on a trip back to Caesarea after this stop, but now. . ."

"Things have changed?" Sheel wondered if he wanted to hear what Halsey was planning. *If it involves Darame?*

"It depends on how this all falls out. If Brant lives or dies, returns to Caesarea or does otherwise. . . . I am much, much older than I look, Atare. I still do my work with finesse and cunning, but I am no match for Brant, or his friends, should someone swear out a 'contract' against me."

"After your life?" Sheel clarified.

"Most likely. Yet running from planet to planet does not particularly appeal to me, either." Reaching for a fresh biscuit, he commented: "A bit simpler than the upheaval about to occur here."

"They would want vengeance, even though Brant was the betrayer? I wonder if Brant has any Dielaan heritage," Sheel murmured softly. Halsey's choked laughter was the only response. "Do not borrow trouble, Halsey, we have enough right here. Perhaps you should consider settling on Nuala. If Brant has succeeded at all in setting up a united underground, it could survive him. I would make you a very rich man, and you would smoke out and dismantle the criminal organization."

There was a pause. Finally, Halsey said: "It is something to consider. I have other employees to speak with, and Davi has some idea about breeding horses."

"Horses?" Puzzled, Sheel looked at him.

"Loves them. But never talks about them; no point in it, she always says. They aren't a part of her business. From her father's blood, the horse thing. His people were magic with horses." Halsey's expression grew distant, and Sheel wondered what the man could tell of Darame's past, if he chose.

"Do you think they will be there?" Halsey asked abruptly.

"Oh, yes. Seedar will surely send someone, as will Kilgore and Andersen. As for the others . . . Wallace will come. That means almost eighty percent of Nuala represented. The others? I sent out a spy—other than Fergus's band—and he should be back sometime today."

"To think you got three clans to agree to the same words. . . . Even your mother and that other one didn't quibble over it, just signed it." Halsey sighed. "You may go down in history as The Great Communicator."

Sheel could not stop his grin. "Halsey, this thing may last a year if we are lucky. Hardly a great bridge-builder. But that may be enough." His attention was caught by a commotion at the edge of the camp. Several *guaard* were walking toward the fire.

"Atare?" He turned to see Stephen Se'Morval. Lifting his eyebrows inquiringly, Sheel tilted his head at the man. "Avis had an uncomfortable night. Can you do anything for her?" The Caesarean was threatening to become clipped once again.

"Possibly. She has reached her time, Stephen. Fortunately it will be late, as first ones often are—we need my mother, among others, as witness to the birth." *By The Path, we need half of Nuala as witness, once Leah's condition is known.* "I will be there in a few minutes." *Damn.* They had borrowed all-terrain vehicles from the closest villages, had driven as easily as possible. . . . There was nothing left they could do to increase Avis's comfort. A swarm of *guaard* was waiting when Sheel politely dismissed Avis's lover.

Ayers! Sheel felt something tighten inside: he had not expected Ayers for hours yet. "Atare," the young man said, nodding politely. He was mud-spattered and worn, but his eyes were alert. At his side was an unfamiliar *guaard*, though surely if he had seen her he would have remembered her: a tall, long-legged woman with a sweet face. She was just as grimy, dark shadows under her eyes. "A stroke of luck, Atare—we were able to acquire two cycles in the city. I have brought Kari back with me. She was one who could not determine our direction and so chose to stay in Atare in hopes of gathering useful information."

"Excellent." Sheel gave a long look to the crowd gathered around them, and people slowly melted away. Finally only Crow, Ayers, Kari, and himself remained. "Have a seat and some tea. Tell us, have any of the clans arrived?"

A pixie grin spread across Kari's face as she accepted Crow's offer of a steaming mug. "Oh, yes, Atare. Kilgore and Seedar have been outside of town for days, and Wallace stormed in yesterday. Valdez and Montincol sent highborn as emissaries, and rumor has it Boone's private guard has been spotted in the area."

"How is this being received?"

Kari dimpled. "It is hard to say, Atare. I was not on duty when Kilgore arrived. You know how precise they are; they sent a copy of your message to Serae Leah and asked her to explain it. She denied all knowledge of it, and told them their honor guard could be interpreted as hostile. So Kilgore went back to their ships and anchored offshore. They have informed her they plan to be at the palace at Sext tomorrow."

Sheel slowly sipped his tea. *I can always count on Kilgore to keep things lively. How lovely.* "Riva Ragaree has not come down from her retreat?"

This stumped the lithe *guaard.* "Ayers saw two of her regular *guaard* in the city, but they could have come ahead, even as Ayers did. I told my sister that I was leaving and to keep her ears open—she has been on Serae Leah's doors lately, so if the yelling starts again, she will know," Kari added.

"Yelling?"

"Whenever the ambassador comes, there is usually a fight. Even . . . sometimes when the captain pays his compliments," Kari finished, her voice suddenly colorless.

Worse and worse. . . . Will my guaard *ever recover from this?* "Thank you, both of you. Did . . . you have time, Ayers?" Sheel said, but the man forestalled him by reaching into a side pouch and withdrawing the chain of office. He dropped to one knee to offer it, but could not hold back a sunny smile.

"I also saw the high priest, who sends his compliments," Ayers announced. "And says he will try to keep the lid on things until you arrive. Everyone was smart enough to approach under a white flag, so at least things will start out benign enough."

"Good for Jonas." As Sheel reached for the necklace, Ayers's face fell visibly.

"High Priest Ward, Atare. . . . High Priest Jonas died—before Yule?" He looked at Kari for confirmation. "Things were handled quietly, as he wished."

No one thought to mention it. . . . "Excuse me, I must see to Avis." Rising from the makeshift seat by the fire, Sheel flipped the chain around his neck and walked quickly toward the nearest tent.

There was little he could do for Avis except help her into sleep. He planned on approaching Atare in darkness; she might as well rest until then. Darame still slept—Sheel found himself back in his own tent before he'd recognized his intentions.

She slept deeply, perhaps dreamlessly, motionless as a delicate porcelain figurine. Settling down next to her, Sheel quietly took one of the long silver curls and wrapped it around his fingers. *You need sleep, and it needs sleep.*

Afraid to probe deeper. It had been chance that he'd found out. Sitting by a fire one night, rubbing the tense muscles of her neck, he had explored every knotted muscle in her system, making sure it was merely nerves over the coming confrontation—and found the change. Withdrawal, then—and fear. Fear to check her system, fear to ask her the question. Did she know? How could she not know? Even if she was free of any discomforts, she must have missed at least two bleeding cycles by now. Or was she so preoccupied that she, too . . .

Speak to her. Three days of miserable silence had been superseded by a new thought. Darame had said something to him once —that first night they met? Something about not being interested in a family, about not pursuing him for that reason, unlike others. *Could she think I would be angry with her? Think it was her motive all along? How foolish. . . .* As foolish as some of his own fears. *I want you to tell me. Whatever else happens, do not try to leave without telling me.* She probably would not remember that a woman could not travel Cold Sleep with a fetus *in utero*. The child would have to be arranged for separately . . . or left behind.

Mendulay, let her remember the law! It terrified him, that she might try to "lose" the fetus—murder by Nualan standards. And there was no way to waive that offense. . . .

"Is it morning?" That soft, low voice he loved, like the purr of one of his cats. . . . Looking down, he saw her half-open an eye as she stretched, a smile tracing her lips.

"If you do not hurry, the food will be gone," he replied, smiling in spite of his unease. Darame had that effect on him.

"Then go save me some tea, silly child," she told him, poking him in the side. The hand rose, touched the chain. "Where did that come from?"

"Ayers has returned. The clans have come. We will be in Atare late tonight."

Nodding, a frown suddenly crossed her face that had nothing to do with their words. Rising from the mass of furs, trying to force the spasms in his stomach to cease, Sheel said: "Sleeping on fur, and now tea and biscuits, served by an Atare. Could anyone want more?"

"Never." A whisper, as she closed her eyes again.

Never? He pulled the tent flap aside and stepped out to greet the starrise.

MENDULARION S ATARE   THREEHUNDRED THREEDAY   TIERCE

"Why do things never go as planned?" Sheel asked it rhetorically, but his mother lifted her head and looked at him.

"Anything specific in that question?" Even now, she managed a gentle smile. Early morning starlight caught her eyes, making them glint like the surface of a pool. . . . How deep were the waters. . . .

"I had not counted on Quenby and Livia insisting on attending," he admitted, moving to her side. Chuckling, Riva gestured for him to sit. "If you and Stephen had not pounced on Avis, she would also have demanded to accompany us. Good thing you remembered the viewing line between the temple and the palace."

"If she can see, she will not complain," Riva agreed. "And a bird's-eye view might keep Tobias from following us!" Her smile faded slightly at the mention of her grandson. According to Riva, Tobias had been withdrawn lately, which was not too surprising. Perhaps he would talk to Darame. The boy seemed afraid of *guaard*, which could be a problem. . . .

I am afraid of guaard, *too.* Three dead, Dirk and White known. . . . How many others deeply in this? Guaranteed to stand by Dirk, no matter what? "Have you decided what you are going to say?" Sheel asked, focusing on his mother once again.

"You did not warn either of the ragarees about this business, did you?" Riva fixed him with her "mother" expression.

"Of course not. But I did not count on them wanting to be in on the confrontation. Careless of me."

"You hoped they would sign, and wait? Unlikely, Sheel—even Quenby cannot trust us that far. The trade of her provinces is at stake." Riva looked distant again. "Sheel . . . can you rebuild our house?"

Again she avoided answering his question. Riva was nominally ragaree until Sheel named his co-ruler; she had demanded both the burden and the privilege of confronting Leah before the clans. *All the clans, Sheel,* she had told him when he explained things at the dawn. *What Leah dared to do threatened all of us. She tampered with the genetic basis upon which our houses were founded. If she remained barren, or a child died, would she have lied and taken someone else's child as her own, leaving us open to blackmail and dissension?*

Sweet Mendulay, the burdens I place upon you. "I will try, mother. Avis is supportive, and . . . even Leah may bear again, if I am not too late."

"Her children can never rule." Riva's voice was final.

"No . . . they can never rule. I imagine Tobias will be relieved about that." As he spoke, he glanced over at Mailan. Like a figure carved in stone. Had she said a single word in days? Crow was worried about her. *Justice as the* guaard *deals. I suppose Fion would tell me not to interfere.* Standing, he moved to her side.

"I want Dirk alive, if possible. I have a few questions for him." He waited; finally she looked at him, her gray eyes like granite. "Agreed?" Mailan nodded once.

"Atare?" The word echoed in the groined ceiling above. Turning, Sheel waited for the shadowy figure to approach. It was Fergus, the mock-Sini, dressed now for summer in desert robes proclaiming his hot city. "It is time, Mindbender." He chuckled. "Andersen arrived this morning. Most of the remaining *guaard* in the city are on the outer walls. Seems Andersen came prepared for some excitement."

"There will be no excitement. I want the palace secured against anyone not inside by fifth bell. When whatever happens is over, I will have to spend some time taking oaths." *So will you use drugs on your own* guaard? *Will both of us or just Avis be sharing the oaths?* "Where is Darame?"

"Here," came a soft voice. She was walking in from the back, Halsey by her side. He wore the look of a man who has lost an argument. "Tobias is with Avis and the other children." She spoke Caesarean out of courtesy to Halsey.

"I was afraid Livia would insist on taking them." The group chuckled at Sheel's sally, which was also in Caesarean. "We have a bargain, you remember that?"

"You are a target, so I am to stay away from you," she paraphrased. "I remember." Tugging at tight off-world clothing, she fingered what looked like a cat knife sheathed on her hip.

What guaard *had given her? . . .* Looking around, Sheel saw that Mailan was looking vague again. *Conspiracy everywhere. . . .* "Halsey?"

"I have the mag gun Ayers gave Darame earlier, but I do not expect to be a target. I am dead, remember?" He looked like he might say more, but Darame poked him.

"Time, Fergus?" Darame asked.

"Time, Serae." Turning, the mock-Sini started for the double doors leading to the temple grounds.

Now is the time. . . . Sheel wanted to kiss her, but both Quenby and Livia were coming up the aisle behind them, and he did not want an audience.

She was not so inhibited. Getting a firm grip on his tunic, she pulled him down to her level and quickly, lightly kissed him. "Be careful. I am a terrible nurse, remember?"

That memory dredged up a smile. "Careful, yourself. No heroes. And watch the tunic, it is the only one I have." Smoothing the wrinkles, Sheel turned and started for the door before Livia could question that statement. *Going to retrieve my throne when I cannot risk returning to my house for fear of activating alarms or setting off a bomb!*

"May Mendulay watch over us all as we march on the palace," came Fergus's voice from the head of the line.

"The back gate of the palace, Fergus," Darame reminded him. "Lower your voice. Do you want someone shooting at The Atare?"

Sheel had a dangerous desire to start laughing.

ATARE PALACE   THREEHUNDRED THREEDAY   SEXT

It is going to be fast. Riva Ragaree will say what she must say, and then it will be very fast. The words ran through Mailan's head like a litany. Walking briskly, avoiding people's eyes. . . . *Hardly anyone out today. Is everyone so nervous? What has been going on here?*

She could see four *guaard* on the back gate as she approached, one of them trainer Edan. The man did not hesitate, walking up to Mailan and smiling briefly. "They are both within the palace walls." "They"—Dirk and White. It was all the *guaard* knew for now, that these two were traitors. "All guns are accounted for; White checked out one recently, and returned two. The second was one of four checked out to Sheel Atare last winter."

Fion's mag gun. . . . Mailan removed her own weapon and handed it to Edan. "Stay close to The Atare. I have something to do."

Sheel, Darame, and Riva Ragaree finally arrived, Riva's ever-present *guaard* at her back. The Seedar and Dielaan ragarees were a bit further behind, surrounded by their own entourages. Unfortunately they were attracting attention, but it could not be helped. Into the palace and through the halls. . . .

Crow came up beside her, one hand on his knife, one on his mag gun.

"Not yet," Mailan whispered as they passed into the entrance near the library. Straight ahead through the entry, past the double staircase and stained-glass window, on toward the petition room. . . .

Crow visibly tensed as they heard shouting. "I think they started without us," he said into her ear. They began moving at a brisk walk.

"Slower, Crow," came Sheel's voice. "We must wait on my mother."

Both Crow and Mailan halted, flattening themselves against the wall until Sheel, Riva Ragaree, and her dozen *guaard* had passed by. Darame winked at them as she followed, and then glanced over her shoulder at the ragarees reaching the entryway.

"Which way do we send them?" Darame asked.

"Left when they enter the room; a table should be waiting for them, if I know the Seneschal," Mailan replied absently, falling into step behind her. "Keep out of trouble, Darame, I may not be in a position to rescue you."

Darame shot her a penetrating look. "Do not get yourself killed—Sheel would be very annoyed with you."

A smile was all Mailan offered as an answer.

"I will stay with The Atare," Crow told them softly. "Where is Haven? You need help."

"White is mine," Mailan announced as they walked through the archway and paused before the huge oak doors of the Petitioning. "Keep the group around The Atare tight."

The *guaard* on the door were loyal—startled, but loyal. Sheel waited only until the ragarees reached the end of the entry hall before indicating that the doors should be opened.

Sound hit them like a wave, washing across them with the harshness of seawater. The room was packed; entirely too many people were at each curved table, their brilliant house colors hanging over their portion of the room (evenly divided, Mailan noted—smart of the Seneschal). The galley above was filled with local nobles of Atare, their own whispering a constant undertone. One ambassador—Wallace's, she thought—was actu-

ally standing on his chair yelling at the dais. Lights across the
corner beams indicated omni broadcasting. *Damn.*

Serae Leah, stunning in a formal dress of pale green and alone
on the dais except for several *guaard*, was attempting to restore
order, pounding a staff on the wooden block reserved for that
purpose. She had had brought out a fine wooden chair from the
library—the two thrones behind her were empty. So, *that* she had
not yet dared.... Too many people in here, and too many clan
guards. Why had Leah allowed them to bring full retinues?

Then Mailan recognized someone sitting at a table. Impossible.... Surely it could not be—

"Is that The Kilgore?" Crow hissed in her ear. "And the guy
standing on his chair is the heir to Wallace!"

"Damn me to The Path," Sheel said weakly somewhere behind
them.

"I guess they figured that if Atare, Dielaan, and Seedar were
going to have their rulers present, they were not about to lose
face by sending lesser dignitaries," Mailan suggested, watching
as Riva and her attendant *guaard* stepped out into the center of
the floor.

The spectacle of Riva in her court gown and twelve *guaard* in
dress blacks achieved what all the pounding had not: silence descended upon the room. Sheel, by the door and surrounded by
guaard, signaled to Crow that he was moving along the wall
toward the front.

*No threat, no challenge—how can Riva be thought to attack
her own descendants?* Mailan began to search the edges of the
room. He was here, somewhere—and he was hers. *Where are
you hiding, White?* There was a possibility he was better than she
was—they were about to find out.

"Riva Ragaree, what means this proclamation?" A sudden
voice rose above the rest, drowning out several other questions.

"All will be explained, Kilgore, in a moment. First there is
other business to be finished." Riva's gaze flicked from the man
at the table toward the dais. "You know why I have come, daughter." Leah straightened in her seat. Leaning forward, she opened
her mouth to speak, but Riva rushed on: "It is very simple. One
live birth in a decade indicates a problem, either with you, my
child, or with your husband. It is time to turn to the healers for
council. All three of them are currently in Atare. Let there be no
more doubts, no more innuendos."

Leah turned absolutely white, her olive skin drained of color.

Mailan paused in her search to see if the woman would faint. *Amazing.... After all you have done, did you think they would not call your bluff? You were lost when you failed to realize Sheel believes in his principles.* For a second Mailan almost pitied the woman, until she remembered that Fion was dead.

Then she located White.

"Ridiculous! Tobias is perfectly healthy! No one conceives immediately after a miscarriage, it is unreasonable!" Drawing herself up, Leah added briskly: "This is not to be discussed before the clans."

"But it is, daughter," Riva insisted gently. "You see, it is one thing to raise our children to understand their responsibilities. It is another thing entirely when they become so obsessed with their role that they will destroy anything that dares to get in their way. Was that it, Leah? You could not wait for Cort to die naturally? Baldwin would not have served your needs? Caleb was always your friend—did you hide this from even him? And then you feared Sheel suspected. Your pride could not bear it, that he would not name you ragaree—and so you acted." Riva actually had tears running down her face. "Could you not have trusted your family? Could you not have trusted me? Child, such things have happened to others, and can often be reversed!"

A counterpoint of sound was building beneath her words, confusion plain on the faces of the assembled landholders. Darame was not certain what this appeal was going to trigger, but she wanted to be as close as possible to the platform when it happened. God alone knew where Brant was in this warren of a building. He was not at the embassy or his own home; *guaard* had already checked. But Leah surely knew, and Darame was going to follow Leah when Leah finally ran.

Leah was on her feet and shouting. "I had nothing to do with it, nothing! I cannot pretend to grieve for that vile old man, I hated him as he hated me, but how could you think I would hurt any of my brothers?"

"Then you did not know that White had Sheel? Was going to kill him if he refused to allow others to control his reign? Come, Leah, we need to talk of many things. Let us leave Sheel and the others to discuss the need for trade agreements." Riva was soothing now, as if talking to a frightened child, but Leah was beyond simple reasoning.

"I only wanted what was mine! Nothing else! He was going to

place her before me!" Leah stamped her foot, abruptly cutting off the speaker's microphone.

"No, Leah." Darame looked up as she approached the dais, and realized Sheel had reached it before her. He was walking toward his sister, his movements slow and precise, holding her eyes with his own. "I was going to examine the problem, and not say anything."

"You would not name me ragaree, I heard you say you would not!" Flaring, angry now, oblivious to the restless crowd below.

"I said nothing would be done in haste. And yes, I would have confronted you. But I could not name you, until I was sure you would bear again."

Lower, scarcely audible beyond Darame's crouched position: "I will! I have chosen badly with men, that is all! Do not be foolish, you need me to control the *guaard*." Leah was actually backing down the length of the dais, while the *guaard* on either side of the chair were frozen in their tracks, immobile in their confusion.

"No, Leah. Dirk is no longer captain. . . . and Avis carries a healthy daughter. I want you, sister, but I do not need you." Cornering her against the far side of the platform, Sheel reached out and took her hand.

A loud crash in the adjoining hallway seized Darame's attention. Looking quickly out the side door propped open for ventilation, she saw a blur of *guaard* uniforms tear by the opening. *Has Mailan finally caught up with White?*

Conversation erupted on the floor of the petitions room, several courtiers leaping to their feet and trying to reach Riva Ragaree. Her *guaard* held them back, creating a walking space for her as she slowly approached the dais. Looking over her shoulder, Darame saw *guaard* entering the balcony to establish order up there.

Leah. Don't forget about Leah. Turning back, she was in time to hear Leah cry out: "Reversible? You are certain?" Her face glorious with color, Leah pulled free of Sheel's grip and dashed behind the arras hanging on the throne wall. Darting past the bewildered *guaard*, Darame was right behind her.

"Darame! Wait!" was all she heard someone yell before her hands were thrusting against a small door. It opened easily and noiselessly; the sound of quick footsteps told her in which direction Leah had run. To her right was the sound of fighting—someone had just been thrown into a mirror or window.

No time to think, no time to plan. This pathetic woman actu-

ally thought they would still let her be ragaree—what a mess.
Was it Sheel who had called? He had enough to do, calming the
hysteria in that room. Brant she could handle. . . . Or, if things
looked awkward, she would simply follow him until the proper
people caught up. *But if the opportunity presents itself, a knife in
the back* would *be convenient.* An important fact rose in her
memory—the mag gun. Brant always smuggled a mag gun on-
world. It was not in his office, which meant he probably had it
with him. . . .

Leah's scream jarred Darame out of her thoughts and sent her
scurrying for cover. The sound continued, terrified, heart-broken.
Darame slipped out of the alcove she had ducked into and continued down the hallway. A huddled form down at the end of the
corridor—good God, what had happened? Darame stopped
abruptly, seizing the banister for balance. Leah's sobbing form,
and the body sprawled across the doorsill was . . .

"Dirk." Who could best the finest of *guaard?* Someone Dirk
never thought would turn on him. Stepping up to the body, Darame bent past the sobbing woman to check for a pulse. Only a
mag gun could stop a *guaard,* but the gun was lying on top of the
pack just inside the doorway, and all Dirk's blades seemed to be
missing. That meant . . .

A hand reached out and caught a large handful of hair, yanking
Darame to her feet and into the room. *Dumb, dumb, maybe fa-
tally dumb.* . . .

"Darame. I've been waiting for you."

Havoc raged in the hall, and Mailan was helpless to stop it. A
huge number of bodies had surged into the entryway, but she
could not pause to distinguish friend from foe. White had no
doubt what she intended, and was slashing away at her with unnerving accuracy. Far down the corridor she had seen first Leah
and then Darame head toward the back of the first floor, but there
had been no breath to tell others to follow.

Was Crow still with Sheel? Sweet Mendulay, let it be so. The
moment's loss of concentration cost her another slice at her left
arm. Pain caused her to lose track of her feet, and she slipped in
some blood. *Blood? Oh—blood. Not mine, please not mine.* . . .
In the shard of the broken mirror, she saw something strange,
another *guaard* about to interfere. *How many times do I have to
say he is mine?*

The *guaard* was striking at her. Twisting and rolling, she managed to elude the slash, grateful for many hard days on mountain

trails. *I am tougher, White. You may be heavier, more skilled, and more bloodthirsty, but I am tougher.* Several familiar faces surfaced from the heaving sea of black, and she yelled "That one!," tossing a throwing blade with her right arm. It nicked White's phantom assistant in the leg, slowing him as he charged off down the hall, a half-dozen *guaard* in pursuit.

At her back, in the bowels of the building, a woman started to scream. Suddenly the royal house was before her. Several cousins, a few spouses, a babble of voices. . . . *Take these fools away from here!*

She recognized first Crow, and then Sheel. The red tunicked figure detached itself from the crowd and sprinted past them, heading down the corridor toward the back. Distracted, White sent a blade flashing after it, and Mailan threw herself at the *guaard*, forgetting all common precautions, hitting him with all the bone and muscle at her command.

His head hit the marble outcrop with an audible crunch, even as he flailed with both knives. Hands grabbed and seized her feet, pulling her away from him. She fought them, trying to kick free, to crawl back and make sure he could not throw those blades. . . .

"Mailan, it is over! There is nothing left but reflexes!" Someone shouted into her ear, and it was Jude, long-absent Jude, holding her up, trying to stop the blood pouring from her shoulder—her damn left arm was not working very well. . . .

"She stopped White?"

"By The Path! I would not have dared!"

"Idiot, she could have died—"

"Crow went this way, hurry!"

A mass of voices, overwhelming her hearing, drowning her plea: "Is Sheel all right?"

"Alive when he went by," Jude assured her, moving her hand as someone supplied a strip of cloth for Mailan's shoulder.

As she slipped into unconsciousness, Mailan knew that that did not really answer the question.

Got to keep him away from the gun, was all she could think as she kept backing into the room. Damn herself to Seven Hells! Why had she stopped to check for life? *Should have grabbed the gun and started shooting, you prime idiot!*

Fortunately Brant was not interested in the gun. He was interested in killing her, but only his bare hands would do. One of his arms had no strength left to it, and dangled limply, the nerves damaged by a knife. He was carrying another blade in his leg, and it looked like one in his lower back, she could not be sure. . . .

"I must apologize for underestimating you, my dear," Brant was saying. "I made a fatal error when I dismissed the idea that either you or Halsey might go native. Apparently you are not as fastidious as I thought. The idea of taking those pills made my flesh crawl."

"You just might get away, Brant, if you start running now," Darame suggested, wondering if she could inflict any reasonable damage by throwing her knife. Too damned heavy for throwing —it was for stabbing, unless you had wrists like Mailan, which she did not. . . .

"Unlikely. Even if I did, I think this blade is in my kidney. What hospice would treat me?" He was getting a bit close; Darame shifted, placing a small table between them.

"With Leah and myself as hostages, almost any hospice." A step toward the door was countered. Brant was still moving well for a man bleeding so freely. "Why did you kill Dirk? He wasn't expecting it, I take it."

Brant actually chuckled. "Always observant, one of your great strengths. He doublecrossed me, and then was angry when I was going to disappear into the underground."

"Yes, Leah was playing you two off against each other quite well, wasn't she? I didn't think she had it in her." Maybe another blade, from the wall. A feint in that direction was quickly discouraged as Brant lunged at her, knocking the table aside.

"I did not think so, either. So you knew that. What else did you know?"

"Enough to know not to back a losing horse." Leaping to the bed, Darame hit the mattress smartly and bounced to the other side. "You lost me when I figured out you had to be involved with the deaths in Seedar and Dielaan. Did you kill Iver, too?"

"Very clever. I really should have let you into my confidence. Then we would both be rich, instead of dead." Anger was flushing his neck, in odd contrast with his pale face. "What was it to you? Did you really think we would get caught by these provincials?"

"Halsey." Another lunge was too close, and she glanced behind her for the door to the baths. Uh-oh—the room was reversed from Avis's quarters. *So how about a closet? I can't let him close—he'd snap me like a twig.*

"Try again, I do not believe you." He paused, leaning against the bedpost, catching his breath.

"Sheel, and Avis, and even Mailan," she suggested, glancing at the window, which was ajar. *Are you fast enough? . . .*

"Enough wealth to make men forget Midas, and you screwed it up," he gasped, shaking his head in mock-sadness.

They jumped simultaneously, Darame for the window, Brant for her. It was just a bit too far. . . . She felt his right hand close on her throat, and pushed wildly at his thumb, putting all her strength behind it. The knife, where? On the wrong hip. How to draw at this angle? Can't let go of his thumb. . . . The blade in his leg—reach it before the black spots take over—

The shots were deafening, ringing in her ears, more painful than the slug that tore past her arm. Brant stiffened, his grip tightening. She was blacking out. . . .

His hand vanished as blood sprayed her face and chest.

Rising out of blackness, like swimming in a sinkhole, light approaching, growing, a lamp in fog . . . Darame knew the light was changing intensity, and decided she was blinking. *The balls! Spawn of Lilith, why didn't you go for the balls? Because he already had so many knives sticking out of him that a little more pain would have been meaningless, idiot—*

"I'm not dead." It came out as a croak, surprising her almost as much as being alive. *Sweet Virgin, where am I?* There was a rumbling in her ear.

Eyes open wide, a face hovering into view. . . . Crow? "You need ultraviolet, child, you're getting pale," she told him, her vocal cords protesting. The face disappeared. Wait, that was Caesarean, wrong language. She panicked, her mind a blank, and then the right words rose to her lips, even as the awareness of pain struck her. "Dear God, I hurt. What hit me?"

"You hit the windowsill on your way down," came a familiar voice. "I did not realize you had passed out, or I would have caught you." Warm fingers reached to touch her face, moving lightly to her throat. "You are going to have a magnificent collar of bruise, but I was able to control the swelling. Why you do not have a concussion I do not know."

"There is a roaring in my ears." She lifted trembling fingers to check the back of her head and noticed that her arm hurt. "Wha—" A bandage, neatly wrapped from elbow to wrist. Focusing on the body before her—yes, it was Sheel—she saw that he had some sort of white sash across his chest.

"No scar, I think—Capashan got here quickly." He sounded

almost apologetic, removing his right hand from her face and lifting something next to her head. The rumbling sound vanished.

A cat? "She is so big," Darame whispered, staring at the purring feline. "Kittens grow quickly, although Somalis are slower than some breeds. She remembers you, it seems." He set the kitten in his lap.

Not a sash, a sling. Darame reached for him, but he stopped her, laying her arm across the coverlet. "Everything," she demanded. "Now." How long had she been unconscious, and what had she missed?

Dimples creased his tired face, and he glanced over at someone beyond her field of vision. "Weak tea and crackers, I think." Someone started muttering into a wall box—requesting food?— and he turned back to her. "It is about matins, of the same day. You are in the palace, in the room you always have."

"Your arm— Brant—" Darame stopped and tried again. "How did you get hurt?"

"White threw a knife at me as I ran past and got lucky. A small blade, not much damage, but Capashan wants me to rest, which is why I have a sling. You are also to rest your arm—or you get a sling, too."

"Someone . . . there were bullets—"

Sheel suddenly looked drawn. "Leah found the mag gun, and . . . fortunately for you the ammunition was the kind that is destroyed on contact, or it might have passed through Brant instead of lodging in him. One ripped you as it passed."

"Leah shot Brant?" Darame felt her jaw drop.

Shifting uncomfortably, Sheel looked away from her. "I think she was using Brant as much as he was using her. . . . They were disenchanted with each other early on. But she loved Dirk. . . . He was a lot like her first husband, I am told. I thought she married Richard because she could control him, but maybe it was because he was the only one she found whom she liked. If she had found someone as strong as her first. . . ."

"But— All that blood—" Darame shuddered; she clearly remembered a bath of blood.

"My fault. When I realized he still was not dead, I panicked and cut his throat." Sheel looked very pale, and she decided not to push him. Plenty of time to figure it out later. "Leah is . . . Dirk's death only made things worse. We may never know everything, because even if she comes out of it, she may have huge gaps in her memory. She denies having had anything to do with my capture, although she keeps saying Dirk disliked me, and that White is—was—crazy."

"White?"

A tight smile, a quick glance at Crow. "Mailan got him. He almost got her—she is in the hospice. Rather satisfied with herself, I suspect. . . ."

Utter craziness. . . . "Whatever did your mother do with all those nobles?" she asked faintly, trying to keep her voice soft.

"She gave them a nice, tidy story about off-worlders attacking the three great families, and how they all had to go home and clean house, in case Brant sent anyone after *their* families, and then suggested that the trade agreement would be an excellent way to begin covering each other's backs so this does not happen again. All while Mailan and White were destroying the entry hall. Only two others, if the one we caught can be believed— White's son Sandal died during an excess of zeal after Mailan's cohorts saw him try to stab her in the back. The other is a quiet fellow named Erik, who was watching Avis. When he lost her that night, he reported to Dirk, of course, and lost a few teeth for it. That was the biggest blow-up, when Dirk saw no need to pursue Avis, while Brant did."

"Dirk . . . could not have known Leah was sterile," Darame said slowly.

"No. He based his entire conspiracy on an impossibility, that he could give Leah the heir she needed. Maybe he will. . . . If she is out of the succession, I do not care how many children she has or who fathers them. If Dirk left anything at the labs, she can pursue it, if she still wants it." Sheel sounded very tired.

"If she ever springs back enough to want anything?"

"Yes."

God, he looked half-dead. "Can that *guaard* tell you anything?" She felt curiously alert, and wondered if she would remember any of this tomorrow.

"Several trainers have been recording everything. I wish I could banish him, but . . ." Sheel paused, swallowing, as a servant entered the room with a tray. In the time it took her to arrange it on the end table Sheel composed himself, settling the kitten next to Darame's hip. As the woman departed, he asked Darame if she wanted to try sitting up.

"Maybe I should have waited," Darame admitted a few minutes later. Still, the pillows were soft and her head had stopped spinning. A twitch at her hip was the kitten, sneaking into her lap. The tea tickled going down; funny, she thought it would hurt more—Sheel or Capashan must have tinkered with her windpipe. Studying Sheel's back as he stood near the window, she said: "If you let him live, will you have trouble with the *guaard?*"

"There is no way to make him live. We had to take his blades away from him to keep him from falling on them." There was a hollow quality to Sheel's voice as it echoed in the alcove. "He talks to try to make up for it. Then I will give him back his blades, and let him be buried on the planet of his birth."

"Why?" As Sheel turned slowly, she added: "Why did he help with this?"

"I think . . . Dirk decided that our house was deteriorating. Cort was ready to fall into his dotage—why else spare Dielaan?—and Baldwin was not Dirk's idea of a war leader. Brant probably suggested eliminating everyone except Iver, who could be controlled . . . and then Dirk fathers the next heir, proving himself superior to off-worlders, etc. Brant would have the underground, and a cut of what Dirk and Leah were doing . . . or so it seems. That is the original plan the three of them had. But as you suggested, I think each one of them had a plan of their own, and we could speculate on it forever. Brant needed the *guaard* at first, but if he had married Avis—" Sheel shrugged. "So many possibilities, so many plans. . . ."

"So your mother negotiated a treaty for you?" Darame reached for a cracker, and after thought dunked it into her tea before tasting it. Maybe it would stay down. Memory returned. *Dear God, is the baby all right?* Had all the excitement . . .

No. Sheel would have said something.

"Riva got a good start on one. After Capashan patched me up, I went in and kept an eye on things while Livia did her 'haughty and holier-than-thou' act. We will continue tomorrow. Now that we have the different groups installed at separate hostels, we might even work something out among us. Riva went to sit with Avis." For the first time, Sheel actually smiled.

"Avis? Sheel, she—"

"Just a few hours ago. Mother claims it is a beautiful baby, but that is probably grandmother talk. Once things blew up, Avis became so excited she went into labor. Stephen was nervous, but there was never a problem. I am just sorry I did not get to deliver her." The smile vanished, and an anxious look crossed his face. "She . . . Avis would like to call her Davi, if you do not mind. She heard Halsey call you that, and liked it."

Darame opened her mouth slightly, but nothing came out. "Of

course," she finally managed to whisper. "If she wishes." *Now is as good a time as any. . . .* "Speaking of babies . . ." *A joke, or a statement, or a question*— "I am pregnant," she said abruptly. "Congratulations. Being around all these mock-Sinis has not bothered you in the slightest."

A very slow smile. . . . "I did not think it had," Sheel replied. There was something not quite right in the look he was giving her.

"I . . . cannot travel back to Caesarea in this condition, of course, so I guess you will have to find a hostel with an extra room," she started carefully, looking down at her mug.

"Over Avis's dead body." That was unexpected, and Darame looked up. "Stephanie has a new baby boy, and will not rejoin the court for a time. Who will my sister coddle if you are not around? One baby to mother is not enough for her heart. She will want to return your favors." He came over to the bed and sat down next to it. Taking the wrist of her injured arm, he held it for a long time.

Knowing it was a healer thing, she did not interfere . . . until she saw a peculiar look cross his face. Oh, no. Rigid, she said: "It got hurt when I leapt the bed?"

"No, no. . . . It is fine. *He* is fine." Sheel finally raised his face to hers. "It is the wrong sex. In the dream it was a little girl— with silver hair and one black iris. But I have never had a pleasant dream come true." Shaking his head, he laid her arm back across the coverlet.

"What was the other iris?" Darame asked, suddenly curious.

"Blue. You were there, I had forgotten. . . . And other children: a little girl about the same age; an older girl and boy; two boys, one dark, one red-headed—" He stopped at the smile on her face. "What?"

"My father had a red beard, when he let it grow. So did his father. . . . I was told I had several red-headed aunts, but I never met them. Red or black, always. . . ." *What am I thinking? You know what the mop-up on a planet is like, after something like this. You came here to work with a man who massacred half the royalty of the North, and the Nualans will not forget it. I am not sure it is safe for Halsey to wait for you—maybe transporting the baby separately would be a better idea—*

"So . . . I have Halsey thinking about working for me," he said quickly, reaching for the pot of hot water and warming her drink. "Someone has to make sure Brant did not leave a coherent underground ready to function. If he wants to retire like a king, I can arrange it."

"Are you crazy?" It came out before Darame could stop it. At his wooden expression she blundered on: "We have to get away from here as soon as possible, before Livia finds out we were connected to Brant in some way. You can throw pardons around all you want, but forgiveness is not in her vocabulary. We would be decorating her walls—in pieces—before next winter."

Sheel answered with a bleak smile. "I gave her Brant's head. I think that will tide her over." At Darame's bewildered expression, he said defensively: "*He* does not need it anymore, and it made her very happy. It will make her return to Dielaan's throne assured. I thought it was worth a crude gesture."

"Of . . . of course, you are quite right." Staring at him, she finally said: "You . . . you are not worried about it, are you? About my free-trading history?"

"Have you ever killed someone in cold blood, or robbed an orphan?" Sheel countered.

"Of course not. I am what we call a gypsy, I only con other con artists." Her indignant expression died when she realized he was fighting a grin.

"Then no—I am not worried. You see, you were chasing my distraught sister and were nearly murdered by this psychopath who had already eliminated the captain of the *guaard* and numerous royal members of several clans. Leah and I were perfectly justified in killing him to protect you. We do not know why he went crazy, and we will probably never know. End of statement."

Darame felt a giggle rise in her throat, but it came out squeaky and dry. Of all the idiot disclaimers . . . "It might work."

"Of course it will work. It is true. If the other business surfaces, we say 'So?' and go on from there." At her silence, he said quickly: "What else do I have to think of to get you to stay? Impounding your ship?"

"Sheel . . . do we really know anything about each other, or each other's culture—" she started, watching his face as she spoke.

"No. Which is why we must always talk to each other. I . . . I assumed too much on Emerson, and fell in love with a woman so alien in thought to me, she had an abortion when she discovered she was pregnant . . . without telling me. I suppose she never understood the extent of my healing quirk . . . or worse, she did not think, either, and did not think I would mind."

"It . . . it is a gift of love. I could not destroy a gift of love," she stammered, embarrassed. *Halsey, damn it, you never taught me how to talk about things like this. . . .* "And I was *very* careful when I worked."

"You see, we are more alike than you think." Then, a bit awkwardly: "If I had been work, you would have remembered a contraceptive?"

"Of course." She poked him with her finger for emphasis. *Or don't you know how to talk like this, either?* "Are you sure you want a fishwife like me for a companion? I suspect I will be the jealous type."

As his face relaxed he actually looked relieved, but he managed to respond in kind. "No sharing? Not with anyone?"

Darame started to answer, and then paused. "Maybe with Mailan." *Brant was right—I have gone native.*

Sheel looked remote, and then shook his head. "No. She is *guaard,* and would never give it up. How could she remain detached enough to protect me, if . . ."

"You have excellent labs here, silly. Can you think of a better way to say thank you?" Darame grinned broadly at him, and then winced—her face did not pull that way yet. Sweet Lord, the muscles of her throat!

"We shall see." Fingers suddenly reached out and took her hand. "We are survivors, we Nualans . . . especially we Atares. We are as prone to land on our feet as the proverbial cat. You have proved yourself a survivor—I think you are meant to be one of us." After a short pause he whispered: "All my life I have had to do what was expected, what was needful—now others can live with what I need."

"Hush," she said absently, returning his grip with strength. Bits of plastic and ceramic danced across her memories. Funny, she had forgotten the museum . . . was this then the secret of Nuala? Out of all things, survival . . . out of both tolerance and love. Darame thought until her head throbbed. *All you ever wanted was enough money to enjoy yourself and not worry. All right, it is yours. With something you never had time to think about—someone who likes you as much as you like him. And as for getting bored . . .* A very sly smile crossed her face. "You realize you will be ruling this planet within ten years if I stay?"

Sheel was visibly startled, and then a dimple appeared. "That is not funny."

"You think I am joking?" The humor suddenly fled from her

faces and she whispered: "Sheel, no one ever taught me how to say 'I love you.'"

Purposefully lifting her palm to his lips, he said gently: "Of course they did—in another sort of language. And I know you are good with languages."